TOO *Great* A *Lady*

THE NOTORIOUS, GLORIOUS LIFE OF EMMA, LADY HAMILTON

A NOVEL

AMANDA ELYOT

NEW AMERICAN LIBRARY

NEW AMERICAN LIBRARY

Published by New American Library, a division of
Penguin Group (USA) Inc., 375 Hudson Street,
New York, New York 10014, USA
Penguin Group (Canada), 90 Eglinton Avenue East, Suite 700, Toronto,
Ontario M4P 2Y3, Canada (a division of Pearson Penguin Canada Inc.)
Penguin Books Ltd., 80 Strand, London WC2R 0RL, England
Penguin Ireland, 25 St. Stephen's Green, Dublin 2,
Ireland (a division of Penguin Books Ltd.)
Penguin Group (Australia), 250 Camberwell Road, Camberwell, Victoria 3124,
Australia (a division of Pearson Australia Group Pty. Ltd.)
Penguin Books India Pvt. Ltd., 11 Community Centre, Panchsheel Park,
New Delhi – 110 017, India
Penguin Group (NZ), cnr Airborne and Rosedale Roads, Albany,
Auckland 1310, New Zealand (a division of Pearson New Zealand Ltd.)
Penguin Books (South Africa) (Pty.) Ltd., 24 Sturdee Avenue,
Rosebank, Johannesburg 2196, South Africa

Penguin Books Ltd., Registered Offices:
80 Strand, London WC2R 0RL, England

First published by New American Library,
a division of Penguin Group (USA) Inc.

First Printing, February 2007
10 9 8 7 6 5 4 3 2 1

 REGISTERED TRADEMARK—MARCA REGISTRADA

LIBRARY OF CONGRESS CATALOGING-IN-PUBLICATION DATA:
Elyot, Amanda.
    Too great a lady: the notorious, glorious life of Emma, Lady Hamilton: a novel/Amanda Elyot.
        p. cm.
    ISBN-13: 978-0-451-22054-7
    1. Hamilton, Emma, Lady, 1761?–1815—Fiction. 2. Nelson, Horatio Nelson, Viscount,
1758–1805—Fiction. 3. Hamilton, William, Sir, 1730–1803—Fiction. I. Title.
PS3603.A77458T66   2007
813'.6—dc22   2006029841

Set in Adobe Garamond • *Designed by Elke Sigal*
Printed in the United States of America

PUBLISHER'S NOTE
This is a work of fiction. Names, characters, places, and incidents either are the product of the
author's imagination or are used fictitiously, and any resemblance to actual persons, living or
dead, business establishments, events, or locales is entirely coincidental.

    The publisher does not have any control over and does not assume any responsibility for
author or third-party Web sites or their content.

For Scott,
my hero and soul mate

GONE ARE THE SIRENS FROM THEIR SUNNY SHORE,
THE MUSES AFTERWARDS WERE HEARD NO MORE,
BUT OF THE GRACES THERE REMAINS BUT ONE—
GODS NAME HER EMMA, MORTALS, HAMILTON.

—Walter Savage Landor, 1801

ANYONE WHO BRAVES THE WORLD SOONER OR LATER
FEELS THE CONSEQUENCES OF IT.

—Lady Melbourne

My sin has found me out.

But it was a sin born of devotion to the greatest man England has ever produced, to protect the glorious name of Horatio Nelson from the taint of his detractors.

I owe the world a confession. It is true that last month I publicly denied the authenticity of a two-volume compendium purporting to be the love letters written betwixt myself and Lord Nelson. At the time, my vehement refutation proceeded from the earnest desire to honor the dead, who cannot speak for themselves, as well as to respect the reputations of the living. I have a child to look after, who must command my devotions—Horatia Nelson, the only offspring of England's greatest hero since St. George and a mother, who, as I once told a shopkeeper, was too great a lady to be mentioned.

In truth, I am the woman. I am the heroine of the greatest real-life love story in England's long and tempestuous history. Robin and Marian, gamboling on the greensward in Nottingham, are perhaps more famous than Nelson and Emma, but they are quaint creatures of folklore, when all is said and done. The passions of Arthur, Guinevere, and Lancelot delight our senses, but they are merely glorious inventions of the writers' pens. *My* passions are not fancies on the silver tongues of medieval minstrels. *My* passions live and breathe at this very moment, in the shadow of a guttering candle resting on a rickety table within a squalid flat in the confines of a debtors' prison. I am the woman who began her life as the daughter of an illiterate farrier and his wife, only to rise, rung by slippery rung, through the ranks of society to become the most talked-about woman in Europe. I am she for whom the gallant Nelson risked all in the name of true love, bravely hazarding the censure of his monarch and his peers. When he sailed forth into battle to defend his king and country from their greatest enemies, it was my portrait that he wore about his neck as a talisman from his guardian angel, and he died with my name upon his lips.

As I write these words on the evening of my forty-ninth birthday, from my two windows overlooking Temple Place I can glimpse the grand illuminations outside the Surrey Theatre, and, in front of the marquee, the Surrey's acrobats performing their circus tricks for the cheering crowds. All day, the bells of London have rung as any man will tell you they have not done in living memory. But the fanfare is not for me, though I have done many services for my country. They are celebrating Napoleon's enforced abdication, thanks to England's new champion—Arthur Wellesley. "Rule Britannia" is being sung boisterously in every tavern. Cries of "It's all up with Boney!" echo through the fetid, narrow streets of the Rules. But as a condition of my imprisonment I am not permitted to attend a theatre or partake of the jubilation; a visit to a tavern or to a place of entertainment is deemed by the authorities to be "escaping."

Yet perhaps it is just as well, for on this still-chilly night my heart cannot soar with those of John Bull. I despair to think that only a few short years since Trafalgar, the name of Wellington has already dimmed the star of Nelson in the memory of the common man. But it shall not *eclipse* his name—no! Not while I live to fan Nelson's flame and remain the stalwart and protective keeper of his living legacy to his country.

If the particulars of my extraordinary life, including the confessions of my intimacy with the illustrious Lord Nelson, are to be disclosed with verisimilitude, they must perforce proceed from my own pen, and not from the greedy presses of scurrilous scandalmongers. I was the one who lived it, and my story is not a prize to be boarded and taken at will. Before heaven I vow to defend the truth, mine honor, and my heart with such unceasing broadsides that it will make the very devils of hell deaf from my cannons' thunder. I am writing for my life, and that of my thirteen-year-old daughter, that I might earn enough from the sale of this memoir to break the debtors' shackles and raise Nelson's only child in a manner befitting her birthright. Whether to exalt or to excoriate, I intend to spare no one my candor.

Begging your indulgence, I hope you will be entertained, if nothing greater, by my extraordinary adventures on this earth, and I wish you every felicity.

Emma Hamilton

Nature

1765–1786

One

***

The Earliest Days

"Oh, Emy, it's just a bit of fun is all!"

"Let go, Peter! I mean it, let me go!" Though he tried to hold me down, I kicked as hard as I could, and my long bare leg made contact with his belly. "Quit it, John Buckley!" Like a feral cat, I clawed at pimply Peter Flint with one hand whilst with my other I clutched at my calico, trying to keep my skirts down.

The boys pushed me onto my back in the mud by the edge of the road, heedless of my tears and shouts. I was nigh on twelve years old and they was fifteen or sixteen, taller than I was; and I knew they wouldn't have thought twice about using their swagger sticks to beat me had I continued to refuse them. "Just give us a squeeze and a fondle," John insisted. "Show us your pretty, round bubbies." John grabbed hold of my bare feet and began to drag me into a ditch where we mightn't be spotted from the road and where for certain my virtue would become just a memory.

"We just want to see what else it is you're selling!" Peter reached into my apron pocket and grabbed a few lumps of coal. I peddled the coal by the roadside, helping my gammer, Sarah Kidd, put bread and bacon on the table for the seven of us who dwelt crammed together like coop hens in her little cruck cottage, "the Steps." Laughing, as if to mock me, Peter lobbed the precious cargo across the road.

"I'm not on offer!" But the two country boys, loutish and poorly shod despite Hawarden's windy damp, had taken the notion to misunderstand me.

Through the years, the same life lesson has appeared in my copybooks and recollections. In the world of men, it appears to be a maxim that a beautiful and charming woman is—regardless of her station or fortune—available. In their view, it all depends on her price. A truly extraordinary beauty, such as I was—for all the greatest painters of the day said so, and my portraits hung in every fashionable salon—was simply more costly to afford.

The ugly childhood memory returns. Just as I thought I was done for, along come Gammer up the Chester Road on her way back from the market in her rattletrap of an empty wagon, a picturesque peasant woman in her striped woolen garments, her graying hair hidden by a kerchief and a soft-brimmed hat. I heard the *whish* of her whip before I saw its long leather tongue catch fat John right between the shoulder blades, landing with a crack like the snap of a dry twig.

"Get!" she yelled, scaring the shite out of them. They backed away from me like jackrabbits, fumbling with their plackets. Leaving me lying in the ditch, they tried to scramble up to the road, but Gammer's whip caught 'em both across the cheeks with a single blow. "*There's* summat to remember the afternoon by," she added. "And if I catch you near my Emy again, I'll bost your heads afore you can come up with your next thought." Then, for good measure, she took the whip to their hides again while they tried to outrun its reach. "Did they 'arm you, girl?" she demanded when she saw I was covered with scratches.

"No, but they was trying. You come just in time, Gammer. These cuts come mostly from fighting 'em off, though maybe John managed to brush one of my bubbies when he was reaching to tear my frock away. It's too small for me anyhow, y'nau," I said, looking down at the straining fabric. "Would'a bost itself soon enough."

"I should 'ave noticed it myself, child," Gammer said, clucking her tongue against her teeth. "I expect I just didn't want to see what was plain as the nose on my face. You outgrew that bodice months ago and your skirts is barely reaching your ankles, but I was 'oping we might get 'em to last a mite longer." She climbed down from the wagon, undid her kerchief, and dried my tears before folding me in her arms.

"You're getting far too old to stand in the Chester Road anymore. You're becoming a beauty, Emy, and I'll not 'ave your charms exposed to everyone as passes. It's time for me to find you a proper situation."

"No!" My eyes filled with tears. "I love it 'ere! You can't make me go!" I said, growing angrier by the moment. Truth was, I hated Hawarden and dreamed of a grander life filled with color and warmth, exactly the opposite of our chilly, damp, gray corner of North Wales. My father, Henry Lyon, died when I was but two months in this world, and Mary, my mam, had gone down to London in the hopes of better employment when I was but a tot. But Gammer was my world. I loved her more than anyone and could not begin to imagine being without her.

Gammer tenderly stroked my head until my sobs subsided into whimpers. Then, after scrutinizing my disheveled condition, she concluded, "A lick and a promise'll do for washing these cuts clean, y'nau? Now 'op up beside me, girl, so we can get on 'ome afore the deeleet fades."

After supper she tucked me into bed as if I were still her little Emy. My grandfather and Uncle William dozed over the table, Grandpa snoring enough to shake the rafters loose. My aunts knit stockings by the guttering flames of our tallow candles, and, muttering almost silently to themselves as they counted their stitches, took no notice of anything else. Gammer sat beside me and struck up a pretty, rustic air. I joined her on the second verse, inventing a light harmony. When she turned her face to mine at the end of the song, there were tiny teardrops in the corners of her eyes. "You've truly the voice of one of the angels, my girl," she said softly. Her words sounded like music, despite—or perhaps because of—her countrified speech.

"I don't want to be leaving you, Gammer," I sniffled. "I don't want to take a position anywhere else."

"Husht thee naise," she said gently, smoothing a curl off my forehead. "Hawarden's no good place for you anymore. The world's a big wide thing, child, and you best be moving into it, so's you can begin to make your way on your own. You might even learn to curb that fierce temper of yours, which could only be to the good." Gammer leaned down and kissed the top of my head. She smelt of the turnips she'd boiled and mashed for our supper and I was missing her even before I was gone. "Now, shut those deep blue eyes of yours, Emy, and we'll talk more about it in the deeleet."

Two

❧

London Town

After I'd spent half a year as an undernursemaid in the home of Mr. Thomas, a local doctor, Gammer found me a better situation in London. The prospect of visiting the bustling capital was as exhilarating as my departure from Gammer was painful.

I'd never traveled anywhere before, much less on my own, and was unprepared for the unusual reception I encountered along the journey, though in some measure it reminded me of the days when I was even younger, a lass of eight or nine, peddling coal from my apron pockets. On occasion, after our transaction a gentleman would try to steal a kiss. I dared not tell him off, so as I curtsied I would turn my head, and his lips would land on my coal-smudged cheek instead. And oftentimes a lady remarked on my uncommon prettiness, coyly asking if I had a sweetheart yet, to which I could only stammer and blush, for at that age how could I imagine myself feverishly ponshyn anyone, which is what I thought sweethearts was all about?

At the first posting inn, I thought they was all mutes, because I couldn't hear a word of chatter once I stepped inside. The silence was so strange, it set my nerves aflutter. A sweaty serving wench cleared a table for me in a twinkling, as if I was a royal.

"A plate of ponsh meip, if you please," I said politely, wishing I'd more in my meager purse so that I might be able to afford a joint or a half dozen bangers instead of the mashed potatoes and turnips we ate all the time in Flintshire.

A corpulent woman slapped her husband's upper arm. "What're your eyes poppin' at? Am I no longer to your fancy after fourteen years?"

"She's so tall," someone murmured as I tucked into my mash. "Have you ever seen hair like that?"

I'd brushed it till it shone, like Gammer taught me, so I didn't know what was so wrong with it. I stole a glance about the room at the other patrons, whose hair—wigged, dark, fair, and gray— peeked out from under their millinery. No one else's hair was red with just a hint of brown. Nor were the women's locks even half so long, but then I was a country girl of twelve and as far from fashionable as I was from living in Windsor Castle.

"Look at 'er eyes, Mum," a little girl whispered. "They's almost two different colors."

The youth who brought me the mash remained, slack-jawed, by my table. He was staring at my face, though once or twice his gaze flickered a bit farther south.

"This eye 'as always 'ad a spot of brown amid the bright blue," I explained, thinking perhaps he was fearful of me. "Gammer used to say it's a bit of mud from the Chester Road, so's I'd never forget where I came from. Oh—I'm not a *witch*," I assured him, suddenly realizing why they all regarded me so oddly, though in this modern day and age I should have thought they'd know better. "Red hair i'nt always a sign of witchcraft."

The boy went crimson. "It's j-just that you've b-bewitched *me*, miss. You're the prettiest miss I've ever seen."

And so it went, to my astonishment, heads turning each time I ventured into the posting inns, from the Golden Bowl to the Angel to the Red Lion to the Swan. The closer to London we got, the less people understood my dialect, though I apprehended their whispers and their whistles of approbation well enough, and soon learnt to be quick on my feet at the various posting inns, else through my petticoats my arse'd feel the pinch of some roving hand.

The London coach rattled into the yard of the Nelly Gwynn in Covent Garden, its final destination. The miasma was so thick that you could scarce see more than a few feet in front of you. A distant church spire pierced the fog as if it were reaching for a breath of fresh air. The city stank to heaven of every imaginable odor: offal and dung, animal sweat, urine, frying fish, rotting meat, and roasting potatoes. I covered my nose and mouth with my hand. The unfamiliar sights and smells—and the noise—were nothing akin to what I had known back in Hawarden. The Chester Market was but a country fair compared to Covent Garden: such a hubbub, what with the fruiterers, root vendors, ballad sellers, and flower girls; bunches of carrots and barrows of cress destined for the dinner table; cart after cart of turnips and onions, apricots, exotic dates and plump fresh figs; and the flies! Horrid black flies everywhere, landing with impunity on the barrels of beans, the piles of potatoes, the mounds of oranges and lemons, and on the bunches of roses. And I had never seen so many people in my life. Almost as many souls as flies! Pushing and jostling and all talking at once, shouting over one another, everyone eager to talk and no one willing to listen.

I dragged my trunk through the narrow streets, asking passersby where I might find Chatham Place and the home of Dr. Richard Budd. The closer I got to the river, the more its smells enveloped me, eclipsing those of the market: fish, of course, and brine invaded my nostrils until they stung. Wood and pitch and turpentine. The Thames was nearly as crowded as the streets. Dozens of ferries and wherries transported goods and passengers from one place to another, and the small merchant vessels sailed so closely together, they seemed a giant's toys, being pulled down the river and out toward the channel by an invisible string.

At Chatham Place, I paused to catch my breath before I began my search for the great brass door knocker shaped like a lion's head, marking the entry to Dr. Budd's home.

The building was handsome, though plain, yet the bricks looked as though they had been scrubbed with soot. Was everything in London so gray and grimy? Even in Hawarden, where one continually inhaled the dust from the fields and country roads, the air never painted things brown. Had I hoped for finer weather, expecting London to be some version of Paradise? In that respect, it was as dreary as North Wales, and just as damp, too. I climbed the steps and made use of the knocker, whereupon a mobcapped maid opened the door, and I introduced myself as Miss Emy Lyon of Chester.

"The new norsery maid is here, sor!" Her Irish brogue was as thick as the miasma. "Come this way, gorl." She ushered me inside and the door shut behind us with resounding finality.

Dr. Budd's home was much grander than Mr. Thomas's. For one thing, it had more than one story and the high-ceilinged rooms seemed so airy and light. From the parlor on the second floor, one could look across the river and chronicle all the comings and goings, an endless parade of activity. *Were I to live in that room, I should never look away from the window!* I thought.

But I rarely saw the daylight, much less the water, as the nursery was situated just under the eaves. I took my meals in the servants' quarters belowstairs, whilst I slept in an alcove adjacent to the nursery in case one of the children should awaken during the night. So obstreperous were the Budd brood that though I was not quite thirteen years old, I was convinced that these unruly and ungovernable children were going to send me to an early grave.

My saving grace proved to be Jane Powell, an underhousemaid a year or so older than I. Soon after I began my employment for the Budds, Jane befriended me, sensing in me a kindred spirit to her own wild temper. Our nocturnal adventures began after I had been in the household for nearly a month. Once the children were fast asleep (for only my lullabies could quiet them), I would creep down to the servants' quarters, and Jane and I would climb through a window, tiptoe up the outer stairs to the street, and then make a mad dash across Blackfriars Bridge for the fairgrounds in Southwark, just across the river. It was there that I developed a taste for beer and revelry, and Jane and I never needed so much as a ha'penny in our pockets, for there was no dearth of gentlemen, young or otherwise, happy to treat a pretty girl to a glass or two. Then, giggling with beer and triumph, we would stumble back to Chatham Place in time to be in our beds before dawn. Thank heavens for Jane Powell, or I should have been entirely miserable at the Budds'.

One day, she sneaked away from the house, swearing me to secrecy. On her return, she crowed, "I've been to see the managers at Drury Lane. But, shhhh, you mustn't say a word to Dr. Budd, for I don't know what's to be. Mr. Sheridan's father-in-law, Mr. Thomas Linley, is in charge of the musical direction, and he wanted to hear me sing. I sang for him once—just three days ago—and he suggested that I work a little harder before coming back so he might hear me again. O, Emy, you must help me practice!"

"Singing?!"

"Yes! Every night from now on, we'll cross the river. At Cocksheath Camp we'll claim that we're ballad singers and stand on a wooden box with a collection basket at our feet!"

But you can't sing, I was about to say. Yet I needed no compelling excuse to attend a fair. I adored them: the gaiety, the music, the games of chance, the acrobats, and the smells, both sweet and savory, of roasting joints and fowl, of frying fish, and of viscous batter fried into airy sugar cakes that burnt your tongue for an hour if you didn't wait for them to cool before you devoured them. How could one not enjoy a place where everyone acted so blithely? For a few brief hours, no matter who you were or where you came from, life was magnificent.

That very night, I joined Jane in sneaking off to Southwark. Cocksheath Camp was bristling with energy. Tradesmen mingled with farmers, red-coated soldiers strolled the fairgrounds in pairs or trios, or sometimes on their own with a tart or two hanging off their arms, and no one minded if two pretty girls commandeered an old cress crate, upended it for a stage, and commenced to sing for their supper. We drew the listeners in with our renditions of "There Was a Lass of Islington" and "As Oyster Nan Stood by Her Tub." The bawdier the lyric, the bigger the crowd. Though Jane was surely not going to favor Mr. Linley with her interpretation of "Blowzabella, My Bouncing Doxie," the more she sang, the greater grew her confidence—as did the appreciation of two young gentlemen with unpowdered hair and scarce old enough to require a shave—whose eyes we had caught soon after we set up shop.

"I'm fagged," I complained to Jane after we had been singing for upward of an hour without respite. "And my windpipe is parched."

"May we suggest that a pint might be in order," said one of our two admirers.

Jane and I exchanged glances. "Well, I've 'eard tell that a glass of porter is good for the vocal cords," I said boldly, and we descended our makeshift stage. The dew-laden grass was damp beneath my feet, so I removed my slippers against their becoming soaked through, and stowed them in our bag of coins.

"I'm James Perry," said the young man who had suggested the refreshment. He slipped his arm through mine. "And a young lady should never be unescorted in places such as these."

"And 'ow would you know that, Jimmy? You come 'ere often, then?"

Mr. Perry blushed to his roots. "No—no," he stammered. "In faith, this is the first time my friend and I—allow me to name Mr. Jonathan Beecham," he said, indicating the cove who'd already managed to slide his arm about Jane's waist.

"Your secret is safe with us!" Jane assured him.

The men bought us beer and sausages, and then suggested that we repair to a less crowded spot, the better to enjoy our repast. On a damp knoll a few yards from London Bridge, our cavaliers spread their cloaks and urged us to sit beside them. At first, they behaved quite properly, but soon the brew made them bolder. Jimmy found my hem and began to insinuate his way up my skirts, pressing against my thighs, caressing them on a too-direct path to the point twixt temptation and ruination.

"Oh!" I exclaimed, slapping my hand down over his, and startling him when I broke our embrace. "Excuse me. . . . I need to take a piss."

When I sprang to my feet, Jane jumped up as well. "It's terribly dark down by the river, Emy. You shouldn't go alone. You must let me accompany you."

I accepted her outstretched hand. "We shan't be but a moment." I gave our admirers my most angelic smile as Jane began to pull me toward the river.

A shilling apiece purchased us the good offices of a wherry boatman, who was tickled to take part in our jest. As he rowed us away from the shore, we shouted to the young gentlemen on the bank. "Ho there, Jimmy and Johnny!"

At the sound of our voices, they rose to their feet and raced along the bankside all the way to the center of London Bridge, cursing us as they gasped for breath.

"Thought we was easy, didn't you?" I called, thumbing my nose at them as we approached the bridge.

"That'll teach you!" cried Jane, mimicking my gesture.

Flushed with the evening's triumphs—of voice and virtue—and with a heavy bag of coins as proof indeed of our artistic talents, we laughed all the way back to Chatham Place, just as dawn was breaking over the dome of St. Paul's.

Three

My First Love

*T*he following morning the Budds were quick to show Jane and me the door. I was done for indeed!

"I'm going back to Drury Lane," Jane announced bravely. "Could be this is God's way of telling me I'm not meant to be in service."

"But what if Mr. Sheridan and Mr. Linley don't take you?"

"They will!" she insisted, as if the thought of rejection had never crossed her mind. "But where will you go, Emy?"

There was just one person in London to whom I could turn.

I had not seen my mother since I'd come to town, though I had heard she was working for the Earl of Warwick. Truth told, I had not seen my mam in years. I was dismayed to see how much hard work had left its marks upon her. Her brown hair, mostly hidden by her mobcap, had already begun to lose its luster. Although her cheeks still bore the pink of youth, her countenance showed traces of the lines of care and age. Her waist had thickened into matronliness, and to my great astonishment, I was now the taller of the two of us!

"Hurry, put wood inth hole, afore someone sees you," urged my mam, anxiously looking in every direction. I quickly shut the door to the earl's kitchen and poured out my tale of woe between hysterical sobs.

"I conna meke thee out, you're crying so. Here, dry your eyes and start all over again."

"But we was really good, Jane and I. Look at all we took in!" I took the bag of coins from my skirts. "And this is but 'alf, as I shared it with Jane afore we parted ways this morning."

Mam didn't take to my crowing over my success. "O, Emy, you got me tampin'! A *singer* indeed! Where's your 'ead? You'll 'ave to make those shillings stretch, my girl, until you can find someone else to take you in. Certain, Dr. Budd won't be inclined to provide a kindly reference, neither." She shook her head and sighed, deeply annoyed. "I'm moidered with myself just as much. I'm in part to blame for your wildness," she added dolefully. "An I could, I would relieve you of your distress. But there's no place for you in the earl's 'ousehold. For me to force the situation would put us both in a bad light, and if I'm to do my best to make sure you don't go starving, I can't risk my place 'ere."

For the next few days, Mam found ways to sneak me food when she could, stowing away a blanket that I could unroll every evening by the kitchen door, having bribed the earl's cook with some of her own saved wages. And at night Jane and I would return to Cocksheath Camp to sing our hearts out, more mindful now in choosing our male companions.

When I met up with her at Blackfriars Bridge on the fourth night of our unintentional liberty, her face was aglow with enthusiasm. "I've done it, Emy! Mr. Sheridan engaged me! I'm just to be a supernumerary for now, but soon"—she glanced heavenward—"soon, I'll be as famous as Nelly Gwynn! And I owe so much of it to you, Emy," she added, throwing her arms about me. On learning how fearful I was at not having found a new situation, Jane insisted that I speak to Mrs. Linley, for between the management of her household as well as the theatre, there must surely be a place for a girl like me.

At their house in Norfolk Street, just off the Strand, a red-eyed and harried Mrs. Linley, clad in mourning for her eldest son, was too distracted to conduct a proper interview. She asked merely if I had a good memory (to which I replied in the affirmative), then promptly took me on, sending me straight to the theatre with a message for their leading lady, Mrs. Pritchard, delivered in such a rapid torrent of words that I hoped I would be able to con it after all.

"Tell her she can't have a cloth-of-gold dress just for her Lady Macbeth. We aren't made of money here. We're in the business of entertaining folk—business—and I have the wardrobe of an entire company to supervise. Tell her I said the red gown she wore in *The White Devil* will suit just as well. While you're about it, you can add from me that she might consider leaving off the beer and mutton if she wants to remain a credible Jane Shore: the character is supposed to be *starving*. And if she throws something at your head, duck."

In no way did the Linleys permit their grief to interrupt the business of running London's greatest theatre. The bustle and hubbub never ceased, and I took to the glamour and gossip of their world like a canvasback to water. I adored the aromas of powder and paint, the majesty of brocade, the subtlety of damask, the sensuality of velvets, and the rustle of silks! How magical were the transformations! Within minutes a homely woman might become a tragic heroine, while a man with a face and figure so common you wouldn't look at him twice in the lane outside the theatre could become, with a spirit-gummed beard and pasteboard crown, a king. Everyday troubles were laid aside in this world of make-believe. No wonder a lowly serving wench like Jane Powell dreamt of dwelling here forever.

During rehearsals, I would wear out my slippers dashing hither and yon from Mrs. Linley's private box to the dressing rooms backstage. And in between fetching fans, arranging flowers, combing out and dressing wigs, delivering all manner of notes, bearing the brunt of an actress's temper—or worse, Mrs. Linley's—locating mislaid scripts, and running interference for love-struck admirers with their painted ladies, I stole every spare moment to stand by the curtain man, silently observing the actors at work from his darkened offstage alcove. I did not think of becoming an actress myself; I was studying the behavior of the players both on and off the stage—for example, the way a woman with rustic roots could make a prince of the blood believe that she, too, was of his ilk. I marked how the actresses used the fans I fetched, how they walked, sat, balanced a teacup. It taught me that to act well-bred did not require breeding.

My arse was worked to the bone, and I'd scarce seen Jane Powell since my employment began, but I'd never been happier. And I didn't give a fig if the people weren't considered respectable, being theatricals. But suddenly, in early December, my duties once again returned to the domestic sphere.

The household was in an upheaval over the unexpected arrival of the Linleys' second son, eighteen-year-old Samuel, who had contracted a fever as a midshipman and was sent home to recover. Despite the illness that was taking its toll on his already-fragile physique, he was the most exquisite man I had ever seen, an angel incarnate with a milky complexion flushed rose with fever, soft golden hair that flopped impudently across his brow, and the palest blue eyes I had ever seen. I was in love from the moment I saw him. And Sam was as instantly smitten with me.

"Let's run away together, Emy," he suggested. "I want to spend the rest of my life with the kindest, sweetest, prettiest girl in all of England."

"Take me with you on your ship," I murmured lovingly. "If you was my captain, I'd sneak aboard as your cabin boy, just to be by your side, no matter where we went in the world. And if 'Is Majesty kicks up a rumpus about 'aving girls in 'is navy, then I'll stow away!"

Mrs. Linley—who, in a lifetime spent among performers, was no stranger to an employee falling arse over tit in star-crossed love—did not favor our match. A servant was still a servant and had no business to go about seducing the scion of the family.

But it went hard with her to refuse her son when he insisted, with ever-weakening breath, that Emy Lyon be the only one to nurse him. I administered his physick, bathed his sickly body, cajoled him into taking nourishment, and sang him to sleep while he clasped my hand to his flushed cheek. When he was awake and sentient, with feverish kisses he would vow to wed me as soon as he regained his strength, so long as I understood that a sailor's life was a hard one and his wife's was too often lonely.

"But one day, Emy," he'd promise, clasping my hand in his cold, damp palm, "we will sail off together to a distant land where the sun always shines."

"I've never seen a place like that. Do you think such a paradise truly exists?"

"I've been there. The water is warm enough to bathe in, and fruit as big as your head falls right out of trees shaped like monstrous upside-down umbrellas!"

"Surely you are quizzing me, Sam! Your fever makes you delirious."

But God had other plans for Samuel Linley than a life on an island idyll with Emy Lyon at his side. Ten days before Christmas, He snatched the darling youth out of my arms and took him to His bosom. My heart cracked. I had been powerless to save him from the fever, despite my tenderest ministrations, and not only despised myself as a failure but also despaired of my ability to ever do a soul any good again.

The family doctor, arriving for his daily visit, found me on my knees before Sam's cot, clasping his lifeless torso in my arms. With the utmost gentleness, he sought to pry me away, but I grew hysterical. I could not accept that Sam was gone from this world, and with him all the love my young soul could ever express.

Blinded by tears, I stumbled through the doorway, elbowing past the Linleys, who, upon hearing my sobs, had their worst fears confirmed. Racked with grief, I fled their home, racing across Norfolk Street until I turned the corner onto the Strand, where I could no longer see the house of death and sorrow.

Four

To a Nunnery, Go!

"Mind the tom tit, luv!" shouted a gent just as I was about to stumble headlong into a horse turd. My eyes were so bedimmed with tears, I could scarce see where I was going. Responding to the unusual warning, I stopped myself short and picked my way over the steaming pile. "Tom tit?" I looked at the man, bewildered.

"Cockney rhyming slang for what you nearly stepped in." The fruiterer took in my tearstained face. "Well, aren't you in a two and eight!" Another uncomprehending look won me the translation. "A state. Aren't you in a *state*? 'Two and *eight*' rhymes wif 'state.' You'll catch on soon enough." He clapped a friendly hand on my shoulder and took a piece of fruit from his cart. " 'Ere, 'ave an orange and tell old Simon Lovett all about it."

Within a quarter hour, the costermonger had become my Samaritan, offering me a job as an orange girl. I trolled the streets near the Covent Garden Market, attracting customers with a pretty smile and sometimes a wink, and by announcing my presence with a far sweeter voice than any of the other costermongers possessed. As soon as my tray was empty, I'd return to Mr. Lovett's barrow and restock. But by the end of the day, my shoulders felt as though I'd been carrying the weight of the world on them, my back ached, my legs and feet protested with every step, and—lacking a shawl to protect me—the late-December chill was piercing my bones.

Mr. Lovett had made me purchase the fruit from his stall at cost with the money I'd earned from selling it in the confines of the market earlier in the day. Whatever I made off the contents of the last tray of the day would go into my own pocket, and I was to show up at Mr. Lovett's barrow first thing in the morning with my empty tray and we'd set to work all over again.

There was no place to rest. I tried to bribe my way into a sedan chair, just until someone called for it, but the men wouldn't hear of it, though they crudely indicated that if it was a lie-down I wanted, they'd be happy to find a more secluded place to accommodate me.

At the corner of New Compton Street, I found a free post. At least it might provide a bit of support for my groaning back, so I leaned against it for a while. A man approached and asked my name. "*Emily*," I replied. I have no idea what made me say that; looking back on't, I expect I didn't want to give him my real name, for he had no business learning it. Thinking, rightly, that I might be hungry, he offered me some biscuits, which I hastily devoured. Then he claimed my acquiescence as his due to engage me in conversation. Pressing his suit, he inquired whether I would still be there at eight in the evening; and not as yet having searched for a place to lay my head, I sighed and replied in the affirmative. I suppose he mistook it for a trollop's response, for with a quick glance at his watch fob, the gentleman hurried off, expressing the fervent wish to encounter me again.

A passing chaise kicked up a cloud of dust, and I began to choke. A few feet from my post, the carriage halted suddenly and a handsome woman of indeterminate years descended, making straight for me in an enveloping miasma of rose water. Much of her face was obscured by her voluminous feather-trimmed bonnet, but a peek under its wide brim told me she was no more a stranger to paint and powder, not to mention patches, than any actress at Drury Lane. Certainly, she was a lady of quality; only the finest women replaced their shorn eyebrows with toupees of mouse fur.

"You look like you could use a warm meal and good wash, my pet." Her lilting brogue was sympathetic, and strangely comforting to my ears. I marveled at how, when she knit her brow, the toupees behaved just as if they were her own hair. "What have you had to eat today, luv?"

"Biscuits," I mumbled. "And an orange."

"How would you like a hot joint instead?" My eyes widened; I could smell it, taste it in the back of my mouth. "Cat got your tongue, lass?"

"N-no. I would love a bit of meat, Your Grace."

The woman laughed heartily. "Your Grace! That's a good un." She extended a hand, gloved in lavender kid. "I'm Mrs. Kelly, and I'm no duchess, though my friends do call me an 'abbess,' seeing as how I make it my business to take care that uncommonly pretty girls like you—specially those innocent lambs from the country, as I can tell you are by your accent—aren't left to starve on the streets of London, prey to the passing fancies of unscrupulous gentlemen. Especially with the winter coming on. Tell me your name, my pretty child."

"Emily. Emily Lyon."

"Well, Miss Lyon, I consider it my duty to take you under my protection; truth told, I couldn't live with myself another hour if I didn't see to it that you were properly fed and clothed by nightfall."

I still had Mr. Lovett's tray about my neck. 'Twould have been proper to return it to the fruiterer on the morrow with my thanks for his kindness and trust in me, and yet here was an opportunity for a warm bed. Still . . . "Are you taking me to a convent, then? For hungry and tired as I am, I assure you I have no wish to—"

"You'll find my 'nuns' have more freedoms and pleasures at their disposal than any of their ilk, my pet. If you enjoy fine frocks, the loveliest in London will be made to fit your charming figure.

Should it be entertainments you fancy, the delights of the gardens—Kensington, Ranelagh, Vauxhall—shall be your Eden. If you've an epicurean bent, the best meats and dainties, confections and ices—not to mention such copious quantities of champagne as might fill your dainty slippers—will tempt your palate."

A Chester lass of thirteen, even one who has spent several months in the service of theatricals, must be forgiven for entertaining Mrs. Kelly's rather convincing pitch that such nunneries existed within the confines of London and that an "abbess" might parade the streets in her own barouche, attired and painted like a stage actress. The vast capital offered surprises at every turn; thus I was prepared to accept Mrs. Kelly as a genuinely charitable woman and her establishment as a respectable place for unmarried young ladies. A cannier wench than I would have recognized that the triumph in her eyes betrayed her pleasure at having made so quick a conquest.

Her house on Arlington Street in fashionable St. James was but a stone's throw from Piccadilly, and just around the corner from the Green Park. A door the color of Sam Linley's Royal Navy coat marked the entry. Inside, all was grace and elegance. Well-dressed young women, not much older than I, sipped tea from delicate china cups as a handsome mulatto girl seated at a gilded harpsichord entertained them with soft melodies. The entire "nunnery" smelt of flowers, whether emanating from the sumptuous displays of fresh blooms that could be found on every little table and mantel (how she got them in December I couldn't begin to imagine), or from the perfumed beauties themselves, for the girls were apparently quite liberal with their scent bottles. Mrs. Kelly ushered me up a flight of stairs, leading me to a tiny bedroom at the back of the house: a modest, though prettily appointed, chamber.

"You'll sleep here for the nonce," said Mrs. Kelly. She pointed to the ceramic ewer and basin. "Have yourself a good wash and I'll see to it that you get a more suitable frock. Dinner for the girls who aren't yet spoken for is in half an hour. In the morning, after you've gotten a good night's rest, I'll explain your duties."

I commenced my unusual employment for Mrs. Kelly as a glorified domestic by day. Toward evening, she had me change out of my gowns and into an exotic costume, usually consisting of a short jacket, cut to push my breasts out as much as possible, and pantaloons, split at the sides to reveal the entire length of my legs. I resembled something out of a Turkish hareem, or a Drury Lane production of *The Arabian Nights*. Sometimes Mrs. Kelly would have me wear an elaborate gown that looked much like those of the other girls from the back, but it was cut short at the front, exposing the entirety of my legs (clad in white stockings to the thigh, and silk-heeled slippers) and just brushing the bottom of my bare quim as I sashayed through the salon offering brandy and tobacco to the evening's guests. Mrs. Kelly had made it plain that these gentlemen were free to look, but not to touch, as my virtue remained unsullied. At first I balked at such displays of my charms, but it did not take me long to grow accustomed to the mode of life at Arlington Street. For much of the time, very little was demanded of me, other than to be an ornamental beauty, and I enjoyed being admired. I was well dressed and accoutreed, and well fed, with a soft place to lay my head; all things considered, it was a situation that was vastly preferable to any I had previously undertaken, including life at the Linleys'.

Men of all stripes—politicians and parliamentarians, barristers and bankers, actors and actuaries, from the self-made merchant to the idle heir, and even a celebrated London physician—were well acquainted with Arlington Street. A gentleman of the town attached no shame to a visit to Mrs. Kelly's. There he would meet a multitude of beautiful young ladies, some as accomplished at the pianoforte as they were at flirtation or French. The establishment was in general respects not a brothel, but a rather respectable place to find an evening's entertainment. What the gentlemen purchased was the pleasure of our company. What then took place beyond Arlington Street was understood betwixt each couple and carefully negotiated with Mrs. Kelly in advance. The gentleman might enjoy a meal with a girl on the premises, or invite her to join him (with or without his comrades and their own companions) in a rustic pic-nic or a fashionable stroll in Kensington, a pleasant afternoon of boating in Marlow or Henley, an evening of dancing and frivolity at Ranelagh (more aristocratic) or Vauxhall (more lively), or even a trip to the theatre. Such a treat it was for me to see the plays at Drury Lane from a box instead of backstage, and dressed as fine as any of the actresses I was watching.

I was something of a "nun in training," for I was permitted to be engaged for an outing, but not to go upstairs with a gentleman, nor to repair to a similar location of his choosing. I learnt that it was not uncommon for Mrs. Kelly to "rescue" a girl as young as I. One of the "nuns," who called herself Sophia though her given name was Mary Ann, had been taken in by Mrs. Kelly when she was only twelve. She had been there four years when I arrived and retained a very practical and decidedly unromantic view of things.

"It don't matter if he fills up your cunny. The important thing is for him to fill up your pockets." She and the other "nuns" schooled me in the rudiments of "romance," demonstrating their jades' tricks on an exotic yellow-skinned fruit called a banana. Under their aegis I also learnt exercises that strengthened my cunny muscles, that I might provide my lover with the most tantalizing massage—a lesson I could practice in utter secrecy, even in a seat at the opera! They also taught me how to pleasure a man in every way beyond the obvious: how to capture his full attention with the merest glance or the slightest touch, and how to maintain and nurture his fascination; how to listen to him with every sense alert and alive, to learn his moods like the weather and then be able to effortlessly shift mine to suit them, to make each admirer believe that he was the most interesting and appealing creature on God's earth.

"And when you disagree with a remark, unless it is cruel, don't let on, for it costs you nothing to agree, but may lose you everything to venture your dissent," Sophia counseled. "A man requests your company and pays handsomely for't because you make him feel like a king, not because you remind him that he's the ignorant dolt his wife thinks he is!"

"And then, of course, you've got to bathe regular!" the girls would laugh. "Armpits, quim, and arse as clean as a pennywhistle; bubbies you could sup off of; teeth polished; hair clean, and dressed with fresh powder and just enough pomade—no man likes a handful of bear grease—and be sure the scent is subtle. Rose water and bergamot, when used judiciously, are the most favored. And if the gent stinks to heaven, suggest a remedy: turn the washing of their parts into a tantalizing pleasure."

By the latter part of the spring, Mrs. Kelly's hints about my "promotion from postulant" grew increasingly more frequent and less couched, and it was impossible for me not to be anxious about the impending event. I knew that since my arrival men had been bidding for my virginity and that my benefactress was allowing the process to tarry in order to press her advantage to the utmost.

Would I like the man who would eventually win the right to deflower me? If he was as lively and well made as Lord L—ton, I should not much despair of the momentary twinge of pain Sophia had described, for she also made the act of coupling sound quite pleasurable as long as the man was as gentle as he was lusty and as clean as he was endowed, "in his 'privy purse' as well as in his wallet." The Neapolitan Prince An—otti was rather dashing in his way; in fact I very much enjoyed the week we spent almost exclusively in company, enjoying the pleasures of Vauxhall every night, for many *baci* were then freely exchanged. Bartholomew Hack—ley, Bt., was a bit too effete for my taste, having returned from the Continent a complete Macaroni, with a foot of false hair to rival

Mrs. Kelly's piled upon his head, his high, stiff collars and cravats, his yellow striped waistcoats cut so slim that he was compelled to make use of a pair of stays beneath 'em, breeches that left nothing to one's imagination, and a silly high hat that somehow managed to stay perched atop his ridiculous perukes. Yet the young baronet was not the worst of the lot; if my champion should be someone like the wizened Duke of D—shire, with a pallor as yellow as his teeth and breath as fetid as a bucket of slops, how could I bear it?

One afternoon, whilst I was walking in Kensington Gardens on the arm of one of my admirers, I spied an agitated figure rushing toward us.

Mam! How had she discovered where I'd been and where I was that very hour? There had been no communication between us since I'd worked for the Linleys. I told my companion that the approaching woman was a servant of my acquaintance and begged a moment or two of leave to converse with her.

Rather than quickening my own pace, which would demonstrate to my cavalier that something was amiss, I maintained the demeanor of a lady of quality, as I had been schooled, strolling languidly toward a knot of trees where Mam marveled and clucked and tutted over my new turn of fortune. "So long as you're 'appy, I don't begrudge it, Emy, girl—"

"I'm Emily, now," I told her. "It just popped out of my mouth one day and I thought to keep it. Leastways," I added, smoothing my gloved hand over my skirts, "Emily's more elegant."

"Well, as I say, I don't begrudge it. Lud knows, it's better than working your body to the bone in someone's scullery or becoming a factory girl and turning into an old woman afore you're twenty." She glanced about before clasping my hands in hers. "Something terrible 'as 'appened, Emily. Last week your cousin Thomas—my sister Betty's boy, I know you've never met 'im but 'e's kin all the same—was taken by one of them press-gangs. Clocked on the head as 'e left a tavern outside Deal. It's the war over in the colonies that's to blame for all of it. A man's afraid to stir out of 'is own 'ouse nowadays, for fear 'e'll get 'imself pressed. Betty's in a dreadful state. I wouldna moidered you about it, but seeing 'ow you know so many fine gentlemen these days, Betty and I was 'opin' you could put a word in the proper ear and get young Thomas released. 'E's only fourteen, gal, same as you. What right 'as 'Is Majesty to go about kidnapping young boys, I ask you?"

"You told Aunt Betty I was a 'nun'?" Suddenly I felt dirty, soiled by my present state.

Mam looked pained. "I didn't say as much *right out*, y'nau? I said you'd been lately introduced to a number of men of quality . . . and I conna say what she took from that."

I promised to think on how to help my cousin, but the truth of it was, I hadn't a clue where to go or how to proceed. "Don't go sending word to Aunt Betty just yet," I cautioned Mam. "You know 'ow I 'ate to disappoint."

"You're a good girl, Emily," she said, taking a last look at my finery. With maternal concern she added, "And all I can say is that I *do* 'ope you've been disappointing all them *beaux* you've been entertaining!"

Five

A Bluejacket at Whitehall

I resolved to begin my quest with a visit to the Admiralty.

Whitehall was an easy walk from Arlington Street, and I departed unremarked from Mrs. Kelly's, wending my way past the Spring Gardens Mews, taking the utmost care that the dust from the narrow, tree-lined lane would not mar my frock and slippers. But the three-storied Admiralty building, with its complement of sashed windows like so many watchful eyes, possessed a forbidding authority that nearly made me turn back from my purpose. Braving a nasty look from the poor man in the pillory, I took my fear in hand and crossed the way, striding through the entry between the imposing row of columns that shielded the raked cobblestone courtyard from the street. Venturing inside, I arrived in a black-and-white-tiled foyer. At least it provided a welcome respite from the stifling July heat.

The place was silent as a tomb, except for a cacophony of discontented voices emanating from behind an open door; it was shut suddenly with such force that the sound reverberated through the empty corridor. Dashing past the glazed door of that crowded and smoky waiting room, I scuttled up a narrow marble staircase. Reaching the first-floor landing, I glanced down the corridor. Every door was closed and looked the same: polished oak with a brass handle. Each was unmarked and anonymous. There was no way of knowing whether the person behind it could entertain my plea.

Daylight shone from a doorway nearly opposite me. Hoping to locate a friendly and sympathetic ear, I banished my trepidation and boldly approached it. A man in a blue-and-white naval uniform smoking a long clay pipe stood rapt in thought, his back to the door as he gazed out the window toward the verdant expanse of St. James's Park. His powdered hair was worn long, in the sailor's queue, and tied at the back with a length of black ribbon.

"May I inquire 'oom I might be addressing?" I said, my words piercing the tranquillity.

Startled, the man spun around to face me. "Captain Jack Willett Payne's the name," he answered reflexively, adding, "Damme, girl, you scared the bloody shit out of me!"

It didn't require half a year at Arlington Street for me to appreciate that I was not speaking to a gentleman. It was plain as an unbuttered bun. The man was relatively young, the south side of thirty for certain; no paragon, but pleasant enough to gaze on, although he displayed the early signs of dissipation: a ruddy countenance, a nose that betrayed a penchant for tippling—and though he was by no means portly, he'd begun to run to fat.

"How the devil did you get in here?" He crossed the width of the room to brush past me at the doorsill and cast a glimpse down the hallway. "Deuce take it! Not a man at his post. I don't suppose you saw any porters on your way up here."

"I saw no one, your lordship."

"Capital! Then no one will see you leave!" As he gripped my elbow to escort me away, his eyes strayed to my bosom, only partly obscured by the organza fichu.

I seized my opportunity. "Sir, my name is Emily Lyon and I come about my cousin Thomas Kidd."

"What about him?"

"Let me step inside and tell you. Please, sir. I won't be taking too much of your time."

The captain stole another glance down the length of the corridor before waving me into the room, locking the door behind us. "Sit down, Miss Lyon."

I perched on the edge of a chair, overwhelmed at first by the grandeur of the room. The walls were polished oak from top to toe, with a high coffered ceiling, while richly carved cherubs cavorted about the fireplace amid nautical paraphernalia; the carved sextants and compasses looked so authentic, I wondered if they might actually work. Surely there were churches that weren't half so magnificent.

Recovering my wits, I recounted the particulars Mam had related to me in Kensington Gardens, then threw myself on his mercy.

Captain Willett Payne sucked his teeth and looked studious. "Accepted the king's shilling, did he? Where are you from, girl?"

"Flintshire, sir. But my cousin was taken in Deal, where my aunt Betty lives now. I'm certain 'e wouldn't've downed that pint of beer if 'e'd known 'e was being tricked. Please, Captain, there must be something you can do about it!"

"Releasing a press-ganged youth is outside of my purview, I'm afraid, Miss Lyon."

"But there must be something—you're an important man, Captain Jack, I can see it. . . . Why, 'ere you are in this splendid room with its carvings and its Turkey carpet—and you've got three windows! A man such as you makes a suggestion and people listen to 'im, I'm sure of it." He made to protest again and I grew more desperate. "If you can't 'elp my cousin Thomas, I don't know where else to turn!"

"Good God, child, don't look like such a frightened rabbit."

" 'E's but a boy of fourteen, no older'n I am, your lordship. And my aunt Betty being widowed and all, and what with 'er eyesight failing these past five years, Thomas is 'er only hope of putting bread on the table and seeing 'er through 'er declining years."

Without taking his eyes from me, he opened a pretty wooden chest and withdrew a cut-glass decanter and two sherry glasses, which he filled to the rim. He offered me a glass, and watching him down the contents of his own in a single draft, I made to imitate him, enjoying a pleasantly searing sensation as the sweet amber liquid slid down my gullet.

Captain Willett Payne refilled his glass and, taking the decanter with him, approached my chair. Placing himself between the long table and my legs, he bent down to pour me another glass, which permitted him an excellent view of my bosom. "Drink up!" he urged. I downed two more glasses of sherry in quick succession, keeping pace with the captain. He slid an open nautical chart farther down the table. "You're quite a handsome young lady, you know that?"

"Thank you, Captain." Suddenly I felt rosy all over. I'd been tipsy before, but usually on champagne or claret, and always when high times and plenty of guttling were on the bill of fare. I was unused to imbibing this early in the day, and on an empty stomach; the sherry was having a powerful effect on me. I struggled to keep my head.

Suddenly, I found myself pulled to my feet and pressed against the captain's body, forced into a semicircular niche at the end of the table from which I could not escape. "And I might be able to effect . . . your cousin—what's his name?"

"Thomas. Thomas Kidd, first of Hawarden and late of Deal."

"Young Master Kidd's . . . *release* . . . if you could see your way around helping me with something."

" 'Ow could I possibly help you?"

Captain Willett Payne drew me closer. "Don't play innocent with me, Miss Lyon. You know perfectly well how you can help me." He boldly insinuated his hand under my bodice and, forcing his way beneath my stays, pressed groping fingers against my bare flesh. "Nicely made, too," he added, groping for my other breast. With a sudden motion he flipped me around so that I was pressed against the grand mahogany table, and he roughly unlaced my gown and stays, pulling them, along with my chemise, down over my naked shoulders. His hands once again found my breasts. "Yes . . . I believe you're going to be most accommodating to your Captain Jack." Soon tiring of this activity, he flipped up my skirts, shoved away my cork bum roll, and, cupping the globes of my arse, declared, "Most accommodating indeed."

If I kicked him in the shins—or higher—and bolted for the door, my cousin's hopes would be dashed forever and I knew it, yet I knew just as well that my submission also guaranteed nothing. A man who'd abuse the privilege of his office to fornicate with a helpless (or hapless) petitioner, no matter how long her hair or bright her eyes or high her bosom, was not a man of honor.

He bent me over the table and I stifled a cry as he made to enter me, muttering imprecations of surprise when he realized that my unyielding quim was virgin territory. The discovery fired up his blood even more, and I released a yelp of pain when after several repeated attempts, a powerful thrust pierced my maidenhead. My sweating hands gripped the top of the table, while Captain Jack tried to grab hold of my breasts without releasing the position he had fought so hard to gain.

"Tighter . . . than a . . . hen's . . . *arse*," he grunted between thrusts.

" 'Ow . . . would . . . you . . . *know* that?" I gasped as he drove me once more against the table.

"Figger . . . of . . . *speech!*"

The pounding seemed interminable. I derived not a whit of pleasure from it, and had no way of knowing whether Captain Jack's catalogue of guttural rumblings during this unpleasant assault was an indication that he was well on the road to the ultimate expression of ecstasy. Somehow, he managed to pour, and then toss back, another glass of sherry without missing a stroke, then picked up speed, his thrusts matching his panting breath, gasp for gasp. With a loud groan, he near to collapsed on top of me, crushing my breasts against the tabletop. A moment or two later, he pulled away. Humiliated, I scarce dared to turn around and look him in the eye.

He had already straightened his clothing. "Here. Clean yourself up." He tossed me a white handkerchief, and I wiped my legs and quim and handed back the bloodstained cloth, which he took between thumb and forefinger and dropped onto the pile of glowing sea coals. I straightened my skirts and turned my back on Captain Jack again. "I'll need 'elp with this," I said, indicating my gown and stays. He relaced me, then, seating himself behind the table, sharpened a quill and removed a sheet of parchment from a large folder. I stood and watched him write something, to which he added his signature and affixed an impressive-looking seal; then he sanded the paper and waited for the ink to dry before addressing me.

"This, Miss Lyon, is an official instrument of release for one Thomas Kidd." He folded the paper and sealed it with a wafer. "It will be delivered this afternoon to Lord Sandwich, the First Lord of the Admiralty." He glanced about the room, and his gaze landed on something outside one of his windows. "You are quite an astute—as well as an exceedingly obliging—young woman. The First Lord does not, as a rule, concern himself with the manning of a vessel below the rank of captain; however, I am persuaded to present him with the particulars of your cousin's situation, and, adding that I am an especial friend of one of Master Kidd's nearest relations, have requested that the youth be released and returned forthwith to the bosom of his family."

"I would take pains to thank you for't, Captain Jack, but I 'ave already done so for these past ten minutes!"

The captain took a moment to think on what I had said, then bosted out into a braying laugh. "By gad, girl, you're something different! By all that's holy, I won't forget you if I live to see a hundred!"

He escorted me to the door, and checked the corridor before letting me leave. "Bloody porters. Still nowhere to be found," he muttered. "Probably sleeping one off in a closet somewhere." He gave my arse a playful smack, tho' I could scarce feel it through my skirts. "Mind the captains' waiting room on your way out. Now off you go, girl. In your prayers tonight, don't forget a little mention of old Jack Willett Payne."

"Believe me, sir, I will remember your name tonight and forever!"

I raced back to Mrs. Kelly's and made immediately for my room, where I gave myself a proper wash and changed into an afternoon frock, suitable for taking tea in the downstairs salon. I rapped on the door to Sophia's room and she opened it and pulled me inside.

"Well?!"

"I did it!"

She clasped me about the waist. "O happy day!"

"Not quite." Suddenly I burst into tears.

"What is it, lovey? What's happened?" She knelt down and took my hands in hers.

"I won Tom's release, but I lost—" I looked into her face and tried to stop my lip from trembling. I could more easily have reconciled myself to the surrender of my maidenhead to one of Mrs. Kelly's patrons—though I'd hoped to somehow avoid it—than suffer the rape I had endured to save my cousin. "I've got to find a way out of 'ere," I announced. "As soon as I possibly can without arousing suspicion. The abbess will think I'll 'ave been fooling 'er deliberate all this time and taking advantage of 'er generosity. There'll be 'ell to pay, I know it!" My tears commenced afresh.

"Shhh, Emily. Take a deep breath and try to calm yourself. There are ways around it, you know, and none will be the wiser."

"Mrs. Kelly will be. If *you* know the tricks, it's certain *she* knows the same and more besides."

Sophia remained unsuccessful in her repeated efforts to soothe my fears. From that hour I resolved to be alert to the slightest opportunity that might present itself, allowing me to quit Arlington Street without the distasteful necessity of returning to my former life in service. Having enjoyed a grander existence for the past half year, I would sooner be damned than regress my state!

Six

The Temple of Health

I began to notice the numerous handbills advertising the educational lectures and beneficial cures offered by Dr. James Graham, at the Temple of Aesculapius—also known as the Temple of Health—located at the Adelphi on the Royal Terrace in Bond Street. I even puzzled my way—for I read so poorly at the time—through Dr. Graham's pamphlet on "The Wondrous Effects of the Celestial Bed in the Curing of Impotency and the Sustaining of Life." A night's enjoyment of the healthful pleasures of the famed Celestial Bed could be had for a mere fifty pounds. *What must such a contraption look like?* I wondered. Fifty pounds was a king's ransom! Although his methods had become all the rage among London's wealthiest and most glamorous citizens, thanks to the patronage of the vibrant and popular Georgiana, Duchess of Devonshire, it was a matter of opinion about town whether the doctor was a quack or a genius.

Having resolved to attend a lecture, I encountered no difficulty in securing an escort from among Mrs. Kelly's patrons; yet I had not realized, until I witnessed it with my own eyes, that the real entertainment took place after the five-shilling scholarly presentation, a lengthy program of a decidedly more sensual (and dearer) nature. Beautiful young women, scantily attired in shifts of the sheerest muslin, struck classical attitudes while—with a liberal employ of sexual innuendo—Dr. Graham, clad like a clergyman in a black frock coat, demonstrated the healthful benefits appertaining to the espousal of mud baths and his radical new electrical treatments.

Back at Arlington Street, unable to sleep, I replayed the events of the evening in my mind, and a course of action revealed itself to me with all the force of Dr. Graham's lightning rods. The doctor was himself a patron of Mrs. Kelly's! Although, to my knowledge, he never privately entertained any of her "nuns," he did enjoy the hospitality of the salon at least once a week, if not oftener. I would audition to be one of the doctor's singers, without his even suspecting my intentions!

Whenever the doctor visited us at Arlington Street, I would stand by the spinet, assuming a posture similar to that of the doctor's Grecian Graces. Though I looked nothing like them, girded in my heavily boned corset, my brocaded hips festooned by panniers, I delivered my songs with immeasurably more expression in my face and limbs.

But after the elapsing of two weeks, the doctor did not take the step I had so anticipated in my design, and my fear was mounting that my plan might fail. A few afternoons later, I paused in the middle of one of my ballads and confessed that I was suffering the ill effects of a sore throat.

Quitting my place beside the harpsichord while the mulatto continued to play, I drew aside the good doctor and asked him if he might be prevailed upon to prescribe a remedy for my condition. I endeavored to engage his interest further by informing him that my visit to the Temple of Health as a mere spectator had inflamed in me a passion to know more about the medical arts and sciences of which he was such a learned practitioner.

"Alas, my responsibilities 'ere do not permit me to attend your lectures as often as I would wish," I sighed prettily. "For I am at the disposal of any of Mrs. Kelly's gentlemen who wish to enjoy my company, and the better part of them would sooner dance and drink the night away at Ranelagh or Vauxhall than spend it in more intellectual pursuits."

Dr. Graham peered down at me, his curiosity now fully piqued. "How old are you, Miss . . . ?"

"Lyon, sir. Emily Lyon. I was fourteen this past April."

"I see no sense in beating about th'bush, Miss Lyon. You have three things that interest me. You have an inquisitive mind, a lovely singing voice, and your figure is incomparably to my liking."

I blushed and curtsied.

"Forgive my bluntness; I'm a Scot. Are you happy here at Arlington Street?"

"I am as 'appy as I 'ave ever been," I replied truthfully, "but I do not dream of spending all my days 'ere. I confess I 'ave conceived a powerful fondness for singing."

"And that is reflected in your talent for it; make no mistake, Miss Lyon. I have been marking you. And were you interested in exchanging your finery for more modest apparel, and your soft bed here, provided gratis I am sure, for accommodations in meaner quarters that you must needs pay for out of your own purse, I would offer you a position as a singer at the Temple of Health."

I struggled to contain the flutter in my heart and keep my smile from bosting out of my face. "At what salary?" I furrowed my brow.

"Two crowns for each performance. Six performances a week."

A heated negotiation ensued, and to my immense astonishment—and glee—I was able to bargain the Scotsman up to a whopping two guineas a performance and the use of his spinet during the day.

My relief was enormous. I had secured legitimate employment at the premises of one of London's most celebrated citizens. And there was nothing Mrs. Kelly could do about it. The "abbess" had lost her opportunity to retail my virginity; however, she had been well paid for the pleasure of my companionship for several months, and it remained in her interest to maintain Dr. Graham's good custom and that of his own elite clientele.

I had my trunk packed and had quit Arlington Street forever by the following noon—a searingly hot day in mid-August 1779, on which a sudden rainstorm produced no effect whatever on either the stifling weather or the city smells. I located a rather spartan room in a boardinghouse in Cork Street, just footsteps from the Royal Terrace, settled in, then, flushed with my own triumph, set out for my new place of employment.

Previously, I had seen only one of the three lavishly decorated rooms known as the Museum of Elixirs, when the evening lamplight had provided a suffused glow over what I now recognized as glorious depictions of heroes and kings, from such grand personages as Orpheus, Atlas, and Prometheus to Alfred the Great, King Arthur, and Richard Lionheart.

In the tinsel chamber of Apollo, the last of the grand chambers, lay the famous Celestial Bed. Gilded dragons gamboled about its columns, meeting overhead in an arched pavilion, and above the bed, an inscription in Latin, which my new employer translated as "It is a sad thing if a rich man has no heir to his property."

My duties varied from evening to evening. On some nights, concealed by lavish draperies, I would stand behind one of the four crystal pillars enshrining the electrical apparatus, and serenade the lovers in the Celestial Bed. Some nights, I was instructed to counsel the infertile and charm them with my songs, often accompanied by additional voices and the dulcet tones of a harp. On other evenings, I participated in the doctor's demonstrations as a "warbling chorister," trilling my odes from beyond the performance area, unseen by the glamorous spectators who clamored for seats and ringed the galleries. How I would have preferred to be one of the barely clad young ladies who struck poses in imitation of some classical and healthful theme. After a month or so, I begged the doctor to promote me.

"Your beauty should be seen, 'tis true," he agreed, "but I have more need of your voice, lass. My goddesses are mute."

But it was the goddesses who received all the attention from the gentlemen. My enjoyment wasn't nearly the same when I was stuck behind the scenes, or providing the musical accompaniment to a fifty-pound fuck.

However, with all the delights of London competing for the attention, and the coin, of his particular clientele, Dr. Graham was compelled to develop new programs with some degree of frequency. Toward the latter part of 1779, as a new way of endorsing the nourishing benefits of frequent mud baths, the doctor introduced Hygeia, the Goddess of Health, to an eager public.

My wish to step out from behind the scenes was less than half-granted, however, for the doctor immersed me to the shoulders in a vat of warm mud—which in truth felt quite delicious against my skin, even through my shift. The audiences could see naught but my head (adorned in the old style in an enormous powdered wig trimmed with feathers, flowers, and pearls) and my face (powdered, patched, and painted like a lady of the court) while I gazed out at the mural of the brave King Richard the Lionhearted clad in the tabard of a crusading Knight Hospitaller.

After the performances, I would reappear in clean drapery, with my own hair falling nearly to my ankles, and the doctor would introduce Miss Emily Lyon to them. From then on, I never lacked for attention and was offered no end of opportunities to dine out, or to visit Ranelagh and Vauxhall just at the time of the evening when the wild and adventuresome crowd would make its appearance, and the grounds truly lived up to their description as pleasure gardens.

Never was a young lady so feted as I was on my fifteenth birthday in 1780. A sandy-haired buck of twenty-six whom I knew only as "Uppark Harry," one of Dr. Graham's frequent patrons—and a man I had also seen at Mrs. Kelly's several times—invited me to

join him and a number of his set at Vauxhall after my appearance
as Hygeia that night. What guttling we enjoyed! Capon and roast
meats, and exotic fruits and delicacies, all washed down with copious quantities of champagne.

"Emily, girl, favor us with a song! *Tu chantes comme un ange.* Celestial!" Uppark Harry stretched his long legs and pulled me onto
his lap. He was one of those Englishmen who, having completed
their grand tour on the Continent, began peppering their speech
with French upon returning to their native soil. They believed it
lent them polish, even as they belched through their words.

"Sing that one you used to do at Mrs. Kelly's," he whispered in
my ear, thoroughly bathing it with his tongue.

"Ooh, 'e's got it for fetching!" I remarked to one of the other
bucks, a slender, rather sober fellow whose name I learnt was
Charles Greville.

"I'm sorry, I don't speak the cant," Greville condescended, with
his eyes on my bosom the while he insulted me.

"It's just one of our expressions back in Flintshire. Means 'e's a
lovable rogue. Ain't you, 'Arry?" I said, giving old Uppark a tickle
in the ribs.

I was living a fine life for a barely literate girl. Though I had not
the fancy clothes and furbelows I was afforded at Arlington Street,
my body was my own and I could bestow it upon whom I pleased.
I had no dearth of admirers to chuse from, and I was earning
enough on my own to pay my landlady, never going hungry in the
bargain. No life of a browbeaten serving wench or filthy, over-
worked factory slut for Emily Lyon!

But below the surface of the glittering town life lurked rumblings I could not apprehend. I began noticing, throughout the
month of May, that more and more people from all stamps of life
walked through the streets of London sporting a blue cockade on
their hats. Their number grew and grew until their religiously in-
spired fervor exploded during the first week of June.

On June 2, I was leaving my room bound for a stroll in Piccadilly when I quite literally bumped into my landlady.

"Quick, gal, there's no time to lose," exclaimed an excited Mrs. Budge, thrusting a blue cockade into my hand while, with her other, she gripped my wrist and drew me into the street.

"Whatever for?"

"Don't just stand there dawdlin'. Stick it in yer 'at. Hurry now, there's a girl. Shows you're one of us!"

"One of who?"

"Protestants, gal."

"But I don't know if I am—I never went to church as a girl."

"Then yer a Protestant!"

Outside, the streets were teeming with cockade-bedecked people rushing toward Whitehall. This much I learnt as I was borne through St. James by the tide of feverish humanity: these preservers of Protestantism, as they considered themselves, were seeking to compel the House of Commons to repeal the Catholic Relief Act, passed two years earlier, which granted Papists equal rights to their Protestant brethren. "But don't everyone 'ere believe in the same God?" I shouted to Mrs. Budge, yet she didn't hear me above the din. Like the other citizens chanting "Down with popery!" at the top of their lungs, she had become infected with agitated zeal: the power of the mob. I tried to duck into an alley or a side street, but it was impossible to avoid the rushing crowds that jostled and shoved and shouted their way toward Parliament. When we reached Whitehall, a retired naval lieutenant named George Gordon, hoisted high upon the shoulders of two burly supporters, delivered a rabble-rousing anti-Papist speech exhorting us to destroy the Catholics and all they held sacred.

That night, linkboys' torches were commandeered as the mob, sixty thousand strong, hungry for Catholic blood, and bent on destruction, battered down the doors of Papist churches, smashing or stealing everything they could lay their hands on, leaving charred rubble and shards of jewel-colored glass in their acrid, noisy wake. Known Papists were dragged from their homes and beaten with brickbats until their heads and limbs were reduced to bloody pulp and their abodes looted of all valuables before they were set ablaze. Word spread like disease that no Catholic, his family, or his property was safe in London.

The rest of us were imprisoned by fear, for the city was under mob rule. Dr. Graham suspended his free treatments of the poor and his costly lectures to the elegant until peace might be restored. For days, the streets teemed with anger and ran with blood. London's miasma became even thicker and more odiferous from the billowing smoke and smoldering rubble. I barricaded myself in my room for fear when I learnt that Gordon's followers had burst the gates of Newgate gaol and released the prisoners, who had quickly blended in among the rioters. The next target was the Bank of England. Five days after the Gordon Riots began, King George summoned the militia, and after John Wilkes ordered his troops to fire upon the crowd gathered outside the bank, the unrest was finally halted.

The human toll was 290 dead. Twenty-five of the riot's ringleaders were hanged, tho' George Gordon himself was found *not guilty* of treason.

I had not known what it was like to experience war, and could not comprehend the complexities and nuances of the politics behind all the violence. But I was certain that I wished to avoid another encounter with such brutality and destruction. I began to suffer nightmares in which I became the victim of a vitriolic mob. For the first time since my arrival in London—a city not unknown for its criminal element, regardless of the political climate—I found myself frightened to live there. I feared that others would feel the same as I and seek their pleasure before their own hearths rather than venture of an evening to an establishment like Dr. Graham's. If times grew lean for him, my employment would not be secure, and to be one step ahead of being tossed into the gutter, I had to devise an alternative plan, should that unhappy day come to pass.

One evening, gazing upon the mural of Richard Lionheart as I impersonated the Goddess of Health, the yearned-for epiphany arrived. It was time for Emily Lyon to seek greener pastures. Out of the warm mud emerged Emily Hart, the young woman to whom, by summer's end, the cavalier Uppark Harry had made a most advantageous offer.

Seven

Uppark Harry

"You're a 'sir'?" I squinted at his card. "*Sir 'Arry Fether . . .* Fetherst—"

"It's pronounced 'Fanshaw,' " said Sir Harry, relieving me of my distress at being unable to make out the pronunciation of "Fetherstonhaugh," his impossibly long surname. And how could anyone, having only heard it, be expected to spell it correctly!

"I'm not a man prone to elaborate preambles, Emily, but you've quite struck my fancy. I find that I enjoy your companionship tremendously. And I should like to know whether you would find it amenable to provide it to me on a more frequent basis."

My breath caught in my throat. "You're not asking me to marry you, are you?"

Uppark Harry laughed, baring his long teeth. "Oh, my dear, you are a wit! I hope I do find a wife half as clever. I offer you a pretty cottage of your own in the country, provided you let me come and visit you whenever it suits my pleasure; and you will entertain me and my guests at table—when my mother is in town, of course, or in Bath for the season. *Fait-il plaisir?*"

"I 'ave no idea what you just said to me," I confessed.

"Does that make you happy?"

Of course I should have preferred a proposal of marriage, but for a girl of my stamp, with little breeding and less education, I had fallen arse over tit into a field of clover.

Within two weeks I had given my notice to Dr. Graham and informed Mam of my intentions to become the mistress of Uppark.

"I suppose you know what comes with the territory."

I nodded my head. "Would I 'ave a brighter future stuck in the mud at the Temple of 'Ealth? Living in one gloomy room in Cork Street with a popery hater for a landlady?"

"I can't say as to that, Emy, and I don't know what difference popery makes to you, but if you kept your situation in Adelphi Terrace, you might chuse to bestow your gifts where you may."

"I'm chusing Sir 'Arry," I said stubbornly.

"Is it far you're going? I don't want you to get so far away you won't be able to get out of trouble if it's brewing."

"It's in Sussex, in the valley of Harting. Eight hours from London with a coach and pair," I recited from memory. "Just think, Mam, I'll be doing all the duties of a country squire's wife—and 'e's a nobleman in the bargain!"

My mother took me to her bosom and, releasing me, grasped me by the shoulders. "Mark me, gal. I know your flights of fancy. You and your 'Arry may be ponshyn like rabbits in your little cottage, but when 'is mother decides to put an end to 'is frolics, you'll be standing in the road before you can remember 'ow to spell 'is name, y'nau." She cocked her head to regard me askance. "It's my own damn fault. I've said it afore and I'll say it again. I love you to pieces, but what the devil will become of you, Emily Lyon?"

I grinned. "Something wonderful, I expect. I'm Emily Hart now! A new name for a new life!"

Harry met me at Petersfield in the yard of the Red Lion. I endeavored to conceal from him how fagged I was from bouncing about for so many hours in the Portsmouth Coach and greeted him with my widest smile. "Miss Hart! I trust your journey was a pleasant one." He swept me off my feet—quite a task since I was near as tall as he—and spun me about, planting a passionate kiss on my lips. "What a jolly time we'll have, my girl. Let's slip a few glasses past the ivory before we set off for the manor, shall we? Come, you mustn't say no, for I know you to be quite the little toper on occasion."

Thus having been answered for without uttering a word, I was ushered into the bustling inn, where he commandeered a large round table at the center of the room.

"Come, a pint of porter for my fair companion, and a bottle of claret for yours truly!" he exclaimed, and within moments our drinks had been set upon the table. When he noticed I was nearly salivating over a roast joint being devoured at the next table, in a twinkling a plate of mutton appeared before me; and I gave him a most grateful grin, for I was famished. Scarce had I downed more than a quarter of a tankard's worth of stout when Harry ordered a second bottle of wine for himself. I prayed he did not expect me to match his pace.

But after the last drop of the second bottle had "passed his ivories," he called for his chaise, and we clattered out of the inn yard as though the excise men were on our trail, driving to the top of the Sussex Downs, along a steep incline, until we reached the iron gates of Uppark itself. How grand it all was, and what a vista it commanded! The sun was beginning to set, but I could still see Portsmouth and the Isle of Wight and just make out a mast or two poking into the sky.

The redbrick main house, four stories high, had so many windows that a delightful view of the estate might be commanded from any room. One entered by a sweeping stone staircase leading from a terraced and verdant park so smooth that a mighty game of bowls could be played upon it. Before the house and gardens lay a charming pond that Sir Harry kept stocked with fish. Grass and gravel walks led to every part of the property, including the new stables and kitchens, which could also be reached from the main house through subterranean passages. As his private races held along the Downs had earned a large measure of renown, the stables boasted some of the finest horses in the county. Beyond the great house lay his orchards and the forest in which Sir Harry and his friends enjoyed their frequent shooting parties.

And this paradise was what I was to be mistress of! Much as I enjoyed town life, the sight of glorious Uppark reminded me how much I'd missed the country. I wanted to roll down the hill the way I used to do back in Hawarden when I was naught but a wild and barefoot child.

With a mischievous grin Sir Harry offered me his arm. "Come, my girl, let me show you inside."

"And this is all yours?" I gasped, agog at the fine staircase, the gilded surfaces, and the elaborate plasterwork. The furnishings looked fit for King George himself.

"I inherited Uppark from my father six years ago. Much of what you see was purchased on my grand tour in 1776. The gilt-edged mirror you see above the fireplace is French, of course; the porcelain figurines on the mantel, Capodimonte—from Naples. Now, my widowed mother still resides here; her rooms are at the far end of the upstairs hall. But," he added gaily, "she is happily ensconced at Bath *à ce moment*, and there I hope she stays—for several weeks. I mean to have a card party this evening; tell me, do you play faro?" I shook my head. "Macao?"

"I'm afraid I must disappoint you there, too. But I should like to learn. I should like to learn everything! 'Arry, teach me 'ow to ride! I'd love to go chasing over the Downs like the wind. I'll win your derbys for you and you'll be so proud of me—"

"I'm sure you shall and I'm sure I will," interrupted Sir Harry. "But you've only just arrived. And there's so much more for you to see."

When he brought me to his own *chambre à coucher*, as he called it, it was not long before my gown was lying on the Turkey carpet, my petticoats and chemise in a heap beside them, and I was watching him as well as feeling him take me before the enormous looking glass.

Uppark Harry was a man of large appetites in every way, possessed of a remarkable amount of energy for one who consumed food and drink with the same abandon he displayed during fornication. "Egad, but you're delicious," he said, helping me into my stays as his tongue followed the laces along the length of my spine. "I must congratulate myself. I don't know which of us has got the better end of the bargain, eh?"

It was a bargain indeed, for I did not love Sir Harry. But in my youth, men and women entered into every sort of arrangement where the benefits inured to all concerned and a legal love match was not in the hand that was dealt.

"When my mother is in residence, you'll take this route," he explained, pressing on a length of wainscoting and escorting me through a cunningly disguised door that took us from his bedroom down a dark and narrow back staircase that led to a discreet rear entrance of the main house. "Don't fret, pretty Emily, you'll find that your own quarters are monstrous charming." We took the dogcart down the slope toward the little village of South Harting, halting at a pretty cottage at the base of the hill. "Rosemary Cottage is your dominion, my girl. You'll have a maidservant and the run of the place, and it shall be our little rustic hideaway."

The cottage's low ceilings were stifling in comparison with the lofty ones found in the main house, and the view from the mullioned windows was not nearly as breathtaking as the vista from Uppark's main house and gardens, but it was indeed delightful—and it was to be mine! Had an unschooled Chester lass ever been so fortunate? Sir Harry assured me that the mahogany wardrobe would be full to bursting with frocks as charming as those I had worn at Arlington Street. I would have a riding habit made up, and like a fine lady I could have the use of one of his carriages to journey to town for fans and gloves, perfumes and cosmetics, and whatever else might suit my fancy.

I took to Uppark Harry's horses like a pig to slops, in short order as adept in the sidesaddle as I was—having borrowed a pair of the master's breeches—at riding astride, which titillated the derby spectators as much as it scandalized them. But the sport of kings was not even the most popular of pastimes (if you don't count a good fuck) among Uppark Harry and his set of country gentlemen. Sir Harry bred fighting cocks, and the matches—which he held in his drawing room when the weather was unfavorable—were from rake to squire as well attended as any at the Cockpit Royal in London.

And the wagering was fierce. Some men knew their Staffordshire jet-blacks from their Shropshire reds; others just threw their coin at any contender, for it was the betting itself that fired up their blood. Those were the gents who would bet on the speed of a raindrop coursing down the windowpane of their London club. But among the cognoscenti, a prodigious amount of attention was paid to the trim of the wings (sloped), tails (shortened), hackle and rump feathers (reduced), combs (filed down to the merest ridge), and the type of spurs (metal or bone) that were strapped over the cock's own talons to ensure a fight to the death.

I wished my attendance was not required during the fights, but I was there to provide further amusement to Uppark Harry and his friends, decorating the room with my presence, breasts nearly spilling from my bodice, cheeks and lips fetchingly rouged, powdered hair tumbling askew—which it would have done at any rate from the sheer weight of my knee-length tresses under all the powder and pomade that was required to coat them.

I'd lay the matting over the carpet; then the owners of each of the two cocks in the match would hold their birds on interlocking fingers close to the matting and swing them thrice forward before my command of "Go!" at which point, the cocks would be released to have at each other, feinting and falling back, strutting and tilting, the scratching of the spurs against the matting sending chills along the insides of my teeth. Meanwhile, the clink of coins against one another as bets were feverishly placed heightened the excitement. The wine flowed freely; if someone overshot his limit, he often went unnoticed as he slipped from his chair or slumped in a corner. A cheer sprang up at first blood. Shouts of encouragement drowned out the cries of derision. Had Harry's mam ever witnessed this spectacle, she would have curled up her toes on the spot.

And when the owner of the loser congratulated his opposite number, and more bottles were opened and poured, it was a mournful Emily Hart who gently placed the corpse of the vanquished into a little box, swept up the errant feathers, and sent the matting to be scrubbed by the servants.

We hosted many dinners at Uppark, and the atmosphere often turned hedonistic during the latter portion of the evening. Sometimes, a few of Mrs. Kelly's "nuns" would be invited, to provide additional company for Sir Harry's friends, and as the meal drew to a close and the gentlemen lit their clay pipes, we girls would favor the guests with a song or two, a dance, or a little skit of our own devising.

My performances, above all, were greeted with the lion's share of admiration. One evening, fired by one such prodigious reception, and perhaps a bottle or two of claret, I surrendered to Sir Harry's drunken request to dance for him and his guests; and when he declared to all and sundry that he was the most fortunate man in the county, tying his tongue in knots in the attempt to spontaneously compose a panegyric to my beauty by rhyming "Sussex" with "lucky" and "fuck," his friends began to clap and stamp their feet as though they were witnessing a prizefight.

Aided by the host himself, I climbed atop the long table in

Harry's richly gilded saloon, and carefully placing my feet between the platter that held the remains of a particularly tasty suckling pig and a large dish of discarded prawn shells, I raised my skirts to display my ankles and calves, temptingly inching the petticoats higher and higher.

"Sing for us, Emily!" commanded Uppark Harry, and thus encouraged by rhythmic shouts of "Sing! Sing! Sing!" I accompanied my dance with a flirtatious rendering of "When for Air I Take My Mare," daintily picking my way amid what remained of the dinner's delicacies. Kneeling before Uppark Harry at the head of the table, I struck up "Come Jug, My Honey, Let's to Bed."

To the accompaniment of loud clapping and stamping, I led my lover out of the saloon, and before we got as far as his bedchamber, he was upon me in a trice.

My little postprandial performance was such a sensation that I was requested by my protector to repeat it on subsequent evenings, and soon, some variation of the original repertoire became part of the customary bill of fare.

Oh, there was guttling and tippling beyond description! One night, the dance went so far that, like Salome, I shed my clothes entirely. The payment I received in admiring glances and vociferous approval of my singing and dancing were to my fifteen-year-old soul the equivalent of a shower of molten gold.

And there were evenings when were it not for the sumptuous surroundings, you might think you'd stumbled into one of the old Southwark stews instead. My sixteenth birthday, in 1781, remains forever woven into the fabric of my memory, for the impact it was to have on my life. As the meal drew to a close, and my health was toasted with many glasses and bumpers, Uppark Harry insisted upon a contest wherein each of his guests would bare his fair companion's bosom, slather it with a liberal coating of syllabub, and thence, using only his tongue, remove every drop of the sweet, viscous beverage from her *poitrine*. Sir Harry's friend the saturnine

Charles Greville was at the table that evening and evinced no inclination to have a filly in the race, for which he was greeted with
such jeers of derision that I could not reckon how he had the for-
titude to remain so calmly in his chair.

"Then you must be the judge, man!" exclaimed Uppark Harry.
"For with this lot, there is bound to be some cheating."

I was of course to be Sir Harry's partner, but scarce had a
minute passed since Greville dropped his handkerchief, signifying
the commencement of the contest, when I found myself rather
abruptly pulled from Sir Harry's lap, and onto the knees of Sir
Roger Ainsley, who sat beside him. As a pawn, rather than a
knight, in this scenario, I was unsure how to behave, for at Sir
Harry's behest I was there to please and entertain, the which I
rather tipsily believed I was doing. Sir Roger's gesture precipitated
a number of similar exchanges and the contest continued to pro-
voke much jollity among the participants, until Uppark Harry—
suddenly realizing that he had lost control of the game—became
violently enraged, as was his wont once a certain number of bottles
had passed his lips. Rising from his chair, he tossed my old friend
Sophia onto her arse. Grasping me first by my hair, and thence by
closing his fingers about my arm, he pulled me to my feet, and,
producing a glove from the pocket of his coat, tossed it down on
the table before Ainsley and demanded satisfaction.

The most ungentlemanly ructions then ensued, as the guests,
including the doxies, instantly chose sides.

Naming me an embarrassing little slut and no better than a gutter whore, he berated me before the entire party, and I fear he
would have slapped me had not Greville raised his arm to
intervene.

"It is one of the hallmarks of a gentleman to be able to finish
what he began in the same spirit in which the enterprise was first
undertaken," scolded Greville. "Harry, this sport was of your own
devising, and while Emily must own her share of the blame, you

cannot excoriate her for her wantonness when the entire game suddenly turned round-robin. Your incomparable cellar is the envy of every man at this table, but given this evening's excesses of food and drink, surely you cannot wonder at the disintegration of common courtesies, even within the limits of the lately interrupted pastime."

An uncomfortable pall descended upon what had begun as an evening of bonhomie and joviality.

"Damme, but you're a prig, Greville."

"If you do not lead by example, how is a girl with the background of Miss Hart's to learn the finer points of gentry manners and be worthy of her responsibilities as your hostess and chatelaine?"

"Enough!" Uppark Harry snarled. "When you are fortunate enough to induce a mistress to share your chilly bed, you may play the tutor and scold or coddle the chit as you wish, but I'll thank you to keep your oar out of my affairs." Then clasping me about the waist, he drew me to him with such force that my bubbies were nearly crushed against his chest, and planted a kiss upon my lips so ferocious that my breath was almost stop'd from the strength of his passion. Releasing me, he declared, as much for my ears as the others', "*I'm* your protector, Emily; remember that. And I will remain so until I chuse to release you from our arrangement."

His words made me shiver; Sophia and I retired to a corner of the saloon to relace each other. "Is Sir Harry often this spiteful?" she whispered.

I cast a glance at the disarray: upended bottles spilling the last of their contents in violet rivers upon the damask cloth; shards of crystal and items of plate that littered the Turkey carpet; bits of meat and fowl that clung to the chairbacks; and syllabub stains on the upholstery. " 'E 'as a temper when 'e drinks too deeply," I murmured. " 'Is capacity is prodigious, but once the line is cross'd there is no vouching for 'is manners."

For many months I had been enjoying a life of untrammeled gaiety at Uppark, but Sir Harry's behavior that night shone a bright light into the dark corners of my dreamworld. My knight was not always the hero of Dr. Graham's murals. But Charles Greville . . . now, here was a revelation. I, too, had oft thought him a prig, but perhaps I had been too hasty to condemn a man who so consistently and assiduously behaved like a true gentleman amid a swarm of so many wild boys. Greville's demeanor, his evident distaste for Sir Harry's more raucous frivolities, and his ability to so deftly defuse the volatile encounter between Ainsley and Sir Harry had impressed my girlish heart, and from that evening on, I was greatly disposed to look upon him—with no small degree of interest—in a new, and decidedly more attractive, light.

Eight

The Wind Changes

During the weeks that followed my birthday I began to notice a gradual cooling of Uppark Harry's ardor. So keenly did I sense his increasing indifference and brusqueness that I felt no shame in meeting Greville during an excursion to London on the pretense of visiting Creed for a bottle or two of scent.

He began our acquaintance by leading me on a tour of the enormous town house he was having built on Portman Square, and then, with furtive sighs and whispers, he expressed the desire to show me his "stones"—which I'd learnt at Mrs. Kelly's was cant for a man's balls. I can't imagine what poor, proper Greville thought when I bosted out laughing at the sight of a bunch of old crystals, gemstones that looked like rock sugar candies, some of them still in what looked to me like half a coconut shell.

"Why 'aven't you scooped 'em out and made 'em into jewelry?" I asked. And then Greville explained—with such a grave expression on his face that I was near to bosting a stay—that the minerals, as he called them, were even more rare and precious in their natural state.

"But what use are they if you're not going to 'ave 'em made up?"

"What use? Why, to look at! My child, you cannot begin to imagine the pleasure one derives, the exquisite enjoyment, from looking—looking at such treasures—in their natural simplicity. How much more attractive, how glorious, they are, the way Nature herself intended, rather than in a gaudy incarnation one might purchase at Asprey. For something in its natural state is far more beautiful than it is after the application of artifice."

Charles Greville fascinated me. I wondered why such a refined gentleman, a member of Parliament, would take the time and the pains to instill a sense of delicacy and education in someone like me. Never had a man cared for me in such a manner, and his generosity in this regard overwhelmed all my senses. We commenced a clandestine affair that continued throughout the summer months of 1781, and into the fall. Early on, while I was still ensconced at Uppark, I would come down to London on some pretext or other, which Sir Harry, increasingly losing interest in my company, would never question. Greville's lovemaking—unlike that of Sir Harry, who rode me as if I were his prize mare—was slow, almost elegant. The time he took to explore my body as though it were a work of art was new and different to me, and I allowed myself to find delight in it. How I enjoyed giving myself to him! After I'd experienced the excesses of Uppark Harry, Greville's restraint was intoxicating to me. He neither overate nor gambled nor drank to excess. And for the first time in my life, here was a man who was keen on broadening my interests, that we might have more to do with each other than romp between the bedsheets. To gain such a fine and amiable protector was akin to being taken to the bosom of God.

Having secured a position with the Admiralty Board a year previous, Greville had the advantage of free accommodation in the King's Mews. His Portman Square town house was being erected upon the speculation of grander things to come, and I own that I permitted my fancies to fly to an imagined existence within those high-ceilinged rooms with their white plaster moldings and their fine marble mantels.

In August, I was struck with the realization that my courses had not arrived in well over a month. By early September I was sure that the best and the worst had occurred sometime in June or July and I was no doubt with child. I was certain the babe's father was Sir Harry, for Greville always took the greatest pains to glove himself and then to withdraw at the moment of ecstasy, with a basin at the ready for me to thoroughly cleanse our parts. Uppark Harry never took such precautions.

A few weeks later, I was absolutely certain of my condition.

At that time, we were all in town, Harry having quit Uppark for his Mayfair establishment; but as I was unable to join him there in all propriety, he lodged me in a small set of rooms in Whitechapel. It was horridly lonely, for I had no friends to call my own; those of Sir Harry's acquaintance did not visit me in London. Sir Harry called on me only once. My body had not yet begun to betray my secret, but in my naive girlish fancy I believed that once Sir Harry learnt it, he would clasp me in his arms, smother my breasts and belly with burning kisses, and bring me to Rosemary Cottage with all due haste. Instead, we had such ructions that day that the landlady came up to see what it was all about. He berated me fiercely for several incidents of poor conduct and a string of infidelities. It was then I suspected that Sir Harry had discovered my meetings with Greville, though he did not name him. But there had been no others in my arms, and were it not for Sir Harry's increasing neglect, I would not have thought to set my cap elsewhere, for well I knew the delicacy of my situation.

In a frightful panic I turned to Greville, the only person I believed would be able to relieve my extreme distress. Coolly, he advised me to throw myself upon Sir Harry's mercy and seek to patch things up between us.

All through the fall I endeavored to contact my protector—praying that he would relent, for I truly believed Sir Harry to be the father of my babe—and each of seven letters went unanswered.

I had deceived myself that I was standing on solid ground, when i'faith, I was on naught but a shoal; my happy world was like so many granules of sand being swept out from beneath my feet by the encroaching tide.

Uppark Harry had left me no money, nor could I count on more than the occasional guinea from Greville. My landlady permitted me to remain as long as she received her blunt on time; but to keep the roof above my head, I was compelled to sink to the lowest and most sordid degradation, stooping to that which even the meanest, lowest woman in England should not have to abase herself to perform. I am ashamed even to confess it now. I own I was in real distress, accepting "guilty support" from anyone who could provide me with a few quid for food and lodging. Even as my belly swelled I frequented the pleasure gardens if the weather was mild enough, and haunted taverns on both sides of the Thames, each time hoping against all hope that I would catch no disease on the lice-ridden straw mattresses.

All through the Christmas holiday I was beside myself with every anxiety, lonely and unattended, drinking a bumper in the parlor with the landlady and her pustule-faced son to celebrate the birth of the baby Jesus. I remained terrified to confess my distress to Mam, whom I had not seen in months.

Through one of his manservants, Sir Harry eventually sent me a guinea wrapped in a scrap of paper without so much as a word scrawled upon it to ease my heart. It was scarcely enough to get myself from London to Chester. I arrived at the Steps looking as though I had swallowed a pumpkin of prodigious girth, and soaked to the skin to boot, for Sir Harry had not given me enough to ride inside the coach.

Weeping, I fell into Gammer's sturdy arms.

"Just look at you, gal! What the devil 'ave you gone and done?" I felt Gammer shake her head as she pressed me to her bosom. "Do you know who the father is, then? Does 'e know you've gone off?

Will 'e at least give you a few bob to care for the babe once it makes its way into the world? It won't be too long now, y'nau? A guess is as good as a promise and I'd say the little one'll be poking 'is head into 'Is Majesty's realm by March at the latest, mark my words on't. But first off," she added, unseating my uncle William so I could avail myself of the best chair in the cottage, "you'll 'ave to fill that big belly of yours with a good meal. We anna any meat, but I've a pot of one of your favorites, Emy, gal: a bit of ponsh meip." Gammer ladled a generous helping of mashed potatoes and turnips into a trencher.

Over the mash and a glass of porter I told her all about Uppark Harry.

"And you say 'e's answered not a one of your letters to 'im?" I shook my head. "O, 'e's got me chawin' the fat now," she grumbled. Thinking on it further, Gammer stamped her foot in disgust. " 'E's got me *tampin'*! If 'e weren't gentry, I'd take my 'orsewhip to 'is stubborn 'ide."

"Don't be making it any worse for me than it already is," I moaned, hungrily shoveling in the last mouthful of potatoes.

Gammer fetched a stool and a cushion and raised my feet before the fire. "Y'aven't gone and blarted out your business with this Greville fellow, 'ave you?" she asked anxiously. "Could be the reason why your dear 'Arry's not of a mind to see to his responsibilities. Though even if 'e didn't suspect you'd been ponshyn on the sly wi'another, 'e wouldn't be the first and Lord knows 'e won't be the last to leave a girl in distress once 'e'd gotten 'er in a family way." Gammer knelt beside me and looked deep into my eyes. "Do y'love 'im, Emy?"

My tears began to drench my cheeks. "Which one?"

"The one as got all them fields and 'orses."

"Sir 'Arry Fetherstonhaugh. No, Gammer, I don't love 'im, though I was fond of 'im when we was good together. Yet I'd still go back to Uppark in an instant if 'e'd 'ave me."

"And what about t'other gent? Charlie?"

"The Honorable Charles Greville. Yes, I *could* love 'im. Very much. 'E's a gentleman through and through—not like Sir 'Arry—and Greville would sooner lose 'is right arm than see me and a babe left to rot in the gutter."

"Are you certain of that, Emy, girl?" Gammer smoothed her callused palm over my brow, wiping away the trickles of perspiration.

"I want so much to believe so," I replied, biting my lip in hesitation. "And, any rate, right now 'e's my only hope."

Toward the beginning of the year, full of anguish, I penned a frantic note to Greville, in response to a sympathetic letter I had received from him the previous day. Would he be willing to become my protector? After enumerating an elaborate set of conditions, first among which was the procurement of a true copy of my baptismal certificate, for he wish'd to be certain that I was of the age I had warranted, Greville indicated to me that he might be persuaded to entertain the prospect.

> *10th Jan. 1782*
>
> *My dear Emily,*
>
> *If you should come to town free of all engagements & take my advice, you will live very retired, <u>till</u> you are brought to bed. You should part with your maid, & take another <u>name</u>, by degrees I would get you a new set of acquaintance, & by keeping your own secret, & nobody about you having it in their power to betray you, I may expect to see you respected and admired. Thus far relates to yourself. As to the child, its mother shall obtain it kindness from me & it shall never want.*
>
> *I inclose you some money, do not throw it away, you may send some presents when you arrive in Town, but do not be on the road without some money to <u>spare</u>, in case you should be fatigued and wish to take your time: God bless you my dearest lovely girl, take your determination soon & let me hear from you. Once more Adieu my Emily.*

Gammer looked thoughtful. "You could do worse than to follow everything 'e says in that letter you're 'olding. It's not too late to mend your ways, Emy gal, and let the gentleman turn you into a fine young lady, fit to mingle with the cream of the crop . . . though I don't know for the life of me what you'll change your name to, as 'e's asking you, y'nau? With a little one in the oven, you should call yourself a 'Mrs.'—of that much I'm certain. Y'can always be a widow, and there's none that'll question it. Or a sailor's wife. They's always at sea for so many months—years, even—that they don't even know they got a babe back home. And they get all kind of disease on them ships. . . ."

I stopped hearing Gammer's words when I thought of poor Samuel Linley, pale and sickly from the fever, plans for our blissful marriage the last words on his parched lips.

"Like I said, you could do worse than put yourself under this Greville's protection. I 'ear you've been calling yourself Emily Hart these past months. So, with a 'Mrs. Emily—' "

"Not Emily. 'Emily' is a silly girl, and I'm leaving 'er on the shelf. Gammer, if I'm to begin a new life as a respectable young lady, fit to be the companion for the likes of a man such as the Honorable Charles Greville, my new name must be dignified as well. I'm meaning to become *Emma*. Mrs. Emma Hart."

Nine

Edgware Road

In early 1782, dusty Edgware Road on the outskirts of London was nearly as rural as Chester, for all its countrified rustication. Situated at the edge of Paddington Green was a row of modest houses, newly built, and it was at Paddington Road, No. 14 Oxford Street, where Greville ensconced me and my mam, now calling herself Mary Cadogan.

Mam told me that she fancied the name after learning that her employer, the Earl of Warwick, favored the powdered wig with clubbed curls nicknamed the "Cadogan wig" after the lordly gentleman who first sported the fashion. The name Cadogan sounded terribly upper crust to her, so she adopted it for her own. Mam was to be my chaperone as well as the housekeeper of the establishment, seeing to the cooking and the accounts, and supervising the servants that Greville would engage after I gave birth.

Greville still dwelt in the King's Mews. Our arrangement was such that he could come to stay with us as whim and leisure directed. In keeping with his "system," he had his own set of rooms apart from ours, which were sacrosanct and not to be entered whilst he was in residence unless we had received permission to disturb him. Another element of Greville's plan was that in order to curb my wild ways and learn responsibility, I should study to keep the household ledger, even in my advanced condition, as he thought it would distract my mind from my physical discomfort and distress. By degrees Greville undertook to educate me, teaching me the properties of arithmetic, as well as correcting my faults in grammar, orthography, and speech. My Flintshire accent appeared to trouble him no end, for he was forever lamenting my pronunciation.

"Emma, one takes a *bahth*," he would scold, emphasizing the broad *A* that proper ladies and gentlemen employ—the *A* that sounds like one is opening one's mouth wide enough to insert an object of sizable girth. "And stop dropping your aitches like a country bumpkin or a Whitechapel costermonger. It's *him*, not *'im*; *has*, not *'as*. You are the loveliest girl in the world—until you open your mouth and mar the celestial image with your mangled speech."

Though I was proud of my origins, he was absolutely right, of course, and thus I would try my level best to mend my faults as much to improve myself as to please him. If I could only adhere to Greville's system in all things, I would be fit to mingle in society—except that my new and adored protector forbade me to do so. No more heavy brocaded frocks, nor powder in my hair, nor paint on my face. For a time I felt miserably unfashionable in simple muslin gowns, fretting my lot to Mam, who reminded me that there was no one but the serving girls to see me, and that Greville himself extolled my fresh, natural beauty, even in its first flush of feminine ripeness.

In any event, despite all the exuberance of youth and my new station, my condition soon rendered it difficult for me to go about. I was not long at Edgware Road before my lying-in commenced. Shortly before St. Valentine's Day in the year of our Lord 1782, the pains began to come, and with all the skill of a practiced midwife Mam made the necessary preparations. Stretched out along my hip, I lay on my bed crying for mercy whilst Mam rested my raised right leg upon her shoulder; and in what seemed like an eternity—

though Mam swore up and down it was naught but a few hours—
she delivered me of a rosy baby girl.

"Lud, but she's a beauty, y'nau," Mam said, placing the babe at
my swollen breast.

"She is indeed," I whispered.

"And look at that 'ead of 'air. That way, she do take after her
mam. What 'ave you a mind to name 'er?"

"I suppose—look 'ow she's latched on; there, now, that reminds
me of her papa—I reckon I could call 'er *'Arriet*, but I never fancied the name."

Mam smiled at us. "Course you could always call 'er *Charlotte*."

"Greville would bost 'is seams! 'Sides which, memory serving
and all things considered, I'm almost certain she would 'ave been
an 'Arriet sooner than a Charlotte." I kissed the reddish down that
covered my babe's soft pink crown. "Emma. She's little Emma.
Aren't you, my pet?" And don't you know, just as if she knew what
I was saying, she cooed a soft assent that set me weeping?

"Do you think—now that she's come—that Greville will let me
keep 'er 'ere?"

"You know 'im better than I, girl. Now quit frowning, or it will
affect your milk."

Youth is nothing if not elastic. By the end of February, not only
was I on my feet and looking as fit as if I had never given birth, but
I was taking little Emma, swaddled in woolens, for walks under the
elms at the edge of Paddington Green or in the quaint little
churchyard abutting the green itself, where my mam loved to stroll;
and as spring whispered its annual promise into the brisk air, I sat
with my little one in our charming garden, where Greville grew
and nurtured the myriad specimens of flora that he assiduously
shared with his precious London Horticultural Society.

Although grateful that I'd come through childbirth as healthy
as a horse, Greville had studied to avoid our cottage since little

Emma's birth, and I missed him dreadfully. My figure was as handsome as ever, and I was eager to welcome him back to our bed; besides, Edgware Road never quite felt like home unless we was all together under the same roof.

In early March, my adored Greville surprised us with a visit, announcing that he had arranged for me to sit to the celebrated portraitist George Romney. On the twelfth of the month, he brought me in his coach to Romney's studio in Cavendish Square, an easy distance from our cottage in Edgware Row. I can still recall the odors of turpentine and linseed oil that assailed our nostrils as we entered the high-ceilinged room. Unfinished canvases lay everywhere: portraits of women and children, women and dogs, children and dogs, and each of them radiantly depicted in lush colors against a muted sky that emphasized the subject as a setting does a jewel. Many of the portraits, tacked to their stretcher bars, were haphazardly stacked three or four deep against one another along the floor moldings, whilst a half dozen or so rested on wooden easels as if anticipating the next brushstroke. Languishing along an entire wall, a large canvas bore the rudiments of a rugged landscape and, only partially realized, a castle in flames.

I thought at first that the studio was curiously empty, save for Greville and myself, but in response to a "Halloo, there!" from my protector, a stocky man of middling years with a kindly countenance presently appeared from behind a vast canvas.

"Greetings, patron," Romney said gloomily. "Forgive me, Greville, for my lack of good cheer this morning. Just one of my usual bouts, nothing more."

Despite the painter's morosity, I felt immediately at home, for Romney's Lancashire accent, not too dissimilar to my own speech, was as pronounced as though he had never left his birthplace. My protector made the introductions.

"Such a pleasure, Greville! Your servant, Mrs. Hart." Romney inclined his head in a subtle show of courtesy. With a newfound glee he examined every detail of my face and figure as if he were to paint me on the spot.

"Did I not tell you she was as unspoilt as the first flowers of May?"

"Exquisite. Simply exquisite. Such a shame that you have been keeping the bloom all to yourself, Charles."

"I mean to remedy that; in fact, such is the purpose of my visit this morning. I intend, George, to commission you to paint Emma as you see fit, to display her beauty to its best advantage, and to effect the sale of such portraits to your other patrons. Although propriety dictates that under my protection Mrs. Hart should live as retired a life as I think meet, I raise no objection to her likeness gracing the drawing rooms that her person may not enter."

"A pity, that," replied Romney, "for she would eclipse 'em all, mark my words on't."

Greville glanced at me before addressing the artist. "The arrangement is a mutually beneficial one, my dear Romney." And lowering his voice, though not enough for me to avoid hearing, he added, "If only I could do something about that accent."

"Though it's true I don't care to go about much, I can't say as country vowels 'ave done me much 'arm in the world." Romney smiled, and I thought in that instant that if my father had lived, I would have liked him to be just like this gentle man from Lancashire.

Romney circled me the way Uppark Harry used to inspect his fighting cocks. "I think I should like to begin just the way Emma looks today: in all the bloom of youth without the affectations of artifice."

"Egad, we are of a mind!" exclaimed Greville. "Emma is at her best just as you see her, all sweetness of feature. And you, my good man, will be a pioneer of portraiture indeed, for I have yet to see, even from my dear old friend Reynolds, a young woman of Emma's stamp—or even a woman of quality—depicted without the good offices of her hairdresser and the prodigious application of lip rouge."

A bargain was then struck between the two gentlemen. I was to sit regularly to Romney, in the company of my mother for propriety's sake, while Greville would give us a shilling each for the hackney coach from Paddington Green to Cavendish Square.

But Greville's "dear old friend" Sir Joshua Reynolds, who had painted my old soul of a protector when Greville was but a boy of thirteen, was not to lose out entirely on the opportunity to enrich both himself and Greville by turning portraits of Mrs. Emma Hart into guineas. We called upon the great painter at his celebrated studio in Leicester Fields, an exceedingly fashionable salon as different from Romney's messy and haphazard premises as Greville's Portman Square town house was from our modest arrangement in Edgware Row. "Remember what I told you in the carriage," Greville cautioned. I nodded my head in assent. "Which was . . . ?"

"Don't gawk."

"Even if you were not born with breeding, I am convinced it is not too late to instill it in you, Emma. You're a quick study, my dear. You soak up knowledge like a dry field after the first spring rain—when you put your mind to it."

"Thank you, my love!" I beamed, squeezing Greville's arm.

"And don't hang upon me so."

"I'll save it, then, till we're back at 'ome. But just one kiss," I insisted, stopping him long enough to press my lips to his. "Oh, Greville, I am the 'appiest woman in London! In all of England, even."

"And why is that, my dear?"

"Because I think you love me."

The corridor echoed with the footsteps of our host, a short, barrel-chested man. Under hooded lids, his small dark eyes missed nothing. His burgundy coat and white neckcloth were immaculate, his breeches of fawn-colored silk as exquisite as those worn by his wealthy patrons in their portraits.

Over tea it was determined that Sir Joshua would depict me as a Madonna, a radical departure from his customary compositions, not merely in subject, but in appearance. Greville's eyes nearly popped, but he was too much the gentleman to otherwise indicate his astonishment at such an ironic twist.

"I've got my very own babe!" I blarted before Greville's warning glance could stop my mouth. "Please, Sir Joshua, paint me with my daughter. She's scarce more than a month in this world, and it would mean everything to me if I could sit to you with my own little Emma in my arms."

With worldly aplomb, the artist did not so much as raise an eyebrow. "Well, at least the bond will appear quite natural," he muttered. "Charles, is this child under your roof?"

"At present."

"Is it your wish to permit Mrs. Hart to pose with her infant daughter?"

"As a man who prefers that his arrangements enable each party to derive an equal sense of satisfaction, I raise no objection. Sir Joshua, I also am a man who is jealous of an opportunity for quietude."

I saw Sir Joshua's portrait only once after it had been completed. He titled the composition *Girl with a Baby*. Bathed in what passes for moonlight, little Emma and I look ghostly and ethereal, while behind us, in scratchy brushstrokes of deep greens and blues, the perceptive and imaginative viewer can make out a sylvan glade and a stone bridge, beyond which looms a distant castle.

Those were happy days we passed, little Emma and I, in Reynolds's grand studio, for not only was I able to spend so much time with my little daughter at my breast, but in that brief period I came to believe that I could indeed pass for a Madonna, resurrecting my wayward reputation. "Being totally clear from all the society and habits of kept women, creditable and quiet people will come to respect you," Greville assured me.

If only he'd enlarge his "system"—by permitting little Emma to continue to reside with us in Edgware Road—my journey toward responsibility and respectability would not have felt like such an arduous one.

Ten

Growing Pains

After Mam brought little Emma up to Hawarden that spring and left her in Gammer's care, I was brokenhearted and dreadfully rudderless. With Greville absent as well, I had no one to shine for. Now that the house was childless, we had two maidservants—Molly Dring and Nelly Gray, the former as plump as the latter was spindly—but under his system, I was not expected to converse with the two girls other than where it concerned the scope of their household duties. Having been in service myself, I was still unaccustomed to my new role on the other side of the great societal divide; it caused me discomfort, like a scratchy garment.

My visits to Romney in Cavendish Square became our mutual saving grace. The portraitist was both a dear friend and a sympathetic ear. "You're a tonic to my soul, girl," he would declare contentedly as he ground his colors, whilst I wandered about the studio inquiring as to the subjects of his unfinished canvases. Then he would tell me the story behind the painting, all those wondrous tales of the Greek and Roman heroes, of their battles and victories, of their gods and goddesses.

On April 13, two weeks before my seventeenth birthday, I was sitting on the painter's stool, gazing out the window, when Romney suddenly exclaimed, "Oh, lud love you, child!"

"What?"

"Sit there, just as you are! Now turn your torso to me—no, no, just your torso—leave everything else where 'tis." After another moment or two of prodigious study, Romney came over and adjusted the angle of my head. "Much better. That slight tilt of your chin, Emma, gives you the most exquisite jawline. Your face becomes a perfect 'eart. You 'ave a receding chin, my dear—it's your only feature that does not approach the feminine ideal. Nevertheless, once you learn 'ow to pose yourself to best advantage, I assure you no one in Europe will be the wiser."

Truth be told, I was already aware of—and secretly displeased by—my weak chin; it was my least favorite feature. "Blame my mam," I teased, pointing to my mother. "It's 'er chin what I've got."

"Well, there's no giving it back, gal, so you two will just have to content yourselves—and Greville as well—with a mark just short of perfection. But that's what gives a person character, so I shouldn't fret over it, Emy. And I reckon even Georgy 'ere, though 'e's in the perfection business, will agree with me." Mam reached into a deep pocket and discreetly withdrew a flask from which she allowed herself a tot of gin.

From then on, I almost always posed with my head tilted at such an angle that I appeared to have the perfect chin!

Romney worked so slowly that for several sittings there would be little for my protector to view. Our sessions formed one of the choicest aspects of my enjoyment, but I bit back my frustration that this was the only sphere beyond Edgware Road that I might share with my beloved Charles.

I confess that I would have very much appreciated the privilege of entering the salons of polite society, for Greville went about in town alone, but I dared not press my advantage, particularly when he suggested a rare excursion to Ranelagh, knowing how much it would delight me to celebrate my birthday there. Endeavoring to please him in all things, I thought myself entirely content in my new, quietly retired life, but the truth was that I missed the gaiety of the pleasure gardens, though not the acquaintance of my prior companions there. To share every experience with my Greville— and only Greville—formed the chief cornerstone of my desires.

We had been enjoying the excitement of Ranelagh. . . . The orchestra, which at that hour was playing polkas and other lively airs, struck up a tune that was familiar to me. In short order, I was singing full voice, and on my feet dancing giddily to the spirited tune, and then two more, receiving a raucous approbation.

As the final note of the third country ballad died upon the air, Greville broke through the cluster of admirers and clasped my elbow. With the sternest expression I had ever seen grace his noble countenance, he trotted me out of the pleasure gardens without another word, except to call for his carriage when we reached the gates.

All during the ride back to Paddington Green, my beloved Greville's silence pained me; he would not hear a word of explanation, nor, can I admit even now, was there much defense to be made on my own behalf.

Greville assailed me once we set foot inside the cottage. "Your conduct this evening was intolerable," he scolded in a tone so severe that it sent chills along my spine. Seating me by the parlor fire and instructing me not to speak a word until he had finished his admonition, he added, "I have no desire to harbor an ungrateful hoyden under my roof, Emma. You have breached the particulars of our agreement, causing me undue embarrassment and monstrous regret that I allowed myself to be tenderly swayed by your predicament. There appears to be no end of young bucks to fawn upon you, if the lascivious attention of such vulgar company is what you prefer to my companionship. You have only to say the word and I will leave you to them without a moment's remonstrance. I will admit to you that at present I find no reason not to cast you off in the morning for your childish ingratitude and your failure to honor the terms of our ménage."

Convulsed with sobs, I rushed into my boudoir, and closing the door behind me, I threw myself into Mam's arms. "Oh God, what shall I do now!" I wept. "It's all over. . . . I've lost 'im . . . and all because I was a stupid, giddy girl. And I . . . want . . . 'im . . . so much . . . to love me," I spluttered. "I'm so scared. What will become of us?"

"Husht thee naise. 'Ere." My mother withdrew her handkerchief and handed it to me. "Dry your tears and make your face pretty again for 'im." I followed her advice, then permitted her to help me out of my embroidered bodice and overskirt. "Put this on instead, pet," Mam said, handing me a plain, long-sleeved white dress. "You know 'ow much your Greville admires you when you present 'im a picture of restrained simplicity."

It was as a penitent that I gently knocked on the door to Greville's study. "I'm so awfully sorry, my love," I whispered through the oaken barrier. "Mayn't I come in?"

Greville opened the door and I sank to my knees before him, tears of contrition trickling down my unpainted cheeks as I looked up into his pale and serious countenance.

"You 'ave taught me nothing but good, Greville," I sniffled. "I own my error, and will 'enceforth strive in every way to emulate your goodness. But please, my love, *please* forgive me! Don't cast me out. I don't know what will become of me if you do." My sobs returned with vigor. "From now on, I will walk in your ways with every step I take, for I know you are in the right." I pressed my lips to his. "Oh, 'ow I love you, Greville. Thank you, my beloved. Your Emma will never again betray your trust in her."

At my next sitting for Romney, I shared everything that had transpired that night.

"I knelt before him," I said, sinking to my knees, my white skirts billowing about me as though I sat astride a saintly cloud. "And raising my eyes thusly, I beseeched him to forgive me."

Romney studied my imploring gaze. "I should like to paint you like that. 'The Penitent.' For that expression would melt even the most adamantine heart."

"And so from now on, you will find me dressed just as you see me now: in 'sweet simplicity,' as Mam calls it."

"My dear child, you would eclipse the sun in sackcloth, but surely you do not intend to go about for the remainder of your days attired in a housemaid's frock?"

"Indeed I do." I nodded. "Oh, my dear friend, for a time, I own, through distress my virtue was vanquished, but my sense of virtue was not overcome." I laid my hat aside to prepare for the morning's sitting. "Greville restored my sense of virtue. 'E believed that it was not too late for me to recover my dignity, and in his eyes—and arms—I 'ave been graced with a second chance. Do you not agree that I should be grateful every day for my dearest Greville's protection?"

Nodding his head, Romney donned his smock. "In some ways I am in the same boat you are, my dear. Now, let us return to the Circe," he said. "We've scarce begun and I should like to 'ave more of it completed by now, for Greville is expecting to view it before the month is out. Your costume is behind the screen where you left it last."

"Tell me 'oo she is, again?" I asked, retreating behind the folding screen, where I seated myself at a small dressing table. First brushing out the lengths of hair that framed my face, I then began to secure them atop my head—a soft corona of auburn.

"Circe was an enchantress, my dear Emma. After the fall of Troy, the great Ulysses sailed for 'is 'ome in Ithaca to return to the arms of 'is wife, the faithful and patient Penelope. But Circe waylaid 'im, luring 'im to 'er shores, where she made love to 'im and kept 'im sated for many months, turning to swine any of 'is sailors who sought to escape."

I allowed this description to sink in. "And you think I look like this Circe?"

"Mrs. Hart, your beauty could enchant the pope 'imself to 'and you the keys to St. Peter's."

I saw George Romney, thirty years my senior, as my friend and more than father, and he was eager beyond measure to see me as his muse. With great delight he told Greville that my features were capable of exhibiting all the gradations of every passion with absolute truth, yet all the while maintaining an uncanny felicity of expression. Oftentimes Romney's good friend, the actor Henderson, would pay the artist a call and stay to observe my sitting, offering me the odd professional tip or two, strengthening my interpretative ability. Soon I was able to seamlessly and effortlessly make the transition from one character to another, holding each attitude and its corresponding emotion for as long as the artist required.

Using my blossoming talents to every advantage, Romney sketched me as Medea, bloody dagger raised, faced with the horror of the infanticide she has just committed. As Thetis, I stood below the walls of Troy and, with the knowledge that his future foretold a violent death in Ilium, pleaded with my son Achilles to return to Thessaly. As an impassioned Cassandra I struggled with the agonizing despair of the doomed Trojan prophetess. I embodied the seductress in Circe; posing with a spaniel pup, I was the youthful personification of Nature; and kneeling in prayer, I became the virginal Penitent.

From mid-March through early August, I sat to Romney fourteen times. Although I missed little Emma and thought of her—and Gammer—often, at Edgware Road I was content to act more like Greville's wife than his mistress, superintending the household with Mam, and assiduously adhering to my lessons with a newfound diligence. My mother, as eager to learn as I, would sit beside me; soon she, too, became a proficient reader—Mam, who had had to sign her wedding certificate with an *X*! Her orthography and penmanship quickly outshone mine, and I was never to catch up!

Now secure in Greville's affection, even if he had yet to tell me that he loved me, I believed myself at peace with my insularity. But my youthful exuberance, my zeal for every ounce of life I could lay my hands on, could not remain dormant forever.

In the dark winter months of 1783, when the elm trees were bare and the grass on Paddington Green was hard and unyielding beneath my feet, a warm presence from the sun-drenched south appeared like the first breath of spring on our doorstep.

Eleven

Pliny the Elder

"Egad, Uncle, they're practically pornographic!" Greville swiftly attempted to close the portfolio of sketches that Sir William Hamilton had spread before him.

"Won't they change shape in my 'ands if I 'old 'em too long?"

"Good God, Emma!"

"Well, they're made of *wax*, ain't they?" I grinned impishly and placed the two phalluses into the velvet-lined chest.

"Greville, I love you because you are my flesh and blood, but you can be an abominable prig."

My protector inclined his head in my direction while I poured their tea. "Under the present circumstances, Uncle, I cannot pretend to be your kindred spirit in all things antiquarian."

"It's not like I've never seen a cock before, my love," I said gaily, bestowing a gentle kiss on Greville's forehead.

"You two suit like a pair of candlesticks," Greville grumbled. "Go ahead, then, Uncle, and enlighten Emma about the Festival of Priapus. My aunt dies and all my uncle can think of is to immerse himself in pagan pornography. And for God's sake, Vesuvius has burnt you to a crisp! For all your silks and brocades and your Order of the Bath, you're as nut-brown as a peasant."

"And you, my dear nephew, are as pale as parchment. It would do your health a world of good to enjoy a sunny day. Lud knows they're rare enough in Albion!"

What a rare specimen of humanity was this man! His princely bearing was impressive enough, but never had I encountered an older man of the upper crust—not among the titled oglers at Mrs. Kelly's, and certainly not among Uppark Harry's set—who comported himself as befitting his rank, yet treated me with the utmost respect and never looked down his nose at me. William Hamilton, envoy extraordinary and ambassador plenipotentiary to the Court of the Two Sicilies—the man who called King George his foster brother, because they had shared a wet nurse—raised his teacup to me as if in a toast. "I'll have you know, Mrs. Hart, that the ex-votos, as they are called, represent a slice of ancient history that will henceforth be relegated to obsolescence. I amassed these artifacts at the final pagan Festival of Priapus—"

"Who the devil is that?"

"Priapus—the phallic Roman god of gardens, viniculture, sailors, and fishermen. Later this year, I intend to present them, with my notes and sketches, to the Society of Dilettanti—"

"You're saying they worship cocks?" I interrupted, unable to suppress a blush. "Then again, I daresay there are sillier things to venerate."

"Emma," warned Greville.

"Let her alone, Charles. Mrs. Hart is a charming creature, all the more entertaining for her spirited curiosity. As you seek to elevate her aesthetics, I can only express the hope that she will chip away by degrees at your asceticism. It will do the both of you a good turn."

Through pursed lips Greville said, "And this is what you were doing while your beloved Catherine was dying."

"My dear nephew, until the world as we know it is radically altered, there is nothing a man can do to stop the progress of the Grim Reaper. My studies of the Priapic cult relieved my agitated mind from the pain of watching the woman to whom I had been married for nearly a quarter century being carried off in a matter of weeks by a putrid fever. She left me last August. One can stew in one's grief or one can immerse oneself up to the chin in the business of living. It is my philosophy to embrace the latter."

On the twenty-third of February 1783, Sir William buried Lady Hamilton, née Catherine Barlow, in the family crypt at Slebach, in Wales. She had been embalmed upon her death, and the ambassador had convinced a Swedish sea captain to bring her body to England with the proviso that the coffin be boxed within a crate labeling its contents as a statue, to allay the sailors' superstition about carrying a corpse on shipboard.

"And in spite of all my philosophy"—Sir William paused to dab at a tear or two that had suddenly overtaken him—"I miss the woman. Catherine found the Neapolitans coarse and vulgar, and assiduously avoided the court life there, leaving me to attend the gala nights alone. I confess I had believed she sometimes cared as little for my society as she did for the boisterous Italians'. It weren't until she was in her final days that she revealed the depth of her love for me. Like many a man of our stamp and set, I was no stranger to the numerous—though discreet—delights to be enjoyed in the arms of an *amour tendre*. Had I known all along that Catherine's affections went so far beyond those of duty and respect—" Sir William was too much the diplomat to give voice to his unexpressed conclusion. Evidently, despite his lengthy marriage, Sir William had been quite the accomplished debaucher in his day.

"It is true that after Catherine's death I was casting about from pillar to post for a while, but at bottom, Charles, I am very much a creature of the Enlightenment. My study of antiquities has kept me constantly mindful of the perpetual fluctuation of every thing. To a humanist such as myself, the whole art is, really, to live all the days of our life to the fullest! There is nothing to be gained from either dwelling in the past or planning for the hereafter. Catherine was forty-four when the fever took her. I turned fifty-two December last. And should I live to a thousand, damme if I won't grab on to the next nine hundred and forty-eight left to me!"

"If you keep climbing Vesuvius, Pliny, you may cut that time short."

"I think Sir Willum is the most juvenile gentleman I have ever met," I said diplomatically. "Why do you call him Pliny?" I asked Greville.

"Pliny the Elder, to be specific. An ancient historian, Emma, who, like my uncle, became fascinated with vulcanology, and specifically Vesuvius, which lies but a few miles from the present city of Naples. He lost his life when, on an attempt to reach the summit during an eruption, he was overcome by the onslaught of smoke and burning lava. It was left to his nephew Pliny the Younger, a kindred spirit—though not so much of a fool to play with fire—to record his uncle's experiences."

"Not so much of an *adventurer*, I believe you mean to say, Charles. Mrs. Hart, I have been to the crater of Vesuvius over two dozen times, and have made at least four excursions to other parts of that grand laboratory of nature. Yet I am not ashamed to own that for all my observations, I comprehend very little of the wonders I have seen there."

"There's many would consider you daft, Uncle, for imperiling your life so."

Sir William favored Greville with another of his wry smiles. "I see no reason for you to fret, Charles. For the sooner Vesuvius reduces my mortal coil to cinders, the sooner your inheritance will be in your hands." Greville winced. Sir William had other nieces and nephews to consider when it came to naming his heir, but his intellectual bond with Greville gave my protector the edge. He stood to inherit his uncle's vast and priceless art collections and his lands in Scotland and Wales. The late Lady Hamilton's Pembrokeshire estate income alone was eight thousand pounds a year.

"Besides," continued Sir William coolly, "thanks to the knowledgeable offices of a half-blind Neapolitan guide named Bartolomeo, I can walk like Jesus of Nazareth over rivers of lava. It's all a matter of how to step, you see. If you tread lightly on the cooling crusts of the scoriae, you'll be home safe and sound and in time for tiffin."

"Your years among the heathen Neapolitans have turned you sybarite, Pliny."

The ambassador smiled. "You wouldn't do too poorly to have a bit of the sybarite in *you*, Pliny."

"Not in England," replied Greville curtly.

As he desired to remain in Sir William's good graces, Greville reluctantly agreed to his uncle's invitation to attend the theatre that night. Since the Ranelagh disaster, he had kept me away from all public entertainments.

I was over the moon at the prospect, and sailed even higher as soon as we set foot inside Drury Lane. For all eyes were upon us that evening! Owing to Sir William's connexions with His Majesty, we were permitted the use of the royal box, and I fear my pen cannot adequately express my delirium at being looked upon as a personage of rank and distinction. Giddy with joy, I felt like a princess! My looks, my gown, my smiles, attracted the admiration of all and sundry, and Sir William could scarce contain his amusement at Greville's struggles with his conscience over the public reaction to his "fair tea-maker," as the ambassador now wryly called me.

"You should be proud, Charles," Sir William whispered to him as the curtain went up on Goldsmith's much admired comedy *She Stoops to Conquer*. "I'll warrant every man in London wishes he were the Honorable Charles Greville tonight."

Greville, his gaze fixed upon the stage, replied softly, "Do *you*?"

I nearly bosted my stays applauding at my dear old friend Jane Powell's performance as a clever young lady of quality who pretends to be a barmaid in order to induce her noble but shy admirer into a declaration of love. I wept tears of joy for Jane's good fortune. So proud was I of her achievements that with the closing of each act, I was on my feet with cheers and huzzahs, despite the dignified comportment of my companions, and the reticence of the other spectators to give the actors their due. How could it be considered proper to titter politely when the comedy merited a guffaw? Smile tepidly where a broad grin was warranted? Perhaps there were things about "polite society" I would never apprehend.

Greville laid his hand upon my arm and drew me back to my chair. "They are all looking at you, Emma."

"Yes! Isn't it wonderful?!"

"I agree with Mrs. Hart, Charles. It is wonderful. In my view, the whole art of going through life tolerably is achieved by keeping oneself eager about anything. The moment one is indifferent, on *s'ennuye*. Emma could have the world in the palm of her hand tonight. Look how the people admire her."

"As one admires a circus performer, perhaps. They are in awe of the spectacle, but do not wish to dine with the acrobat."

"Come, come, nephew, don't be so hard on the girl. She is fresh and unspoilt—unstintingly eager to please—and naive in so many respects, despite her past. Mrs. Hart is passionate, generous, and adores you as if you bestrode the heavens yourself. Can I not persuade you to regard her exuberance as just another jewel in her diadem?"

With monstrous glee I watched my beloved Greville wrestle with an assent. "I've always said that such a woman, if she control her passions, might rule the roost and chuse her station."

"As long as you were by my side, Greville," I added enthusiastically, kissing him full on the lips. I don't think I had ever been more in love.

After that auspicious night, Sir William became my champion; at his urging, Greville arranged for a singing master to come all the way to Edgware Row to give me lessons, for old Pliny thought my voice as sweet and natural as a nightingale's; it only wanted training. Truth told, my singing then seemed so grand to people because I always stayed in a comfortable range. Had I performed in higher or lower keys, where I lacked confidence in my abilities, my flaws would have soon become apparent. Under a music master's tutelage I learnt the harp and grew more proficient at the pianoforte. A drawing instructor was at my disposal as well, and although Sir William had departed London to inspect his estates, he had promised that upon his return my sittings with Romney (curtailed during the spring due to Greville's economies) would be renewed, a glad event indeed.

Yet for all his generosity, Sir William was no Croesus. While he madly collected virtu—a word explained to me by Greville to refer to sundry curios, paintings, and antiquities—he was on occasion compelled by his own constraints to part with some of his dearest treasures.

Sir William returned to London in mid-August, intent on completing the business he had commenced during his earlier visit: that of divesting himself of one of his grandest assets—a rare Roman artifact known as the Barberini Vase—with an eye toward convincing the elderly Duchess of Portland, herself a rabid collector, to purchase it from him. Sir William had already sold off a priceless collection of ancient vases to the British Museum, which, in a gesture of gratitude, had then made him a trustee.

By this time, Greville was in renewed spirits, having received a new appointment with the court. As Treasurer of the Royal Household, he moved back to the King's Mews; therefore he did not object overmuch to an excursion into town, where we met up with Sir William at Nerot's hotel in King Street.

Pliny the Elder carefully uncrated his prized possession and placed it before us on a table near the window, the better to admire how the daylight illuminated the milky white figures besporting themselves in relief upon its surface of cobalt blue glass.

"Quite an exceptional piece, Uncle," murmured Greville, tracing a delicate fingertip over one of the figures.

"A perfect first-century artifact, found by a farmer hundreds of years ago, completely intact, in a sarcophagus a few miles outside the old city wall in Rome."

" 'Tis a very pretty joug indeed, Sir Willum!"

Greville sighed. "Proper ladies pronounce the word '*jug*,' Emma. Your *U*'s are deplorable. And how often have I reminded you that my uncle's name has an *I* in it. Say it as though it had a *Y* in it if it's the only way you can remember to say it properly: *Willyam*."

"Oh, I'm sure Sir *Will-um* don't mind," I teased. "And it's still a pretty joug."

"You know, Mrs. Hart, the story narrated by the figures on the Barberini Vase is still in dispute. All the experts who have examined it cannot agree upon a single interpretation. Would you care to take a stab at it?" Sir William relaxed against the back of the sofa, languidly draping an arm along its crested rim. "Tell us, what do you think the figures represent?"

"A parlor game, then!" I had learnt the rudiments of classical allegory from Dr. Graham when I performed nightly at his Temple of Aesculapius, and my adored Romney had increased my education in that subject. Yet even under Greville's astute tutelage my store of knowledge was still sorely wanting. Would these two learned worldly gentlemen laugh at my tyro's interpretation? I turned the vase in my hands and beheld the figures forever frozen in a single moment of their lives.

"Well, 'ere you've got a serpent between a maiden's legs—there's your phallus—and right above the maiden, you've got a cupid with 'is bow and arrow, which to my mind is saying something about the temptations of love. The old man with the beard is probably 'er husband, or at least 'er lover. The young man that's coming through the archway is a visitor. And see, 'im and the maiden's got their arms entwined even before 'e reaches 'er, like they've made a special connexion even before they've 'ad the chance to make love. I think the young man's 'er new lover, see? And the bearded man, leaning 'is foot on a rock like a proper philosopher, don't know whether to be upset about it all or whether to acknowledge that it's the way of the world when you're an old man what 'as got a beautiful woman 'oo is tempted away from 'im by a young and 'andsome 'ero. Besides, I doubt the young folks can 'elp themselves, as Cupid is aiming 'is bow at them; and the old man can't 'elp it, either, because everyone knows that mortals are powerless when Cupid takes it upon 'imself to loose his arrows. What's not to comprehend?"

"*Bravissima*, Mrs. Hart." Sir William applauded. "I daresay the antiquarians could learn a thing or two from you! But what do you make of the figures on the other side of the vase?"

"Oh." I examined the rest of the jug. "Well . . . 'ere you've got a pretty lady, all in 'er dishabille, sitting on a pile of rocks—or maybe it's a stack of books. And she's outdoors, because she's reclining under a tree 'alf-dressed and all, so the climate can't be England!" I received a laugh, even from Greville. "And the men are sitting on the same rocks or books, excepting one of 'em looks a bit like 'e's on a throne, but they're both looking at the 'alf-naked lady, so she must be very important as well as very beautiful, or why would a man on a throne be looking at 'er for centuries? And the man 'oo's not sitting on the throne, 'e's got a staff in 'is 'and, so maybe 'e's a shepherd. Or a mountain climber, seeing as the staff ain't got a crook in it." I suddenly grew uncomfortable, with Greville and Sir William watching me so intently. "Oh . . . my 'ead is too full to bosting to tell you any more. Can't we just go to the theatre again?"

Twelve

Indeed I Truly Am a Mother

Sir William was as good as his word, not only arranging for me to sit to Romney again, but I once more sat to Sir Joshua Reynolds, who, at Sir William's commission, depicted me as a bacchante. Poor Sir Joshua was no longer the man he had been when we first met several months earlier. A paralytic stroke had left him ailing, and his left arm now dangled like a useless appendage. Sir William had Romney paint me as a bacchante as well, and ordered the finished canvas crated and shipped to the Palazzo Sessa, his home in Naples.

When Greville announced that he and Sir William intended to inspect the ambassador's property in Pembrokeshire and Scotland that summer, he made it clear to me that in all propriety, I could not accompany them. Perhaps I might use the time to visit my relations in Hawarden. I knew he was referring to little Emma. My anxiety over her welfare (though I knew she was in good hands with my gammer), and my renewed fears of losing Greville, had manifested themselves in a rash on my elbows and knees, an ailment that recurred whenever I found myself a victim of my anxieties.

"A bit of sea bathing would be quite restorative as well," added Greville.

I confess I had no choice in the matter. A decision undertaken by the Honorable Charles Greville might just as well be law. Thus, on the sixth of June 1784, although I was inconsolable with weeping at the thought of being parted from him for so many weeks, Mam and I set out for Hawarden. Dear Gammer was overjoyed to see us, insisting on hearing every detail of our life among the upper crust, for I had often mentioned the ambassador in my letters to her, not failing to remark upon Sir William's urbanity, his lively wit, and his gentlemanly ways.

She tried to push the money away when I repaid her the five guineas she had laid out for little Emma's care. "Husht thee! 'Tis a pittance, gal. Save it for a new frock or bonnet; you'll 'ave more use for such a sum than your poor old gammer, y'nau?"

"If Greville 'as instilled nothing else in my daughter's lovely 'ead—and mind you, 'e 'as 'er learning music and drawing like a proper lady—it's the importance of keeping accounts and repaying one's debts," my mother said. "Take it, Mam, so's you can put some meat in the pot with the ponsh meip."

Mam and I brought little Emma with us to Parkgate, a bathing resort in Chester. Creating the fiction that I was a widow left with a young child to care for alone, we let rooms from Mrs. Darnwood, whose husband was away at sea and who dwelt with her mother, taking in guests to make ends meet. A guinea and a half a week covered our room and board.

During the day, I took the cures for my rash, drinking Peruvian bark that was boiled down into a liquid called tang, and also applied it to the affected areas of my limbs. I drank the salt water as well as dipping in it, donning a bathing dress and entering a bathing house—which rather resembled a privy—rolled by an attendant down to the sea. It was a treatment that I was scarce able to afford on the meager allowance Greville had given me.

My heart was so torn apart during those long weeks. For the first time, I was afforded the opportunity to form a bond with my little daughter, but how I missed my Greville! He had left me with a number of franked sheets of paper so that I might save money on correspondence. On June 15, as soon as we reached Parkgate, I penned him a letter. But then a week passed and I received no response. Heart aching, I wrote to him again, telling him how dearly I missed him, and how the society of my little daughter had released all my maternal affections, though the tot was as giddy and guileless and wild as I had been as a girl:

> *My ever dear Greville,*
>
> *Whether you will like it or no, there is no telling, but one comfort is she is a little afraid of me. Would you believe on satturday whe had a little quarel, I mean Emma & me & I did slap her on her hands & when she came to kiss me & make it up I took her on my lap & cried. Oh, Greville, you don't know how I love her, endead I do. When she comes & looks in my face & calls me "mother," endead I then truly am a mother, for all the mother's feelings rise at once and tels me I am or ought to be a mother, for she has a wright to my protection & she shall have it as long as I can & I will do all in my power to prevent her falling into the errors her poor once miserable mother fell into.*
>
> *Emma is crying because I won't come & bathe, so Greville adue tell after I have dipt. May God bless you, my dearest Greville & believe me faithfully, affectionatly & truly yours only.*
>
> *Emma Ht.*

" 'Ow many letters 'ave you written to him now?" my mother asked on June 26.

"Three times this week alone," I sobbed. "Why does not Greville write to me?" I was desperate for a kind word and even the merest show of affection.

"Now, what kind of example are you setting for the little one with your weeping like a baby yourself?" my mother soothed. "Sure there's a good reason your Greville 'asn't been able to scratch out a letter. You 'ave to acknowledge, Emy, gal, that 'e may have more on 'is mind at the moment than your lovesickness. My advice to you is to stop being so moonish and turn your attentions instead to your daughter."

I acknowledged the truth of Mam's wisdom, allowing little Emma to grow dearer to me by the day, and when a letter finally came from my beloved Charles, I replied immediately, expressing the hope that he would allow me to bring little Emma back to live with us in Edgware Road. This request was met with such a violent letter of reproach that my rash returned with a vengeance. My lover even reprimanded me for my dreadful orthography and my poor penmanship. And what a choice he left me with: himself and his continued protection, or the companionship of my daughter! I daresay even Solomon would have been devastated by such a decision!

Panicked, I scribbled a reply, accepting with the heaviest of hearts Greville's demand that little Emma be sent away to receive a proper education and a better upbringing than my poor relations could ever have afforded her.

> *You shall take her, put her there where you propose. Lett what will happen; I give her up to you to act as you think proper by her. Take her Greville & may God reward you tho her mother can't.*

Greville's offer to provide for little Emma's schooling was one that a woman in my position—barely nineteen years old with nothing to call my own—was scarcely able to decline, despite being compelled to leave all of the particulars in his hands. To provide for his lover's child, when the tyke's parentage was clearly so uncertain, was an act of angelic generosity. But the cost—to me—was enormous in every way. Propriety—*bienséance*, as Greville termed it—made it an absolute necessity that little Emma be raised elsewhere.

Although I genuinely believed I was capable of abiding by these terms for the sake of my prodigious love for him, I confess that in a corner of my heart, a mother's devoted heart, still dwelt the hope that once he made my daughter's acquaintance, Greville would find a way to honor his pledge to provide for the girl . . . and still keep her close to home.

Thirteen

An Unexpected Proposal

But it was not to be, although Greville did relent ever so slightly, permitting us to spend the autumn months together in Edgware Road. Yet in December 1784, little Emma was packed off to Manchester, to be raised and educated by a Mr. and Mrs. Blackburn who had a modest house in Market Street Lane and two young daughters of their own. Such tears and cries filled the house for a week before her departure, an eavesdropper might have thought that one of the residents was at death's door! Knowing that Greville's arrangement was all for the best in the main did not relieve my anguish at the inevitable. Just as I was coming to know the child, delighting in her every new discovery, her melting smiles, even her tears—for they gave me the opportunity to dry them and kiss them away—*bienséance* compelled me to bid her adieu.

Sir William had departed for the Continent three months earlier and though sympathetic to my distress, he had been unable—on my behalf—to sway Greville from his plan. Our parting was more than cordial, for in his gentlemanly and diplomatic way, he tacitly promised me his protection should anything happen to my beloved Charles, or if Greville should inflict some slight upon me. Effusively, I thanked him for all his kindnesses, expressing the wish that he should not stay away too long, though I knew he had to get about the duties with which His Majesty had entrusted him. His leave had ended and his business in England been accomplished. Sir William had presented the British Museum with his wax ex-votos in June, the Dilettanti Society had voted to publish his account of the Festival of Priapus, complete with the illustrations my dear Greville had found so lewd, and he had at long last persuaded the elderly Duchess of Portland to purchase the Barberini Vase. Once again, this priceless, graceful object changed hands. I wondered if the duchess would read the same story I did in its translucent figures.

Toward the middle of 1785, unpleasant rumors swirled about, suggesting that Greville was hunting for a wife. He had been seen at the theatre with the whey-faced heiress Henrietta Middleton. Of course I confronted my lover, but he refused to countenance my hysteria. Secretly, I knew that the rumors had to be just that, as Greville's financial situation could not permit him to afford the high cost of matrimony. I was the one who scrupulously kept his ledgers in Edgware Road, so I knew to the farthing where his money was spent. In fact, Greville had once chided me for giving a ha'penny from the household purse to a poor beggar man, and had suggested on more than one occasion that we seal up some of the cottage's twenty windows to avoid Prime Minister Pitt's increased taxes upon them.

But the fact that Greville no longer came to Edgware Road as often as he had done at the beginning of our arrangement added fuel to the speculative fire. He had sold his grand house in Portman Square in September and was living once more in the King's Mews. When Greville did visit Mam and me, his presence was so welcome I practically wagged my tail upon greeting him. For all his fears that if I was out in society, my head might be turned by another, whether a vivacious buck or a moneyed decrepit, he need never have concerned himself, for I belonged to him, and him alone, body, heart, and soul. Sure, I had chafed at his system from time to time, but I was coltish then. He had all but cured me of my giddy, girlish ways and my inclination (if left unchecked) toward dissipation. I had been a fallen woman and Greville had rescued me; I vowed I would never stumble again. He had made me good and my gratitude—as well as my love for him—was limitless.

But one late-autumn afternoon, Greville summoned me into his study. "Sit, please, Emma. I have something of great moment to discuss with you. Now, don't look like such a frightened rabbit," he added, as my eyes welled with tears, "for this is good news indeed."

"What is it, then?" I snuffled, reaching for a handkerchief.

"I will soon be obliged to spend a number of months in Scotland—"

"Are you off to inspect your property again?"

"Emma, it is impolite to interrupt. Yes, I will inspect my property—my uncle's property, that is—but my interests are taking me in a new direction at present. I intend to embark upon the study of chemistry in Edinburgh. It will keep me away from you for a substantial length of time."

"But it can't take just a few months to learn chemistry!" I wanted to believe that my beloved Greville was telling me the truth, but the sour feeling in my gut told me something did not quite tally. "If Sir Willum was here, I could bear your absence better, for 'e is a kind and courtly companion, and 'e loves my singing so—but oh, Greville, what shall I do all alone 'ere without you? With no society to speak of, I want the opportunities to prove that I 'ave bettered myself. Such a separation for so long a duration will seem to me a *total* separation from you, Greville."

"I am very much aware that you find Edgware Row a lonely place from time to time—"

"Not 'from time to time,' " I blarted, interrupting him again, "but whenever you're away. Which is more than 'from time to time'!" I could not bear the thought of losing him.

"I am not about to indulge in semantics with you, Emma—"

"How can I indulge in—when I don't even know what that is?" I replied, hurt to the core.

"What I have been endeavoring to tell you is that I think a change of scene might benefit you in every way. As you are fond of Sir William, and as he appears not unamenable to the pleasure of your company, I propose that you and your mother journey to Naples, where my uncle will provide a modest lodging for the both of you, no less comfortable than what you have enjoyed at Edgware Row. He will see to it that your instruction in voice and music is continued, and in Naples you will be able to avail yourself of the finest masters. Sir William will also arrange for you to be tutored in Italian so that you may communicate with the servants."

My lip trembled. "And 'ow long is this 'oliday to be?"

"Six to eight months. You will start off next March. It is a very pretty climate, Emma, with much to recommend it."

I considered the proposal for several moments. "But Naples, without you, will be no more tolerable than Edgware Road."

"Please don't cry, Emma. I offer you—my uncle and I offer you—a shining opportunity to enjoy a charming holiday and improve your education tenfold. Certainly you have derived much pleasure from Sir William's companionship."

"But not without you! Without you, 'ow shall I bear it! No! I shall not stir a foot if I am to go alone."

"With your mother, of course, which is not quite what I would call—"

"Alone. Without you, I am alone, and that's that!" In a display of temper and tears, I fled the room.

It took several more conversations, many of them fraught with sighs, weeping, and lengthy negotiations, before I finally acquiesced. On December 3, 1785, I composed a letter to Sir William, which in truth was mostly dictated by Greville. It was franked and posted, setting in motion our plans to embark for the Continent. The following March 13, in possession of new linen, a new dress, and a smart bonnet, courtesy of my beloved Greville, I bade him—and Edgware Road—a tearful farewell. From that moment, I lived for October, and the opportunity to step into his arms again.

Bacchante

1786–1791

Fourteen

Nasty Surprises

On my twenty-first birthday, April 26, 1786, I entered the city of Naples. I confess that my initial view was a disappointing one. Sir William's head footman, Vincenzo, who had traveled with us since Geneva, apologized for the squalor that surrounded the round towers of the Porta Capuana, the portal though which we passed into the city.

"There's more costermongers and balladeers than in Whitechapel!" Mam exclaimed, for every square foot of space was taken up by a vendor's stall or a street singer, peddling their wares.

"I think they're singing for the sheer joy of doing it, Mam, as they don't seem to have a care about making a penny off it. Lud, look how colorful everything is! Even the people! Can you imagine wearing a red skirt with a yellow petticoat about London and not be taken for a doxy?"

"Don't look there, Emy!" Mam warned, reaching over to shield my eyes, but she was too late.

"When did you get so proper?" I quizzed, and immediately my eyes became moist, thinking of my darling Greville. "It ain't like I never saw a naked man before—though I confess I've never seen so many at once—and not so many brown ones."

"The sun," Vincenzo began to explain. "Of course when you live out of doors in a climate such as this . . ."

"They live out 'ere? On the streets?"

"It is the way of the lazzaroni, signora. Our underclass. Many of them sleep along the quayside and out on the mole that stretches into the bay. They receive free bread from His Majesty, and thus feel no compunction to work for it. They loaf about the piers, catching fish when they are hungry, entertaining the pedestrians if they are talented, and going about as nature made them, with their straw sun hats and their many tattoos their only adornments, for the Neapolitan heat is exceedingly *forte*—strong, you say in English. And the English are surprised to see them without their shirts and breeches, but I assure you that here in Naples, the Italians never wink an eye. Wink? Is correct?"

The buildings in the center of the city were as tightly packed as those in any impoverished London quarter, and nearly as gloomy; and the streets, paved with square-shaped stones made of the dark Vesuvian lava, were as narrow as a lane in Southwark or Soho. But the nearer we drew to the Bay of Naples, the sweeter and more fragrant the air and the larger and prettier the houses—painted in the pale cream, peach, and rose colors of refreshing ices and terraced into the hillside, their flat roofs and balconied facades dripping with lush and vibrant bougainvillea. Looking at them made me thirsty.

We passed the vast and imposing Castel Nuovo and the Palazzo Reale, the royal residence, and turned into the Vico di Cappella Vecchia di Santa Maria, a narrow way not much larger than an alley. Passing under an old Roman *porta*, we entered a larger courtyard, where the horses were halted and Vincenzo alighted from the carriage to help us descend.

"This way, signore," he said, gesturing toward a vaulted passageway, just as another carriage, bearing an impressive emblem and driven by a fully liveried coachman, rumbled into the outer courtyard. I waited to see who would step out of this most elegant conveyance—Sir William, perhaps? But the passenger was a tall and slender woman, attired like a man in breeches and surcoat, a riding crop tucked under her arm.

"This way, signore," Vincenzo repeated. *"Andiamo, per favore."*

I hadn't a notion of what he'd just said to Mam and me, but his meaning was clear enough, and hastening to follow him, I employed the only word I had learnt in his tongue, mimicking perfectly the Italian pronunciation. "*Grazie*, Vincenzo."

The head footman beamed, displaying a shoddy set of choppers. I believe I had made a friend for life.

"*Aspettate!* You wait. Here." We had passed through the inner courtyard and entered the Palazzo Sessa, a grand three-story residence with a gleaming white facade: England's embassy and the home of Sir William, His Britannic Majesty's ambassador. Vincenzo seated us in an antechamber, graceful, and rich in detail. White plaster pilasters, decorated with a raised motif of painted ivy, lent the room the air of a most elegant conservatory.

"Look, Emy, gal, you can see the ocean from 'ere! Imagine sea bathing in *that*, eh?"

"That is the Bay of Naples, Signora Cadogan," Vincenzo corrected politely. "Is it not the most beautiful thing you have ever seen?"

The waves looked like diamonds dancing on azure silk. I walked to the window in as stately a manner as I could muster, having just spent several hours in a cramped and stuffy carriage, and found that I could not pull my gaze from the view. " 'Oo was that woman we saw in the courtyard?" I asked Vincenzo as coolly as possible. I felt a fillip in my stomach.

"The one descending His Excellency's coach?"

"Yes, of course. The one dressed in gentlemen's apparel."

"Ah, *sì*. That is Signora—Mrs.—Damer. An Englishwoman. She is an artist. A sculptress."

"*Mrs.* Damer? Then she is married?"

"She is a widow, Signora Hart. Her husband . . . he—"

Vincenzo put his fingers to his temple as if to pantomime a pistol. "Bang." He cleared his throat in an obvious display of discomfort. "She will pack her things and leave the late Lady Hamilton's rooms by the end of the day, I assure you."

"Did not Sir Willum expect us?" What call had I to feel a glimmer of jealousy that this strange woman, mannish, odd, and unconventional, had been residing under Sir William's roof, sleeping in her ladyship's boudoir (if not elsewhere as well), and freely granted the use of one of his carriages—I, who had been thinking all afternoon about how I would have liked my precious Greville to have been at my side so that we might have shared the excitement of reaching this exotic new city on my birthday? "Where is Sir Willum, Vincenzo?" I admit I had expected him to greet us on the doorstep with open arms.

"I believe he is bidding his farewell to Mrs. Damer. It should not take long, I assure you." He made a courtly little bow first to me and then to Mam before leaving the room. *"Pazienza, signora e signora."*

Vincenzo brought us a pot of excellent coffee and some almond-flavored biscuits that damn near broke my teeth. Mam decided to dunk hers in the steaming coffee to soften it. "Can you imagine that a man who lives like this serves stale biscuits?" I whispered to Mam in amazement.

Presently, the doors to the antechamber were thrown open and an uncharacteristically flustered Sir William entered the room, apologizing profusely for the delay. "The time—I—," he began distractedly, and, upon greeting me, became even more disconcerted. "Mrs. Hart—and good afternoon, Mrs. Cadogan—Mrs. Hart, you are even lovelier than the image of you that is imprinted upon my memory . . . and of course the bacchante, Romney's bacchante—well, I daresay it's my bacchante, as I am the owner of the portrait. I look at you every day, but I had scarce dared to dream that the original would be standing before me—under my roof, I mean. . . . Damme! Mrs. Hart, please forgive me; a man of fifty-five, and I suddenly feel like a giddy schoolboy. I am keenly aware that you once referred to me as the 'most juvenile man' you ever knew, but perhaps you may wish to reconsider the remark as an intended compliment. Now, I understand it is your birthday today. May I be the first to say *buon compleanno*? I trust you had a pleasant journey?"

Mam and I exchanged a glance, and off I went on every detail of our long excursion, omitting nothing, including the bedbugs at the posting inns, despite Mam's frantic waving of her hand.

Sir William seemed much amused by both my verisimilitude and my vivacity. "Evidently, you did not arrive fatigued. And I hope the weather held?"

"Is the sky always this blue?" I wondered aloud.

"On most days. Quite a change from an English sky—if you can even glimpse it through the London miasma! I should caution you, it may take several days before you become accustomed to the Neapolitan climate. It can, on occasion, be unpredictable—we live in an active volcanic region of course—but in the main, particularly in the spring and summer months, the word that comes to mind is 'sultry.' Once you become acclimated, you will begin to comprehend the Neapolitan tendency toward indolence, even among our foreign visitors."

"Well, we've already gotten a gander at Neapolitan nekkidness," Mam said, bosting into a laugh.

"You will find that everything in Naples is substantially more . . . voluptuous . . . than back home in England," Sir William added. "From the manners and pursuits to the opera and the wine. Our Lachryma Christi—the 'tears of Christ'—is heavier and sweeter than we are used to imbibing; to the northern palate it is often thought too like a syrup."

Mam furrowed her brow. "Don't people drink gin, then?"

Sir William laughed. "As His Britannic Majesty's envoy I am

more or less obliged to entertain every English man and woman who set foot in Naples, from the dignitary to the scholar to the curiosity seeker, and like as not, they are forever requesting me to procure some local extravagance and send it back to England to await their eventual arrival. Naturally, the better-mannered of the lot wish to thank their host with a modest gift, something that will remind him of home, perhaps."

"I think 'e's saying it won't be too 'ard to arrange, Mam," I whispered loudly.

"I have settled it so that you will have two lady's maids to help you both. Giulia and Laura. They will unpack your trunks and get you settled in your rooms. You have nothing to do here but enjoy yourselves."

Our holiday commenced with a tour of the spacious Palazzo Sessa. Sir William's private study was crammed from floor to ceiling with paintings and curiosities, so much so that there was scarcely an inch of space left for anything more. My feet was getting tired from standing as he lovingly described each of several items from his numerous *Wunderkabinetts*, one more dear to him than the last.

"'Ave you ever seen such a deal of bric-a-brac?" Mam whispered to me. "And he treats each one of 'is things as if it were 'is child. Pity the poor soul 'oo 'as to come in 'ere with a dustrag."

The cornices around the walls of the study were inscribed with various homilies that Sir William considered precepts for his life. One in particular puzzled me. Sir William translated *La mia patria è dove mi trovo bene* as "My homeland is where I feel at home."

"Seems to me you're even more at 'ome 'ere," I remarked. "Even in the past 'alf hour you've seemed 'appier than you ever was in London."

Sir William smiled warmly. "I attach no shame in admitting that I do love my collections. I could spend many hours at a time—and do—in this room. This is where I usually breakfast. I find that beginning my day in the chamber where I derive such comfort and satisfaction, being surrounded by my dearest possessions, makes for a more amiable remainder of the time."

In the library sat Sir William's two British secretaries, Mr. Smith and Mr. Oliver, who greeted us with a curt nod of their heads as if to say that unlike their employer, they were busy, busy men. It was here that Sir William met with those on official business—where lengthy discussions of moment on matters of great import took place. This room, too, boasted a prodigious number of paintings, and leather-bound volumes lined shelf after shelf.

Thus far, each of the rooms offered a spectacular view of the Bay of Naples. In the distance was the island of Capri, rising like a knuckle from the Mediterranean. "I think if I was Mr. Oliver or Mr. Smith, I should never get a lick of work done, with such a vista to behold at every moment," I murmured.

We stepped out of the library into a corridor, where Sir William proudly pointed out the water closet. The plumbing in the Palazzo Sessa was the most advanced to be had, and owing to his studies of the sciences and the elements, he had also caused a lightning rod to be installed on the roof. "Ladies, it gives me pleasure to say that you will be residing in the safest house in Naples."

Sir William opened a door onto another suite of rooms, where the two Italian maids were hard at work unpacking our baggage and airing our gowns, stopping only to drop a curtsy. So much for Greville's intention that Sir William relegate us to some remote outpost. There was a large sitting room, painted white, with a ceiling fresco of gold wreaths and stars—a hero's room, I thought—and two smaller rooms, one of which was to serve as Mam's bedroom. My favorite was the last chamber, with its generous fireplace and ceiling of robin's-egg blue. This delightful boudoir boasted a sumptuous bed fitted up with a demicanopy of cream-colored silk.

And with two windows, what a view! "You are looking out upon the Chiaia quarter, one of the most beautiful and verdant spots in Naples," Sir William explained. From the second window one could admire the water lying at the foot of the hill below us, where it forked into two gulfs, separated by one of three great Neapolitan fortresses, the Castel dell'Ovo, which jutted out into the sea. "The Neapolitans are a very superstitious people, as you will soon discover for yourself. For example, the Castel dell'Ovo got its name because the locals believe that it was built on an egg provided by a magician named Vergil."

We passed the strange Mrs. Damer and her servants on the staircase leading to the upper rooms. She paused to gaze at me, studying my countenance with a good deal of intensity before continuing on her way without so much as a how-de-do to Sir William. Greville would have been mortified if I'd asked his uncle about her, so I bit my tongue.

On the upper floor, in addition to Sir William's bedroom and sitting room and those belonging to his late wife, were the enormous dining room, the salon, and the ballroom—where up to three hundred guests could wear out their slippers dancing away the night. Here Sir William did his private entertaining, presenting his frequent musical assemblies. The ambassador employed his own quartet of chamber musicians, and he was himself an accomplished cellist.

"And here," Sir William said as he left the salon, "despite my passion for virtu, is my favorite room of all: the entire observation tower was just recently added to the palazzo at my own instigation and expense."

It offered a grand semicircular view of the Bay of Naples, the mirrored interior walls creating the illusion of being surrounded on all sides by the glistening sea. In the late-afternoon light, the water looked violet; and as the sun began to set, the sky turned from rose and gold to vermilion to lavender and indigo. "What a paradise!" I exclaimed, taking care not to stumble over the telescope perched upon its tripod.

"I sit here as often as I can," replied Sir William. "Nothing can compare to the enjoyment of a good book in so enchanting an atmosphere. There is Capri, opposite us; to the left, the seacoast from Sorrento to Cape Minerva, named for the Roman goddess of wisdom; to the right, Mount Posillipo, where I have a pretty little summer villa right on the sea. Closer to hand you can see the Villa Reale. Imagine Hyde Park at five p.m., Mrs. Hart, as one grand stretch of roadway where every Friday night all the fashionable men and women parade about in their fine carriages just to see and be seen. Tomorrow evening, we will join the promenade and you will get a taste of life among *il meglio del raccolto*—the cream of the crop—of Neapolitan society."

Seated together on the curving upholstered banquette, we watched the light change. "If you find the vista to your liking at present, it is pure magic at night," assured Sir William. "The bay by starlight is breathtaking, one of life's most agreeable pleasures. On some evenings the moon appears to be rising right from the mouth of Vesuvius."

My romantic heart was full. "If only Greville could be 'ere to see it!" I sighed.

A silence settled over the room. "Yes. Well." Sir William crossed his hands behind his back. "Shall we dine?"

Fifteen

Settling In

I could not wait to compose a letter to my beloved Charles, but the post for England was not scheduled until the first of May. Certain that Sir William would be compelled to spend the better part of his days engaged in weighty affairs of state, I would have felt honored should he have been able to take supper with me on any single occasion, but to my astonishment, he joined me at every meal. He did not even breakfast in his beloved study.

It was impossible not to notice how besotted he appeared. I could not stir a hand or a leg or a foot but he was marking it as graceful and fine. This I could not wait to impart with some pride to Greville, as well as the way the Neapolitan people praised my beauty when, on my second night in Naples, we rode in Sir William's carriage along the crowded Villa Reale, an avenue so crammed with coaches carrying the local nabobs that it took hours to traverse its length. I hoped to be able to hold my own amid these exotic and extravagantly attired foreigners who chattered like magpies at breakneck speed, in a language I did not know, emphasizing their words with wild gesticulations of their hands.

We strolled amid the lush gardens of the Chiaia, admiring the classical statues lining the graveled walkways. Everywhere I looked there was color and fragrance so heady it whispered of lust, of illicit assignations among the boughs of white-starred myrtle and black cypress, between the stiff-leafed palms, or amid the nearby citron, bergamot, and tamarisk groves. What need was there to wear scent when the very air carried the aromas of roses and orange blossoms? Syringa and oleander bloomed everywhere. The gilded balconies of the houses near the bay were dressed in bright shades of pink, purple, and yellow; passing beneath the pots of herbs nestled among the planted blooms, one could catch a savory whiff of basil or rosemary.

It was as if every day were a feast day. Music was everywhere—not just at the Teatro San Carlo, the grand opera house, where the most celebrated prima donna of the age, Brigitta Giorgi Banti, reigned supreme. Sweet strains sifted through slatted shutters, and musical Romeos serenaded their balconied Juliets with guitars and mandolins. Sometimes the evening breeze would carry their voices as far as the Palazzo Sessa.

However, it was not long before I learned that lurking beneath this shimmering surface, where the music of Mozart and Haydn was heard nightly in salons such as Sir William's, and where the nobility clad themselves in Venise lace, Lyonnaise silks, and Genoese velvets, there was something more sinister. While the lazzaroni seemed as carefree as the nobles and the priests, in truth they were a filthy mass of miserable-looking humanity, begging when they wanted to, stealing when they needed to, no better off than any of the wretches who lived on the streets of London.

On my third day in Naples, Sir William took me down to the quay. Inhaling the briny air, we picked our way among the dozens of fishmongers counting their catch, hawking their wares, gossiping with one another, or merely lazing about. In their picturesque red caps, striped trousers, short jackets, and gold earrings, they resembled a band of pirates in a panto at Drury Lane. One of them, a remarkably ugly man—an inch or two shorter than I, and not old by any means, but with a protruding belly, a sallow pallor, a thatch of dull, coffee-colored hair, and an enormous hooked nose—

grinned at Sir William and tossed me a cockleshell, smelling his hands after releasing it. Laughing, he rubbed his crotch and gestured lewdly at us. I had to stare at him, for his looks were so striking. His prodigious nose began all the way at his forehead, gradually swelling into a straight line until it nearly hit his large mouth with its jutting lower lip. His brow was low; his eyes small and piggy; his cheeks lacking in the delineation marked by a prominent bone structure; and his neck, without a stock or cravat to blur the line between collarbone and chin, was uncommonly long.

"Lud, Sir Willum, what a crude man! And so hideous!" I was less insulted than nonplussed by his antics.

"Lower your voice, Mrs. Hart. Remember that man's face, and in future, keep your thoughts about him to yourself."

"But why?"

"He's the king."

Only thirty-five years old, King Ferdinand IV of Naples was the third son of King Carlo VII of Spain and one of the only siblings not to be declared a congenital idiot. In fact, even this was up for dispute, Sir William added, as he commenced my education in Neapolitan affairs. "Later nicknamed *Il Re Nasone*—'King Nose'— as well as *Il Re Lazzarone* after his affinity for the underclass, he was placed on the throne of the Two Sicilies when he was all of eight years old, with a regent, the Duca di San Nicardo, who was told that too much education would damage the lad. Thus, given only a bowing acquaintance with breviary, he learned to hunt and to fornicate, and those remain his greatest passions," sighed Sir William. "He fancies himself a practical joker, putting marmalade in people's hats, forcing his servants to swallow live frogs—and then there was the occasion when he cut up a live pregnant deer to see what her young looked like—of course, that was when he was a boy. But the people love him, chiefly the lazzaroni. And like the lazzaroni, Ferdinand is terribly superstitious. In order to ward off evil elements, he wears all manner of talismans pinned to his undergarments. He only speaks the Neapolitan dialect, would fuck a chambermaid as soon as he'd bed a noblewoman—and has—and adores juvenile humor, the more scatological, the better. I doubt that there is an ambassador plenipotentiary to any other court in Europe who is commanded by the king to keep him company because His Majesty gets lonely during his after-dinner shits."

"No! But you're pulling my leg, Sir William! I admit to 'ave seen quite a bit in my past, but even the rowdiest of my former acquaintance were never so uncouth."

Sir William chuckled. "Welcome to Naples."

I was treated, if one could possibly use that word to describe such a spectacle, to another of His Sicilian Majesty's customary antics when Sir William first took me to the opera. The Teatro San Carlo, built by King Ferdinand as a tribute to his father, was an impressive edifice with a glorious rococo interior of red and gold. I noticed that the heavily jeweled, rouged, and powdered patrons spent as much time using their quizzing glasses to pick out friends or enemies as they did in watching the performance—when they weren't talking or eating during the arias. But their manners were nothing to their sovereign's. Supping in his seat, with stains on his brocaded waistcoat, and his brown hair unpowdered, he plunged his lace-cuffed hands up to the wrist into a silver bowl of steaming macaroni smothered in a gravy redolent of cheese and garlic, and gleefully tossed handfuls of it onto their heads. His hapless victims then turned around to face the royal box, and, cheering loudly, did applaud him! I had never been so astonished by a thing in my life! And Greville had found *me* too boisterous at the theatre! What would he have made of this?

When he was not desecrating the coiffures of the first families of Naples, King Ferdinand's eye strayed to my person. Every night we were in attendance at the opera, I caught his gaze. "*La più bella inglese,*" he called me, in good enough Italian to make himself clearly understood.

All this and more I longed to share with Greville. My first letter to him, completed on April 30, was filled with expressions of homesickness for him, details of the sights I had enjoyed thus far, my reactions to the colorful Neapolitans, and reports of their high opinion of me. And I did not neglect to mention his uncle's generosity:

> *I have a carridge of Sr. W's, & new liverys & new coach man, foot man & the same as Mrs. Damer had. If I was going abbout in 'is carridge they would say I was either 'is wife or mistress.*
>
> *I know you will be pleased to hear that he as given me a beautiful goun, cost 25 guineas, India painting on wite satin & several little things of Lady Hamiltons & is going to by me some muslin dresses loose to tye with a sash for the hot weather, made like the turkey dresses, the sleeves tyed in fowlds with ribban & trimmed with lace, in short he is all ways contriving what he shall get for me.*

I had more good news to impart: Sir William had made his will and named my beloved Greville his heir. How delighted I was that he no longer needed to fret about a future income. Yet Sir William claimed to know nothing about Greville's plans to come for me in October. I was gobsmacked, for this was the original arrangement, agreed upon to the letter by all of us! Sir William was far too young for a lapse of senility. From his expression I could tell that something was afoot, though he was loath to reveal it. He came and stood beside me and made a move as though he wanted to stroke my hair, but thought better of it and restrained his impulse.

"Mrs. Hart, your tears wound me to the core of my being. I would give anything in the world to relieve you of your unhappiness and distress. Forgive me for what may seem a cold comfort at the moment, but in time the pain will ease until you have transcended it entirely." Puzzled, I gazed at his placid countenance. "Mrs. Hart—Emma—I beg you to accept the circumstances. I am not such an ogre; indeed I flatter myself to think that you may even love me a little."

"As an *uncle*, Sir William. *Never* as anything more than that!" I felt my heart rise into my throat. "You mistake my character if you think me light or inconstant and do me an injury to believe so. If not for the 'love' you bear for me, such as you may term it, then for the love you bear to Greville, I beg you to never speak of such a subject again!"

Hysterical, I fled from his study and locked myself in my boudoir, closing the heavy draperies. I did not even wish to see the bay. Full of panic and confusion, I penned a coda to Greville's letter, gasping for breath as if someone had placed his hands upon my throat and begun to strangle me.

> *I have had a conversation this morning with Sr Wm. that has made me mad. He speaks half I do not know what to make of it, but Greville, my dear Greville, wright some comfort to me, pray do, if you love me, but onely remember you will never be loved by any body like your affectionate & sencere*

> *Emma*

Sixteen

Betrayed

Over the next three months I wrote fourteen more letters to my beloved Greville. None were answered. "Remember Uppark 'Arry," cautioned Mam grimly, but I would hear not a word of detraction. Convincing myself that he must be traveling, I tried to maintain as cheerful a manner as possible, so as not to insult Sir William's hospitality. He feared to broach anew the subject of his attraction to me, as well as his suggestion, however couched, that he was now my protector in every way.

I admit that Sir William never asked me to account for every penny I spent, nor carped, nor scolded, nor criticized. He spared no expense in clothing me and making me presents of no end of pretty trinkets such as brooches and hatpins and gloves. I felt guilty accepting the gift of the twenty-five-guinea gown, for here I was wearing such an extravagance for just a few hours, when that kind of money would have enabled Gammer and the Kidd family to live tolerably well for several months. But I had neither requested nor coveted these fine things. He took me to the opera several nights a week, and when we entertained at home, he encouraged me to sing for his guests. Sir William paid for so many lessons I thought I was at an academy. I found that drawing came to me as easy as ABC and when I made a little sketch of his beloved Vesuvius, he was enraptured. To my own astonishment, my progress was just as swift in my Italian and French lessons. Within weeks I was practicing my French with Sir William and conversing in Italian with the servants, who agreed that my ear was so fine, I spoke like a native. Sir William praised my French as well, amused at the perfection of my accent when I still sounded like a country wench in my own tongue! I expect I could have gentrified my speech if I'd set my cap at it, but the truth of the thing is that I was proud of my Flintshire roots—fiercely so—and it would have been a slap in the face of my dear gammer as raised me, to admit that a Hawarden accent wouldn't do among the so-called upper crust.

At Sir William's expense, my dear, dear Romney came all the way to Naples to paint me, but still no word from Greville. What a marvelous reunion we had, Romney and I, and it delighted me beyond measure to see him in such excellent spirits. In short order it became the rage for artists visiting Naples to pay a call upon Sir William in the hopes of gaining a commission to paint (or sculpt, or sketch) his English protégée.

"As an artist myself, I can explain the attraction," Romney told me. "You are uncommon tall and long-limbed, and the proportions of your figure the beau ideal. From a purely aesthetic vantage, your features are perfectly symmetrical, their size and shape considered perfection. Your hair is extraordinary, not just for its length and texture, but for its color. Find me, Emma, another beauty of the day whose tresses are completely natural and the color of flame mahogany. Find me another whose eyes can appear to be anything from brownish to indigo violet, depending on her mood."

"You forget my horrid weak chin. There are mornings I make my toilette and I can see nothing else in the glass before me."

"Ah, but my dear Emma, it is by such flaws that we become our fullest selves, for what is man without the vulnerabilities that make him truly human? Now, find me another whose eyes convey the vivacity of yours as well as the depth of the soul behind them. The sorrows and pain that have made you vulnerable to injury, my poor girl, can be read in your eyes as easily as one can read your enthusiasm and exuberance. Even to the dispassionate observer, the combination of these qualities in a single charming body make you an uncommon beauty, whom not even Lady Betty Foster or the Duchess of Devonshire herself can rival. Add to that your expressive voice, your talent for drama, your zest for life, your generous nature, and your gift for making everyone you speak to feel as though you admire them and care deeply for their welfare."

"But I do!"

"Even *more* uncommon!"

"Lud, Romney, I can scarce recognize myself; you take my breath away with such compliments! My own father, 'ad he lived, could not have been so proud of his daughter."

My sweet, dear friend smiled wistfully. "You said yourself that the Empress of Russia has commissioned a cameo of your head. Do you think everyone would want to own an 'Emma' if I were just flattering you up?"

We began to spend much of our time at Sir William's charming summerhouse in Posillipo, just three rooms and a kitchen, practically jutting into the sea. From May to September the heat in the city was oppressive, so we would drive out from Naples, arriving at the villa in time for lunch, lingering until sunset, when we were obliged to return to Naples to attend the opera or to entertain at the Palazzo Sessa. In my honor, Sir William christened the little house Villa Emma, and in truth it was always my favorite of his three establishments. I would bathe every day there, and sometimes go sailing with Sir William, for fishing was another of his passions. I also loved to dive among the rocks in the *piscina* he had built, swimming underwater to admire the sea flora and fauna that dwelt in this special pool. Sir William was nearly as fascinated with marine life as he was with vulcanology. To him, every one of Nature's formations represented a laboratory.

At night, the sky was ablaze with fireworks, ignited from the balconies of the Posillipo grandees. They burst into the heavens like fiery blooms, cresting like fountains before falling into the purple darkness of the bay.

Of course I told Greville that his uncle had named his little coastal cottage for me, but still I received no word from him. I told him about all the servants we had at the Palazzo Sessa as well as at Sir William's *capannina*, his hunting cabin in Caserta, where he routinely went with the king on their massive hunts, excursions that Sir William described as wholesale slaughter. The king employed thirty-two hundred beaters to chase the poor beasts into a pit just within range of His Majesty's rifle. Dressed like a tradesman in a leather apron and hat and standing in a roofless sentry box, he could kill dozens in a day, hundreds in a weekend, and enjoyed repulsing his guests by plunging his muscular bare arms up to the elbow in gore and cutting up the animals himself with his coarse brown hands. "If only he were as good a monarch as he is a butcher, no one need despair about the future of the kingdom," sighed Sir William.

Our servants numbered nowhere near the thirty-two hundred beaters, but we did employ many, as wages were so low. And I was surprised to see men handling such ordinary household chores as changing the bed linens, but this was the Neapolitan way. At least changing the linens was not dangerous business. Other servants daily risked their lives for us. Sir William's *volanti* were employed solely to run in front of his carriage shouting and waving their arms to shoo away the freely roaming cows, chickens, street vendors, and lazzaroni.

Not too long after Mam and I arrived, Sir William asked us if we should like to see Vesuvius.

"I can see it right from where I'm sitting," Mam replied pragmatically.

"I meant *climb* it, Mrs. Cadogan."

"I know you did, Sir Willum. I was just quizzing you. But my hip i'nt what is was but a few months ago, so I think I'll admire the view from this chair. And if I feel like stirring, your cook or chef or whaddyecallim 'as promised to show me 'ow 'e makes his salt cod. Back-allow, 'e calls it."

Naturally I was mad to climb the volcano, but my first visit was to be no ordinary day trip. Sir William chose to show me his precious Vesuvius at midnight, which he vowed was even better sport. 'Twas a good thing my feet was big, because I had to don a pair of Sir William's thick-soled boots. No dainty slippers for picking your way amid the changing topography, now crunchy as gravel, now spongy where the lava had begun to cool, now ashy as a massive pile of cinders. Even through the boots I could feel the heat beneath my feet.

" 'Ow I wish Greville was here to share this with us!" I exclaimed into the night as I gazed at five miles of flame. The light of the moon was nothing to the lava, the finest fountain of liquid fire.

"It may spoil your opinion of my nephew, but I must tell you, Mrs. Hart, that he was less intrepid than your imagination would have you believe. In fact, when he was here some years ago, he was terrified to climb the volcano."

" 'E wouldn't be affrighted if I was to 'old 'is 'and," I insisted.

"Look!" Sir William cried as an enormous cloud of smoke belched forth from the crater. "Now do as I do!" I crouched down and turned my body toward the foot of the volcano, shielding my head with my arms. A moment later, we were pelted with a shower of stones, as though the sky were raining black hail and soot. I crept closer to Sir William, who struck a flint and glanced at his pocket watch. Several minutes later, he helped me to my feet. "Give me your hand. It's safe to go all the way up to the crater now. We are between eruptions."

How thrilling it was! Slowly and carefully, we picked our way to the summit. The breeze had caught the smoke and was blowing it westward, yielding us a better look at the crater itself.

"It looks like a bowl of steam now," I remarked, trying to hold my breath so I shouldn't have to hold my nose against the sulfuric gases.

"It's coming from the numerous fissures inside the crater," Sir William explained. "I'm afraid that's the best view we're going to get tonight."

"O, I shall never forget it! Thank you, Sir Willum." I leaned toward him to press my lips to his cheek.

Well into our descent, we met none other than the Prince Royal with his tutor, who evidently had shared the same thought we did. "What did you think of the sight?" I asked him in my rudimentary Italian.

"*Bella, ma poca roba,*" the youth replied, shrugging his shoulders.

"Not such great stuff?!" I could not believe my ears. Then I learnt that at the urging of his tutor, they had stopped well below the lip of the crater. No wonder he had been less than impressed. "Did you hear that, Sir Willum? Five hundred yards 'igher and 'e could 'ave watched the noblest, sublimest sight in the world. But the poor frightened creatures beat a scared retreat. O, I shall kill myself with laughing!"

After three months in Naples, I had not received so much as a single word from my beloved Greville. Sir William had begun to appear once more as though he desired to break something to me, yet he always changed his mind moments after the cloud had darkened his usually placid brow.

Let me have onely one line from your dear, dear hands, I begged Greville in July.

> *I find life is insupportable with out you.*
> *I have a language master, a singing master, musick, etc, etc,*
> *but what is it for; if it was to amuse you I should be happy, but*

Greville what will it avail me. I am poor, helpless & forlorn. I
have lived with you 5 years & you have sent me to a strange place
& me thinking you was coming to me; instead of which I was
told to live, you know how, with Sir W. No, I respect him, but
no, never, shall he peraps live with me for a little wile like you
& send me to England, then what am I to do, what is to become
of me.

I told him that an Austrian prince was besotted with me, and
the King of the Two Sicilies himself fawned over me like a cicisbeo
over his married mistress! But all I desired was Greville. His silence
had broken my heart and rendered me miserable, despite the warm
reception I had received in this foreign, faraway land. I endeavored
to be cheerful for Sir William's sake, for he was being so kind to
me, but in truth, my smiles were naught but a mask that concealed
my real distress.

Meanwhile, Sir William continued to tutor me in local history.
If King Ferdinand was the "King of the Lazzaroni," the Queen of
the Two Sicilies, Maria Carolina, was known as the "Queen of the
Illuminati" for her support of the freethinking societies formed by
the intellectuals of the Neapolitan noble and middle classes.

A daughter of Empress Maria Theresa of Austria, Maria Carolina had the cream and rose and gold coloring of the Hapsburgs.
I found her a great beauty, for she was uncommon intelligent, and
this can go a long way to turning a plain woman into a striking
one. But no one would compare Her Sicilian Majesty to a statue of
Venus. Her watery blue eyes were red-lidded, small, and too close
together. Her forehead was too high, her mouth too small, and the
Hapsburg jaw too prominent, with too great a distance between
the mouth and chin. And her unfortunate underbite had a way of
strangling her speech so that the Neapolitans nicknamed her
polpett mbocca, for they thought she sounded like a gobbling turkey
when she spoke.

The king possessing neither the head nor the stomach for governing, it was Maria Carolina, along with Sir John Acton—the kingdom's English-born secretary of war and minister of the marine, and also rumored to be the queen's lover—who were the true sovereigns of the Two Sicilies. After the crown prince was born in 1775, Her Majesty claimed the prize she had coveted upon her wedding and which had been inserted into the marriage contract: her seat in Parliament and a controlling interest in the government. And it was the *queen* who, during the Bourbons' long and fruitful reign in Naples, had instigated the creation of libraries and the opening of universities, as well as freeing the roads from tolls and enacting reforms to encourage industry and agriculture. How I wished that I might come to know this fascinating creature!

According to many, the queen and I could boast of the best complexions in the kingdom; our milk white skin was much admired by the swarthy Neapolitans, who slathered so much paint upon their faces that they resembled oil portraits and covered their pox marks with patches. After I attempted to duplicate the Neapolitan fashion, Sir William kindly suggested that my true beauty would be better revealed were it not so masked by prodigious quantities of paint and powder. At his insistence I wore my hair completely natural, too. And in his amiable, diplomatic way, Sir William also suggested that I refrain from trying to *dress* like the ladies of high society, who reeked of pomade and perfume, piled copious amounts of false curls upon their heads, girdled their necks, wrists, and fingers with heavy, precious stones, and over their numerous petticoats and underskirts wore gowns trimmed with tinsel and spangled with sequins. The men were no less gaudy. And the grander the rank, the more colorful the picture. One aspired to be vastly overwhelmed by one's accoutrements.

"Their heads will turn, Mrs. Hart, if you looked markedly different from them. Should you emulate their style, you will run the risk of fading into the crowd. Simplicity is all. You will flaunt your beauty the most, my dear, when you least appear to do so."

Finally, at the end of July I received a letter from Greville, which at least was warm, if not effusive, but then that was never his way. Yet he scolded me for not being receptive to Sir William, which sent me into a panic. On the first of August, I replied hysterically, admitting that I had always harbored a dark foreboding that our connexion would come to no good end, then threatened to return to England and descend into dissipation, as an example to other women of what can befall an innocent country girl who is betrayed and abandoned by her lover. Then I grew contrite, offering to do anything to secure his love, and by the time I penned my postscript, I was desperate:

> *P.S.*
> *Pray write, for nothing will make me so angry & it is not to your interest to disoblidge me, for you dont know the power I have hear, onely I will never be his mistress. If you affront me, I will make him marry me. God bless you for ever.*

I kept my word: it was indeed the last letter I wrote to Greville in which I groveled for his love.

A few days later, just after breakfast, Sir William asked if he might speak with me quite candidly on a subject that he confessed had been troubling his mind for some time.

"It pains me no end to see you in distress, Emma. You may believe that you are concealing the ache in your heart, but the vivacity of your smile cannot conceal the sorrow in the depths of those dark eyes. I have struggled with my conscience night and day for several weeks now, and I have come to the conclusion that it is for the best that you know all."

I felt my knees begin to tremble and placed my hands upon 'em to disguise their wobbling.

"What has been hinted at—or perhaps more than hinted at— by Greville and myself ever since your arrival is not meant to tease you, or suggest an alternative to your situation, but has been a way of informing you, by degrees, that things have changed."

"Wh-what do you mean 'things 'ave changed'? Is not my Greville coming for me in October?"

"I think you take my meaning, Emma, but your trusting heart is too devoted to believe it. Greville will not be coming for you in October, nor in any month in the future. I regret that my nephew was too craven to say it outright, for his obfuscation has caused you no end of anguish these past three months. However, I cannot remain insensible to your distress. Chuse to hate me if you will, but someone must tell you the truth."

"Greville means to give me up?" The realization settled upon my bones like a funeral shroud. I went numb. "But don't 'e know I love 'im and would go to the end of the earth to please 'im?"

"You poor child," Sir William said, handing me his handkerchief, for I had forgotten mine. "Sweet, beautiful, loving Emma, you could turn yourself into calcified amethyst if you thought that's what Greville desired, and still you could not regain him."

I sobbed noisily into the embroidered cambric square. "What're you about, saying such falsehoods about my Greville?"

Sir William shook his head sadly. "For your sake, though not my own, I wish it were a hoax, but it is the unvarnished truth, Emma. My nephew and I came to a gentleman's agreement some months ago. He needed enough capital to set about getting a wife—"

"But Miss Middleton refused 'im! That is, Lord Middleton did, for Greville 'adn't enough in the banks!"

"Which is precisely why he recognized the gravity of his situation. My nephew was also overextended on his credit to the tune of several hundred pounds, particularly indebted to those who had procured the newest additions to his mineral collection."

" 'Twere better 'e 'ad lost me in a game of whist, only 'e don't frequent the gaming tables."

"If I would secure Greville's debts, and name him in my last will and testament as my heir—which you are aware I have indeed done—then I would inherit Emma Hart, placing her under my full protection in every way, and the matter would be concluded, to the mutual benefit of all concerned."

"Yes, Greville is a great one for 'is arrangements of 'mutual benefit,' " I cried. "If I've 'eard 'im use the words once, I've 'eard 'em an 'undred times! But 'ow could 'e be so cold? So cruel?! No, I shall not believe it! Tell me you are lying to me, Sir Willum. Tell me my Greville is true to me!"

Sir William sighed. "My dear child, it sits ill with me to make apologies for my nephew—or to make excuses, either. I can express the wish that the matter was handled in a better manner—"

"There is no 'better way'!" I blarted. "You tell me that you and Greville 'ave treated me just as you did the Barberini Vase or any one of your other precious jougs or dead rocks. Sir Willum, did you and Greville think nothing of taking me into your confidence before you engaged in your cloak-and-dagger transaction? I am no piece of pottery to be sold off or bartered away in order to satisfy debts! I am flesh and blood, as Greville is keenly aware, my 'aving been no stranger to 'is bed these past five years. I cannot conscience 'is . . . 'is manipulation. That 'e should stoop to such machinations to deceive me." My face was wet with tears.

"In the only words I can offer—not in his defense, but perhaps by way of explanation—I believe that Greville misjudged you. It is no compliment. I believe he was certain that you would find Naples so much to your liking that you would desire to stay of your own accord, should the opportunity be presented to you. And the happier you became in your new surroundings, the more acquiescent you would become to receiving the inevitable blow."

" 'Ow could he ever expect that of me, when I 'ave offered him proof upon proof of my devotion? I cannot understand it."

"It was, I fear, yet another way in which he misjudged your

character. You have a temper, Emma, and knowing my nephew, it is likely that he took your pledges of undying devotion with as much salt as he took your histrionics on other occasions."

"I 'ate the both of you!" I railed.

"Precisely my meaning. For you don't hate either one of us, at least not beyond the present moment." For what seemed like several minutes, Sir William respectfully remained seated in his chair, whilst I remained in mine, too stunned to stir, weeping as though my heart had been demolished into tiny shards, as irrevocably shattered as one of his priceless ancient vases.

Seventeen

Moving On

"Though it would sadden me greatly to see you depart, naturally I remain true to my word to settle an income of a hundred pounds a year on you and your mother, matching a pension of a hundred pounds to come from Greville. The funds would be held in a trust administered for you by Romney, whether you chuse to remain here in Naples, or whether you decide to return to England."

"I appreciate your generosity, Sir Willum. But where shall we live? I don't suppose, as Greville is endeavoring to recover some of his honor by offering me an 'undred a year, we could go back to Edgware Road."

Sir William shook his head. "That, I fear, is out of the question. As a consideration of the arrangement, you must close the door forever on that chapter of your life. Perhaps you would like to retire to the countryside, where you might stretch the income farther. A quiet cottage, perhaps in Flintshire near your grandmother? That might suit, would it not?"

"No, it would not, though I love my gammer dearly. I daren't answer for Mam, but you 'ave spoilt me, Sir Willum. 'Ow can I go back to dreary, damp Hawarden, to a life even duller than Edgware Row—especially as there is no Greville there to greet me—after I 'ave been so admired in Naples? 'Twould be like asking a derby winner to pull your plow!"

"You have time to more fully consider it," replied Sir William, "so long as you inform me of your intention by Christmas. That will permit me the time to make the necessary arrangements, should you indeed find it more amiable to return to England. I give you my word that your annuity will continue with no ill will on my part, until such time as you chuse to marry."

"Marry! To some country lout, I expect you mean! You've spoilt me for that, too. Kings and princes 'ave paid court to me. Back home, the best a girl such as I could do is marry a tradesman."

"You are a delightful companion, Mrs. Hart. I confess I should hate to lose your society. Of course you might meet a young Englishman here, not a pup, of course, but a mature man of means between the ages of twenty-five and thirty-five, perhaps. If only you had been given a proper education in your early youth, you would indeed be, as they say, a consort for a king."

Somehow, I took comfort in those words. "I'm getting a proper education *now*, a'nt I?"

I spent the rest of the day deep in thought, wandering the rooms of the Palazzo Sessa, wondering whether I should miss them. From the balcony just off the late Lady Hamilton's boudoir I could see the double peak of Vesuvius rising majestically from the fertile plains beyond the little town of Portici. Had I not been wearing a straw bonnet to shield my complexion, the sun would have kissed me in the Continental fashion, dabbing each cheek with a spot of Nature's rouge. I leaned against the iron railing and inhaled the aromas of Naples, both sweet and savory, pungent and delicate. A gentle breeze from the sparkling bay wafted essence of bergamot past my nostrils, and a moment later gifted me with the scent of sweet basil. Off to the west, the coast curved toward the grotto of Posillipo—Posillipo, where His Britannic Majesty's envoy had renamed his delightful, ivy-covered villa in my honor; where we often swam naked in the *piscina* with only the starfish and each other for company.

My mother joined me on the balcony. "I've been looking for you, Emy, gal."

As though her words had released the plug on a dike, I flung myself weeping into her arms. "I've lost 'im forever," I sobbed. "How could my beloved Greville betray me so? Excepting Sir Willum, of course, I 'ad thought that 'e was the only true gentleman I've ever known. P'raps if I had learnt to better control my temper, Greville wouldna been so quick to cast me off."

Mam stroked my hair. "Husht thee naise. You mustn't blame yourself, girl. You 'ave a grand 'eart, as big as all of England, Wales, and Scotland all rolled into one. If anything, although you've seen a lot, and p'raps too much for a girl of twenty-one, you still have a lot to learn about men, is all. I know you're 'urting like the devil, but wunst you've dried your tears, you'll look at things the way Greville 'imself and 'is uncle do."

"Meaning what?"

"In that detached way these uppity crusts do. *Their* sort of cynicism, softened by your *own* benevolent 'eart, becomes a kind of pragmatism. Which ain't a bad way to go through life when all is said and done. And a lot easier on your tender sensibilities than flinging yourself at life like a romantic."

I sighed deeply. "Would you miss this, if we was to go back home next spring?" I gestured toward the purple vista.

"Well, these Neapolitans don't know the first thing about cooking, for one. All that macaroni and gravy. Someone needs to teach 'em what's what. A good joint and a passel of potatoes and turnips, or a good 'earty Irish stew is what does a body good." She looked out at the pristine bay, where merchant vessels bobbed about, their colored sails like enormous festival pennants. "I go where you go, Emy. Don't make your decision based on what you think is best for your poor old mam, for what's best for me is what's best for you, and I ain't jesting when I say it."

"We can't afford to live well, if at all, in London on two hundred a year. And if I was fortunate enough to find another protector, I'm certain Greville and Sir Willum would cut off our pension."

"Is that what you want?" asked my mother. "A new protector?"

"No. 'Tisn't. Not really." I shook my head. "Do you really think we can go back to Hawarden, or some place like it, after this?"

"It's not for me to answer that question, y'nau?"

"It's rather a different climate from home in nearly every way," I mused aloud. "And Naples is as different from London as London is from Hawarden. All that bustle of London, still everything so gray and dreary most days. I confess I've grown rather accustomed to sunshine."

"I can't say as it's done any injury to my aching hip," Mam concurred.

"Smells better here, too," I added, enjoying the redolent fragrance of the coral-colored roses that bloomed beneath the window. "And I've become rather acclimated to the indolent pace . . . dinners as take four hours . . . all the musical entertainments. . . . You 'ave to agree that my singing 'as been greatly improved and much admired. . . ."

"That I do. And it's not your only attribute to be praised to these blue skies. I know you've no rival for beauty in the entire city, and Sir Willum takes care that everyone sees that. And the king hisself, though 'e's as ugly as an 'alibut, has an eye for you. What do you bet 'e's thinking of you when 'e's ponshyn that homely wife of 'is?"

"Mam! I think the queen is at least tolerable-looking, if not more than that. Those stiff court gowns with all their gems and pearls and embroidery become her figure, for you'll admit at least that she's got a majestic carriage. Besides," I added, beginning to weep again, "Maria Carolina knows 'ow to 'old on to 'er man when she wants 'im. Unlike your daughter."

"Husht, pet, don't be too 'ard on yourself, now. It ain't quite the same thing and you know it."

"All 'Er Majesty needs to do is display 'er pale white arms to 'Is Majesty and 'e salivates like a mongrel. It tantalizes 'im so when she sits before 'im and slowly dons her opera gloves, 'e would willingly make 'er the pope if it was in 'is power to do so! She's smart as the sting of a whip, Mam, and I would count myself blessed to ever find myself in the merest shadow of 'er favor."

"Which of course there'd be little chance of if we was to be living in England or Wales."

"Well, that's true enough!"

"So, 'ere you've got weather that 'appens in England wunst every blue moon. You've got a coach at your disposal, a passel of comely gowns and frocks, days spent lazing in the countryside, and nights strolling along the elegant Chiaia with all eyes upon you, or at the opera or the musicales, where your presence alone is one of the chief attractions. There's no end of admirers, starting, not with 'Is Majesty, but with our 'ost. Sir Willum values you for more than your looks, Emy, and that's not to be sneezed at. 'E's come to rely on you over these past few months, and one would 'ave to be blind not to see it. Sure, 'e no longer sees you as 'is 'ouseguest but as the *chatty-lane* of 'is establishments, if I may borrow a word from that French valet of 'is. And 'e's arse over tit in love with you, though 'e keeps 'is cards close and is clever not to tip 'is 'and about 'is intentions. But 'e could be yours, gal, if you wanted 'im. Just give 'im time. Old folks like us, we get set in our ways; now and again it takes us a bit more time to acknowledge the truth of a matter even when it's been staring us in the face bright as the sun and twice as large." Pausing for breath, Mam gazed off toward Posillipo. "Naturally, the decision is yours, child. Though I'm guessing it might be'oove me to go down to the kitchen and start teaching that fancy French cook of Sir Willum's 'ow to whip up some ponsh meip if I want to eat proper for the rest of my life."

Eighteen

A Change of Heart

I did not give Sir William my reply right away, for I knew that it went hand in glove with the presumption that our society would no longer proceed beyond an affectionate and respectful cordiality. Dear Sir William had been nothing but kind to me, yet at that time I was not in love with him. Truth told, I was tampin' over the way things had transpired, too angry to enter Sir William's bed even if I'd been of a mind to. Both men bore a share of the blame for hurting me so, and at least it did the diplomatic Sir William an ounce or two of credit not to press his amorous suit, even when it appeared evident that I planned to remain in Italy.

This decision more or less taken, I spent the summer like any Neapolitan lady of quality, yet adding by degrees the responsibilities of Sir William's chatelaine, supervising the household (when I wasn't delegating Mam to do so) and entertaining the ambassador's guests. Oh, did we have dinners and dances then! My head went dizzy from the political intrigues involved in what should have been the simple preparation of a seating chart: Count So-and-so could not be placed anywhere near Prince No-name or for certain one would find a reason to call the other out. This marquess was left-handed; that ambassador was deaf in his right ear; Ladies X and Y were notoriously not speaking, though they attended the same parties and conversazioni, one not to be socially outdone by

the other. By September, I might as well have been a minister without portfolio.

My days were also taken up with my schooling, for every day I
had Italian and French lessons, music and singing; and my drawing lessons continued as well. Sir William much enjoyed my renditions of English and Scottish country airs, but his true
sensibilities lay with the great German and Austrian composers; to
please him I applied myself to learning the lieder of Mozart and
Handel, and further increased my repertoire with some of the Italians' popular opera buffo pieces.

From November to March, the boar-hunting season, the entire
court would ride out to the town of Caserta at the foot of the
Apennines. The vast royal palace there, with its gloomy facade, resembled nothing so much as a barracks. Sir William would reside
in his *capannina*, accompanying the king each day for the quotid-
ian butchery, while I strolled about in the magnificent English
Gardens adjacent to the royal palace there. But without Sir
William's companionship at Caserta, for all the gardens' beauty
and the charming views they afforded, I was terribly lonely. The
capannina, though it boasted fifty rooms, was dull and drafty and
not conducive to a comfortable ménage, for it had never been designed with a woman's amenities in mind. Sir William was gone all
day, and my social position—for by that time they all assumed I
was Sir William's mistress—did not permit me to be formally recognized or received at court. Caught between acceptance on the
one hand and avoidance on the other, I was teetering on the verge
of returning to England after all.

"What can I say that will induce you to remain here?" Sir
William asked me.

"Say you'll come back to Naples with me."

"You know I can't, Emma. Duty. The king expects me to accompany him at every hunt."

"Every bloody one of them?"

Sir William chuckled. "Aptly put, my dear. And yes, I'm afraid, every bloody one of them. It may not sound like much of a privilege, but I am the only foreign emissary to receive an invitation from King Ferdinand to accompany him every day. As His Britannic Majesty's envoy, my job is to get as much as we can out of the Two Sicilies, whether it comes in the form of commerce or military aid, or simple goodwill—whatever *our* king might require at any given time."

"Well, then, I 'ope Farmer George appreciates the service you do for England!"

Before we knew it, the Christmas season was upon us, the first Mam and I had ever spent outside of Britain. The climate, so lush and sultry during the summer months, turned inordinately cold. In Naples there was snow on the streets, and Vesuvius was now as white-capped as was Mont Cenis when we'd crossed over it in early spring.

"I expect this is God's way of keeping us from getting 'omesick," Mam grumbled, rubbing liniment on her aching hip. "If we'd wanted to spend the Lord's birthday in a frosty, gray country, without enough 'eat in the fires to warm our bones, we'da stayed back in England! Just in case you 'aven't 'eard, Emy, girl, I ain't the only one chawin' the fat over it. Everyone's talking 'ow it's never been so monstrous cold 'ere. Them superstitious lazy-ronis, 'oove all gone underground to catch a bit of warmth in the catacombs, think the Almighty is punishing the Neapolitans for something or other; leastways that's what Vincenzo told me. Cat got your tongue, gal? Why, you're as silent and thoughtful-looking as one of Sir Willum's statues."

Mam ambled over to embrace me. " 'Appy Christmas, Emy." She handed me a prettily wrapped package. "It ain't much, but I thought you should 'ave something to open on the Lord's birthday."

It was a handsome Kashmir shawl. "Mam," I gasped, "this must 'ave cost you a king's ransom!"

She shrugged. "I've yet to see the need to use up Sir Willum's clothing allowance on fripperies for myself." She tucked the shawl around my shoulders. "I'm a practical sort, my girl. Mayhap I had a sense you'd need a little something extra to keep you warm this season."

Our modest celebration was interrupted by Sir William's friend, the landscape gardener John Graefer. Graefer was a frequent visitor to the Palazzo Sessa, enjoying our musical evenings as well as a good rubber of whist.

" 'Appy Christmas to you," Mam told him. "You're welcome to stop by tomorrow evening if you can find yourself a partner, for Sir Willum ain't at 'ome this week, tho' my daughter and I would be most obliged to take you on. As whist ain't her best game, I don't expect you'll be parting with too many ducats."

"I've something for you as well," I told Mam after Graefer had departed. Opening a drawer in my jewelry chest, I withdrew a bottle of spirits. "Romney brought it with 'im all those months ago and I've been saving it up for today."

"Oh, Emy!" Mam said, her eyes misting over with homesickness when I handed her the bottle of gin. "What an 'oliday this is turning out to be after all!"

"If only Sir Willum were 'ere to share it with us!"

I took my thoughts to my bath. Soaking in the tub as the verbena-scented water clung to my chemise, I thought about how to tell him what was in my heart. I had missed him dreadfully these past few weeks, and I had finally come around to acknowledging that my feelings ran far deeper than an affection born of gratitude for his many kindnesses to Mam and me. I loved him, not merely because of what he had done for us, but for his own myriad merits. Sir William was everything a man should be: educated, courtly, witty, charming, solicitous, athletic, adventurous, artistic, and beloved by all who knew him, for never had I heard an ill-tempered word spoken against him.

Since we had démenaged to Caserta in November, I had permitted him certain liberties of my body: caresses and kisses and intimacies of a further nature that taught me that Sir William was prodigiously skilled in the art of making love. Whilst in every other situation he was the detached ironic observer, in the boudoir he was playful as well as ardent, and the recollection of those nights—and days—in the *capannina* when we'd found much to delight in each other fired up my blood anew. With a sudden rush of passion, I realized that I wanted him, wanted to give myself to him fully and completely.

"*Buon Natale*, Vincenzo *e* Giulia! Happy Christmas, Mrs. Cadogan!" Sir William's voice resounded through the ground floor of the palazzo.

" 'Ave you come 'ome for the 'oliday, sir?" I heard my mother inquire. "What a pleasant—"

"Where's Emma?" he asked enthusiastically.

I suppose Mam had forgotten that I was bathing, for she flung open the door to our rooms. Startled, I stood up to greet him, momentarily unmindful that my shift was clinging to my nude body in clusters of sodden folds. Sir William was apparently just as stunned by the unexpected manner of welcome, for he halted immediately, remaining rooted to the spot.

"My . . . good God . . . no . . . *goddess*. Emma . . . my dear, have you any . . . ?" Sir William's eyes were misted with tears. "Damme . . . you are the most beautiful creature I have ever beheld," he whispered. "If my statues could weep with jealousy, surely they would do, for never was there a womanly form so flawless . . . so exquisite. . . . Emma, you take my breath away."

I held out my arms to him. With a cry of joy and not a fig for his fine garments, he strode across the tiled floor and flung himself into my embrace. I held him fast, raining tears and kisses on his cheeks, eyes, and lips. Mam stepped into the corridor and discreetly closed the door.

"My Emma. My own," murmured Sir William as he lifted me from the tub, divesting me of my shift, which remained all but forgotten in a soggy heap beside the basin.

Sir William's ardor and energy were exceptional for any man, let alone one of his years. Suffice it to say that we were both immensely satisfied with our Christmas gifts to each other. Unfortunately, however, our holiday was to be short-lived, as Sir William was expected to join the king at Caserta the following morning for another day of wholesale slaughter.

"I promise to steal away again as soon as I can, my love." We shared a last embrace before Sir William climbed into his carriage. It was not yet dawn. Still Christmas, to my mind.

"Wait!" I tugged at his sleeve. "Do they celebrate Boxing Day 'ere? For tho' they are robbed of your absence tomorrow, I should not wish the servants to be deprived of their gifts."

"What a girl you are! And an angel to remind me, for you have so addled my brain, I can think of nothing but the past few hours of unimpeded bliss." Sir William imparted his instructions concerning the servants, urging me to ask his valet, the dapper Abraham Cottier, for help should I require it, and with a final parting kiss, he was off to the countryside.

It gave me such pleasure to see our servants so delighted with their Boxing Day gifts and the rare holiday for themselves. Mam and I were quite content to make do without them for the day, our having been long accustomed to taking perfectly good care of each other without the necessity of a retinue. We supped in the kitchen, enjoying one of her Irish stews: good home cooking in a faraway fairy-tale land.

That night, I seated myself at my escritoire to compose a letter to Sir William. I wrote so many drafts that the floor was littered with crumpled pages.

> *Yesterday when you went a whey from me, I thought all my heart and soul was torn from me, and my greif was excessive I assure you. I saw Graefer yesterday and he said he would come this evening to play wist, but I would rather play this evening at <u>all fours</u> with you; oh! I forgot, cribige is our game, it's all the same, you like <u>crib</u>.*
>
> *Adio, my dear Sir William; laying jokes aside, there is nothing I can assure you can give me the least comfort tell you come home. I shall receive you with smiles, affection and good humer, & think had I the offer of crowns I would refuse them and except you, and I don't care if all the world knows it. I know you mind temper more than beauty, so if sometimes I am out of humer, forgive me, tell me, put me in a whey to be grateful to you for your kindness to me, and believe I will never abuse your kindness to me, and in a little time all faults will be corrected. I am a pretty whoman, and one can't be everything at once; but now I have my wisdom teeth I will try to be ansome and reasonable. God bless you, my ever dear friend, etc, etc, etc, etc, and believe me yours and onely yours for ever sincerely.*

And to think that not a half year previous, Greville was the sun, moon, and every star in the firmament of my heart! Now that resilient organ beat only—and most devotedly—for my dear Sir William.

Nineteen

❧❧❧

The Attitudes

All through an astoundingly cold January Sir William and I remained parted, yet we corresponded nearly every day. And our love for each other deepened with each letter.

The boar-hunting season ended with the bitter weather. The lazzaroni emerged from the catacombs, and the royal court returned from Caserta. Sir William came back to Naples with a most unusual proposal. "I have not been able to shake the image from my mind," he confessed, "from the moment I saw you standing in your bath, with your shift clinging to your body like the drapery on a Grecian caryatid: a statue come to life. Think on't, Emma! What if we was to have you act the part of a living statue, a modern piece of virtu, as 'twere."

I puzzled over it. "You mean imitate the classical figures like I did when I sat to Romney? Medea and Cassandra and Niobe and all? And at Dr. Graham's Temple of Aesculapius, I sometimes wore draperies and stood-stock still just like that while 'e gave his lectures on 'ealth."

"What do you say, my dear Emma?"

"I can't see why not—so long as my draperies isn't wet when I'm performing. I ain't shy, mind you, but there's certain things that are for your eyes only!"

Sir William clasped me to his heart. "Oh, Emma, you are a dear!"

We set to work on it right away. A thorough grounding in the classics became a mainstay of my schooling. Sir William read to me from all the Greek and Roman myths and legends, from the histories of the Caesars, from Ovid and Catullus, from Aeschylus, Sophocles, and Euripides. I came to know Lucretia and Antigone, Echo and Andromache, Calpurnia and Dido, as if they had been my playmates back in Hawarden. The men, too—Achilles and Pythias, Orestes and Adonis—for Sir William was convinced that my height, combined with my depth of feeling and empathy for the personages he coached me to portray, would enable me to play man or woman with equal dexterity and compassion.

Below the ground floor of the Palazzo Sessa lay a number of storage rooms, filled with crates and statues and paintings and assorted curios that there was no place upstairs to display. Among these assets was a lidless sarcophagus, as large as a hip bath. In the dark of night, illuminated only by torches and tapers, the sarcophagus and the other haphazardly arranged artifacts would lend an unearthly feel to the ambience.

One night, we descended the staircase to experiment with the concept amid these ancient treasures. I was wearing a sheer Grecian tunic of my lover's designing, flowing like gossamer about my body and down to my ankles. "Every time you assay a new pose, hold up the Kashmir shawl, and then draw the curtain again, as 'twere, when you are ready to assume the next role," Sir William proposed. He thought that I should not depict just one personage, but move from character to character with seemingly effortless grace.

"And 'ow long do you want me to 'old each . . . each attitude?"

"How long can you manage it without moving a muscle?" He glanced at his pocket watch and began to count the minutes.

"You've turned Pygmalion, Pliny," I teased, when in raptures Sir William described the Attitudes to the assembled guests at Casa Coltellini.

"Quite the reverse, my dear," corrected my lover. "For Pygmalion desired that a statue should become a real woman, whereas I am turning the flesh-and-blood woman into the statue."

"And remember the besotted Pygmalion's fate," warned my frequent admirer, the Austrian Prince Dietrichstein. "His ungrateful Galatea left him for another man."

We were attending one of the Coltellini sisters' famed musical soirees, and I had been asked to sing, an honor not to be taken lightly, given the illustrious nature of the company. I gave them one or two Scottish airs, performing them with such passion and gusto that though the Neapolitans had not our language, there was no mistaking the ebullience of their approbation. And then I favored them with a bit of Paisello's *Nina*, which I had been working on with my singing master, Galucci. The finest judges of musical talent in Naples could not have been more impressed.

The following day the rooms on the ground floor that Mam and I had been occupying since our arrival the previous April were swiftly transformed into an entire academy for music and voice, while we moved our things upstairs to the rooms that had belonged to Lady Hamilton. To my immense delight, I would now sleep in her late ladyship's boudoir with its charming balcony and magnificent views.

Within the week, Sir William had invited each of my admirers from Casa Coltellini to visit the Palazzo Sessa and witness the debut performance of my Attitudes.

Enacted in the palazzo's supernatural subterranean gloom, that first presentation became an overnight sensation. Word quickly spread throughout Naples that Sir William's young and beautiful English protégée, Mrs. Hart—she of the charming voice and passionate interpretations, both comic and dramatic—was equally deft with her *silences*, needing but a few hand props, such as a dagger and a goblet, to achieve her flawless mimicry of the greatest personages of antiquity.

However, the morning after our great triumph, Sir William, in his ever-diplomatic way, delivered his own review of the performance. A straight razor was left on my dressing table.

"I 'ope to God 'e doesn't mean for you to kill yourself with this!" Mam exclaimed, puzzling over the message.

I bosted out laughing. "I think I know what 'e means. Did you watch me last night?"

"Well, of course I did," Mam replied, much affronted.

"And could you see my quim through that little slip of a frock?"

"Well, now that you mention it, Emy, gal . . ."

"Look at the Venus," I said, pointing to a foot-high marble effigy on the mantelpiece.

"I'm looking."

"What do you notice about 'er? All right then, I'll make it easy for you. Can you see 'er quim through 'er draperies?"

My mother squinted, then approached the statue, peering at the juncture between its thighs. "Well, she don't 'ave any 'air on it, so it's hard to tell—no! Do you think Sir Willum wants you to shave your cunny?"

I nodded my head. "Though 'e don't quite know what he's saying. Or not saying. If I take a straight razor to my quim, I'm liable to do myself some lasting injury, to be sure." I examined the razor. "These was never designed for curves."

"What will you do, then? Sure, 'e wants you to do it because it looks vulgar to be seeing through your draperies when you're supposed to be a statue and all. Given that girl statues 'ave no 'air down there. And 'e don't want prying eyes to be getting the wrong idea, as you're giving 'em something high-tone and artistic."

Once again, my dubious past provided the key. "Warm honey and lemon juice, Mam," I said, recalling how the "nuns" at Mrs. Kelly's took care of business in order to achieve the same result. "It's called *sugaring* and they've been doing it ever since Cleopatra was a girl."

Together, we mixed the concoction, and ripped numerous strips of muslin as I had seen Sophia do all those years ago. "Might as well make the other parts resemble marble as well," I sighed, raising my arm. I yelped in surprise, not having considered how painful the process would be. "Shite, Mam! That smarts like a raft of bee stings."

My mother gazed at me, her expression one of bemusement and sympathy rolled into one. "In that case, my girl, you'd better stuff a bunch of these muslin strips in your mouth so the servants don't 'ear you cry out and think you're being tortured by your own mam."

"But I am!"

However, the pain soon passed and was outweighed by many rewards, both within and beyond the boudoir. In short order it became clear that the original venue for my Attitudes was too cramped to accommodate such a large audience, even though the performances were intended to be offered only to favored guests. Sir William and I abandoned the gilded frame and the sarcophagus and reconfigured the presentations, offering them in the salon upstairs, where there was significantly more room. I performed on a low platform—ten to twelve Attitudes in succession—whilst the chairs were grouped before me in a semicircular arrangement. Sir William, ever my *cavaliere*, stood off to my right and held the torch as though it were a greater honor than the Order of the Bath. We entertained foreign travelers as well as local artists and dignitaries, and a performance of Mrs. Hart's Attitudes at the Palazzo Sessa soon became known as an imperative for anyone of note passing through Naples.

One such visitor was a celebrated author from Germany. Johann Wolfgang von Goethe was a rather humorless man in his late thirties, who could not for the life of him comprehend the English fascination with tromping up Vesuvius—for Sir William, being his host, was naturally keen to show the writer the sights immediately

upon his arrival. Goethe had arrived in Naples with the painter
Tischbein, who was eager to immortalize me in oils.

"How are you enjoying Italy?" I asked the writer.

"Ach! In Rome I have found myself for the first time," he
replied, his command of English far better than my German. "I
have made many drawings—there and here—and found myself
moved beyond comprehension by the classical form. An ancient
temple I visited—modeled on the Greek—left me in tears; its
power was so primitive I could scarce imagine such a thing existed
in the modern world. And Naples." He clutched his heart. "Naples
is a paradise. In it everyone lives a sort of intoxicated self-
forgetfulness."

"And the people?" I smiled as charmingly as possible.

"You English are such a strange mixture, Frau Hart," Goethe
said. "You are both coarse and refined all in one. What a treat for
a student of human nature! You and the ambassador are . . .
lovers?" Blushing, I nodded. "Fascinating!" exclaimed the writer.
"And he is . . . how many years do you have between you?"

"A bit more than thirty-four, *mein Herr*."

"Fascinating! Your eternal beauty keeps *him* eternally *young*.
What a wonderful way to become an immortal." Goethe made a
polite bow. "I am very much looking forward to your performance
this evening, Frau Hart."

Months later, Goethe sent me a copy of the thoughts he had
recorded in his diary after witnessing my Attitudes.

> *The Chevalier Hamilton, so long resident here as English Am-*
> *bassador, so long, too, connoisseur and student of Art and Na-*
> *ture, has found their counterpart and acme with exquisite*
> *delight in a lovely girl—English, and some twenty years of age.*
> *She is exceedingly beautiful, her figure fine and pleasing. He has*
> *a Greek dress made for her, which suits her wonderfully well. She*
> *undoes her hair, takes a couple of shawls and goes through such*

a changing succession of poses, gestures, looks etc, that really in the end you think you are dreaming. You see what so many artists would have been glad to achieve, here perfectly finished in movement and change. Standing, kneeling, sitting, lying, serious, sad, teasing, extravagant, penitent, seductive, threatening, fearful etc, one flows into and out of the next. She suits the folds of her shawl to every expression and with the same two or three of them can invent a hundred different dressings for her hair. The old lord holds the lights for it and has given himself wholeheartedly to his subject. He finds in her all the statues of antiquity, all the lovely profiles on the coins of Sicily.

I—Emma Hart, the once-impoverished daughter of an illiterate farrier from North Wales—had become the most talked-about woman in southern Italy! That same season, the Society of Dilettanti in London published Sir William's letters on "The Feast of St. Cosimo or Priapus in Isernia" within a compendium that included numerous illustrations of wax, clay, and bronze effigies of "the Organ of Generation in that state of tension and rigidity which is necessary to the due performance of its functions."

What a pair we made!

Twenty

A King Unwittingly Plays My Hand

As the months passed, Sir William and I grew more and more inseparable. We traveled about the town and countryside together, explored the ancient ruins of Pompeii, even studied botany together. Arm in arm we attended conversazioni, nodding our greetings to the hobnobbing nabobs by torchlight. In order to improve my Italian, I challenged myself not to utter a word of English, and my proficiency increased with astonishing rapidity. Frequently invited to perform with the orchestras at a conversazione, I favored the guests with solos, and sometimes a duet or two with the finest opera singers of the day. Even the Banti, la prima donna at the Teatro San Carlo, a woman jealous of her reputation, singled out the nuances of my phrasing and the passion of my interpretation. How terrified I had been that night to follow her performance, for she was universally considered to own the finest voice in the kingdom. An army of butterflies invaded my stomach. This was no giddy balladeering on a wobbly wooden crate in Southwark. But—to my immense relief—how well my songs were received! I was floating on air. From that night on, I had no fear of singing before such a discerning crowd.

On occasion, prince and commoner alike would sidle up to me, their flirtatious remarks often no more than frank propositions. "*Mi scusi, signori, ho solamente uno cavaliere servente,*" I told them, beaming proudly at Sir William. My lover was the only man I needed.

One evening I was approached by the maestro of the Italian opera in Madrid, offering me a three-year contract at the rate of two thousand pounds a year to be the first woman there. It was an enormous sum, nearly two-thirds as much as Sir William's annual stipend after twenty-two years as His Britannic Majesty's envoy to Naples. But as I gazed across the room at Sir William, I heard myself decline the engagement. "I know no one in Spain, nor do I know the language," I told the maestro. Sure, I had gained a passable proficiency in both Italian and French in a matter of months; learning Spanish would not have presented many difficulties, but the truth was that I could not leave Sir William. I had grown to adore him and could not bear to be separated. Accepting the offer to perform in Madrid would have put an end to our arrangement, I am certain of it. And one thing I had always known about myself was that I was not made to walk the world alone—happiest always when I was half of a loving couple.

Also visiting us at the time was Gallini, the commissioning dancing master of the London Opera House. "Please, Mrs. Hart," he pleaded, "permit me to engage you for a series of subscription concerts back home in Hanover Square. It will be very ladylike, I assure you." This, too, was a tempting suggestion, and difficult to ignore.

"Begging your pardon, Maestro," Sir William said affably, "but *I* have *engaged* Mrs. Hart for *life*."

My heart sang at his words.

A few years earlier I would have jumped with alacrity at these offers. To be paid—and handsomely—to do nothing but sing? Had that not been one of my girlish dreams when Jane Powell and I warbled and trilled our young hearts out at the Southwark fairgrounds?

Despite my popularity in certain circles, my presence was still not accepted at the royal palaces, nor was it tolerated by some of the other English hostesses in the city, who, for all the amorous intrigues that infested the ranks of the upper crusts, made an elaborate show of refusing entry to the ambassador's mistress. To these hypocrites, my low birth and unfortunate past rendered me a pariah; and in a world where a woman's reputation was a far greater asset than her beauty, her virtue a more valuable commodity, shame on Sir William for parading me in public! Not to be outdone, the Neapolitan ladies of quality—the very same women who sought to emulate my English complexion of roses and cream—also barred their doors to me.

But I put a gay face on it and tried to mask my feelings, which were colored at various times with anger, disappointment, and regret. *Let them keep their dreary evenings to themselves*, I thought, stuffing back tears, *for no one wants their little entertainments anyway. It's Mrs. Hart they all want to see.*

My third spring in Naples was dawning, and once again the city bloomed with fuchsia and oleander, and *canzoni d'amore* wafted on the breezes that blew off the azure bay. On April 26, 1788, my twenty-third birthday, Sir William presented me with a box bound in red Moroccan leather tooled with gold. I opened the catch and was stunned speechless.

"You've often mentioned that you would like diamonds . . . as all the fashionable ladies of Naples wear 'em." He permitted the tiniest smile to play upon his lips.

"Oh, Sir Willum!" I jumped up from my dressing table and threw my arms about his neck. "If you are not the dearest, sweetest, most generous, most wonderful man in the world, then such a one does not exist!"

Later, I was to learn that the diamonds cost Sir William five hundred pounds, more than double the amount of the annual allowance he permitted Mam and me for clothes and washing. We had the brilliants set into a suite comprising a choker and a pair of earrings and I wore them to every gala we attended that year, as proud of my glittering acquisition as Sir William was of me. "Can you imagine Greville or Uppark 'Arry doing such a thing?" I marveled to Mam.

She clucked her tongue dismissively. "They wasn't gentlemen, Emy, gal, despite their fancy birthrights. Sir Willum knows your value, that 'e does, and 'e also knows *it's* worth an 'ole lot more than them stones you're wearing, no matter what they cost 'im. 'E's arsey yarsey in love with you, pet. He don't spend that kind of money willy-nilly unless it's something 'e really wants, like a statue or a painting or another one of them old jugs."

"Five 'undred pounds was Greville's entire yearly income when we was together," I mused. "It's been two years, y'nau. Do you think Sir Willum will ever ask me to marry him?"

"Dunno," Mam replied. " 'Is mind's distracted by them newspaper reports about 'is 'foster brother,' as he calls 'im."

"Do *you* think King George 'as gone mad, Mam?"

"With an heir such as 'e's got, I wouldn't blame the poor sod if 'e 'ad!"

Sir William's mother had been a lady-in-waiting to the king's father, Frederick, back when Frederick had been the Prince of Wales. I confess I always wondered if Sir William was really a Hamilton and not a Hanover, but in all my life I never heard a word contradicting his legitimacy, and I never dared broach the subject. Sir William had become quite distressed over the accounts that surfaced throughout 1788 regarding King George's bouts with madness. His Majesty would suffer an attack, then recover his wits after enduring the most horrid cures, only to relapse again. I felt sorry for him. That such a powerful man should be reduced to such pathetic wretchedness wrung my heart.

My importance to Sir William and the value he placed on my love for him had been steadily increasing as the months progressed.

No longer did he fear that I might wish to return to London, or seek another protector. We were now as secure in one another's affections and first place in each other's hearts as any pair of devoted lovers.

Another sea change had taken place over the past several months. What had been at first a nodding acquaintance with Queen Maria Carolina, with careful and fastidious nurturing, was blossoming into a true, burgeoning friendship between us, though I was still unwelcome at official court functions, such as the *bacio mano*, or hand-kissing, ceremonies that Sir William was required to attend. And I remained unable to enter the front door of the palace as did the ladies of the Neapolitan nobility. If Her Majesty and I wanted to converse, I had to employ a subterranean passage that connected the Palazzo Sessa to a backstairs entrance leading to her private rooms within the Palazzo Reale.

Yet outside of the city, things were slightly less formal. In the fine spring and summer months Sir William and I would ride out to Caserta every Sunday, along roads redolent with the aromas of orange, melon, lily, and rose and the strains of mandolin and guitar coming from nearly every garden and window. In the vast palace we dined *en famille* with the royal household. And when the men would retire to talk of hunting (for that was the king's only subject that was fit for family ears), the queen and I would discuss everything from politics to her children, to the fashions of the day. "I am a mother first," Her Majesty would always remind me. "The Queen is just a court dress I put on." As she had brought seventeen children into this world, it was impossible for one to doubt her sensibility.

To my utter astonishment, the queen took an interest in my life. "*Êtes-vous heureuse?*" she would sigh, solicitous for my happiness. Although an Italian monarch, she derided that language as coarse, insisting on speaking mostly in French, the courtliest of tongues and the universal language of diplomacy. "I wish I could

do more for you, *ma chère*. The rules are silly, but without protocol, you have anarchy."

Although it bothered me that I had to sneak about like a thief
to see her, our visits soon became everyday events. I was with her
that awful day in July when the news arrived about the storming of
the Bastille in Paris. She threw herself weeping into my arms, terrified for the safety of her beautiful younger sister, Marie Antoinette. I held her and stroked her hair as though she were my
little Emma. But once the *woman* dried her tears, the *queen* vowed
revenge. Although several French émigrés resided in Naples—
royalist nobles as well as those with republican sensibilities—there
had been no political rumblings of any sort here. Nevertheless,
from that day forward, Maria Carolina resolved to maintain a
tighter scrutiny on the Illuminati societies she had once strenu-
ously supported.

Perhaps it was the rumors of my close friendship with the
Queen of Naples that gave rise to other tales about me. "There is
talk that you and His Excellency are secretly married," she disclosed one afternoon as her youngest children played at hoops in
her private drawing room. The queen did not flinch when their
boisterous game caused a Meissen ware shepherdess to topple from
an end table, smashing to bits when it hit the highly polished floor.

I smiled. "Is that why more doors are suddenly open to me?
Not too long ago the same hostesses made a point of not including
Mrs. Hart on their guest lists."

"Alors?" Her Majesty smiled like a cat.

"If Sir Willum and I were married, would I not 'ave visited you
this afternoon by entering the palace like *Sua Eccellenza l'Ambasciatrice*, instead of like a serving maid?"

"He made you a present of five hundred pounds' English worth
of diamonds. Was it not a wedding present?"

"It was *not* a wedding present, Your Majesty." I laughed. "Don't
you think I would have known it?"

The subject came to a head nearly a year later on a gloriously beautiful summer afternoon in the English Gardens at Caserta. I had brought my sketch pad and pencils and was strolling along one of the numerous winding pathways, in search of the perfect vista to immortalize. A furious crunching of gravel betrayed the presence of another, rapidly gaining on me.

"Signora Hart! Signora Hart!" The panting voice was unmistakably that of the king. He had somehow run afoul of his servants and was completely alone. I stopped and waited for him to catch up with me. At least he had the manners to mop his brow before plunging into his theme. In all my years in Naples I never learned more than a few words in the local dialect, but I did not require a proficiency to take His Majesty's meaning.

"You are . . . a very beautiful woman," he said, still panting. "You . . . very desirable."

"I am your dear friend's lady," I replied, expecting no need to elucidate any further. After all, when I'd first arrived in the city four years earlier, he admitted regret that he could not make me any overtures, for I belonged to Sir William's nephew. For years now it was abundantly evident that Sir William was my protector, and even though he was The King, Ferdinand must have realized that it would be unwise to attempt such a seduction.

But he did! Like the country louts in the Chester of my childhood, his majesty tried to steer me into a secluded grove with every intention of having his way with me in the bushes!

"*Aspettate!* Wait, Majesty!" I held up my drawing tablet, creating a barrier between my person and the king's. In a flurry of pantomimed gestures and rickety Italian, I asked him to put his proposition in writing. Something as simple as "*Ti voglio bene*" would have sufficed.

"In Eenglish—*Inglese? Italiano? Napoletano?*" The king was very keen on getting it right, as he was undoubtedly certain that if he did so, his wish would be granted and I'd lift my petticoats and open my legs just over the next rill.

"*Non fa differenza.*"

In his boyish scrawl, King Ferdinand took the tablet from my hands and wrote something in Napoletano, the only language in which he was as comfortable as he was in the subject of his text. Making sheep's eyes at me, he offered the protestation of, if not his *love* for me, his unmitigated *desire.*

"*Mille grazie*, Majesty!" I spied a pair of royal servants huffing and puffing toward us, still some distance away. I hallooed them, waving grandly but gaily. "Were you looking for 'Is Majesty?" I shouted. With all the subtlety of an opera buffo performer I pointed to his person. "*Ecco qui!*"

Unscathed, I was thus able to effect a polite escape.

I brought the king's declaration straight to the queen. "Were I indeed married, would I be subject to such unwanted overtures?" I asked her. " 'Ave I not always been the picture of fidelity? Do you know 'ow many years I 'ave 'ad to endure the jests and jabs about my 'dubious past,' when in truth my relationship with Sir Willum is thoroughly untainted by scandal and my 'ighborn critics are themselves adulterous and unfaithful? Now your own 'usband seems to have declared it 'open season' on Emma." I dissolved into a flood of tears. "Your Majesty, since I came to Naples all I 'ave ever asked of life is to enable me to show my gratitude to Sir Willum for what 'e 'as done for me and given me. You are not a jealous woman. Can you not believe that a young beautiful woman, tho' of obscure birth, could 'ave noble sentiments and act properly in the great world? I own I made mistakes in my youth—and many of 'em—but I assure you that I can be—have been—am—as virtuous as anyone born to the purple."

"*Ma petite pauvre,*" replied Maria Carolina sympathetically as she wiped the jam from the sticky palms of one of her young princes. "I wish it were within my power to allow Sir William to make you a proper offer of marriage. But that rests with your English sovereign, as His Excellency is a servant of King George. However, my dear Emma," she added, with the sly smile of a consummate politician, "I will see what it *is* within my purview to attain. And as for my husband—you need not fear that he will renew his entreaties and advances. How is it you English say . . . ? I shall 'take him well in hand,' " she purred silkily, slowly peeling off a long white glove.

Twenty-one

A Modest Proposal

*I*t soon became known throughout Naples and beyond that Emma Hart had been taken under the protection of the ever-astute Queen Maria Carolina. Owing to her influence, more doors opened to me socially. Several other artists came to render me in oils, clay, or watercolors, for Sir William never ceased to brag about his piece of "modern virtu." We even fitted up a chamber in the Palazzo Sessa as a painting room. Among our artistic visitors was the German Wilhelm Tischbein, who had first come to Naples back in 1787 in the company of his countryman Goethe. I called him "Willie," because he was such a serious little man I thought to quiz him out of his stuffiness. In 1790, Sir William offered a commission to a talented, though highly self-important, Frenchwoman named Elisabeth Vigée Le Brun, who painted me a number of times. She depicted me twice as a bacchante: in one portrait I am dancing with a tambourine, my hair flowing behind me while Vesuvius smokes in the background. In the other bacchante, which has always remained one of my favorite portraits, I am reposing before a cave with a leopard skin draped over my hips. Mme. Le Brun's painting of me as a Sibyl eventually became a calling card for her talent. For some time she carried the canvas with her as she traveled throughout the Continent in search of further commissions. But it saddened me to learn that Mme. Le Brun was quick to taint me with tawdriness once she stepped away from her easel, for word got back that she found me enchanting when costumed for any of the numerous roles in which she painted me, yet thought my usual wardrobe loud and vulgar. She could scarce believe it was the same woman, so she said. Well! All I can say to that is she comprehended very little of our Neapolitan society, where fine ladies were not afraid of color, or strangers to fancy trim.

And this was from a woman who sought to enrich herself by promoting likenesses of my person! A brilliant portraitist, to be sure, but a common Frenchwoman when all was said and done.

A year after the storming of the Bastille, Jacobin sympathies surfaced in Naples. Secret societies were unmasked and a number of Frenchies—shopkeepers, cooks, tavern keepers, and even artists—were deported for holding discussions on "The Liberty of the Subject." Queen Maria Carolina wasted no time in prohibiting such sensibilities from festering. Sir William broached the subject of a journey to England, but foreign travel became inadvisable for several months.

So we spent the rest of the year entertaining as usual at the Palazzo Sessa. It was not uncommon for us to have fifty or sixty to dinner several times a week, and one evening we threw a ball with four hundred in attendance, including many of the Neapolitan and foreign nobility. An invitation to the British embassy was by any account the most prestigious ticket in the city, for our gala nights were as much fun as they were festive, and dear Sir William took especial care that I should outshine even the most glittering of our guests. A simple white satin gown showed my figure to perfection; I applied a minimum of cosmetics—just enough to maintain the rosy bloom in my cheeks—and wore no powder in my hair, which Sir William desired me to leave unbound, loose, and flowing to my heels.

Hints, winks, nudges, and nods—and occasionally the outright question—regarding our marital status continued to plague me. To all the world, Sir William and I appeared the most loving and devoted couple, and even my detractors were compelled to admit that the ambassador had a renewed spring in his step when he was in my presence, and positively glowed when he extolled my virtues. But for all these concessions, there remained a substantial contingent who still disapproved of the match, for whom my present conduct could not atone for my past, even though they had never known me when I was young and wild. Daily, I offered proofs of my complete reformation, but their prejudices trumped the truth. The wife of Sir William's good friend Heneage Legge was ailing and Sir William suggested that I would make an excellent nurse and an entertaining and compassionate companion. Yet the invalid tartly refused his offer, saying that while she was certain it was well-meant, she did not think my present position in society too different from my past, and therefore would have been hard put to welcome me into her home.

"I don't know 'ow much longer I can go on this way," I'd tearfully tell Sir William once the guests had departed, the torches and candles been extinguished. The slights, the digs, the little mortifications, added together became insults of far grander magnitude. It was affecting my health, too. My rashes had returned.

The cuts wounded me—even tempted me to strike back in one of the only ways that was available to me: my performances. Herder, the noted poet and Lutheran minister, insisted on an invitation to see my Attitudes. I can't imagine why, as his discomfort and disapproval were immediately evident. The more this pedantic prude frowned and fretted in his chair, the more I was tempted to play the seductress, retailoring my performance on the spot to ensnare him in my shawls the way a spider traps a fly. The more he squirmed, the more I wormed, until the rest of the audience was exploding with laughter at his expense.

Another night I positively scandalized some of our guests when I introduced a popular native peasant dance into our postprandial concerts. Proper ladies did not dance the tarantella; it was considered far too risqué, so none of our guests would join me when I exhorted them to stand up and dance off some of their fine dinner. Thus refused, I was left with no alternative but to call for my maids, Laura and Giulia, and we gave them quite a show. Sir William pronounced my performance "downright erotic, by gad!" and demonstrated the full measure of his delight once we retired for the evening.

"I do believe it is time for a holiday," he sighed, nestling into my arms.

I slept late the following morning, exhausted from all the hullabaloo of the previous night. Looking for Sir William, I found him in his observatory tower, gazing at his precious Vesuvius. "My love?"

Startled out of a reverie, he turned around, his face a reflection of emotions that flowed into and over one another like the sparkling waves below us. He took my hands and seated me beside him on the upholstered banquette. "Emma . . . my own dear Emma . . . it pains me more than you know to live with the awareness that you are hurting inside. You are so good, so gracious, so loving, so . . ." His voice trailed off while he gathered his thoughts. "I turned sixty last December. We will celebrate your twenty-sixth birthday in April. I have long desired to be able to grant you what I have been fully aware for some years now is your greatest wish. And I have struggled to appreciate how the consequences attendant on the manifestation of this desire will affect each of us. For you must believe me, my beloved Emma, I never want to spend a day outside of your sunny company. There might have been a time when the opinions of others would have carried a degree of weight, might even have affected my decision, but I am beyond all that now." I felt my heart quicken. "Emma . . . my angel . . . my darling girl . . . I should like to make you Lady Hamilton."

My lips began to tremble and my eyes moistened. I gazed into Sir William's face, more composed than I had expected it to be after so stunning a declaration. "Oh, Sir Willum!" I flung my arms about him and smothered him with kisses.

"You realize, my dear," he said modestly, between passionate embraces, "that I will be entering the twilight of my life just as you are approaching your zenith. And what a mismatched pair we shall be. It is no small trifle to consider. What will the world say when the glorious Emma must excuse herself from our grand dinners to attend to her 'slippered Pantaloon'?"

"Faugh!" I rested my head against Sir William's chest. "You are 'the most juvenile man I have ever known,' remember?"

But this most devoutly wish'd-for turn of events was to remain a secret until the eventuality might become the reality. As Queen Maria Carolina had so astutely observed, Sir William required King George's consent to our union, and His Majesty's permission was no certainty, their "foster brotherhood" notwithstanding. Queen Charlotte, fastidious about protocol and other societal niceties, had a tremendous influence on her husband, particularly since he had begun to slip in and out of madness.

"Whatever will Greville say?!" I exclaimed through happy tears.

"Given all that has transpired over the past few years, this will undoubtedly come as no shock to you," Sir William replied. "One of the reasons my nephew was so insistent that I assume the responsibilities of your protection was *precisely* because he feared I would remarry and jeopardize his chance of inheriting what can laughingly be categorized as my 'wealth.' "

"But you named him your heir soon after I came to Naples. Was that not part of the *bargain*?" The memory still lingered somewhat bitterly.

Sir William looked amused. "He had worried, particularly when I was entertaining Mrs. Damer, that I might marry some lady of quality and that would be an end of it, for I would settle an income on her and diminish his legacy. But if it was *you* that brightened my days and warmed my bed, he would have the best of all possible worlds: the ability to reduce his expenses while pursuing an heiress, and I would have a lively companion and 'the cleanest bedfellow' that he 'had ever known,' as he called you. Given your history, no matter how besotted with you I was, he was certain I would never be so foolish as to make you my wife. Nor, given the magnitude of the hurdles I must overcome to do so, did Greville ever believe such a thing might come to fruition."

"He does us both little credit. And what manner of man describes the woman who adored him no end for 'alf a decade as 'the cleanest bedfellow'—never mind, I already reckon the answer. You know, 'e never said 'e loved me," I added quietly. "For all the times I told 'im during the years we was together. So I guess 'e never did." I took a deep breath before broaching the other subject on my mind. "And what of the unusual Mrs. Damer? Would you 'ave proposed to 'er?" I steeled myself for the reply.

"She wouldn't have me, you know." Sir William chuckled. "Actually, 'Don't even take it into your head to ask me' was what she said. And what a lucky escape she permitted me, for Mrs. Damer prizes her independence—and her breeches—above 'the domestic prison of matrimony,' I believe she called it."

"Then I shall try not to be jealous, but rather thank 'er for releasing your 'eart."

"My heart was not pledged then, Emma, nor was it ever engaged where Mrs. Damer was concerned. An amiable companionship was all I ever expected from any marriage to her." Sir William pressed my hand to his cheek. "But that was a hundred years ago. You are as different from any woman I have ever known as—"

"As Mrs. Damer in trousers is from the genuine article!"

Sir William laughed loudly. "I *am* besotted, you know. Entirely enchanted. When you first arrived, I couldn't take my eyes off of you, remember? And as the weeks and months passed, infatuation gave way to admiration and it gives me the most unalloyed pleasure to tell you, my precious Emma, that I stand before you now never having been more in love." Sir William placed one of the brocaded cushions on the floor and dropped to one knee upon it. "Dear, dear, Emma, my love . . . my life . . . will you do me the greatest happiness of becoming my wife?"

"My own adored Sir Willum . . . 'ow I love you! 'Ave I not already said yes?"

I helped him to his feet. "But I had to make it formal, my dear, or I shouldn't deserve the name of lover. A few minutes ago I made a *declaration*, an expression of *desire*. This time I was asking your permission!"

"It was such a long time in coming, but I knew it would happen someday, Emy, gal, y'nau?" Mam was overjoyed when I imparted the good news and rushed to extend her felicitations to the prospective bridegroom. It took a good deal of persuading to convince her of the importance of keeping our confidence.

We set out for London—and destiny. On April 21, 1791, just five days before my twenty-sixth birthday, Sir William, Mam, and I arrived in Venice, a fairy-tale city that rose out of the mists, and so unlike Naples it was hard to believe we were still in Italy. By midday the mists had lifted, as if La Serenissima, playing Salome, had shed her veils. Serenaded by gondolieri, Sir William and I held hands as we drifted under the Bridge of Sighs; at night we gambled at the casino that Casanova himself had habituated. And we saw many French émigrés who had fled their own country. They despaired not only for their own safety but for the entire future of their homeland.

We reached London a month later, on May 22. That evening, my lover's anxieties about this undertaking gave way to fear that his endeavor would fail. "Old Lady Spencer and Lady Bolingbroke are in our camp, my dear—as was the late Duchess of Argyll though of course they each married for love—but there's many I thought to call my friends, Heneage Legge among them, who think I'm a fool and you're considerably worse."

I knelt beside him and massaged his tired feet. "Damn them all, then," I smiled. "There's only one person that really counts."

"And by all accounts he's a madder man than I am!" sighed Sir William.

Twenty-two

Lunacy Triumphs

While Sir William set off for Windsor to begin his campaign, I commenced my English holiday by paying a visit to my old friend in Cavendish Square.

"Emma!" exclaimed Romney, laying aside his brush and wiping his hands with a rag before rushing to greet me. "What a splendid surprise! What brings you to the city of stench and fog?"

I kissed him on both cheeks in the Continental fashion. "The truth?"

"Well, of course."

"I missed the stench and fog. Terribly boring in Naples with all that blue sky and the sparkling bay," I added gaily. "Everywhere you go you are overwhelmed by the perfume of roses and one could go positively deaf from all the mandolins. Nothing but love songs night and day. And that dreary, irresponsible volcano always threatening to erupt but never seeing the thing through."

"What a wit!"

"Sir Willum and I are 'ere on business, and you may 'ave me all summer, or until our—'is—affairs are completed and we once again set forth for foreign soil. We plan to return through France. Queen Maria Carolina insisted that I extend 'er sympathies to 'er poor sister. Why, Romney, *perchè* the frown?! Are you not beside yourself over what is 'appening across the Channel? To treat their king and queen with such disrespect—it makes me ill to think on't!"

Romney looked thoughtful and I feared he was beset with another bout of melancholy. "I 'ad the good fortune to do a portrait of Thomas Paine. And I am not a politically minded man, but I found much merit in his philosophies—the abolition of slavery, permissible divorce, and divisible property laws, for example. I would hazard a guess that even a royalist like Sir William would welcome a change in the property laws. 'E and Greville, being regular clients of mine, I know 'ow they stand in the world. They are both second sons, wrestling with perpetual financial woes, because a gentleman ain't supposed to work; yet they must make their own ways in the world while their elder brothers sit on their arses and inherit. Now, I don't conscience murder, of course, as a stepping-stone to Liberty, but between you and me, Emma, absolute monarchy don't sit quite right, either."

"Well, you might be right about Sir Willum and the in'eritance question. But don't ever let 'im 'ear you talking like a Frenchy!"

Sir William did not return from Windsor with an answer in hand. He had induced the king to make him a privy councillor, which entitled him to certain perquisites, but he had not received a response to his primary request. "These things take time," he sighed, but counseled me to keep my chin up. "One of the first rules of diplomacy, my dear, is that nothing happens overnight."

In the meantime, we went about our holiday.

In August, the prime month to be there, we set off for Bath, while Mam journeyed to Manchester to visit little Emma, who for some reason was now calling herself Emma Carew, though it was not the name of the family that raised her. I considered joining her, rather than going to Bath with Sir William, but I admit that I thought it would be better for the poor dear child if her quiet, simple life was not upended by my sudden appearance, when I should only have to tear myself away from her after a few days. Were I to suddenly swan into the girl's life now that she was nine years old, I was certain, my arrival would raise more questions than it would answer.

Sir William and I had made it our plan to remain in England for a few months so he might introduce me to certain influential members of British society. They were not to know of our engagement, of course, nor of Sir William's petition to His Majesty, but if his suit was successful, he wanted the leaders of the fashionable world to know firsthand that I was as worthy of taking my place in society as any of them.

To my astonishment and delight, some of the leading lights of the day scorned the hypocrisy of their contemporaries and welcomed me into their midst. I could have leapt for joy. At the Duchess of Devonshire's salon, I met Her Grace, as well as her best friend, Lady Elizabeth Foster, who was also the duke's mistress, an open secret among their set. There, rather than being disdained as vulgarity, my displays of emotion and exuberance and my unaffected spirit felt entirely at home. The duchess and I took to each other immediately. And her mother—who was one of the few to have been taken into Sir William's confidence—was most encouraging regarding our marriage. But Georgiana was the liveliest and most generous and charitable soul—not to mention the most beautiful—that I had ever met. I remembered how I'd admired her when she'd been a frequent patron at the Temple of Health so many years earlier. What a different life I'd had then, counting myself lucky for earning my own way as neither a servant nor a Cyprian!

I treated their coterie to a performance of the Attitudes, which were roundly praised, as were the simple, neoclassical gowns I had begun wearing daily during my visit. Within a few weeks, it seemed as though all the fashionable ladies of Bath were copying my ensembles, seeking to emulate the ancient heroines brought to life by the fresh and vivacious Mrs. Hart.

Among the venerable guests who enjoyed my Attitudes in Her Grace's salon was the Prince of Wales. Georgiana was amused at the way he practically fell over me with compliments. I knew his reputation, as well as the nature of his friendship with the duchess, and permitted him only the most benign of flirtatious gestures. "Well, then, I must have you in my *boudoir* any way I can," he whispered suggestively, "even if it means I must hang you in effigy."

"Good 'eavens!"

"A portrait, Mrs. Hart. Romney is the artist who captures you best, I believe. You see, I have become something of an Emma *connoisseur*. I think as *Calypso*, for you portrayed her so cunningly in your Attitudes, tho' I wish'd you'd have sung, for didn't Calypso enchant Ulysses with her voice?"

"But the Attitudes are silent, Your Royal 'Ighness."

The heir to the English throne pouted like a petulant schoolboy. "Nevertheless! I should like to hear Calypso sing. In fact, I command it!"

For a command performance of *that* sort, I was happy to oblige. I gave him a bit of *Nina*, a young woman driven mad by the death of her lover, and since the aria was in Italian, His Royal Highness didn't know what the words meant anyway. But he was in raptures afterward and declared himself my eternal servant. Sir William congratulated me on having made yet another conquest.

"Yes, but it's 'is *father* 'oo counts."

"We are getting closer." He handed me a copy of the letter he had written to the Archbishop of Canterbury on August 22.

> *My Lord,*
>
> *As Your Grace is at Scarborough and I have but a short time to stay in England I am under the necessity of solliciting a favor of Your Grace in this manner instead of doing it personally as I cou'd have wished.*
>
> *In short My Lord it is my intention to marry a young person*

with whom I have been acquainted several years & whose be-
haviour I think fully merits all that it is in my power to bestow.
Her name is __Amy Lyon__, tho' better known by the name of Hart.
Will Your Grace at the request of an old Friend grant me a Spe-
cial License as speedily as possible—as I wish my marriage to be
secret untill I have left England. I flatter myself that Your Grace
will hear from many quarters of the merits & talent of the per-
son that has induced me to take this Step so late in life, inshort
it is my own affair and I shall be much mistaken if this Event
does not insure my happiness. Excuse the confusion which I find
in reading over what I have written—it is an awkward subject
to write upon. I beleive my being a Privy Counsellor entitles my
application to Your Grace but I shall take it as a very particular
favor shoud you grant me the request & speedily.

My heart was racing. "Do you think 'e'll grant you the special
license?"

"I pray he does. But if His Majesty does not approve, it scuttles
the whole affair, regardless of the archbishop's acquiescence."

On August 28, Sir William revisited Windsor, returning to our
rooms in Somerset Street late in the evening. His face betrayed
nothing of his emotions.

"Well?" My heart was pounding in my chest.

"I have good news and bad news."

"What did the king say?"

"Let's say I got off better than I expected. I'd expected a thorough dressing-down, you know, 'Duty' and all that humdrum. The
king knows well enough that some years ago, after he denied my
requests to be transferred to the more vital embassy in Spain, I reconciled myself to remaining in Naples, out of the international eye,
growing old and quietly living out my dotage in the shadow of
Vesuvius amid my virtu. As long as I am never to have the post I
coveted, why not at least have the happiness I deserved?"

"But what did 'e say?!"

Sir William hunched his shoulders a bit in mimicry of King George's posture. " 'You're not quite as religious as you were when you married the *late* Lady Hamilton, eh, wot-wot?' "

"A quizzing?"

"I assure you, though it could have been much worse, it was not altogether pleasant."

"But it's a *yes*!"

"It's a *yes*!"

"Oh, Sir Willum!" I drew him to me with such passion that we collapsed together on the settee. "You have made me the 'appiest woman in England."

King George's consent to our marriage came with a number of caveats. I was not to be received at the Court of St. James. Not now. Not ever. I would be Lady Hamilton in name, but the marriage would not entitle me to be the ambassadress in any official capacity as was the first Lady Hamilton, who had been of gentle birth. The oddest restriction of all was that while Sir William Hamilton, private man, was free to marry the woman he loved, the person of His Britannic Majesty's envoy was for all intents and purposes to be considered a celibate. Translated out of diplomatic language, it meant that the king had given Sir William his consent, while at the same time retaining his privilege not to recognize the marriage in any formal, official way.

It was a triumph of love, if not of lunacy.

The archbishop split hairs as well, permitting us to be married "by license," thereby dispensing with the posting of the banns, which would have ruined our attempt to keep our marriage a secret until we left the country.

Our wedding was not a grand affair. Sir William, the secular humanist, had little use for churches and religion, so we exchanged our vows in a quiet ceremony at St. Marylebone, a charming little church so small that it had no room for a freestanding baptismal font.

I wore a white satin gown accentuated with a wide sash, and a large pink bonnet with a white panache. The officiator was the Reverend Dr. Edward Barry, rector of Elsdon. Standing by as a witness was the elderly Marquess of Abercorn, one of Sir William's relations: a thoroughly delightful gentleman who developed an immediate fondness for me. Mam was there of course, and to my surprise, Greville honored us both with his attendance.

The briefest of congratulations were exchanged. There was to be no wedding breakfast. No sooner were we pronounced man and wife than Sir William and I dashed off to Cavendish Square.

"Our business here is done," Sir William declared, producing a bottle of champagne from a wicker hamper. "We depart for the Continent as soon as practicable. How fast can you paint?"

Our dear old friend appeared utterly bemused—as much by Sir William's uncharacteristic ebullience as by the flying bottle of champagne that landed in his hands.

"Romney, my man, congratulate us. And allow me to be the first to commission a portrait of—dash it, I don't care what the king says—of Her Excellency, the Ambassadress." Sir William slipped his arms about my waist and lifted me into the air. "By gad, I am the happiest man in the world today. Kiss me, Lady Hamilton!"

The Ambassadress

1791–1800

Twenty-three

The Frenchies Give Us a Fright

On September 8, 1791, two days after Sir William and I were wed, we arrived in Paris. Just five days earlier, King Louis XVI and Queen Marie Antoinette had been permitted their liberty, having been imprisoned in the Tuileries by the National Assembly, following their disastrous flight to Varennes in June. Despite remaining heavily guarded, Their Royal Majesties retained their dignity and maintained their hauteur, holding court three times a week as though nothing had changed.

But in truth, there were *many* changes in the city's perfumed winds. Shop windows displayed grotesque caricatures and political cartoons ridiculing the monarchy and the members of the royal family. As Sir William and I wandered the streets, we noticed many men with short, unpowdered hair, wearing the striped trousers or "sans culottes" popularized by the revolutionaries, who condemned any man in knee breeches as an aristocrat, though Robespierre himself wore them. Men and women alike sported the red Phrygian cap, which denoted their Jacobin sympathies, and the "tricolor" of the new republic was flown from windows and balconies in nearly every neighborhood we visited.

Sir William's friend Lord Palmerston, in Paris on some sort of official business, somehow managed to get us admitted to the meeting of the National Assembly on September 14, a most auspicious day for the new order. That afternoon, King Louis appeared before the governing body to publicly declare his acceptance of the new constitution. The king spoke only briefly; to me it sounded as if his words had been scripted, his unhappy demeanor unmasked by his native dignity. I found myself pitying him. Sir William, so customarily placid in every situation, was prodigiously agitated by the rude treatment His Majesty received from the President of the Assembly.

"By gad, that ill-mannered upstart is acting like he's the equal of a king!" Sir William muttered angrily. "Where is his deference? Where is his respect? If this is a taste of the fruit which their trees of liberty have yielded, I'll have none of it!"

On the following day, Sir William and I were presented at court. Having been prohibited from appearing at the Court of St. James and barred thus far from the Court of the Two Sicilies, I was unaccustomed to the magnitude of the preparation that went into such an event. I was up at dawn to begin my toilette. Both Sir William and Greville had always preferred me to leave my tresses natural, so I was also unprepared for the length of time it took to affect the expected coiffure without a wig. My hair was so long and heavy, I must have used up all the bear grease and bergamot in Paris in the making of my pomade, and enough powder to fill a miller's flour sack.

But how grand it was! I wore the diamonds Sir William had given me, and it took Mam over an hour to help me into my numerous underpinnings and petticoats and lace me into my court dress of mustard and rose-colored satin and brocade. Sir William had chosen my robe and underskirt, thinking the colors set off my complexion to perfection. Since I had grown accustomed to very light boning under my neoclassical gowns, the corset, fashioned in the old style, so constricted my movement that I felt like an exotic insect in a silken carapace.

The king and queen were still holding their audiences in the

Tuileries. To reach the twin thrones at the far end of the great hall, Sir William and I had to traverse the length of a pale blue runner accentuated with golden fleurs-de-lis, the Bourbon colors. The queen's perfume—a concentrated essence of tuberose—invaded my nostrils long before I reached the dais. To my immense relief I managed my very first court curtsy without incident, sinking gracefully to the floor, lowering my head without losing a single hairpin, and then rising without a trace of a wobble. Only then did I gaze into Her Majesty's eyes. They were a deeper color than her sister's, and less watery, without the red lids that made her elder sibling too often resemble a bunny rabbit. On the whole, Marie Antoinette was a much prettier woman than Maria Carolina, more doll-like, with proportionate features, larger eyes—though not as keen as those of her elder sister—and a sweet mouth. By the grace of God she had escaped the Hapsburg forehead and jaw. Her artfully applied cosmetics enhanced her natural beauty, rather than obscured it, as it did to so many of the ladies of her court who slathered their faces with white lead. While the elaborateness of her coiffures was legendary, this one was modest by comparison, rising only some eight inches from her scalp and adorned with an enormous diamond aigrette and a pair of stuffed songbirds. She was by no means dull when she spoke, but was clearly without the intellect of Maria Carolina. In almost every family there is a "smart sister" and a "pretty one." It did not take long for me to determine which was which of the two.

King Louis had something in him of the Bourbon physiognomy: the nose that began high on the forehead, the small eyes, the cheekbones that appeared more long than wide. Yet he possessed more regality in his little finger than did King Ferdinand in his entire loutish person. Where the King of Naples gloried in being a man of the people, anyone could tell from his demeanor that the King of France detested the common citizen—and with reason.

"*Approchez, ma chère,*" commanded the queen. "*Non, non, rapprochez-vous.*" She motioned for me to come even closer. A bit nervous, I came as near as I could without climbing the steps that led to her throne. Marie Antoinette rose and looked at me curiously. "Lady Hamilton, *je crois que vous êtes une vrai amie de la couronne. De temps en temps, ma soeur bien-aimée avait évoqué votre gentillesse. Je dois vous confier quelque chose d'importance.*"

"I am honored by both you and your sister, for your generous compliments of my person. What is it you wish to give me?"

The queen withdrew a folded paper from her busk. It was already doubly sealed; in addition to the wafer, the Bourbon royal crest was boldly embossed upon the scarlet wax.

"*Une lettre pour ma soeur, la reine la plus puissante de Naples. Donnez-la cet papier en toute confidentialité. Vous n'oubliez pas?*"

"I won't forget to give it to 'er, mum. I promise."

Marie Antoinette kissed the letter before handing it to me. As I slipped it in my own busk, her eyes misted over with tears. "*N'oubliez jamais,*" she said, trying not to cry.

Was she reminding me not to forget to give her letter to Queen Maria Carolina, or exhorting me never to forget *her*? I would have made a dreadful faux pas if I had sought clarification.

To celebrate the *fraternité* that formed the third pillar of the new republic (the other two being *liberté* and *égalité*, of course), September 18 was declared by the Assembly to be a gala day. No carriages were permitted in any of the Parisian streets; all citizens and visitors promenaded about on equal footing. Throughout the entire day and well into the night, everyone in Paris was treated to breathtaking balloon ascensions, spectacular displays of fireworks, and grand illuminations of all the public buildings, gardens, and widest thoroughfares. The Palais du Louvre, the Tuileries, the Champs-Élysées, all glittered with firelight, and everywhere you turned, there was dancing in the streets. Surrounded by such glorious excess, the unfamiliar suddenly felt like home. "Lud, Sir Willum, it's almost like Naples!" I breathed.

Sir William shook his head. "If only it were, my love."

We arrived at the Palazzo Sessa on the first of November, exhausted, but happy to be home. Sir William enfolded me in his arms and fixed me with a tender gaze. "You cannot begin to imagine how much I am anticipating introducing you to Neapolitan society as Lady Hamilton."

"Can *you* imagine 'ow much I am already enjoying *being* 'er ladyship?"

"Then why the frown, my dear?"

"The French queen's letter. Do you think 'Er Majesty knew I'd have to bring it to 'er sister through the back door of the Palazzo Reale? Will the King and Queen of Naples accept me at court now that I'm your wife?"

In fact, the queen did allow me to be presented, though as Lady Hamilton and not as *Sua Eccellenza l'Ambasciatrice*. But the difference mattered little, for upon my return to Naples as an honest woman, she showed me all sorts of affectionate attentions, and I cannot imagine her being any kinder or more gracious to me had I been officially recognized as the ambassadress. The common Neapolitans did not split hairs; they conferred the distinction upon me themselves, and cries of *"Eccellenza!"* greeted me wherever I went. My new life was all I had ever wished for and more.

Just after the New Year, the king embarked on another one of his lengthy boar-hunting sorties, commanding Sir William to join him. My husband had been showing signs of exhaustion since our return from England and France, and I feared for his health during those terribly long days, which King Ferdinand refused to account a success unless he had sent hundreds of beasts to their bloody demise. Sir William entrusted me to handle his correspondence while he was "pigsticking," as he liked to call it. Thus, I opened a letter from Greville, enclosing a bill to Sir William's bankers at Ross & Ogilvie in the sum of thirty-two pounds, eleven shillings, for little Emma's most recent care.

> Now that you have taken possession of Emma under the eyes of God and according to English law, I trust that you will assume responsibility for any expenses in that connexion, whether close or remote. I therefore submit the enclosed for the past several months of maintenance of the child. As bienséance demands that she continue in her present circumstances, & I am certain you will agree, there is no longer any reason it should continue to fall to me to shoulder the burden, I trust you will be happy to acquit the responsibility from now on.
>
> Yours, &c
> Charles Greville

Sir William had insisted that I write to him every day whilst he was away. But so angry was I when I told him of Greville's missive, that I misspelt several words and Sir William chided me for my inattention, after so much marked improvement in my orthography. But what was I to do when I was looking at such a petty-minded thing? I was tampin'! Little Emma's board was enumerated, her washing, her staying the Christmas holiday, her teacher and servants, music and copybooks, shoes, use of a pianoforte, haircutting, a seat at church, Evans' worm powders, and the drawing of two teeth—my poor little dear—all understandable expenses, but how small-minded to list a charge for pins, needles, tape, and thread amid the child's expenses? And why the reference to a guinea spent for "one dozen of port red wine"? The child was a whisper shy of her tenth birthday! Who was consuming the spirits?

It was an unpleasant way to begin my first calendar year as a married lady.

Throughout the autumn and winter, and even in the spring, though the French Republic had declared war on Austria, we found ourselves entertaining so many intrepid English visitors that Sir William and I nicknamed the palazzo "the Hamilton Arms."

"Evidently education in England does not improve, for upwards of one hundred British travelers have been here this winter, and I can scarcely name three who have reaped the least profit, for they have lived together and led exactly the same life they would have done in London," Sir William groaned.

So he took a quietly perverse delight in exposing some of our British visitors to the more unusual Neapolitan rituals, such as *I Morti*, the native celebration of All Souls' Day. Every November 2, the Neapolitans would disinter those who had died in the past year. They would dress the decomposing corpses in their finest gala attire and display them in the churches and streets as though they had come back to life. Friends and family of the dear departed, as well as complete strangers, would come either to venerate the bodies or to mock them—perhaps taking the chance to taunt the deceased—an opportunity that they had been deprived of whilst the person lived. Even the hardiest constitution did not fare well when exposed to the bizarre spectacle of *I Morti*.

But while they dined sumptuously at our table and drained our cellars, I knew that behind their snuffboxes and their fans our British guests were sneering at me. My laugh was too loud and came too easily; my countrified accent still redolent of manure; and my broad gestures and frank speech—devoid of *nuance*, such a dreadfully popular affectation among their circle—were deemed vulgar and coarse.

Sir William always endeavored to cheer me. "I am sorrier for them that they have missed your goodness, my sweet girl. So jeal-

ous are they of your beauty that they refuse to admit your generosity and devotion as well as your own brand of wit, and acknowledge that you are ten times more virtuous than any of 'em."

I rested my head against his chest and felt the beating of his
heart against my cheek. "It don't make it any easier to play the
'appy 'ostess, my love."

Seventeen ninety-two was a ghastly year for the French aristocracy,
and, by extension, my dear new confidante, Queen Maria Carolina, who despaired for her sister's safety. On August 10, the mob
stormed the Tuileries, igniting the Second French Revolution.
They massacred the Swiss Guards and incarcerated Marie Antoinette and Louis in the Temple. Although the Assembly called it
a "Convention," to our view, constitutional monarchy had been
replaced with anarchy.

In early September, jailed prisoners, including priests, were
slaughtered by the hundreds. Reports reached our ears in Naples of
the shocking butchery practiced upon their fellow Frenchmen by
the inflamed mob—beheadings and hacked limbs—behavior one
might have encountered on King Ferdinand's hunting parties.

The new republic sent its own minister, Armand de Mackau, to
Naples, but the queen treated him coldly. Enraged by the Jacobins,
Maria Carolina was little inclined to countenance the niceties of
diplomacy under the circumstances. How could she respect the
representative of the terrorists who had toppled her sister from her
rightful throne and tossed her in prison like a common criminal?

In retaliation for this snub, the republic sent a fleet of thirteen
ships to Naples, ostensibly to attack and pillage us like a band of
pirates if the Kingdom of the Two Sicilies refused to formally recognize the French Republic. The royal family were beside themselves with fear. "You must help us," the queen insisted, relying on
me to take an active part in the supervision of their decampment
to the fortress of Castel Sant'Elmo. Terrified that they would be

caused to flee with nothing but the clothes on their backs, and recognizing that they would need as much currency as possible in that unlucky event, the panicked queen began to sell off the treasures of the royal household. Everything from chandeliers to plate, even coffeepots, was exchanged for gold. The king, anxious that the Frenchies might enrich themselves off his stables, gave away three hundred of his dogs and nearly four hundred of his horses. Even Sir William was urged to take advantage of the situation and accept a matched pair of bays. How my heart cracked when Ferdinand commanded that all of the wild animals in his menagerie be slaughtered so as not to fall into the hands of his enemies.

But too fearful to stand their ground, the Two Sicilies soon acknowledged the French Republic—and the mood shifted markedly. Those who had secretly harbored Jacobin sensibilities felt free to openly express their beliefs, going so far as to clothe themselves in "Citizen" fashions (or the appalling lack thereof), sporting the silly red Phrygian caps. Naples, city of sultry breezes and gay parties, of music and merriment, had suddenly gone from a climate of *volupté* to one of dread.

As 1792 drew to a close, I breathed a sigh of relief, in the hope that the coming year would be a better one, for things could not possibly get worse. Or so I thought. We was at Caserta in December when Sir William was overtaken by an attack of bilious fever. I was overcome with fear and fatigue and could not bring myself to leave his side for an instant, not even to sleep.

I had believed myself unloved by the fine Neapolitan ladies, but their generosity in this unhappy circumstance reduced me to tears, for they, as well as the English travelers, were tender and solicitous, driving out to Caserta to visit me—for I had no other society there—and generously offering to help me care for Sir William, even if it was only to permit me to steal a few hours of precious slumber. Their Sicilian Majesties sent messages to our *capannina* twice daily, so eager were they for news of Sir William's recovery.

I knew he was not a young man, despite his athleticism. In fact, he passed his sixty-second birthday in the clutches of the illness. As he lay abed for days, feverish and wet with sweat, I despaired of losing him. What would I do if he left me? Was it God's dreadful design that I should finally be granted my dearest wish only to have it snatched away from me so quickly?

We live but for one another, I wrote to Greville when Sir William finally pulled through and commenced his unhurried convalescence. *Every moment I feel what I felt when I thought I was losing him forever.*

Twenty-four

A Savior Arrives

One morning at the end of January, a servant arrived from the Palazzo Reale with an urgent message from the queen: Come at once!

I did not know how to dress for such a summons. Protocol must be observed at all costs, and to properly attire myself to appear before Her Majesty, even if I was meeting her in her boudoir, took time. I could not very well simply throw on a dressing gown and race through the subterranean passageway like some thief in the night.

I found her in her private sitting room pacing like a tigress, her eyes more red-rimmed than usual. Shreds of silk littered the floor. With nothing else immediately at hand, she had rent her petticoats.

"They have done it!" she shrieked. "*Nous sommes revenus*—we come back from the fortress thinking all is safe in Naples, yes—but we may never be safe anymore!" She thrust an official report into my hands. "My brother-in-law has been executed by the animals in Paris who dare to refer to themselves as a new civilization. Like a criminal, they kill him. Explain to me, *ma chère amie*, how is this *fraternité*? Frenchmen killing Frenchmen! Where does it end? We are going to rid the house of pests," she told me, gathering strength from her tears. Almost immediately, the queen asked her subjects

to send their French servants home. No more lavish dinners prepared by French-born chefs, no French bonnes to properly launder
their linens and dust the Capodimonte figurines. In an attempt to
curb meetings of Jacobin societies, she issued a decree making it il-
legal for more than ten people to gather. A few Neapolitan Jacobins
were jailed, and at the opera house one night, the Banti was nabbed
backstage by two of the queen's secret police just as she made an
exit. She was whisked off under armed guard to the Papal States,
permanently expelled from Neapolitan territory. Her Majesty ordered priests to openly call for death to the French from their pul-
pits and replaced elected government officials with men under her
own control. In this climate of fear and mistrust, she even hired de-
nouncers and informers to spy upon their neighbors for any signs
of Jacobinism.

"We are no longer living in a backwater, my love," I told Sir
William. "The queen believes that the wolf is at our door. The republicans have already taken Toulon and now have garrisons in the
Papal States, right on Naples's northern boundary. 'Er Majesty says
we must fortify ourselves against the possibility that they may
come further. What do you think of that?!"

He remained thoughtful for several moments. "I am not one
to ever conscience violence," Sir William replied. "But before we
rush ahead where angels fear to go, we must take a moment to re-
flect upon why the societies of Neapolitan artists and intellectuals have embraced many of the republican sensibilities. In this
country justice does not exist, the government of it is very defec-
tive, and the people have a right not to be trampled on. I know
you have become thick with the queen, Emma, but you must
caution yourself that your infatuation with her does not render
you blind to these defects. If you wish to behave like a diplomat,
you must consider a thing from every one of its sides. Naples
more closely resembles a decahedron, wife, than a wafer. If this
government does not speedily and seriously set about a reform in

all its branches, the general discontent now silently brooding will probably, sooner or later, break out into open violence. Nature has certainly done more for the Kingdom of the Two Sicilies than for any kingdom in Europe, and yet I have been witness myself of more misery and poverty among the inhabitants of some of its richest provinces than I ever saw in the whole course of my travels."

"But if you, as 'Is Britannic Majesty's envoy, do not seek to protect the Two Sicilies by encouraging England to come to her aid, where will the revolutionaries stop, Sir Willum? Will solid, beef-eating English subjects soon be sipping brandy instead of quaffing beer and singing 'La Marseillaise' instead of 'God Save the King'? You must do something about it, Sir Willum. If ever there was a time for England to seize the present in order to protect 'er glorious future, that time is now!"

Sir William regarded me with studied curiosity. "Egad, my dear, you sound like Britannia herself!"

Yet my impassioned words did have an effect. On behalf of their respective governments, Sir William and Sir John Acton signed the Anglo-Neapolitan treaty on July 23, officially declaring Naples an ally of the British Crown. Suddenly, Sir William and I were two of the most influential people in Naples. For years now, we had set the tone in fashion and entertaining, but now the stakes were significantly higher; securing our friendship and goodwill was of vital *political* importance.

In August, a British fleet under the command of Lord Hood arrived in Toulon, under orders to blockade the port. Invoking the terms of the Anglo-Neapolitan treaty, he sent an emissary to Naples charged with demanding that the Kingdom of the Two Sicilies honor its pledge to provide troops in return for subsidies from the British Crown.

On September 11, 1793, that envoy arrived. Hood had dispatched the thirty-four-year-old post captain of the *Agamemnon*, a slender, slight man named Horatio Nelson, much admired by his men, we were told, and highly commended for his decisiveness and grace under pressure. I could never have known it at the time, but his appearance would change all of our lives irrevocably.

"Nothing could be finer than the view of Vesuvius." Those were the first words he said to Sir William, and had Nelson been a diplomat instead of a naval captain, he could not have ingratiated himself more with the British ambassador.

As for me, when I first saw him, I thought I was seeing a ghost, for he so resembled poor dear Samuel Linley, the young navy officer I was smitten with as a girl, that I was immediately undone. Nelson's size and stature, his almost-fragile physique, the shock of unpowdered light hair that would not be tam'd, the blazingly intelligent blue eyes—and even the outmoded uniform with its wide flaps on the waistcoat—it was as if Samuel breathed again before my eyes.

"Does Lady Hamilton usually have such a . . . passionate . . . reaction to visitors?" Nelson inquired politely.

"Forgive me for the outburst, gentlemen." Covering a blush, I excused myself from the room, for I could not very well have added, *You remind me beyond all measure of my first love.*

I allowed a few minutes to compose myself, reentering Sir William's library in time to hear Nelson request an immediate commitment of six thousand Neapolitan troops. As His Britannic Majesty's ambassador, it was up to Sir William to broker the deal with Acton and Their Sicilian Majesties.

"I do not know if you are aware, sir, that the 'king' of Naples is really the queen," Sir William said smoothly. "I will most assuredly take your demand to Sir John, but to win the unmitigated support of Maria Carolina, it is my wife to whom one must make a petition, for she and the queen are thick as thieves. You said you have no Italian and even less French, am I right?"

"You must hate the Frenchmen as you hate the Devil, Sir William."

"Then I take that to mean you have not learnt the lingua franca?"

"I am just a common English sailor, sir, with no pretensions to much of a formal education. I set aside my books for the smell of pitch and bilgewater when I was but twelve and a half years of age."

"But you see, as much as you detest the lot of 'em, French remains the language of diplomacy. Now, by coming to Naples at nineteen or twenty-one, or whatever it was—you should have seen her then, all emotions and eagerness to absorb everything around her like a sea sponge—Emma has got the language better than I have in twenty-eight years. Although we have had many ladies of the first rank from England here, and indeed such as give the Tone in London, the Queen of Naples has often remarked that my Emma's deportment was infinitely superior."

Nelson bowed politely. "Then I place myself at her ladyship's disposal."

Thus was I drafted to intercede with the queen on Nelson's behalf, but it was Sir William who applied to Acton for the troops, a request that was promptly honored.

"I must say, I admire your husband tremendously," a grateful Nelson remarked.

"As do I, Captain Nelson. 'E 'as many fine qualities. But tell me your reasons for likin' 'im so."

"We are of a mind, Lady Hamilton. Sir William is a man of action who conducts his business in the same manner as myself."

I smiled. "And 'ow is that?"

"With no dithering and a great respect for and trust in those under his aegis. I am speaking of yourself, your ladyship, and your husband's implicit confidence in your ability to carry out your assignment with skill, diligence, and all due speed."

I suppressed a blush. "You honor me, Captain Nelson."

"As does Sir William."

Sir William was equally impressed by Nelson. "He is a little man who could not boast of being very handsome," said my tall and elegant husband in the privacy of our rooms, "but mark my words, Emma, Captain Nelson will become the greatest man that England ever produced."

Accompanying Captain Nelson on his errand was his fourteen-year-old stepson, Josiah Nisbet. "Your Excellency must excuse me for bringing one of my midshipmen. I make it a rule to introduce them to all the good company I can, as they have few to look up to besides myself during the time they are at sea," Nelson told us. "Some of my colleagues think my attention to these young men is madness, but I assure you there is both merit and method in't. For it is my belief that you must be a seaman to be an officer, and alas, you cannot be an officer without being a gentleman."

In the four days that Nelson spent on Neapolitan shores, he was much honored by the king and queen, meeting with them no fewer than three times—and once, he was placed by the king's right hand—a grand success by any account. As a measure of thanks, he insisted on hosting a dinner party for us aboard the *Agamemnon*. Mam was beside herself with amusement that the little captain, as she called him, had asked her for the loan of plate and cutlery from the Palazzo Sessa, for he dared not expose us grandees to the rigors of shipboard life. "He even asked me for butter dishes!" Mam exclaimed. "Don't Farmer George outfit 'is warships with butter dishes?!"

"Fourteen seems terribly young to be away for so many months, if not years, at sea," I mused, raising my glass to Josiah.

"Perhaps 'tis," Nelson replied. "But in fact, many boys are first taken on board when they are only twelve, though the Admiralty has declared it unlawful. However, they wink at it as often as not and the exception has become the rule. When I was Josiah's age I had a bit of a dust-up with a polar bear!"

"But 'ow?!"

"Though no boys were permitted to join up, I talked my way into becoming a member of an expedition to the North Pole, reckoning I might be of service as a coxswain; and there we were, just below the polar ice cap when I took it into my boyish head to bring back a souvenir for my father. He would have been the only rector in Norfolk to have a bearskin rug, you see. But my musket misfired and the bear became rather agitated."

I clutched my heart. "What 'appened?"

Nelson smiled sheepishly. It was charming. "A signal shot fired from my ship frightened the beast and he lumbered off in search of something else to call his dinner." He emptied the last drop from his wineglass onto his fingernail. "An old naval superstition," he murmured, when he caught me watching him intently. "Takes care of the heeltap."

Our party was abruptly interrupted when a man arrived from the shore with a message from Acton: four French ships had anchored off Sardinia. Nelson immediately issued the command to his crew to disembark the guests and weigh anchor. There was not a minute to be lost. In the blink of an eye the captain's table was cleared, and the vessel was once again a warship.

"The *Agamemnon* is the fastest ship in the Mediterranean," Nelson explained as our little party was ushered to the gunwale, where below us the longboats bobbed upon the dark waters, waiting to row us back to shore. "I must make for Toulon immediately."

"But what about the knives?" Mam wanted to know. It had become abundantly clear that the crew could spare no time to comb through all the dinner things and return our dirty cutlery. "And the butter dishes?"

"Permit us to hold them in trust against our inevitable return, ma'am." Though his thoughts were no doubt elsewhere, Nelson managed a smile for his guests and bowed politely. For the first time, I realized that he was a few inches shorter than I. "Duty is the great business of a sea officer. All private considerations must give way to it, however painful it is."

The man might as well have been a prophet.

Twenty-five

Treachery Unmasked

It was a race against time. If the English couldn't hold Toulon, it was a certainty the republicans, with a toehold in the Mediterranean already, would emerge victorious. Sir William and Nelson maintained a regular correspondence, keeping each other apprised of developments. I might as well have been an ambassador without portfolio, for all the negotiations I continued to effect on my own. By now, I was quite obviously the queen's favorite.

I was in Her Sicilian Majesty's salon, translating documents from French into English, when we received the devastating news that the Queen of France had been beheaded on the sixteenth of October.

Maria Carolina shrieked and tore her hair. In her rage she flung priceless treasures onto the floor, smashing them to bits. "Never will I sleep till vengeance is satisfied!" she declared. "*Je poursuivrai ma vengeance jusqu'au tombeau.* 'To my dying day,' as you English say. I will never rest until the last Jacobin tastes the dust."

From that day on, the queen became even more formidable, granting neither clemency nor leniency to anyone even suspected of harboring republican sentiments. She demanded my presence and companionship with ever-increasing frequency, as though she could invent in me a new younger sister. "My beloved Emma, we could never have dreamed to know it at the time, but you brought to me Marie Antoinette's very last letter," she would weep, touching her heart with two fingers. "And for that, you are forever in my bosom." Fearing the loss of her own family, she drew them even more tightly about her. She retired to her favorite palace at Portici, refusing to eat or bathe, pouring out her grief to her forty German maids.

In December, word came that Toulon had fallen to the republican army, due to the efforts of a ruthless young Corsican named Napoleon Bonaparte. Six thousand citizens—women and children among them—had been slaughtered. The Neapolitan troops, never battle-ready, had proven disastrous. "Perhaps our friend Nelson and his superiors are regretting their request," sighed Sir William.

Often during those tense years in Naples I found myself comparing the kingdom's bubbling political cauldron—with its republican sentiments simmering below the surface, ready to blow at any moment—to Sir William's beloved Vesuvius. I had long grown accustomed to seeing the perennial wisp of smoke curling skyward from the volcano's peak whenever I glanced in its direction, like a kettle always on the boil, but all through the early months of 1794, the great mountain had been quiet.

Late at night on June 12, we were violently shaken from our beds by a powerful earthquake. "There's going to be a thumping good eruption, my dear!" exclaimed my husband. He clasped my wrist, and together—Sir William in his nightshirt and cap and me in my shift, with plaited hair—we raced down the corridor to his observatory.

Just as Sir William adjusted his telescope, the clear night suddenly went completely black. "Mark my words, Emma, it's coming," Sir William said excitedly. "We are witnesses to history."

Three days later, a second shock, milder than the first, shook the region. A fountain of bright fire spewed up from the central crater—then another burst of fireworks erupted from farther down—and then—one, two, three, four—fifteen torrents of lava, we counted, commenced their blazing descent toward Torre del Greco. The sky rumbled with thunder as though the heavens had erupted with artillery fire, whilst at the same time a tremendous *whoosh*, like the roar of an angry sea, filled the night. And then we heard another blowing noise, like that of the going up of a large flight of skyrockets, as Sir William described it.

I could not turn my gaze from the rivers of liquid fire snaking down the black mountain, carmine and amber and gold. "I don't believe I've ever seen something quite so beautiful!" I exclaimed.

"Vincenzo, the carriage!"

We dressed in haste and made for Villa Emma, for Sir William thought we could more safely witness the eruption from Posillipo. But for all his experience, he was proved wrong when two fiery orbs, joined together by a small link like a chain shot, came rolling down toward the villa. We held our breath. Would they ignite our home? My heart pounded in my chest and I clung to Sir William's waist as though his strength had the power to protect our property. And then, but a few yards above us, the balls of fire separated, one falling into the vineyard above the house, the other in the sea.

On the sixteenth of June, the lava enveloped Torre del Greco, leaving rubble in its roiling wake, and reached the sea, turning the azure waters of the bay bloodred. The sun was all but blotted out. Day and night had become one. There was not a whiff of fresh air to breathe; with every inhalation we felt as though we had buried our noses in a damp blanket covering a passel of rotten eggs. Buildings crumbled and collapsed like toys under the weight of the ash. The lava traveled from the summit to the sea—a distance of four miles—in all of six hours! As fascinated as I was terrified, I was sure we would become another Pompeii. I dared not sleep a wink for fear I'd never wake, and centuries later I would be found just as I had perished: bolt upright in bed, clutching Sir William's arm.

The volcano's summit did not become visible through the ash

and smoke until June 18. Sir William gasped at its radically altered silhouette. Where the very tip had been conical, it now was flat. One-ninth of the crater had been utterly demolished by the force of the eruption, as though someone had sheared it off with a celestial scythe.

For some weeks, the air in Naples remained unfit to breathe. Sir William insisted we repair to the *capannina* in Caserta. The mountain still gasped and sighed, pouring out a steady column of vapor that filled one's lungs with white ash whenever a strong sirocco blew over the city. From mid-June through August, it descended upon us in torrents of heavy rain, carrying away the already-crumbling walls of fragile houses, toppling trees, drowning livestock, and covering everything with a layer of volcanic mud.

To the monstrously superstitious Neapolitans it was a sure sign that God was angry. But at whom?

The wild ride that had become my life continued to dip and turn like the road from Vesuvius to Portici. The English attempt in July to wrest Corsica from the French had been an unmitigated disaster, but the queen found consolation in toasting the end of the Terror when the villainous Robespierre was executed by his own confederates on the twenty-eighth of that month. She hoped this would bode well for the political climate in Naples, forcing the Jacobins to recant their views. But our rejoicing was interrupted by an urgent message from my maid Giulia: Sir William had taken ill again.

I raced back to the Palazzo Sessa. Sir William was wheezing terribly. I rang for Mam and after a good deal of effort we finally got him resting comfortably. "I fear, my dear, that I have inhaled too much of the sulfurous and mephitic air of Vesuvius, that I have done my lungs some little harm."

"Pliny, don't be mimicking your namesake to the end," I chided through my tears. His bowels wasn't good, either. "You need to rest. At sixty-three years of age, you can't be exerting yourself like a man of twenty."

Sir William coughed so hard, it was several moments before he could regain enough breath to speak. "Nonsense, my dear. My illness comes from a *want* of exertion. I have been *too* sedentary of late. Starting tomorrow, I will resume my regimen of regular equestrian exercise. I warrant you, 'twill be a better physick for my bowels and my lungs than any of your powders and potions."

He coughed himself into exhaustion and I would not leave his side until he was fast asleep. I tiptoed out of the room and found Mam sitting in a chair just beyond the doorway. " 'E's growing old, Mam." A sob came unbidden from my throat and she raised a finger to her lips.

"Husht thee naise," she whispered. "Don't let 'im 'ear you cry. You 'ave to be strong for 'im, y'nau?"

"I never thought about it before; really I didn't. 'E always said 'e'd be on the wane as I was waxing, but 'e was always so energetic that I didn't pay 'is words any mind. I can't lose 'im, Mam. I don't know what I'll do if 'e takes sick and dies. I love 'im more than my life. Sir Willum is the kindest, dearest man—where would we be without 'im?"

He took ill again in April 1795, a few days shy of my thirtieth birthday, this time with another bout of bilious fever. I dosed him with Dr. James's antimonial powder and he finally rallied, but his increasingly frequent lapses of health had weakened him. His elegant physique began to look frail; his healthy sunburnt complexion, sallowed.

More and more, Sir William took to his own bedroom, where I would not be troubled by his sleepless nights when he was plagued with aches and pains and attended by dark thoughts of mortality. I was devoted to him, but I was still a young woman—just approaching the prime of life. Other women would have freely taken a lover, but for so many years I had sought to prove myself a paragon of respectability, and I still loved Sir William passionately, and owed him a debt beyond measure. My conscience would not permit me to toss all of that aside for the sake of a few moments of temporary pleasure. Nursing Sir William through his several illnesses had its effect on my body, too. Mam noticed that I had begun to put on weight. I had taken to the Italian style of cooking almost as soon as we arrived in Naples, and never thought twice about all the macaroni I consumed, for it was on the menu nearly every night. My taste for wine and Champagne—as well as my daily glass of porter—had surely left its mark as well.

Sir William's ailments had reduced his energy and increased his lassitude. Now that Naples was suddenly an important piece in a high-stakes game of international chess, the British ambassador's role was more vital than it had ever been. With my husband frequently indisposed, it fell to me to assume some of his diplomatic responsibilities. He supervised me while I reviewed documents and drafted correspondence, keeping the ministers in Whitehall abreast of the political situation.

I also became even more indispensable to Maria Carolina. By virtue of Sir William's office, he could not be seen conversing too often with the Queen of Naples, or visiting her with great regularity, for it might be construed as collaborating in another country's diplomacy. The actions of his wife, however, were a different story. What an odd stroke of luck it turned out to be that I had not been formally permitted to become the ambassadress! Because I was simply a common citizen, it was perfectly within the bounds of propriety for me to be a frequent companion of my dear friend Maria Carolina.

During those months, I acted as her amanuensis as well as her confidante. She passed me state documents to translate into English and entrusted me with secret dispatches containing privileged information—aware that I would show them, or the fair copy I had made, to Sir William, who would then transmit them to the British government. Many of these dispatches were directly addressed to the king, but Her Majesty would waylay them and deliver the information into my hands before resealing the messages.

One day, we learnt for certain that the queen was being deceived by her husband. A courier brought the King of Naples a private letter from the King of Spain, and the queen contrived to steal it from Ferdinand's pocket. Her hands trembled as she handed me the revealing letter from King Charles of Spain. "Don't let anything smudge it or he will know it has been read."

"I'll be as quick as I can and give it right to Sir Willum," I promised her.

"I only beg of him not to compromise me. *Je vous prie, miledi.*"

What a frenzy of activity thus ensued! The letter was in cipher and I raced against time to translate it out of code before it had to be returned to the queen, for she was playing a dangerous game. Her name was never to be connected in any way to these packets and political intrigues, for spies abounded, just waiting to catch her in a misstep.

When I decoded the stolen letter, I found it to contain the King of Spain's intention to withdraw from the coalition, and join the French against England! Advance warning of Spain's plans would give the English time to send a fleet to Gibraltar and strike a resounding blow against the unsuspecting dons. I immediately dispatched a messenger to the British foreign secretary, Lord Grenville. To ensure the necessary precautions it cost me four hundred pounds from my privy purse. For three days and nights I did not sleep, nor scarcely ate a morsel, and no sooner had I bidden adieu to our courier than I had to host a supper for an assembly of three hundred guests. Never had I been so fagged, but never more exhilarated. I imagined myself heralded by my native country and my adopted one as a true heroine!

On October 5, Spain—newly allied with France—declared war on England. A treaty was entered into between Naples and France. The Neapolitans naively rejoiced in the streets with music, dancing, and fireworks.

All of the Mediterranean ports were now under the control of either France or Spain, preventing their common enemy—the English—from watering and revictualing their ships. With no friendly harbor, the British fleet began their evacuation from the region, and we in Naples held our breath. "It is all a matter of time now," Maria Carolina told me. "Boney's army has taken Rome, and he is waiting for the opportune moment to strike at Naples, dethrone us, and declare the Two Sicilies a republic state under the dominion of France."

One day a packet arrived containing a silver locket, dated and inscribed, *With appreciative thanks to Lady Hamilton. Horatio Nelson.* Though I'd often thought of him with the fondest memories, I had not seen him since we were so swiftly disembarked from the *Agamemnon* back in September 1793. Whatever was the little captain thanking me for?

Twenty-six

I Am of Some
Little Service to My Country

As if there wasn't enough to occupy us, what with the leek breath of the French republican army down our necks, we suddenly found ourselves preparing for a royal wedding and entertaining the English poetess Cornelia Knight and her ailing mother, who had fled the Papal States, fearing the worst from Napoleon.

The nuptial ceremonies for Francis, the twenty-year-old crown prince of the Two Sicilies, and his cousin Clementina, daughter of Emperor Leopold II of Austria, went on for days. Full court dress was mandated for each event, and never had I seen such a display of gowns and jewels, of color and tinsel. Never had so much pomade greased so many powdered coiffures. Not even at the opera gala nights did so much scent hang heavily upon the air.

I wish I had been able to be a better hostess to the Knight women, but the truth was, I was already done in upon their arrival. After the royal wedding I collapsed in a state of exhaustion, suffering from a high fever. I was blistered and cupped, and blooded nine times in as many days.

"My poor dear," soothed Sir William when we found a rare moment of total privacy. "Look at you." He smoothed my hair off my forehead. "You'll always be a beauty, but this business of late is exacting its toll. On both of us, in point of fact." My husband sighed

and looked away, as was his wont when there was domestic un-
pleasantness to be discussed. "Emma, I will be honest with you.
My estates in Pembroke are not measuring up as I had expected—
perhaps leaving Greville in charge of making improvements on the
property was not my finest decision, but that's another tale for another time. I had thought to retire on their income, but I fear that
may never meet my expectations. If I could be assured of a government pension of two thousand pounds a year, I would tender
my credentials to King George and we could return home to a
comfortable existence at a pace that better suits a man in my time
of life."

"But Sir Willum, they need us here. You can't be thinking of
going home now! If we leave 'Er Majesty, there's no one left to keep
the kingdom from falling to the Frenchies. The queen don't even
trust Acton anymore; you and I are the only ones who speak proper
English and can intercede for Naples with our government. And if
we can keep the Two Sicilies allied with England, or neutral at the
very least, Farmer George will assuredly give you more than a pension. 'E'll give you a parade!"

I could not confess it to my husband, but I thrived in all the attention, admiration, and approbation I was receiving—for my
singing, for my Attitudes, as a hostess, and as a diplomat. In Naples
I had been smitten with the English *maladie du pays*, that the farther you go from your homeland, the less you regret leaving it.
After all, what kind of life had I left behind in London? I could endure a fever and a little blooding to remain an important personage within the center of Neapolitan activity. Though debilitating,
what an honor it was that a European monarch daily reminded
me—once-grubby little Emy Lyon—how vital I had become to her
kingdom!

Sir William, however, had spent nearly half his life as His Britannic Majesty's envoy to Naples, and he was fatigued of the whole
business of diplomacy. It saddened me to see my husband aging so

much in so short a space of time. He was now content to potter about his vast collections of virtu all day, sometimes appearing more worried for their security than for the safety of the Neapolitans. His increasing infirmities, as well as his natural inclination toward an English version of Neapolitan indolence, left him with little taste for the exigencies now demanded of him.

But he did derive delight—we both did—in the news of England's outstanding victory against the Spanish fleet in what would soon come to be known as the Battle of Cape St. Vincent. On February 14, 1797, in the waters off the Portuguese coast, our fleet engaged the dons, routing them soundly and scuttling their mission to escort a sizable merchant fleet to Cádiz.

The hero of the hour, we learned, was the commander of the seventy-four-gun *Captain*—our old friend Nelson—who was told soon after the battle ended that due to coincidence rather than any show of valor at Cape St. Vincent, he had been promoted to rear admiral of the blue.

"Listen to our brave and gallant friend," said Sir William, perusing Nelson's letter announcing the good news. " 'I realized in the heat of the conflict that my commander's sudden decision to flout the rules of engagement through a new deployment of his vessels was the right one, but had come too late. The dons tremendously outgunned us. My ship was the second to last in the line of thirteen. How could I wait patiently for my turn to engage, while my comrades got blown out of the water due to a poor tactical decision? I thus took it upon myself to reinterpret Jervis's command to tack. If I had carried out my commander's orders, as issued, it would not mean victory, but would instead have spelt a lost opportunity, both bloody and ignominious, for His Majesty's Navy—' "

"But what exactly was it 'e did to win?" I interrupted. "It's like 'e's dropped one shoe and I'm on pins and needles till the other one hits the carpet!"

"Wait. . . ." Sir William shuffled though the pages of Nelson's lengthy letter. "Eureka! 'I wore my ship,' Nelson writes, 'turning her away from the wind, rather than into it, taking a shortcut past the other British ships ahead of me, to engage the first three vessels in the Spanish van.' Imagine that!" Sir William began to rearrange the breakfast things on the table, in an attempt to re-create Nelson's maneuvers.

Gallant Nelson and his crew had ensured an English victory, boarding and taking two of the dons' largest warships. I could just envision him, sword in hand, cutlass in his teeth like a corsair, dropping from a rope onto the burning deck of our unsuspecting enemies, leaping from one captive ship to the other, and subduing thousands of Spanish sailors without shedding a single drop of blood. I imagined their captains hailing him for his clemency, which a lesser man than Nelson would never have granted them. I wanted to write to old King George and ask him to name my diminutive hero commander of the fleet.

"Raw animal courage," said Nelson's superior, Admiral Jervis, of his performance at Cape St. Vincent, words that struck a chord in my rather patriotic—and somewhat besotted—breast. Yet my partisan heart leapt into my mouth when I read in Nelson's letter that in the thick of battle he'd been knocked sideways by a blow to the abdomen, caused by a flying lump of wood. Would that I might fly to him and nurse his wound! Yet there was some consolation, he wrote:

> *I would I could mask the swelling with the sash that will accompany my Order of the Bath, such distinction which His Majesty accorded me, in recognition of my contribution to England's glorious victory. It pleases me to think that Sir William and I will now have something in common.*

I wished I could have let him know how much it pleased Sir William and Lady Hamilton as well.

Although we were disappointed not to receive another word from Nelson for the rest of the year, Admiral Jervis, made Lord St. Vincent after the resounding naval victory, sent me a letter addressed to "The Patroness of the British Navy." In response to Queen Maria Carolina's repeated petitions to King George—which I had helped prepare—asking for a fleet to protect her kingdom from the French, he was "sending a knight of superior prowess" to determine the reason behind the Frenchies' increasing armaments in Toulon and in other Mediterranean ports. St. Vincent had placed Horatio Nelson in command of a squadron to be plucked from the rest of the Mediterranean fleet and dispatched to Naples. How thrilled we were that Nelson would return!

At six o'clock one morning in June, Sir William and I were awakened by a shout from the servants that there were foreigners on our doorstep. We struggled to get into our clothes as fast as we could. Could the French have arrived and be demanding the head of the British ambassador?

Our visitors turned out to be two captains from His Majesty's Navy, Thomas Troubridge and Thomas Masterman Hardy. Arriving in the *Mutine*, they had been deputized by Nelson to call upon Sir William on a matter of the most urgent importance.

I sat with the two men in Sir William's library, while Troubridge, a pear-shaped man of about forty years, disclosed the nature of their errand. "It boils down to this," Troubridge said, running a hand through his thick shock of lightly powdered hair. His sunburnt complexion grew more ruddy as he became anxious to impress upon Sir William the import of the situation. "Nelson has been given orders to chase down the French fleet in the Mediterranean. But we're running out of fresh food and water, and all of the Mediterranean ports are closed to us. This puts the squadron in a bit of a bind, as I'm sure you can appreciate, Your Excellency. Nelson has charged me with asking you to intercede with Acton and the king."

Sir William gazed at him intently. "Tell me exactly what it is you require. I need details, man, before I can take the thing any further."

Hardy, whose name well defined his appearance, took up the cause. "An official document signed by King Ferdinand asking the governor of Syracuse to allow the English squadron to revictual and water there."

"You realize of course that this will take a good deal of persuading, gentlemen. Opening the Syracusan port to your ships is in direct violation of the treaty that the Two Sicilies signed with France. I'm sure you know that King Ferdinand's elder brother occupies the Spanish throne, and as such is allied with the French."

Troubridge raised a bushy eyebrow. "I am well aware of that, sir, as is Nelson. But the Frenchies are a tricky lot. Nelson's tied himself in knots trying to fathom their intentions. He now thinks their Mediterranean fleet may be headed in the opposite direction—possibly for Egypt—which, if they gained control there, would lay Boney's route to the East wide open. The Corsican bastard—pardon my language, your ladyship—intends to conquer the world, but by gad, we shall not let the devil take England with him. We stopped his allies at Cape St. Vincent, and Nelson will not rest, nor none of us, neither, until we've put a stop to 'em. Which brings me back to the text of my errand. Watering and victualling the British squadron. It must be done, man!"

"Don't you worry, gents. We'll do everything we can," I assured them. "Emma Hamilton don't take no for an answer!"

Neapolitan indolence was difficult to rouse, however, even in the most pressing of circumstances. Although Sir William took the naval officers' request to Acton's house that morning, Acton and the king harangued over the particulars, and whether they should skirt the treaty at all, as the Two Sicilies dared not risk a blemish on its neutrality with the French republican army at our northern border.

When the dust settled, Nelson had not secured the royal mandate he had requested. Instead, Acton—through his deputies—gave him a ministerial order detailing further instruction that contained not a word about watering and restocking.

The whole bloody mess was too vague and indirect. A proper order was an imperative. Nelson needed a hard commitment, not diplomatic dithering. Meeting with Maria Carolina in secret, I urged her to supplement Acton's inadequate document with direct instruction. Sir William dashed off a private communiqué to Nelson, saying, *You will receive from Emma herself what will do the business and procure all your wants.*

I wrote Nelson:

> *17th June, 1798*
>
> *My Dear Admiral, God bless you, and send you victorious, and that I may see you bring back Buonaparte with you. The Queen desires me to say everything that's kind, and bids me say with her whole heart and soul she wishes you victory. God bless you, my dear Sir. I will not say how glad I shall be to see you. Indeed I cannot describe to you my feelings on your being so near us.*
>
> *—Ever, Ever, dear Sir, Your affte. and gratefull*
> *EMMA HAMILTON*

I enclosed a carefully worded letter from Her Majesty that would do the trick, as they say. The English squadron sailed that very day.

But what an unexpected welcome they received! The Sicilian governors made the business of watering and revictualling the English squadron as difficult as they could without engaging in outright treason. I received an angry communication from Nelson dated July 22. His handwriting looked different than I had remembered it, though I thought nothing of it at the time.

I am so much distressed at not having had any account of the French fleet, and so much hurt at the treatment we receive from the power we came to assist and fight for, that I am hardly in a situation to write a letter to an elegant body; therefore you must on this occasion forgive my want of those attentions which I am ever ambitious to show you. I wish to know your and Sir William's plans for going down the Medn. for if we are to be kicked in every port of the Sicilian dominions the sooner we are gone the better. Good God! How sensibly I feel our treatment. I have only to pray I may find the French and throw all my vengeance on them.

However, the queen's letter must have eventually achieved its intended impact, for enclosed with the next packet of letters for Sir William and myself was a note addressed to the both of us:

My dear Friends, Thanks to your exertions we have victualled and watered, and surely watering at the Fountain of Arethusa, we must have victory. We shall sail with the first breeze, and be assured I shall return either crowned with laurel or covered with cypress.

"Covered with cypress!" My eyes welled with emotion as I read Nelson's words. "Impossible!" A single tear escaped, and as it rolled down my cheek I wiped it away with the back of my hand. So keenly did I feel for this brave man I had scarcely met, yet believed I knew so well, that my tender heart could not bear to imagine his death.

Twenty-seven

See, the Conquering Hero Comes

So, yes, I was half in love with him then, but then it was the glossy infatuation that men and women alike feel for heroes or saviors. Their deeds elevate them in your esteem and from there is it but a short journey to the heart. It was easier for me to keep my head by writing to Nelson of others' admiration for him. *Everybody here prays for you. The Neapolitans say mass for you, but Sir Wm. and I are so anxious that we neither eat, drink, nor sleep; and till you are safely landed and come back we shall feel mad.* All the hopes and fears for the future of England, as well as Naples, rested on Nelson's golden epaulets.

Then, on September 1, news of the grandest and most glorious victory reached our ears. A month earlier, Nelson had engaged the French fleet in Aboukir Bay near the mouth of the Nile. It had been a magnificent engagement, culminating in the spectacular explosion of the French flagship *L'Orient*. I was enraptured, dizzy beyond all measure with triumph. And to know that I myself had played some little part in this tremendous success—by securing the permission for our ships to be watered and restocked in Syracuse—filled every fiber of my being with euphoria. I could not wait to hear every last detail from Nelson himself—yet all I received was a cryptic note, reading, *My dear Lady Hamilton, you will soon be able to see the wreck of Horatio Nelson. May it count for a kindly judgement if scars are a mark of honor.*

So great was my excitement that my hand shook as I wrote to
Nelson of our collective reaction to his brave and brilliant conquest. My words tumbled forth as if I were speaking them; my
emotions could not be contained on a mere scrap of paper, nor
controlled by the mean servants of quill and ink.

> *Naples, 8 September, 1798*
> *My Dear, Dear Sir,*
>
> *How shall I begin, what shall I say to you? 'Tis impossible I
> can write, for since last Monday I am delerious with joy, and as-
> sure you I have a fevour caused by agitation and pleasure. God,
> what a victory! Never, never has there been anything half so glo-
> rious, so compleat. I fainted when I heard the joyfull news and
> fell on my side and am hurt, but well of that. I shou'd feil it a
> glory to die in such a cause. No, I wou'd not like to die till I see
> and embrace the Victor of the Nile. How shall I describe to you
> the transports of Maria Carolina, 'tis not possible.*
>
> *The Neapolitans are mad with joy, and if you wos here now,
> you wou'd be killed with kindness. Sonets on sonets, illumina-
> tions, rejoicings; not a French dog dare shew his face. How I glory
> in the honner of my Country and my Countryman! I walk and
> tread in the air with pride, feiling I was born in the same land
> with the victor Nelson and his gallant band.*
>
> *My dress from head to foot is alla Nelson. Even my shawl is in
> Blue with gold anchors all over. My earrings are Nelson's anchors;
> in short, we are be-Nelsoned all over. Once more, God bless you.
> My mother desires her love to you. I am so sorry to write in such
> a hurry. I am affraid you will not be able to read this scrawl.*
>
> *I send you two letters from my adorable Queen. One was writ-
> ten to me the day we received the glorious news, the other yester-
> day. Keep them, as they are in her own handwriting. I have kept
> copies only, but I feil that you ought to have them. We are prepar-
> ing your appartment against you come. I hope it will not be long,*

*for Sir William and I are so impatient to embrace you. I wish
you cou'd have seen the house the 3 nights of illumination. 'Twas
covered with your glorious name. Their were 3 thousand Lamps,
and their shou'd have been 3 millions if we had time. All the English vie with each other in celebrating this most gallant and ever
memorable victory. Sir William is ten years younger since the
happy news, and now wishes to see his friend to be completely
happy. How he glories in you when your name is mentioned. He
cannot contain his joy. For God's sake come to Naples soon. We
receive so many Letters of congratulation. I send you some of
them to shew you how much of your success is felt here. How I
felt for poor Troubridge. He must have been so angry stuck there
on the sandbank and unable to fight, so brave an officer! In short
I pity those who were not in the battle. I wou'd have been rather
an English powder-monkey, or a swab in that great victory, than
an Emperor out of it, but you will soon be so tired of all this.
Write or come soon to Naples, and rejoin your ever sincere and
oblidged friend,*

Emma Hamilton

Finally, after scanning the horizon several times a day, on September 22 I spied Nelson's flagship, the *Vanguard*, limping into the Bay
of Naples. "Sir Willum—'e's 'ere at last!" My husband raced to his
observation tower, wig askew, to see for himself. I made my toilette
as carefully as I could for one in such a state of agitation, and
dashed to the palace to tell the queen that our hero had arrived at
last!

Five hundred vessels went out to greet the *Vanguard* that day,
though the flagship itself appeared much the worse for wear, its
own battle scars evident from the battering its hull and rigging had
received in Aboukir. Not even the Prince Royal's wedding had merited such a festival. The king had commissioned boatloads of
singers and musicians to serenade Nelson's arrival with "Rule Bri-

tannia," "God Save the King," and "See, the Conquering Hero
Comes." Thousands of caged birds—doves and swallows—were released into the air. King Ferdinand wore his finest state-occasion
ensemble, and there was nary a drop of gravy to be seen upon't. For
the first time since I had met the Neapolitan sovereign a dozen
years earlier, he looked every inch a king.

We were rowed out in our own barge amid much fanfare. Sir
William in his burgundy silk coat and knee breeches, with his
Order of the Bath, was the very personification of England's embassy. I wore my costume alla Nelson, and wrapped a blue-and-
white bandeau about my tresses inscribed with the words *Nelson
and Victory* in golden letters. Only my stays kept my heart within
my throbbing breast. Every additional minute of waiting was its
own agony.

We finally reached the ship and I was hoisted up in a bo'sun's
chair, each foot bringing me closer to our hero. But once on deck I
gasped at the sight before me! When I had last seen Nelson, he was
hale and hearty and whole. The picture before me might as well
have been of a different man. His right arm! Gone! Gone! His
empty sleeve was affixed to his blue jacket in a right angle, a delicate
loop securing it to a button of his lapel. And while his left eye fo-
cused on me, his right eye was unseeing, as if clouded over. His hair
was nearly white—at first I thought 'twas from the stress and worry
of battle, but then I saw that it was powder, for Nelson had bedecked himself with as much formality as he could muster; and he
had arranged a lock of hair to flop over his forehead, barely concealing a hideous scar just above the bad eye, nearly fresh, an ugly
slash of tender pink flesh marring the noblest brow in all of Europe.

"O God, is it possible!" I exclaimed, falling in a sudden swoon,
more dead than alive, into his remaining arm.

"You can't say I didn't warn you," he said softly as I bedewed his
fine jacket with tears, just grateful and ecstatic then that he was
alive and had returned to Naples.

The upper portion of Nelson's right arm twitched as though the phantom lower segment was reaching to shake Sir William's hand. "I am Lord Nelson, and this is his fin," he chuckled to Sir William, who was nearly as overcome as I by so drastic an alteration of Nelson's appearance.

I could barely contain my weeping. Tears of joy and tears of sorrow commingled in bittersweet splashes.

Sir William bent to murmur in my ear, "Emma, my dear, you must pull yourself together; the king approaches."

It wasn't seemly for me to be such a jumble of emotions in Ferdinand's presence. I reached for my handkerchief to blot my nose and cheeks, and practically held my breath when His Sicilian Majesty stepped onto the deck and hailed Nelson as "*Nostro Liberatore*, Deliverer and Preserver of Naples."

Modestly, Nelson accepted his accolades. Touching his tender scar, he said, "I confess I should have been done for entirely had I not been wearing my hat," whereupon the king demanded to see it. A midshipman produced the hat, battered and torn to pieces. Gesturing with it toward his tangled rigging, Nelson quipped, "You will see that I am in as much disrepair as my ship."

"Then I insist you stay with us at the Palazzo Sessa while the *Vanguard* is refitted. I refuse to take no for an answer."

Sir William laughed. "She said those very words to Troubridge, and look where it got His Majesty's Navy!"

But Nelson demurred. "You are kindness itself, Lady Hamilton, but I would not wish to turn your residence into a quarterdeck, with officers traipsing in and out at all hours. I am sure your marble floors would be much the worse for it."

He looked utterly exhausted, trying to put a brave face on it. And I could see that he was feverish. "You're ill," I whispered. "And you know it as well as I. Of what use will you be to your men, who look up to you in every way as if you was great Jove himself, if you present them with an invalid?" Now that he'd returned alive, if rather the worse for wear, I thought never to let him out of my sight. Some heroine to my country I'd be if I let the victorious hero of the Nile perish from want of proper care!

Overhearing me, Sir William concurred. "You would do well to let Emma tend to you, my friend. I stand here before you as a personal beneficiary of her soothing ministrations. In fact, were it not for such a fine nurse, the bilious fever would have carried me off years ago."

This convinced him. But the Neapolitans' rejoicing would not permit him to recuperate in solitude. On the night of Nelson's arrival, Sir William and I hosted a lavish dinner in his honor at the Palazzo Sessa. Three thousand candles blazed, while an orchestra struck up the martial airs that had greeted the *Vanguard*'s arrival in the bay. I wrote a new verse to "See, the Conquering Hero Comes" and sang it fortissimo as the entire blazing assemblage of Neapolitan and English nobility raised their glasses in a toast to *Nostro Liberatore*.

"You must tell us all about the great victory," Sir William urged him. "And begin at the beginning."

Though he looked flushed and tired, Nelson could not disappoint the multitude of guests eager to learn from the hero's own lips how he'd bested Boney.

"And with only one eye and one arm!" Mam exclaimed, toasting him with her gin glass.

"And in the dead of night, too!" I added.

Nelson took a prodigious gulp of wine before launching into the story that hundreds of ears were eager to hear. Tears sprang to my eyes when I recalled how he had spilt the last drop onto his little finger on the night he feted us aboard the *Agamemnon*, for that simple little gesture was now an impossibility.

"Best to explain it in laymen's terms," said Nelson, winking at Francesco Caracciolo, the admiral of Naples's own fleet. "Essentially, I made a naval sandwich! You see, the French admiral, Brueys, had left too much room between his line of ships and the shore; I sent some of my vessels to get between them, so that the enemy would end up bombarded from both sides, for all of Brueys's cannons were facing in only one direction—*seawards*. This shocked the devil out of them, but there was no escaping by that time, and in short order, we disabled many of the French ships."

"Bravo!" I cried, clapping my hands. "Hip hip hurrah for Nelson!" The whole room joined me in a rousing cheer and a chorus of "For He's a Jolly Good Fellow."

"It was not quite such an easy victory, Lady Hamilton. The losses on both sides were heavy, so closely were our ships entangled. We had to toss the bodies into the bay, for there was no other choice but to dispose of them as they fell. Stripped to the waist, for the heat was so intense, several of my own gunners were dragged away dead. Powder monkeys dashed to and fro, trying to avoid the darkening pools of blood that colored the decks while taking care not to spill their fresh ammunition or the buckets of water needed to cool the guns. It was so dark that it was near impossible to see one's hand in front of one's face, as they say. Our eyes stung and our lungs smarted from the clouds of billowing smoke that blotted out the firmament with a blanket of soot."

"How ghastly!" remarked Cornelia Knight, who, I was certain, was in the instant composing in her head a panegyric in Nelson's honor.

"Two hours into the battle, as dusk descended, the eighth of the French ships struck her colors, the blasted tricolor left in tatters amid her rigging." Nelson touched two fingertips to his forehead. "I was hit with flying langridge—shards of iron debris—and knocked back onto the quarterdeck as the blood ran into my eyes and down my face. I thought I was done for. 'I am killed!' I exclaimed. 'Remember me to my wife.' "

"Oh God," I whispered. My hands, folded discreetly in my lap, twisted my linen napkin, for I was suffering a pang of jealousy that her name might be the last on his heroic lips.

"I refused to go down to the surgeon, but my men insisted. Their morale was so elevated with our brave showing thus far that I was certain it would plummet if they knew me to be hit. But once below, I was adamant that I wait my turn."

"What a man! No wonder your men respect you so much," said Sir William admiringly, proud to call Nelson his friend.

"Yet, though I'd been hit, as long as there was a breath of life within me, I could not rest, nor consider relinquishing my command to a subordinate. My orders were to destroy the French fleet, and by God I was honor- and duty-bound to see it done! I dictated dispatches from the sick bay in case it proved true that I was a dying man. 'How fast can you sew me up?' I asked the surgeon. 'It won't be pretty if I go quickly,' he cautioned. 'Never mind about beauty, man. And if a sculptor is so foolish as to waste good marble and bronze on my already-disfigured physiognomy, I'd rather have them memorialize a living Nelson than a dead one!' "

How I wanted to reach over and tenderly stroke the still-angry gash upon his noble brow! How many men, thus wounded in the heat of battle, would remain so clearheaded? How many would place their crew's morale above their own survival?

"The action intensified, and the sky above the bay flashed red and orange from the roaring cannon. The finest painter could not have done justice to the scene; he could never have adequately captured the atmosphere—as filled with fear as it was with triumph, every cannonade an angel of death. All through the night, we exchanged broadsides. Just past nine a cry went up: 'The *Orient* is on fire!' "

Everyone in the vast ballroom seemed to gasp at once. The men began to pound the table with their fists, behaving as if they were at a gentlemen's club instead of a state dinner. I feared we'd have to replace half our china and crystal. "More!" they cried, "*Dicaci di più!* Tell us more!"

Nelson became caught up in the moment, buoyed by their excitement. His voice took on a more dramatic tone. "Against the surgeon's better judgment, I raced up to the deck, my head swaddled in bandages. Sure enough, the towering French three-decker was silhouetted in flame, like a ghostly illumination in the night. And when the fire reached the flagship's powder magazine, she *blew*—with a sound so ferocious and so violent that it drowned out the rolling cannonade. Never in all my years at sea, and in the many actions in which I have taken part, have I heard an explosion onetenth as deafening! The men who were not thrown by sheer force into the water, like so many ninepins, hurled themselves into the bay, which was already red with the blood of the dead and dying."

I glanced about the table. The mood had shifted markedly. A number of our guests were quite demonstrably moved by Nelson's vivid recitation. Many had visibly shuddered when he'd recalled the ferocity of the *Orient*'s obliteration.

"The French did not go quietly into the night, even after the report from the dreadful explosion died on the wind," he said. "They were stunned for some time, but after a lull, the ships in the rear resumed their fire. One of the frigates blew herself up rather than strike her colors. All told, ten ships surrendered to us, five were sunk, there was the one that destroyed herself, and three vessels—two ships of the line, and a single frigate—managed to escape. More than one-third of the enemy died that night, but not one of our squadron was irreparably damaged. God had surely been with us." Nelson's eyes welled with tears. "Victory is not a name strong enough for such a scene."

Much affected, Sir William rose to his feet and lifted his glass. "To the hero of the Nile!"

The company followed suit, Nelson, on my right, grasping my arm with his left hand to steady himself. "To the hero of the Nile!" we echoed.

And then the hero of the Nile went pale and I realized that he had become incapable of supporting his own weight, frail as it was.

"We wish you all a good night!" I declared suddenly, raising my voice above the plaudits. "Go to your beds and dream of the Glorious First of August and the extraordinary deeds of the brave Nelson!" Turning to our guest of honor, I smiled to cover my fearful anxiety and whispered, " 'Old on to me as if we was entering a ballroom."

His weakened health thus undetected, I spirited Nelson from the room. But scarcely had I escorted him to the chamber we had prepared against his arrival, when he collapsed in utter exhaustion into my waiting arms.

Twenty-eight

Tender Ministrations

"They will call you Cleopatra," Nelson chuckled. He had refused to let me undress him the previous night, beyond the removal of his shoes, though it was breaking my heart to see him struggle so with his garments. His own valet was still on board the *Vanguard* and Nelson was evidently ill at ease about revealing his battered form to one of our servants.

"I think Cleopatra was the one who *took* the asses' milk baths, not *administered* 'em," I said, reaching for the sea sponge. "But I'll ask Sir Willum. 'E's sure to know. Best way I know for your recovery—inside and out. Like me. I get rashes on my elbows and knees, and sea bathing is the only remedy; drinking the salt water as well as dipping in't."

I feared he might detect the rapid beating of my heart. Never could I have imagined our friendship should become so intimate—that I should be a modern Magdalene and bathe the man who had bested Bonaparte. How was it possible that in his presence I was as nervous as I was calm, as bold as I was timid? I supposed it was the image of the *hero* that intimidated me, while the warm and approving gaze of the *man* had a way of stilling my turbulent soul, making me feel that all was right with the world.

"I can't imagine the benevolent Lady Hamilton being anything less than perfection. To me you are all rapture and rhapsody."

I turned away to hide a blush.

"I fear this question may do me some little embarrassment, but . . . how did I get here?"

"You don't mean in the tub?"

"No, no. In this room. My head wound must have affected me more than I knew."

"You was suffering from an awful fever last night. At the dinner party in your honor. I 'elped you 'ere before you collapsed face-down in your syllabub."

"Your voice, Lady Hamilton." Nelson closed his eyes and leaned back in the bathing tub. His shirt, pregnant with asses' milk, buoyed him up.

"I—"

"It reminds me of home," he added softly. His voice was mild and gentle, despite the flat vowels.

"Would you think me mad if I told you I've never received a greater compliment? Look at me! I'm about to cry. But you're not from Flintshire. Leastways you don't sound it."

"No, Norfolk. But it's a country accent all the same. I've never lost mine despite all these years at sea amongst men of every possible stamp and stripe."

"You're more like me than I'd dared to imagine. You must be as proud of your 'umble origins as I am of my own. They tell me I speak like a native in French and Italian. My German is getting quite tolerable, too. Sir Willum used to cringe a bit at my speech, and so did Gre—" I caught myself before I spoke of a now un-comfortable and embarrassing subject. "But my people are 'ard-working stock. Besides, 'ere, no one knows the difference whether I'm speaking like the King of England or not."

"May I be so bold as to state that I love your country speech, Lady Hamilton. It reminds me what we're fighting like the very devil for. Like a lady's favor a medieval knight wears into battle."

He let me gently sponge his forehead. "Now you've really gone and made me cry," I murmured. A tear splashed into the hip bath and landed on his heart.

"Now help me out of this blasted contraption. I must get back to my ship."

"You're still burning up with fever. You ain't going anywhere, excepting maybe back to bed."

"I know what it is."

"What *what* is?"

"It's malaria. I've had it for weeks. A relapse. To look at me, you might think it would have carried me off, but I've had any number of illnesses and always pulled through. Back in 'seventy-six I suffered a bout of it during a voyage south of the equator. I was all of eighteen then. Nearly died on the voyage home. After a long and gloomy reverie, in which I believed I should never make something of myself and discredit my family by ending up the most dismal of failures—I almost wished myself overboard—a sudden glow of patriotism was kindled within me, and presented my king and country as my patron. My mind exulted in the idea. 'Well, then,' I exclaimed, 'I will be a hero and confiding in Providence I will brave every danger.' And I pulled through the sickness! My captain couldn't believe I'd survived it. He was tying himself in knots trying to figure out what to tell my father when he delivered him the corpse of his little Horace. You see, back when I was twelve, a pasty-faced little runt of a thing, I so yearned to go to sea that I urged my uncle, Captain Maurice Suckling, to take me under his wing. He thought I was daft—thought the notion was my father's, in fact—and accused the rector of sending me to my death!"

"Well, you proved 'em all wrong, that's for sure."

"I was near my uncle Suckling when he died. I owed him a tremendous debt of gratitude, for it was he who enabled me to begin my naval career, and I felt duty-bound to continue to do his legacy proud. 'My boy,' he said to me then, 'I leave you to my country; serve her well and she'll never desert, but will ultimately reward you.' So you see, I am honor-bound to stay alive, as much for king and country as anything else."

"But you still ain't leaving this 'ouse until you're as 'ealthy as the day you was born. I don't believe in 'alf-measures."

Nelson laughed full-throatedly. "Well, hang it, Lady Hamilton, nor do I! Not only that, the boldest measures are the safest, I always say. Nevertheless," he added, climbing out of the tub, his chemise dripping the viscous asses' milk on the red terrazzo. "I refuse to spend my fortieth birthday as an invalid."

"Your birthday! When?"

"What day is today?"

"September twenty-third."

"The twenty-ninth."

I clapped my hands like a little girl. "Then we shall 'ave a party! A birthday party the likes of which no one on earth 'as ever seen. I'll see to all the plans myself!"

Nelson smiled weakly and raised his hand. "Please, Lady Hamilton, no more parties. I appreciate the most generous hospitality that you and Sir William have shown me, but last night was enough celebration to do a man like me in. Enough to make me see in a single evening that Naples is no place for a simple sailor; it's a country of fiddlers, poets, whores, and scoundrels."

I winked at him. "*Fiddlers and poets* ain't so bad."

"But you, Lady Hamilton, rise above them all. You are an honor to your sex. In fact, I should like the loan of some foolscap, quill, and ink, that I might write as much to Lady Nelson. She will be pleased to know that I am being so well cared for after the exigencies of so great a battle."

I swallowed hard and looked away, pretending to be fascinated by a little bird that had landed upon the windowsill and was peering in at us with the utmost curiosity. " 'Ow long have you and Lady Nelson been married?"

"Fanny and I were wed March eleventh, 1787. We'd met two

years earlier on Nevis, where her uncle on her mother's side was president. I had been sent to the Caribbean to enforce the Navigation Acts—though for doing my duty I was roundly despised—and rather soundly disciplined—by the islanders as well as the merchants."

"Is she beautiful?"

"Fanny? I suppose she is tolerably attractive in that retiring English way." It did not sound to me like the ringing endorsement of a man in love, and I found myself suppressing a smile. "She does not trumpet her looks with cosmetics and gemstones," Nelson added. I wondered which of us—Fanny or me—was the lesser in his eyes because of it. "Dark-haired . . . a martyr to colds . . . never have I met a woman who seemed to suffer them with such alarming frequency. One would not characterize her appearance as displeasing. My brother William, a clergyman like our father, says Fanny has a faded prettiness, like a rose that never bloomed." Nelson appeared to be searching for words. "She admires duty as much as I do. I have the utmost respect and esteem for her, and always have."

"But what about *love*?"

Ruminating on this question for a moment or two, Nelson winced in pain when he tried to furrow his brow. "Not what it vulgarly—no, I won't make use of that word commonly called love. . . . My love is founded on esteem, the only foundation that can make love last."

"Sir Willum and I respect and *esteem* one another as well, though I don't blush to admit that once there was a rather prodigious amount of passion between us. Sir Willum is the best 'usband, friend—I wish I could say father also, but"—I touched my belly—"I should be *too* happy if I 'ad the blessing of 'aving children, so I must be content."

Our conversation—so seemingly casual—was pregnant with the mutual awareness of what was not being said. The unspoken, the unshared, hung about us with formidable palpability. I endeavored not to tremble at its power. I feared I had already confessed too much, and so I changed the subject by rummaging through Nelson's trunk. "Where's your clean linen?"

He emitted a grunt of disgust. "I am lost without my valet."

"Never you mind, then. Just sit your arse on that stool until I find it."

"Then you once desired motherhood?" A silence settled between us. "I have always wanted to be a father. But I must content myself with thinking of my sailors as sons, for I care for them with all the fervor any father could muster. And perhaps I was drawn to Fanny as much for her son as for herself. Josiah was a little scamp of five when I first met him, full of beans and mischief." He sighed heavily. "I suppose I wasn't as good a father to him as I had wanted to be, for the beans and mischief, to my immense consternation, remain. His mother wanted a career in the law for him, but we couldn't afford to lay money by for it—after we married I was 'on the beach' for five years and didn't receive another commission until 1793, when the French started making noise in the Mediterranean. So when he grew old enough, I took him to sea."

I found a clean shirt and draped it over the folding screen. "Would you like me to 'elp you dress?"

"No, no, thank you, Lady Hamilton. You have already been goodness itself." The answer came as something of a relief. "But if you can find my green eyeshade . . . a makeshift sort of affair . . . affixes to my hat . . . I will have to have some new ones made up . . . somewhere in that trunk. . . . Your bright Italian sunlight . . . I am ashamed to admit . . . causes my damaged eye no small degree of discomfort as well."

"But aren't you blind in it? I thought—"

"No, not entirely. Imagine a heavy milky film covering it. I can distinguish light from dark and make out shadows and silhouettes."

" 'Ow did it 'appen—if you don't mind my asking?"

"It's not a secret," Nelson chuckled. "The siege of Calvi in 'ninety-four. We were under heavy fire from the San Francesco battery on the shore. I was hit when a ball struck a heap of stones very close to me, shattering them into a spurt of gravel. The surgeon told me that the blow damaged the optic nerve, causing permanent loss of sight, though by some miracle I suffered no structural damage to the eye itself. By all accounts I am told it looks normal, except for some minor enlargement of the pupil. I refuse to cover it with a patch because I have retained a bit of vision in it. Besides, I like to fool my men into thinking I've got both eyes on them all the time, you see! It's still not altogether a pretty picture, for if you inspect more closely, you'll notice that my right eyebrow was singed off during the whole messy business and never quite grew out again." There was a rustle from behind the screen, followed by a muffled oath. "Lady Hamilton, I am afraid I must impose upon your kindness after all. I can't seem to . . . might I trouble you to step over here for a moment?"

It near broke my heart to see the hero of the Nile losing his battle with his chemise. His "fin" was flapping frantically about—something I would come to learn was an almost-involuntary physical reaction to anxiety and agitation—and he was completely tangled up in the voluminous shirt.

From beneath the fabric came the plaintive, embarrassed, and horribly frustrated request: "Would you kindly help me hoist sail, Lady Hamilton?"

"Shhh . . . husht thee naise," I whispered. "As we say in Italian, *pazienza. Non perda la pazienza.*"

I began to dislodge him from his linen prison and to help him properly dress. I confess I feared to touch the stump of his right arm and gingerly endeavored to avoid it. "Dare I ask 'ow you lost the arm?"

"In 'ninety-seven, I was in command of the *Theseus*, sent to

Tenerife to take possession of the town of Santa Cruz by vigorous
assault. The true aim of the mission was to seize a fleet of treasure
ships from Mexico that were supposed to be in harbor there. I was
charged with destroying every vessel I encountered along the
African coast unless a contribution from the inhabitants of the Ca-
nary Islands was forthcoming for their preservation."

"And this was a commission from 'Is Majesty? It sounds to me
like you was being asked to be a corsair."

"Lady Hamilton, every crown seeks to enrich itself in whatever
way it can, just as every sailor goes to sea hoping to capture prizes.
Without the financial compensation that comes with a share of the
spoils, including the head money and gun money for the men and
arms captured, a man can scarce feed his family on navy pay. Do
you know that there has not been a rise in pay for His Majesty's
seamen since Charles II was on the throne! And merchantmen pay
a man even less!"

"Heavens, what a dreadful injustice! Well, then, you was being
a lawful pirate. Go on."

"I made the decision to attack Santa Cruz by night—not my
finest hour, as it turned out, for the Spanish batteries were prepared
for our onslaught, and our men, once we reached the mole, were
trapped and gunned down by enemy grapeshot. Not only that, between the darkness and the heavy fire, we couldn't see a blasted
thing. The surf churned up, smashing our smaller boats against the
rocks and drenching their ammunition. Men were tossed out and
drowned before they had the chance to raise their swords. At eight
p.m. on July twenty-fourth, I sent a message to my commander,
Earl St. Vincent, informing him that after great effort, we had not
been able to secure Santa Cruz. I closed my note with the words 'I
have only to recommend Josiah Nisbet to you and my country,' for
I was sure that night would be my last. I then elected, however, to
have at them a second time, for I could not accept defeat. In the
still-dark hours the following morning, I was in a small boat just a

few yards from shore. As I raised my arm to draw my 'lucky sword,' a gift from my uncle Suckling, I felt a tremendous burst of pain in my arm, and looked down to see that it had been shattered by grapeshot. 'I am shot through the arm,' I exclaimed. 'I am a dead man.' Josiah, close by, tore off the handkerchief that he wore about his neck and swiftly made a tourniquet. The flow of blood stanched, I felt much relieved, and when I spied some of our men floundering about in the water, having been blown out of the *Fox* cutter, I insisted that we divert our boat to rescue them. Josiah was adamant that I have my arm tended to as quickly as possible; but the closest ship at hand was the *Seahorse*, and with Captain Fremantle's wife aboard it and I with no word to give her of her husband's safety—besides which the *Seahorse*'s surgeon was a butcher—I demanded that I be taken back to the *Theseus*, where our surgeon, Thomas Eshelby, was a fine medico. Eshelby took one look at me and determined that the arm could not be saved and there was nothing I could do but submit my limb to the saw. I left the *Theseus* a right-handed hero and was returned to it a left-handed one."

"Does it 'urt?" I asked gently.

"Sometimes the hand that's no longer there feels as though someone was poking it with pins, or it feels like someone is wringing the missing lower half of my arm as though it were a wet rag. Eshelby called it a 'phantom pain.' He said it's because the nerves in my right shoulder were damaged from the shot. But I believe, Lady Hamilton, that I felt the pain most acutely in my soul. Twice had I failed my men; I was not half the leader I aspired to be, nor was I any longer fully a man. 'I am become a burden to my friends and useless to my country!' I told them. Disconsolate, I wrote an exceptionally self-pitying letter to St. Vincent asking him to give me a frigate to convey the remains of my carcass back to England."

"And did 'e?"

"Only because he thought I was too valuable to lose altogether.

He gave me my leave and I returned to Norfolk, where Fanny nursed me for nine straight months till I could bear the life of an invalid no more and begged the Admiralty to take back a one-eyed, one-armed admiral."

"I'm sure Fanny 'ad something to say about your desire to return to sea!"

Nelson laughed. "Fanny has never been able to comprehend, or perhaps come to terms with, my passion for the sea. It calls to me like Calypso. After we married, I believe Fanny expected me to remain shore-bound, living the quiet life of a country squire. I admit to have taken that notion into my head from time to time, but I am certain it is not in my nature to make a career of it. 'Death or Glory' is one of my credos and damme if I shall not suffer one in pursuit of the other. In the last five years, I have been in action on more than a hundred occasions; and though in a few of 'em I left a bit of myself behind, I tell you, Lady Hamilton—this is as true as my name is Nelson—I would never have been anywhere else, nor doing any other service for king and country."

Within the week, Nelson was well enough to enjoy his fortieth-birthday party. Sir William and I spared no expense on the gala, at which eighteen hundred guests supped and danced the night away. The Palazzo Sessa was aglow with lanterns and bedecked with buntings, and every guest received buttons and ribands bearing Nelson's initials. In the center of our ballroom I unveiled a column of Carrara marble into which had been carved Julius Caesar's triumphant words *Veni, vidi, vici*, along with the names of each of the Nile heroes—the captains and commanders of Nelson's victorious squadron.

I made him a present of an engraved silver cup, and in Nelson's honor, Cornelia Knight had penned a new verse to our national anthem, which I then sang for the entire assembly.

As the huzzahs and hip hip hurrahs filled the room, one voice suddenly carried above the rest. "Once a whore, always a whore!"

Josiah Nisbet was raving drunk. "And *you*," he shouted, dramatically pointing at Nelson, "the hero of the hour, the example to us all, allow her whore's hands to sully the flesh that you have pledged to my mother! I can assure you, madam," he said, venting the full measure of his inebriated wrath upon me, "you will never—*never*, do you hear me—supplant my mother in his affections. No matter how often you bathe his wounds or how much you cosset him and cock your ear in sympathy to his tales of war and woe. My mother will hear of all of this, I can promise you that!"

Livid as well as mortified, Nelson clasped my wrist and whispered in my ear, "Blink back your tears, Lady Hamilton, for you are above any of this. And *I* assure you, my stepson will answer to me for his rough manners."

The sweet-natured youth I had briefly taken under my wing back in 'ninety-three was now an arrogant pup of nineteen. Before Josiah could unleash another tirade, Captain Troubridge and another officer removed him, arms and legs flailing madly, from the ballroom. A shocked silence settled over the gathering, but the holiday mood of the bawdy Neapolitan nobility was not to be dampened for long.

"Boys!" exclaimed the Principessa Pignatelli with a hearty laugh, jostling her lover, the Duca di Montenegro, in the ribs.

Twenty-nine

An Unexpected Farewell

Nelson had hoped to depart on his next commission as soon the *Vanguard* was repaired. But Lord Spencer—who was First Lord of the Admiralty—and Nelson's commander-in-chief, Earl St. Vincent, ordered him to remain, and give Naples the most cordial and unlimited support.

Nelson chafed at these orders, which seemed designed to chain him down and waste precious time, rather than letting him loose again on the French navy to finish what he had so triumphantly begun. His official recognition for such heroic service was a slap in the face as well.

"Jervis was made an earl after the action at Cape St. Vincent, and he commanded from the rear—nowhere to be seen in the heat of battle," Nelson fumed. "For what I achieved that day, I should have been named at least a viscount! I should have been granted an earldom after Aboukir—but for such a great feat, I am made only Baron Nelson of the Nile!"

"But why 'ave they stinted you? No man in 'istory 'as gained as great a victory!"

"Why, Lady Hamilton? Dreary, pencil-pushing protocol is *why*! Ridiculous technicalities! Because on the books I was not the commander of a fleet, but rather the commander of a detached squadron, and no such officer has ever received higher recognition."

"Well, if I was King of England, I would make you the most noble puissant Duke Nelson, Marquis Nile, Earl Alexandria, Viscount Pyramid, Baron Crocodile, and Prince Victory, that posterity might 'ave you in all forms," I told him. "And I'm sure Sir Willum feels the same."

Sir William and I were tremendously glad of Nelson's continued presence, as Naples remained in danger from the French republican army and from the Neapolitan Jacobins who, bolstered by Bonaparte's earlier victories across Italy, felt bold enough to step back into the light.

"If the French were to march on Naples, the wisest and safest course is to flee. Convey this to Her Sicilian Majesty that she may make all the necessary arrangements for the evacuation of the royal family, if it comes to it. The boldest measures are the safest," he told me, invoking his credo. "If the Neapolitans remain sitting ducks, waiting to be attacked before they respond, the kingdom will be lost for certain. And I must confess, Lady Hamilton," he told me in utter confidence, "as much as I admire your husband, Sir William's employment of diplomacy has made him too indirect, where decisive action is both wanted and warranted. Now is not the time for circumspection. Now is the time to play Henry V and rouse the Neapolitans from their torpor. It requires the strong language of an English admiral to impress upon 'em the severity of the situation at hand."

Somehow, Nelson's zeal convinced the king to defend his own country—by marching into the Papal States and attacking the French. But Ferdinand's triumph was short-lived. The canny French had bided their time while the fool in his bliss thought himself victorious. Two weeks later, they declared war on the Kingdom of the Two Sicilies and the republican troops marched back into Rome. That evening, Ferdinand slunk back toward Naples disguised as a peasant, and the French reoccupied the city without a struggle.

"Oh, for the courage of the lion Nelson!" cried the queen, weeping and tearing her hair. I wondered if she was thinking it might not have been better for Ferdinand to have been killed, that she might rule the Two Sicilies alone.

But the lion was now at Leghorn, up the coastline, making tactical decisions that would keep the French at bay. He ordered the blockade of Genoa and summoned ships from the north and west coasts of Italy, from Malta, and from Egypt to put more pressure on the Frogs.

What a man! Nelson's vision and skill—and of course his heroism—had utterly captured my fancy. My admiration for him grew by the day, and it made me jealous to think that I might not be alone in my fondness. I'd once heard a rumor regarding Nelson's infatuated dalliance with the opera singer Adelaide Correglia back when he frequented Leghorn in 1795. Was she still there, waiting to embrace the hero? How could I let him know what was in my heart when I had no right to do so? Attempting to conceal the anxious flutter in my stomach, I had handed Nelson a letter before he left for Naples because I had not the courage to unburden myself face-to-face.

> Do not spend time ashore wile in Leghorn. Forgive me dear
> frend if I say there is no comfort for you in that city.

Nelson responded, writing to Sir William and me from his ship.

> My dear Sir William and Lady Hamilton: my gratitude for
> your most gracious and considerate hospitality and kindness is
> more than I can express. You have honored me beyond what I
> have deserved; and dare I say that no two people have ever been
> so kind to me. The world now seems a barren place when I am
> separated from you. Believe me when I say that my dearest wish
> is to return to you and never leave your company.

My heart rejoiced.

With an eye toward our eventual evacuation from Naples, Sir William began to generate a meticulous inventory of his collections of virtu: his vases, statues, cameos, and sarcophagi, and his paintings—which included dozens of old masters, as well as numerous gouaches of his beloved Vesuvius in eruption, and fourteen portraits of me. He carefully catalogued his volcanic minerals and fossils, his specimens of botany and ichthyology, and the ephemera from his *Wunderkabinetts*. Two thousand of his vases, along with five crates of paintings and a half-dozen cases of bronzes and marbles, were sent on to England in HMS *Colossus*, as Nelson would not have room for them aboard the *Vanguard*. Sir William hoped to sell the collection he put aboard the *Colossus*, for he was deeply in debt, the expenses of running the embassy far outstripping his government pay of eight pounds per day. During all those years of lavish entertaining in Naples, we had been living well beyond our means, tremendously dependent on credit.

In mid-December, the city, redolent of holiday aromas, was preparing to celebrate Christmas, whilst the queen and I commenced, in surreptitious increments, to spirit the royal treasures out of the palace. Mam labeled cask after cask with the words "Stores for Nelson," in preparation for their being rowed out to the *Vanguard*.

I helped Maria Carolina remove thirty-six barrels filled with 2,500,000 pounds' worth of gold, plate, and jewels, which were then brought to the mole in unmarked carriages by British sailors disguised as peasants. Ferdinand feared riot in the streets if his faithful lazzaroni were to discover that their king was deserting them. The royal family's flight, if discerned, would be made to look as if they were leaving Naples only to visit her sister capital in Palermo—a simple holiday—yet another reason for the royal treasury to be emptied well in advance of their departure. To escape in the night with so much baggage would ruin the ruse.

December 21 was the date set for our departure. Admiral Carraciolo, in command of the Neapolitan navy, prepared and signed the embarkation arrangements. Maria Carolina became even more superstitious than usual, joining Ferdinand in writing prayer after prayer upon scraps of paper that they pinned to their undergarments, or swallowed, as if God might pay more attention to their orisons if such pleas were secreted within their stomachs. I, too, despaired for everyone's safety, but could not reveal my anxiety, nor voice my fears, for the queen was relying upon my resolve. There were days when feigning optimism called upon all my powers as a performer.

By the eighteenth of the month, the queen was in an utter panic, weeping incessantly and sending me frantic notes several times a day, as much concerned for her brood as for her crown. The situation in Naples was growing uglier by the hour. On December 20, an Austrian attaché, mistaken for a Jacobin sympathizer, was murdered by the royalist mob. His battered body was dragged below the palace windows the way a cat brings a mouse to her master, expecting a dish of cream and a scruff on the head for her grand achievement. The king and queen were appalled, however, and grieved for the innocent Viennese. To reassure their supporters that they were remaining in Naples, contrary to rumor, they spoke to them from the balcony of the Palazzo Reale, as convincing as any actors I had seen at Drury Lane.

The following day, the *Jacobins* delivered a message to Their Sicilian Majesties. Alessandro Ferreri, a French royalist, was seen escaping into a boat. The republicans dragged him out of the skiff by his embroidered cuffs, kicked him to a bloody pulp, tied his buffeted body by the legs as though he were a lamb being brought to market, and laid him on the cobblestones in front of the palace. The noisy rabble soon swelled into an angry mob, reminding me too well of the violent Gordon Riots I had witnessed so many years earlier in London. Visions of her poor beheaded sister swam before the queen's eyes, and Maria Carolina fainted. The king needed not another whit of convincing that it was time to flee.

Shakespeare himself could not have written a more brilliant cover than that which was serendipitously provided to us by the unsuspecting Kelim Effendi. The emissary of the Turks' Grand Signior planned to host a dinner on December 21, to honor Nelson and his gallant squadron for saving the Turkish province of Egypt from French domination.

Hundreds attended the gala at the Palazzo Reale that night. The centerpiece of the evening was Kelim Effendi's presentation to Nelson of a stupendous diamond aigrette—a *chelenkh*, or "plume of triumph," the Turks' version of a laurel wreath. Kelim Effendi also presented the hero of the Nile with a sable-lined pelisse of scarlet-colored cloth. I tried to suppress my amusement, as it had clearly been manufactured for a man of greater physical stature than the diminutive and unprepossessing man of the hour, who was drowning in its long, voluminous sleeves.

Although our secret was both thrilling and terrifying, it was incumbent upon each of us to be consummate actors. As if nothing could ever be amiss, I then performed a selection of Nelson's favorite Attitudes. I was a forlorn Ariadne, pining for Theseus, who had abandoned her to her lonely fate on Naxos; and then Helen of Troy, standing on the crumbling ramparts of her adopted city, courageously facing its destruction.

The dancing commenced after my performance, which allowed our party, one by one, to slip out of the embassy undetected.

When Nelson and I reached the queen's apartments, having made sure that each of the royal party was accounted for, we carefully picked our way down the dark, narrow cockle-stair to the subterranean passageway, which we knew would eventually open onto the jetty. Nelson and I had previously explored that passage together, and it was he who had devised the route. Leading the way—I with one of the lanterns, Nelson with a pistol, and members of his crew with cutlasses—we crept along the dank passage. It smelt of brine, and worse, and the ladies fretted about their delicate noses as well as the state of their hems and dainty slippers. The queen muttered imprecations about leaving in disgrace, and voiced her fears that their flight might become another Varennes. The children, scared of the dark, became hysterical. Everyone had their hands full—with a torch or lantern, a casket of jewels, or a bawling child. Ferdinand tried to calm his wife by assuring her that life would be no different in Sicily, for he had already ordered his kennel master to send the royal dogs on ahead, as there was certain to be excellent hunting in Palermo. The two of them quarreled like a pair of fishmongers, a spat that threatened to betray us all, for their voices echoed through the damp corridor and carried across the water. Finally, upon reaching the mole, we boarded barges that were rowed out to the *Vanguard*—by armed sailors who had muffled their oars by wrapping them in strips of kersey.

Sir William and I left behind three magnificently appointed homes, half a dozen carriages, all our horses, and, of my husband's numerous collections, everything but the best paintings and vases. His eyes moist, my poor dear Sir William could scarcely bear to take a last look at the city he so loved, and in which he had resided for thirty-four years—nearly as long as I was old. I wished to be able to find some words of comfort for him, but came up bereft. I had been in Naples for a dozen years and now found it difficult to imagine what a life beyond or outside it—even in Palermo—might mean. I was accounted the beauty of the age. I had wielded power and influence. Now what? Was my star still on the ascension or had it reached its celestial zenith?

The air on the water was chilly and damp. The ladies, including myself, had left the city swathed in furs. Nelson looked concerned. "My fin," he said. "When the stump throbs, there's a storm coming on. Lady Hamilton, it is quite possible, you know, to truly feel something in one's bones, as 'twere."

We were unable to weigh anchor until more than a day later, as we were awaiting fresh consignments of food and drink and other stores. Not only that, the weather had not been friendly. Nelson had been right. But soon after we hoisted sail around seven in the morning on December 23, a tremendous gale blew up, tossing person and property to and fro. The queen was a poor sailor and required nearly all my attention. In her haste to flee, having concentrated on the removal of her jewels and wardrobe, and having concealed her escape from her own servants for as long as possible, she had forgotten to pack beds and linen for the king and herself. As Her Majesty could not endure the voyage like a common seaman, I put our own things at her disposal, leaving poor Sir William miserably cramped in one corner of a tiny cabin that Nelson had allotted to us. He was suffering from another attack of bilious fever, and I found myself dashing from deck to deck to ensure that the queen and her family were as comfortable as possible in the tempest-tossed ship, and then doing what I could for my poor ailing husband.

The *Vanguard*'s beam was about fifty feet, a moderate size for a warship, but never intended, nor fitted out, to carry passengers for pleasure. In addition to her crew of six hundred, the seventy-four-gunner was carrying fifty highborn travelers, who insisted on commanding more space than could conveniently be spared under the circumstances, though Nelson engineered the logistics like a veritable Solomon. "Where do your men sleep?" I inquired. He showed me their quarters. "Fourteen inches to a man," Nelson explained, raising his voice to be heard above the din of the crashing waves. "Hammocks are strung up side by side and stowed as soon as the men awaken."

"But most grown men are significantly broader than that! Fourteen inches of space apiece? How is it possible?"

"Watches. Mercifully, they are rarely down here all at one time."

The tiny, low-ceilinged cabins were cramped and claustrophobic and stank to hell. By midday on Christmas Eve, the storm was reaching its zenith. The ever-superstitious Neapolitans thought it was an omen, and if they were destined to die, they insisted on doing so in a state of grace. Count Esterhazy gave a parting kiss to his snuffbox, which bore a miniature painting of his naked mistress, before he tossed it into the churning waters. "There is nothing to fear," Nelson assured them, the very image of confidence and supreme command. "The Vanguards are the finest and bravest men in His Majesty's Navy."

Several of the sails were ripped to shreds and Nelson wasted not a moment in sending his men scampering up the rigging, hatchets in hand, to cut away the damage, even hack down a mast if need be. He surveyed every inch of deck himself to be certain that everything was properly lashed down to prevent its being washed overboard.

Swearing it was the worst storm he had seen in thirty years at sea, Nelson ordered all available hands to batten the hatches and place deadlights over the windows to prevent water from sloshing into the ship, but even Nelson was no match for Nature, and the angry waves washed over the decks and down into the corridors. The few heads on board had become unusable; even in normal sea conditions, there was only one seated lavatory per one hundred men. All manner of detritus could be found floating about the decks in more than six inches of water. Nearly every one of the royal party had taken seasick. Although poor Sir William was dreadfully unwell, he gamely roused himself to help Mam belowdecks in the wardroom, tending to the king and the crown prince as well as seeing to Acton and the Neapolitan noblemen. The entire ship smelt of vomit, urine, and feces; it was horrid. I don't know how any of us managed to inure ourselves to the stench. Weeping and shivering despite her furs, the queen was sure we would never make Palermo. Most of her children were now ill;

I soaked rags in vinegar and pressed them to their royal temples, to cool their fevers.

The wind kicked up something fierce, tossing the *Vanguard* about as though she were a toy. The hull creaked and groaned. I had no stomach for food nor time for sleep, besides which, there were no more beds to be had. Fragile little Clementina, the Princess Royal, was recovering from the exigencies of childbirth; the six-week-old future King of Naples was at his wet nurse's breast, prompting the squeamish Acton to remark that "a suckling child makes a most dreadful spectacle to the eyes of the servant-women and in the rest of the family."

Shrieks filled the air with every pitch and swell, yet they could not drown out the deafening howling of the wind through the tattered sails, and the terrifying crunch when a mast cracked and snapped like a twig. So concerned was I for the welfare of others that I hadn't a thought to spare for myself. I found Nelson inspecting the damage on the quarterdeck, wearing a tightly laced broad belt stuffed with a horsehair pad over the belly, a remedy for seasickness. He had once confided to me that he was prone to such bouts, despite his profession and his passion for the sea. "You stride the deck like a heroine, Lady Hamilton. I should call you 'Santa Emma.' Forgive me if a simple sailor cannot conceal his admiration." The spray hit my face and nearly knocked me against the bulwark. "But I must ask you to go below, your ladyship."

"People need me."

I began to slip and he clasped my arm before my knee reached the sodden deck. He was stronger than I ever would have expected. "They need you below. There is nothing for you on the deck but danger, and God help me should you suffer any injury. I know I should never sleep again."

I gazed into his intense blue eyes, the one seeing everything, the other pretending to. At that moment I wanted to clasp him to my breast.

"Lady Hamilton . . . I—"

I swallowed hard. "I must obey the captain." His lips were trembling. "I 'ave not seen to Sir Willum in hours. Please excuse me." I turned to leave, then turned back to him again. "Nelson—" I realized I dared not voice my thoughts and changed the subject. "That tree in your day cabin—I noticed it when I was seeing to the queen."

"That 'tree,' Lady Hamilton, is a piece of *L'Orient's* mainmast. One of my Nile captains, Ben Hallowell of the *Swiftsure*, lifted it off his deck, where it had landed after the French flagship exploded, and made a gift of it to me. I intend to have my coffin made of it. Crowned with laurel or covered with cypress, madam."

"I 'ate it when you say that." Another fierce gust of wind blew my feet out from under me. Rubbing my arse, I looked up at Nelson. "You've got much to live for—not least of which is getting us through this storm."

"And I have been wondering," he said, helping me to stand, "whether I wasn't intended to die in't."

"I won't let you! And anyway, your cabin is so crowded, you couldn't get to that piece of driftwood if you tried."

"My God, what are you about?!" I found Sir William, wigless, in our tiny cabin, his elegant form balled up into a corner, a loaded pistol in each hand. "Give me those," I demanded, trembling with fear that he might really fire them. "Please."

He raised the pair of pistols to his temples. "My dear, I am determined not to have salt water go guggle-guggle down my throat. Being a former military man and a lifelong diplomat, I fully comprehend the importance of being prepared for every eventuality."

Tentatively, I stepped toward him, my palms open and outstretched. "Please give me the firearms, Sir Willum. I could not survive it myself if I lost you."

"I am aging and exhausted, wife. And you never know, widowhood might become you," he added wryly.

Tho' in truth there was naught for me to be ashamed of, a pang of guilt stabbed at my heart, for I had been thinking affectionately of Nelson. "I shan't countenance such absurdity. The pistols, please." Reluctantly, he relinquished them into my hands. I found their box and locked 'em up again. "Your fever is back," I said, kissing his forehead. "I'll get some rags and vinegar to cool you off and a dose of Dr. James's Powder to bring it down."

"You look a sight, Emma. You must get some rest."

"I'll sleep in Palermo, if we ever get there." I gave Sir William his medicine and mopped his sweating brow with the vinegar-soaked rag. "I'll be back as soon as I can. I must see to the queen."

In Nelson's day cabin, Her Majesty's spirits were terribly low. The Princess Royal, three of the young princesses, and young Prince Leopold had rallied about her as she held a shivering Prince Albert in her arms. Sweet-natured little Albert, only six years old, was my favorite of all of Maria Carolina's children.

"I cannot stop the cough, miledi. I don't know what to do. He was all right when we began the voyage, I am certain of it. But the air and who knows what else . . . something has settled in his chest. I tried to offer him some food, but he has had no stomach for it."

I examined the boy, yet I was no medico. Perhaps Mam would have a remedy. I found her in the wardroom and together we managed to brew some tea for the child. The prince rallied for a while, but soon his little body was overtaken by convulsions. "Sing to him, miledi," commanded the queen. "It always soothes him when you sing."

I held Albert in my arms and rocked him as though he were an infant, singing all the lullabies I recalled from my own childhood, one after another, and when I exhausted my repertoire I began again. At seven p.m. on Christmas Eve, the queen's youngest son died in my arms.

Land was sighted just after dawn on Christmas morning. Of the entire flotilla of twenty, only the *Vanguard* had suffered severe damage in the storm. Her three topsails had been split, her staysails had been torn to shreds, and her foreyard, mainmast, and rigging badly damaged. The flight from Naples had been a most dreadful ordeal. As we limped into Palermo, I found it difficult not to enumerate our losses and the tremendous personal price we had paid for our passage.

The tumultuous welkin saw fit to welcome us with a gift of its own. It was snowing.

Thirty

Palermo

Although he had never visited his second capital in the nearly four decades he had ruled it, the king refused to disembark until a cheering crowd of Sicilians could be amassed to formally greet him as he stepped ashore. Maria Carolina was too distraught to leave the *Vanguard*, despite the unpleasant shipboard conditions. Although she had lost a daughter a year earlier, the death of little Prince Albert, so swift and unexpected, had hit her terribly hard.

It was rather an ordeal to unload the *Vanguard* in the snow, and one of the first and greatest difficulties to surmount was the matter of where everyone was going to stay. Two thousand souls had endured the storm-tossed journey from Naples to Sicily, and Palermo—a rustic village compared with its glittering sister capital—boasted but a single inn and some two dozen religious houses, hardly enough to accommodate even a fraction of the refugees.

Upon reaching dry, though icy, land, the royal family, Sir William, Nelson, Mam, Miss Knight, and I made first for the Colli Palace. Its highly unusual and exotic exterior did not hint, however, of the distinct lack of creature comforts to be had within its walls, for every room was dreadfully drafty, lacking both fireplaces and carpets; and none of the windows and doors would close properly, the wooden sashes and frames having suffered from the extreme shifts between sultry heat and icy cold. In short, the Colli Palace, as cold and damp as a Welsh winter morning, was entirely unsuitable for the present climate, let alone a place where convalescing invalids might heal properly.

Within the week, our party démenaged to the Villa Bastioni, a large house in the Moorish style with a magnificent view of the sea, but it, too, wanted the requisites for a comfortable domicile, lacking chimneys as well. Poor Sir William, suffering a relapse of bilious fever, was chilled to the marrow by the villa's dampness. Nelson wrapped him in the sable pelisse from Kelim Effendi, with instructions to sleep in it, if need be, to keep the cold at bay.

Nelson, too, was suffering, but it was his pride that was wounded. He despaired over the loss of Naples and a victory for the republicans. He was a man of two minds that January, one moment vowing like his hero Henry V to thrash the French, and in the next dolefully saying that perhaps it was time for him to consider becoming a country squire after all. He would return to England and die in peace and obscurity.

I refused to let his spirits flag so. "What 'appened to 'Death or Glory'? Though if it was up to me, we shouldn't think about the first part. If you was to return to England, I should miss you every hour," I added softly. "I wish with every breath I have that I could soothe away your pain. Could you sleep at night if I was to tell you that I think you're the greatest son England ever produced? Sir Willum thinks so, too. He predicted it from the first time you met, back in 'ninety-three, and damme if he wasn't right!"

A few weeks after our arrival I made arrangements to let the Palazzo Palagonia, a glorious fifty-room villa nestled into the terraced hillside, with commanding views of the sea. Nelson and Sir William

had agreed to evenly share the expenses, for the hero adamantly refused to be thought of as our guest.

I returned to the Villa Bastioni with news of our new residence,
to find Sir William in his library, collapsed in his chair with a few
sheets of paper clutched in his hand. His shoulders were heaving
with sobs. He looked so old and fragile without his elegant wig, his
hair so sparse he resembled a plucked guinea fowl. We had been
married for years, and I scarcely thought of the vast difference in
our ages, yet I now saw before me the image of a battered and defeated Pantaloon.

I raced to his side and knelt at his feet. "What is it, Sir Willum?"

He fluttered the pages in his hand. "Everything. Gone. Everything. Sunk." He had not spared his silk banyan from his copious
tears.

"What do you mean?"

"Here. From Greville, dated the tenth of January. 'It pains me
greatly to inform you that I received the news of the destruction of
the *Colossus* on 10 December, 1798, off the Scilly Isles en route to
England. . . . It would appear that all of your crates were lost to the
wreck, although a local inhabitant managed to salvage a particularly large box. Believing it contained some of your treasures, he
pried it open, only to discover the corpse, preserved in alcohol, of
a man later identified as one Admiral Shouldham, whose body was
being transported back to England in a crate marked 'Statues.' "
And this letter, written back on November twenty-sixth, from a
Major Bowen, explains that the *Colossus* was wrecked half out of
the water at low tide, and several of my boxes were rescued by
Scilly islanders. But Bowen adds that as soon as they pried open the
crates, the ancient vases disintegrated in the water. A few were recovered, he says, and for these he gave the islanders a guinea apiece
for their efforts. Seawater, Emma, will not harm a piece of glazed
pottery. It is impossible that the vases turned to wet clay in their
hands. Either they stole what they were able to salvage, or else the

whole lot is sitting at the bottom of the sea. In either event, I shall
never see any of it again. Oh, Emma!"

Sir William threw his arms about my neck. "Years. It took years
of painstaking perseverance to amass those collections. Not to
mention the money I spent in acquiring each vase, each painting—
all of it. And now no way to eliminate my debts, for there is nothing to sell. All has been lost forever."

I gazed into the tearstained face of my husband, a man who
had turned sixty-eight just a few weeks earlier, and who had been
dealt one of the severest blows of his long life. For Sir William,
losing his meticulously nurtured collections to the deep was
equivalent to Maria Carolina's losing a child to the icy grip of
death.

He took my chin in his hands. "My life's work. Gone. Including more than a dozen of you, my sweet, sweet wife."

I kissed his long tapered fingers. His hands had remained elegant, despite the slow deterioration of the rest of his body. "You
still 'ave the original, Sir Willum," I murmured with a smile.

"Do I?" He looked into my searching face. He was far too
much the gentleman to give voice to what he might suspect.

"Yes," I replied truthfully. "Yes, you do."

By then, we had become a nearly inseparable threesome, Sir
William, Nelson, and I. Both men were Knights of the Bath,
whose motto was *Tria juncta in uno*—"Three joined in one"—and
that was how we began to refer to our interrelationship and our
ménage. Truly, Nelson and Sir William lived like brothers, each
completely devoted to the other. We were a study in amity. Sir
William even commissioned the Palermitan artist Guzzardi to
paint a full-length portrait of the hero of Aboukir—though I never
thought it was flattering. Privately, however, I was tormented by
my growing passion for Nelson, and I knew the Baron of the Nile
felt the same way. Our gazes held for that extra moment in which

a million things remained unsaid. Melting smiles gave way to furtive and embarrassed glances. Proximity begot knowledge of each other's true character and achievements, with knowledge came admiration, and from admiration it was but a hop, skip, and jump to love.

"Your Excellency, Lady Hamilton appears quite devoted to the admiral," observed Charles Lock, the chargé d'affaires at Palermo.

"Have you had occasion to visit Vesuvius whilst you were in Naples?" Sir William inquired smoothly, and before Lock could reply, my husband added, "Truly, it is an uncommon phenomenon. But of course, to fully acquaint oneself with the volcano, it takes a complete appreciation of the changing of the Neapolitan climate, her shifting topography, her geology, and so forth. It's terrifying at times, to be sure, but nothing can compare to its beauty and awesome magnificence. I speak of Naples, of course, sir. Thus, despite the dangers, of which I remain fully sensible, I could never think of what my life would be like if I were never to see the city again after devoting so many years to it—or abandoning my attraction to the volcano."

Lock, who could not have mistook Sir William's meaning, was rendered speechless.

On the last day in January 1799, Maria Carolina summoned me to the Colli Palace, where the royal family remained in residence. "What is happening?!" she raged before I could rise from my curtsy. She brandished an official communication from Naples. "I learn now that just after we departed, my kingdom's ships in the Bay of Naples were torched—and on January twelfth, that fool of a viceroy, Pignatelli, signed an armistice with the French! The French! An armistice! Who gave him this authority? Not I, I can assure you, miledi. I do not even think my husband could have been so stupid. Now it is Paris all over again, but Paris inside out, where the rebels come from the educated classes and the mob defends the throne. The lazzaroni stormed the palace, demanding weapons to protect themselves against the French. Then they used them to attack the Jacobins. Read this!"

The queen thrust the documents into my hands. They included a litany of brutalities against the rebels. The royalists had broken into the prisons and slaughtered anyone suspected of Jacobinism, beginning with those sporting short hair or wearing trousers. I trembled as I silently read on. Women had been dragged naked through the streets; numerous acts of rape, murder, arson, dismemberment, and even cannibalism were enumerated. It took all of one day for Naples to fall to the French. Of the fifty thousand lazzaroni in Naples, that day two thousand were killed. The French then stitched up a brand-new flag, a tricolor of red, blue, and yellow, made of fabric looted from the churches, and declared the birth of the Parthenopean Republic, Parthenope having been the ancient name for Naples.

Ferdinand blamed their situation on Maria Carolina's fondness for the English. "Had Naples remained neutral, none of this would have happened," he sulked.

"*Now* you want to play king?!" she railed at him. "You *be* the king, then. Take back our kingdom so you have someplace to *be* the king!"

Throughout the spring, the *tria juncta in uno* met with Their Sicilian Majesties to determine the best course of action. The queen—and Nelson, a fervent royalist—was adamant that Naples be retaken at any cost and the French, as well as the Neapolitan rebels, be given no quarter.

As summer loomed, with no respite from the heat, the desultory air turned the daylight hours into a purgatory. At night, the entire city, it seemed, was gripped by a passion for gambling, and at every house party the gaming tables were filled well into the wee hours of the morning.

"Fanny has written to me," Nelson confided one afternoon as we strolled amid the arcades of citrus trees in the Flora Reale, my parasol offering little protection from Palermo's omnipresent flies.

The gravel crunched beneath our feet and I wished it'd been chips of ice instead. "And . . . ?" I was not even sure I wanted to hear the answer.

"She says her doctors have advised her that a change of climate would benefit her health. . . . As you know, she is always suffering colds. . . . On the hottest day of the year, the woman could swathe herself in layers of flannel nightshirts under her gowns." *What a pleasant appearance she must present*, I thought, the green-eyed monster grabbing hold of my senses. Nelson stopped under the shade of an orange tree. A bergamot-scented breeze riffled through his hair. "I . . . I have no wish to see her, Lady Hamilton. Nor would it even be prudent for me to do so, as I told her by return post. For one thing, her departure would leave no one to care for my father, whose age and infirmities preclude him from much activity. Imagine this—I felt compelled to explain to her what should have been abundantly obvious: that I am essentially in the middle of a campaign. 'The Hamiltons and I are the mainspring which governs what goes on in this country,' I told her. She wished to journey as far as Portugal, expecting me to meet her there. I told her that the notion was not only impractical; it was preposterous, for no sooner did I greet her but I would have to strike my colors and bring her right back home again. Which of course would be well out of my commission. She thinks that because I am living on dry land with my two dearest friends in the world, that I must be on holiday."

"Every day with you is a holiday." I smiled, delighting in the curve of his upper lip. Wishing I could touch it. "Perhaps she finally recognizes that."

"You are an angel to say so, Lady Hamilton. But the truth of the thing is"—he glanced away uncomfortably and scuffed the pebbles with his shoe—"the truth is . . . that . . . and I confess that since my marriage I have bedded other women than Fanny . . . but knowing you now, I cannot imagine being in the company of any other woman ever again."

I felt the heat rise in my cheeks and my skin began to tingle as if a thousand twinkling stars had taken up residence just beneath the surface. If my heart could have leapt out of my chest into his hand, I was sure it would have done so. Just as I lowered my head to risk kissing him for the first time, we heard footsteps, and we broke apart. Nelson offered me his arm and the conversation was not resumed. We returned to the Palazzo Palagonia in complete silence, scarcely daring to exchange a glance, both of us, I think, too fearful to speak of love.

Since the loss of his most valuable treasures in the wreck of the *Colossus*, Sir William had also lost the vigor and vitality that had once made him "the most juvenile man I ever knew." More and more, he wished to be left alone. He would wander through the vast rooms of the Palazzo Palagonia caressing the objects of virtu that we had managed to bring with us from Naples, as if they were living things—as though his touch upon the clay or marble could bring back their absent companions. It broke my heart to see him so defeated. And as much as he loved Nelson like a brother, my husband was not a champion of the admiral's vision for recapturing the lost half of the Sicilian kingdom. "I am King George's servant, my dear, not King Ferdinand's," he would remind me. "You know that it will not do for the envoy from the Court of St. James to take an active part in another country's politics nor in a foreign campaign. In fact, such a thing is most emphatically outside my embassy."

His intransigence had the effect of bringing Nelson and me closer together, for the admiral and I—of a single unequivocating mind—spent increasingly longer hours strategizing, either alone or in the company of the king and queen. Given Sir William's frequent absences, I was indispensable as a translator at the latter's discussions, for Nelson spoke no foreign languages.

While the weather, even hotter, more sultry, and more indolent than in Naples, carried its own erotic charge, our mutual involvement in the tumultuous political climate eventually had a heady effect on us as well.

Thirty-one

Rough Justice

Nelson and I spent nearly every waking hour in each other's company. The campaign to retake Naples brought us together by day, but in the evenings, we could not bear to quit each other's side. Everyone who witnessed our behavior, however careful we were not to seem more than the most amicable of friends, could not fail to be sensible of the current between us. Though nothing untoward had happened, I believe we both knew it was inevitable. Yet never had I endured such agony. I had spent thirteen years totally loyal to Sir William, proud to prove to the world that a once-fallen woman could be a paragon of fidelity and a model wife, even, or perhaps especially, amid the licentious and permissive Neapolitans.

Yet every night I went to bed alone. Sir William and I had not shared a *càmera da letto* in well over a year; he now preferred to take a book to his bedchamber and fall asleep at his leisure, rather than disturb my slumbers. Before then, if he desired to visit me, he would gently catch me by the arm as our dinner party was breaking up and run his thumb along the tender flesh in the crook of my elbow, a gesture he performed less and less frequently as the months went by. As I lay in my lonely bed, my thoughts were now filled with nothing but Nelson. I was tormented by my passion for him. Is it any wonder that I stayed up into the wee hours of the morning at the gambling tables? I had the energy of a restless tigress and nowhere else to vent it. So I began to satiate myself instead with high-stakes hands of cards, with gourmandizing, and with copious quantities of champagne. Because I was unable to enjoy a private moment with the man who had captured my head and heart in a way that no one had ever come close to doing in the past, I would fill the house with strangers and laughter and music so that my thoughts and emotions could be directed elsewhere.

I welcomed the morning, for it meant I would see Nelson again. With abandon I threw myself into his plans, believing in them as much as he did. We would all indeed be covered with glory for our achievements. And to me, as to Nelson, glory meant honor. In those tense and terrible months, we both dedicated our existence to Honor, and it brought us even closer together. If only we could persuade the cowardly Ferdinand to see things the same way. After weeks of Nelson's urging the king to behave like a proper sovereign, what finally drew him fully into the campaign was the report that a new Parthenopean law declared that anyone called Ferdinand had to change his name!

"Who is this Cardinal Ruffo whom the king has chosen to replace Pignatelli as viceroy?" Nelson handed me a dispatch from Naples.

"What 'appened to Pignatelli?"

"Absconded. I am beginning to think it is bred in the Neapolitan temperament to be craven. I beg of you, Lady Hamilton, to translate this mumbo jumbo so I may advise His Majesty as to the swiftest course of action."

I perused the paper. "Cardinal Ruffo's title is honorary. 'Is family is as rich as Croesus and 'e was the minister of war to Pope Pius VI. This document states that 'e 'as an army of seventeen thousand—Sanfedists, they are calling themselves, the "Army of the Holy Faith." If I know Ruffo, this so-called army

are really 'is tenants, incited to defend the crown with the promise of relief from taxes, the chance to battle the Devil, and unlimited looting."

"What a helpmeet you are in every way! An angel to behold,
and a true partner in my work . . . as well as in my heart."

My own heart stopped for a moment as we gazed upon each
other, sensible of an equal measure of mutual longing and pain. A
silence settled between us before Nelson returned to the matter at
hand.

"Do you think Ruffo's army can stop the Jacobin terrorism?"
He began to pace the room as if it were his quarterdeck. "I wish to
draft a note to King Ferdinand. Tell him that it is my belief that
the Spanish might send another naval squadron to bear down on
the Two Sicilies by the end of March. England and Naples need to
prepare for such an eventuality. To that end, in His Sicilian
Majesty's name, I am dispatching Captain Troubridge to Procida to
effect a blockade of Naples and take control of the islands in the
bay."

But Troubridge handled this assignment with bloodthirsty zeal,
hanging Jacobins at Procida, and passing a death sentence on a
squad of Swiss Guards who complained at the high cost of food, a
verdict he commuted at the last possible moment. *Was all that brutality really necessary?* I wondered.

"War is no place for gentlemen, miledi," insisted the queen.
"Now Ruffo confesses that he is surprised and appalled by the
butchery perpetrated by his army's counterrevolution. He says he
had never envisioned such a thing. He must treat Naples and these
soi-disant patriots like the rebels of an Irish town. Quash them
without equivocation!"

"Your Majesty, Ruffo's men, the counterrevolutionaries, are re-
sorting to wholesale rape. To *cannibalism*. The Sanfedists claim to
be royalists and yet they looted the Palazzo Reale! They took whatever they could steal and even pried the lead off the mullioned win-

dows. 'Ow does this gain you and the king the respect you need to regain your thrones?"

"Respect? Miledi, *respect* is a word reserved for diplomats, begging Sir William's pardon."

Maria Carolina was deaf to my suggestions for moderation. Fearing a rupture in our most precious friendship, during our subsequent strategizing discussions I began to hold my tongue.

The sovereigns' paranoia increased with their superstition. Now every artisan and aristocrat in Palermo who in any way evinced a thirst for knowledge was suspected of being a secret Jacobin. All literary and scientific meetings were henceforth banned. Anyone who owned more than a handful of books was under suspicion. Theologians, lawyers, chemists, professors, scholars, doctors, and musicians—even the clergy—were now under surveillance. To own—let alone read—Voltaire and Rousseau was treasonous. Someone caught with a single forbidden book was tossed into prison for three years. For a man nabbed with unpowdered hair, the sentence was six months.

Sir William, who read, and owned, several works by both of the banned philosophers, was livid. "Voltaire himself would have been horrified to be thought of as an inciter to riot and violence; to think he promulgates brutality is to entirely misread his writings. This is not the country I ever knew," he muttered angrily, murmuring that perhaps it was time to tender his credentials to King George and return home to England. "If I were not a foreign ambassador, I might well be a victim myself. And so should you, my dear, for I have seen you reading *Candide*."

Nelson had returned to sea to better assess the political situation. A worried Sir William wrote to him that *Emma is unwell and lowspirited with phantoms in her fertile brain that torment her. I fear she has too much sensibility.* It was all too true. I despaired daily for Nelson's safety. What horrors might he witness? What ugly disputes might he be called upon to mediate? Would the rebels respect his British citizenship or would they drag him down to hell?

In mid-May, Nelson recalled the vainglorious Troubridge to Palermo, replacing him with the milder and more diplomatically minded Captain Edward Foote of the frigate *Seahorse*. Nelson prayed that Foote's appointment would restore order and preserve life, but fears for his own mortality rose to the surface, as they did just before an action. On May 25, 1799, Nelson wrote a codicil to his will, and three days later, he was back in Palermo, planning to withdraw some of his ships from Malta in order to concentrate his forces wholly on the retaking of Naples.

I flung my arms about him the moment he set foot in the Palazzo Palagonia. "My dear, dear friend," I murmured into his chest. "Don't ever leave again. Promise me you will never, ever leave."

He looked into my tearstained face. "Duty, Lady Hamilton. A sailor's first obligation."

"I wish it weren't, you know."

Nelson caught a falling tear on his fingertip and brought it to his lips. "Emma. Beautiful, magnificent *Emma*." Our fingers entwined. "*Now* why are you weeping?"

"It's the first time you've used my Christian name."

On the eighth of June, now a rear admiral of the red, Nelson shifted his flag from the *Vanguard* to the eighty-gun *Foudroyant*. Eight days later, Sir William received an alarming dispatch from Naples. "It would appear from this communiqué that Cardinal Ruffo has concluded a twenty-one-day armistice with France— signed by representatives for Naples, Russia, and Turkey, as well by Captain Foote on behalf of His Britannic Majesty, I might add— and Ruffo is also spreading rumors that Nelson fled to Palermo because he feared the French fleet."

"Feared!" Nelson roared. His usually pallid complexion turned crimson with rage. "*I*, who delivered the French fleet the soundest thrashing it ever received?! This shall not be countenanced!" He glanced quickly at the papers. "I never gave Foote the authority to sign treaties, make armistices—he is out of his commission. Sir William—Lady Hamilton—whichever of you can speak that infernal Neapolitan tongue—send a message to His Sicilian Majesty that we must make for Naples as soon as it is practicable. The king's authority and sovereignty must be asserted and this armistice, entered into without Ferdinand's knowledge—let alone his consent—must be undone."

A few days later, the king accompanied the *tria juncta in uno* aboard the *Foudroyant*, and with a total of nineteen ships, we hoisted sail for the Bay of Naples. Maria Carolina, still racked with fear for her own safety, was determined to remain behind in Palermo.

Sailing into the bay, Nelson was heralded as a rescuer. The city was aglitter with illuminations, as if to welcome us. Upon our arrival, the flagship became a kind of central command post from which Nelson sent and received all official dispatches and correspondence, and where Acton and the king would interrogate the captured rebels, trying them if necessary.

I translated Nelson's first dispatch, which contained orders to dissolve the truce immediately, giving the French all of two hours to surrender. Those who did so would be given safe passage back to France, but "as for the rebels and traitors, no power on earth should stand between their gracious king and them."

Thought he met with resistance from Ruffo, Nelson was not one to accept no for an answer.

By the next evening, although the peace had not been fully secured, the fortresses had been surrendered and the royal colors once again flew from their crenellated turrets. Finally able to exhale after months of violence, the royalist nobles rejoiced in the streets with typical Neapolitan vivacity—plenty of music and macaroni—

and the royal standard fluttered alongside the British flag from every loyal home.

Unfortunately, an alarming number of Neapolitan Jacobins had been friends of ours: men and women of high rank and position, including a number of Maria Carolina's former ladies-in-waiting, noblewomen who for years had been Her Majesty's bosom companions. Many of these sympathizers were brought out to the *Foudroyant*, where they begged us for clemency. I confess that it made me feel good to be needed as much as it appealed to my nature to be of some benefit to others. But it was exhausting business. Nelson hated to see me so fagged at the end of every day, referring to the desperate petitions as "Lady Hamilton's teasers." To Greville I wrote, *It's nice to be with the king, but it's better to be by oneself. I am waiting to get quiet. I am not ambitious of more honners.*

The gray-haired, elegant Ruffo was taken on board the *Foudroyant* to account for himself and his actions, and I translated the angry contretemps between Nelson and the cardinal. Ruffo raised a vociferous defense with classic Neapolitan passion. Yes, he had agreed to the armistice—but he had done so in order to keep the peace. The violence unleashed by his Sanfedist counterrevolutionaries had got well out of hand. It sickened him. "You have not seen the hangings, your lordship," Ruffo said hotly. "My army erected makeshift scaffolds in the public squares, employing a particularly vicious form of execution, where it takes three of them to hang a person. In addition to the hangman, one man climbs atop the scaffold and presses down upon the victim's shoulders. The third man, standing on a ladder, grabs the victim by the ankles, and once the trap opens, the condemned is both pulled and pushed to his—or her—death. Yes, your lordship, *women* have not been spared this gruesome torture. Such was the fate of the celebrated Jacobin poetess Eleonora Fonseca da Pimentel. I have seen republican-minded noblemen such as the Duca della Torre and his brother dragged out of their beds, tarred and feathered, shot, stabbed, and set afire, their burning bodies disemboweled as they gasped their last—while remaining alive enough to be fully sensate of their torture. Naked Jacobin prisoners were dragged en masse before me and shot before my eyes. Fifty at a time on one occasion! And you wonder why I make an armistice? True, I did not have His Majesty's authority but—"

"*But.* There is no *but,*" Nelson countered. "And therein lies your error. For every command must issue directly from the king and in taking matters into your own hands"—here Nelson raised his voice—"in taking matters *into your own hands,* you are in violation of your commission and as guilty of treason as any of the rebels."

"With all due respect, your lordship," shouted Ruffo, without the slightest trace of deference in either his voice or his manner, "it is important under these delicate circumstances to be *merciful* in order to restore law and order. Law and order will not be restored to Naples with further acts of violence! You are a foreigner in our waters. I am Neapolitan born, and I understand my own people. I know that order will not be established either quickly or smoothly. Trust must be gained, tempers soothed."

"Sir, I am here as His Sicilian Majesty's servant, acting under his orders," Nelson thundered. "*You,* on the other hand, as His Majesty's viceroy, acted of your own accord, well outside of them. You have no choice but to concede that I am in the right, having been deputized by King Ferdinand to represent his express wishes in this situation."

The two men were at a stalemate. Evidently, Ruffo and his subordinates had attempted to persuade the rebels that once they surrendered, they were free to escape to France *without* having to submit to the punishment of the sovereign whom they had actively defied. Yet Nelson, on the king's behalf, was adamant that the traitors be awarded no free pass. Three days of tense standoff followed.

By June 30, despite Sir William's suggestion that they "keep smooth" with Ruffo, the king gave Nelson the authority to arrest the cardinal if he refused to recognize the canceling of his ill-conceived capitulation.

We soon had another crisis on our hands. To our collective disappointment and dismay, news of Admiral Caracciolo's certain defection reached our ears. In an overt act of war, he had attacked the British fleet at Procida and fired upon the *Minerva*, a Neapolitan ship commanded by one of the king's most trusted nobles, the Austrian-born Count Thurn. Caracciolo was ordered to be brought to the *Foudroyant* for trial, but an exhaustive search of the city was unsuccessful. After several days, a loyalist farmer discovered a bearded, bedraggled man, dressed in tatters, hiding in a barn on the estate belonging to Caracciolo. At knifepoint, the fugitive identified himself, whereupon he was dragged back to Naples in disgrace.

"I don't understand it," the king said, shaking his head in utter disbelief. "I trusted this man. There was no higher officer in my navy. Just half a year ago, he aided our flight to Palermo. Why would he do this?"

"I think, sir," I replied, " 'e was still smarting from what 'e perceived to be an insult to 'is honor and 'is 'eritage, being a proud Neapolitan. 'E took it very 'ard that you and 'Er Majesty was sailing away on an English ship instead of on one of your own."

Ferdinand sighed heavily. "If he is a traitor, he must be hanged."

"I think a proper court-martial would be in order," Sir William insisted. "Let the man tell his side of the story before you condemn him."

The king pounded his fist on the table. "Damn trials! I say hang the bastard from his own yardarm!"

"Your Majesty," Nelson interposed smoothly. "That may very

well be the verdict. But Sir William's plan is well reasoned and appropriate under the circumstances. Besides, we wish to do everything 'by the book,' as we say in England, which will, of course, better facilitate your regaining your rightful place on the throne."

I knew Caracciolo well. He had often been our guest at the Palazzo Sessa. He had supped more than once at my right hand and we had danced together. I wished with all my heart that the accusations of treason were naught but a dreadful mistake, that there was a perfectly reasonable explanation for his flight to the countryside.

Late that evening I sat up with Nelson in his sleeping cabin long after the others had gone to bed. I had become *his* amanuensis, as I had been for the queen: indispensable for my ability to translate documents back and forth from Italian and French into English. And I was a wizard with ciphers. "I have enough correspondence for two arms," he jested, sighing over the mountains of paperwork before him.

"I'll stay up day and night, for as long as it takes," I assured him, rubbing my tired eyes. "I may be fagged, but I find nothing more exhilarating than working side by side with you to restore Their Sicilian Majesties to their thrones. We are doing weighty work and saving millions."

"Well," said Nelson with finality, affixing his seal to a writ, "we shall soon learn whether Caragholillo, or whatever you call him, is a Jacobin dog after all." I laughed. "I don't see what the devil you find so amusing, Lady Hamilton. A man's life might, quite literally, hang in the balance."

"It's not *Caragholillo*," I said, bosting out even harder. Laughter eased the tensions in my heart, provided a tiny respite from the ugly business in which we were embroiled up to the neck. "Watch me, Nelson. It's pronounced Ca´-rah-chee-oh´-lo. In Italian you caress each syllable with your mouth. You taste it. You make love to it. The A's and O's are big and round like a woman's breasts. When you make the *o* sound, think of rounding and softening your lips as though you were about to kiss someone. Ca-rah-chee-*o*-lo."

Leaning closer, Nelson smiled. "Do that again."

"Ca-rah-chee-*o*—" His lips were on mine, meeting them softly at first, as though the tender skin sought first to test its purchase. And then his arm encircled me just above the waist and drew me to him. I cradled his face in my hands and kissed every feature— the scar on his forehead from the wound he had received at Aboukir, his good left eye, his poor damaged right one, his cheeks and chin—and once again I returned to his lips, where I thought to remain forever. "Nelson," I breathed.

"Emma. Santa Emma. My beautiful Emma. My love." He reached for the candlestick and with two fingers pinched the guttering flame dead.

We lay together all night, but we did not make love then, for we both knew the stakes, as well as the risk we would be taking. I did not wish to break my marriage vows, yet I could not bear to quit his side.

"I feel like Lancelot," Nelson whispered as he held me, tickling my ear with the tip of his tongue. "History may remember us as one of many *tria juncta in uno*s: Arthur, Guinevere, and Lancelot. Menelaus, Helen, and Paris. Sir William Hamilton, Lady Hamilton, and the simple sailor who captured—"

" 'Er 'eart and soul."

"Ahh . . . I was about to say 'thirteen French ships at Aboukir.' Not to mention a number of privateers, a couple of Spanish first-raters, and—pray don't tickle me in the ribs, Lady Hamilton, for you put me at a distinct disadvantage. I cannot hold you and defend my midsection at the same time."

Caracciolo was taken aboard the *Foudroyant* in chains and court-martialed by a jury composed entirely of fellow Neapolitans. The charge had been crimes against the crown, and not an Englishman was present during the proceedings. In fact it had not been a Royal Navy court-martial but a Neapolitan one. He was adjudged guilty, though the vote was not unanimous, and ordered to be hanged from the yardarm of the *Minerva*, the ship that he had fired upon. I did witness the hanging, though at the final moment I averted my eyes, for they were filled with tears. When I turned back, I saw the crew weight the corpse's legs with stones and toss it overboard. Thus perished ignominiously an old friend and a once-great man who, like Nelson, bore the greatest love for his country.

The emptying of the forts then began apace. Two thousand Neapolitan Jacobins were evacuated to fourteen polaccas to await sentencing. The same number of rebels were reimprisoned onshore. All things considered, in the aftermath of the counter-revolution the restoration of order had been relatively bloodless. In fact, in an ultimate act of clemency, King Ferdinand permitted the cardinal to remain in Naples and retire in peace to private life.

One morning, a few weeks after the execution of Caracciolo, a shout went up on deck. One of Nelson's midshipmen brought him the news. The king himself had spotted a bloated, sightless corpse bobbing alongside the *Foudroyant*'s anchored hull, floating with the current in the direction of Naples. The ever-superstitious Ferdinand was all atremble, for the body, though partially decomposed, left little guess as to its identity.

"Caracciolo," blubbered the king, fumbling for his numerous talismans. "The stones would not sink him. It is an omen. Look how his feet point to the shore! He was my friend. He has returned to ask my forgiveness. His soul could not rest, nor his body, neither, for we did not permit him to be shriven." At His Sicilian Majesty's insistence, a team of sailors lowered a net and fished the corpse from the water. It was taken back to dry land, where it was given a proper Christian burial in the sand. God had seen fit to give Caracciolo a coda to his once-noble life. I wept for him anew.

Thirty-two

The Nelson Touch

All through the month of July we remained in the Bay of Naples, living aboard the *Foudroyant*, Nelson's "darling child," determined to make it seem as much like home as we could. Our days were taken up with hearing petitions and administering justice. While the officers and crew engaged in sword and sail drills, gunnery, and boarding practice, men disinfected the vessel by scrubbing it with vinegar, and holystoned and swabbed the warship's decks. We broke at noon for dinner, and after the meal, I would sit on deck and play the harp, singing our favorite tunes. Nelson's sailors loved it, for I knew all the old country ditties. Whilst they shed a homesick tear or two, they were happy to be reminded of England, so far away, yet brought so close for a few hours with my music. We must have sung "Heart of Oak" a half dozen times a day. Boatloads of Neapolitan musicians came alongside us nearly every day as well, to serenade their most puissant sovereign and the courageous English who had been his deliverer as well as theirs.

I went ashore only once, to see what had become of our property. Sir William did not wish to accompany me. When I observed the looting and desecration that had taken place at the Palazzo Sessa, I turned back and headed for the mole in tears, too disconsolate to even consider hiring a hack to take me out to Villa Emma in Posillipo. I was relieved then that my husband had avoided the pain of seeing that which he had already been canny enough to surmise. I could not speak a word as Nelson's sailors rowed me back to the *Foudroyant*, nor could I take my eyes from the shore.

I had no way of knowing at the time that Sir William and I would never see Naples again.

On August 2, the city was deemed secure enough for us to weigh anchor for Palermo. We had lain in the Bay of Naples for six weeks, and I had been the only one of our party to ever step upon dry land. The king never once ventured to visit his capital. In many ways I was glad to go back to Sicily, for I missed Mam something dreadful. Upon our return, even in the scorching heat she insisted on cooking me an Irish stew. "I know you've been eating naught but macaroni and marzipan and all them sweet cheesy desserts. You need a proper stew and a syllabub." She gave me a hug. "There's a bit more to squeeze than when you left me, gal. Not enough beef. That's the problem."

The queen was effusive in her welcome. The most grateful sovereign heaped honor upon honor on Sir William and me, rewarding us with presents of gowns and jewels and snuffboxes. But Ferdinand was even more generous, giving Baron Nelson of the Nile the dukedom of Bronte, a small estate on the lower slope of Mount Etna, named for the Cyclops who, as ancient legend had it, lived inside Etna, forging Jove's thunder. "With only one eye on it, no wonder he couldn't stop the volcano from erupting," jested Nelson. Now my hero was formally "Nelson & Bronte" or "Bronte Nelson of the Nile," resolving to use his new European title when he was in Italian waters. The dukedom was reputed to yield an annual income of three thousand pounds. Unlike many of his seafaring brethren, Nelson had never become rich through prize money, so the Bronte income would be exceptionally welcome.

On the third of September Their Sicilian Majesties hosted an enormous fete to honor our grand success in Naples, and to belatedly celebrate the first anniversary of Nelson's Nile victory. And what a grand affair! Life-sized wax effigies of Sir William, Nelson, and me were displayed atop elaborate Roman columns, clothed in our own garments, jeweled and accoutered just as we ourselves would be on any gala night, the figures of Nelson and Sir William wearing copies of the Order of the Bath.

Nelson was lapping up the admiration. I, too, felt the same rush of heady excitement to be the honoree of a king and queen. Mam, in her simple housedress and cap, a ring of chatelaine's keys at her waist, was positively beaming. I glanced at my husband. Sir William looked tired, his once-ramrod posture now stooped, his innate elegance faded as old damask. He looked like he would have much preferred to be home in bed. A pang of regret stabbed at my heart. He had once been so vital, an adventurer undaunted by the encroaching exigencies of age. In Palermo, antiquarian dealers visited him in droves, but he had neither the money—being fifteen thousand pounds in debt to his bankers—nor the enthusiasm for rebuilding his collections. His morale at low tide, no matter how much I tried to cheer him, my husband would not be roused from his melancholy.

So more and more I kept company with Nelson, whose passions in everything so closely matched my own. We promenaded every day in the Flora Reale and sat side by side each evening at dinner, so I could cut his meat. Aware that we were being observed, I was careful not to permit our bodies to touch, however harmlessly, though I was close enough to become intoxicated by his heat, from the scent of his skin and the powder in his hair. Our proximity, combined with the inability to act upon my urges and desires, was slowly turning me into a madwoman.

At night, Sir William retired early and Nelson would sit beside me at the gaming tables. He'd once won a small fortune of three hundred pounds several years earlier, an event he put down to beginner's luck, but Nelson was not a gambler. "While I had won that night, I shuddered to think what might have happened had I *lost* such a fortune," he told me. "The thought alone was enough to cure me before I caught the disease."

But the fact that Nelson never quit my side every evening, regardless of whether or not he was placing wagers, did not stop tongues from wagging, particularly Troubridge's. It was no secret to me that the admiral felt quite proprietary of Nelson's companionship. They had fought together in the same actions, and they had been close friends for years before Nelson had ever heard of the Hamiltons. As it appeared to everyone in Palermo that there was no one Lord Nelson would rather spend his time with than Lady Hamilton, many of his acquaintance—and most especially Thomas Troubridge—behaved, to my mind, rather jealously. Confiding his distress to Nelson from his post at Messina, he wrote:

> I see by your lordship's last letter your Eyes are bad. I beseech, I intreat you do not keep such horrid hours, you will destroy your constitution. Lady Hamilton is accustomed to it for years, but I saw the bad effects of it in her the other day, she could not keep her eyes open, yawning and uncomfortable all day; the multiplicity of business which your lordship has to perform must with the total want of rest destroy you, pardon me my Lord it is my sincerest esteem for you that makes me mention it: I know you can have no pleasure sitting up all night at Cards; why then sacrifice your health, comfort, purse, ease, everything, to the Customs of a Country where your stay cannot be long. I again beg pardon. If you knew my feelings you would I am sure not be displeased with me.
>
> Pray keep good hours, if you knew what your Friends feel for you I am sure you would cut off all <u>Nocturnal</u> partys, the gambling of the people at Palermo is publickly talked of every where. I beseech your Lordship leave off. Lady H— Character will suffer, nothing can prevent people from talking, a gambling Woman

in the Eye of an Englishman is lost; you will be surprized when
I tell you I hear in all Companys the sums won and lost on a
Card in Sir Wm's house, it furnishes matter for a letter con-
stantly, both to Minorca, Naples, Messina, &c, &c, and finally
in England. I trust your Lordship will pardon me.

A glum Nelson handed me the letter to read.

"England?" I questioned. "By 'England,' does Troubridge mean the Admiralty?"

Nelson nodded. "And Fanny."

"Gossip and malicious lies!" I fumed. " 'Ow does someone in Messina or Naples know what was wagered on a single 'and—and by whom?" I lowered my voice. "Sir Willum is up to his arse in debt. Would I dare 'azard a fortune every night? And while you've staked me from time to time, I 'ave never borrowed more than a few quid. And if they knew that the real reason we stayed up into the wee hours at the gaming tables is because we can't spend the night in each other's embrace, their vicious tongues would really be set afire! We know the truth of the thing."

"Yes, we do. Yet I fear, Emma, that Troubridge is not without reason. Whilst the card parties continue, so will the rumors."

I could have gone on being defensive, flouting our detractors by continuing to flaunt our friendship. After all, we were being pegged as guilty, though we were in truth stainless. But I feared the ugly rumors would irreparably injure Sir William, destroying the respect he deserved as a distinguished gentleman and a servant of King George. "Well, then, the remedy is simple, ain't it? No more card parties at the Palazzo Palagonia." It was done that very night, something I was certain to share with Troubridge. But would it stop the wagging tongues of bored aristocrats? I had my doubts.

A few nights later, in the cavernous salon, now empty and still, I turned to Nelson. "Silent as a graveyard in 'ere, isn't it? I reckon we shall 'ave to find something else to do in the evenings."

Those were bold words, but we still did not take bold actions. And yet I could not help but think on Nelson's motto, "The boldest measures are the safest." For our sanity, perhaps, but for our hearts? Summer gradually segued into autumn, which metamorphosed into a mild winter. Both Nelson and I knew he would eventually be given a new commission, for the Mediterranean was now relatively peaceful and free of French warships. Although neither of us ever broached the subject, I daresay we each believed that Time was our ally, and in the leisurely, indolent climate of sunny, sultry Palermo, like the air, It seemed to move more slowly.

The days bled one into the other then, but I do recall a particularly upsetting morning in late December. "Well, it seems I am being asked to give an account of myself," Nelson said tightly. "George Elphinstone, now Lord Keith, has assumed St. Vincent's post as commander-in-chief of the Mediterranean fleet. St. Vincent was not the most courageous C-in-C, but he can make a decision in the heat of battle—however ill timed it might, on occasion, be—and he was a friend. Indeed, when I first heard the rumblings that he wished to return home, I urged him to stay on."

"You don't like Keith, then?"

Nelson gave me a sour look. "Lord Keith is one of those men who, rather than relying on experience and sound judgment, always checks with the Admiralty before doing a thing, no matter how impractical it is to wait for word from London. A man on active duty cannot look to a bunch of pencil pushers in Whitehall who barely remember the smell of bilgewater. We've had a dustup in the past. He refused my recommendation to promote Eshelby, the surgeon who amputated my arm in Tenerife. Damme, the memory still smarts! Eshelby saved my life so I could fight another day for king and country, and by not picking up the pen, Keith ruins the man's chances for advancement. And he's rather fierce when it comes to discipline—you know, fond of the lash. And petty: insists the men wear the queue rather than it being a matter of personal choice." He tugged on his own pigtail for emphasis.

"Well, 'e can't be miffed at *you* for your 'air. What, then?"

"I am being summoned to Leghorn to account for my actions in Naples this past summer—the Caracciolo business, the interrogations of the rebels on board the *Foudroyant*—and to explain what he perceives to be my current inactivity."

"Why, don't he know? The very presence of your fleet 'ere keeps the Frenchies at bay! All they need to do is 'ear the name of Nelson and they 'ave nightmares of the Nile! And isn't Leg'orn dangerous now? I won't let you go!" I dreaded he might succumb once more to the charms of Adelaide Correglia as much as I feared he might get blown to bits.

Nelson shook his head. "Leghorn is neutral territory. Anyway, as it's the Mediterranean headquarters for the Royal Navy, the Frenchies would be fools to attack it." Nelson reached across the breakfast table to stroke my hand. "And I must go. There isn't a question of my disobeying orders this time. Keith wants a full explanation of the Minorca business as well."

"What's to explain there? You was given contradictory orders. How was you expected to dispatch marines to Minorca when they was already fighting the republicans on the mainland and thrashing the rebels that was holding St. Elmo? A man can't be in two places at once, let alone three!" I was disgusted. "But since you've worked miracles before, I suppose the Admiralty wanted you to be a conjurer this time, too. They're punishing you like a schoolboy is what's 'appening. I can see it. The 'letters' Troubridge referred to 'ave reached Keith's 'ands as well. 'E mopes about like a jilted lover, y'nau? Troubridge, I mean. And 'e's trying to come between us."

"*That*, my dear, beautiful Emma, will never, never happen. No matter where I go. This I can promise you."

What happens when you are truly happy with everything in life, when finally, after a long and arduous climb, you have everything you want? You love deeply and are loved deeply in return; you have a talent for admiration that is returned to you tenfold. And then— when you have reached the pinnacle of happiness and can peer into the cup of it, filled near to overflowing—then, you meet the one who can be no other but your soul mate, and everything explodes in a riot of ecstasy?

Our eyes were wide open. We both knew what we were getting into. We had denied ourselves for so many months, both of us at war with our consciences, struggling mightily to resolve our mutual passion, desperate to neither injure nor shame our spouses. We always knew the pot that was on the simmer would eventually boil over—and when it did, our greatest desire and our greatest fear would both be realized.

Did Nelson lead me to his rooms then, or did I take him there, that first time? It's odd that I don't recall that detail. Even with the slight chill in the air, his bedroom, with the sash thrown up wide, smelled of cassia and cloves. We did not rush, expecting somehow to remain undisturbed by the servants and uninterrupted by Sir William.

The room was very light. We sank down on the settee and for the longest time gazed into each other's faces as if to etch an impression of them forever inside our souls. And then, almost as if Time were suspended momentarily, Nelson reached for me and drew me close until our lips met. We had waited so long to make love; every precious moment had to be savored. I buried my face in the scent of his skin, kissing, not only his lips and eyes and cheeks, but his neck and the hollow of his throat where his shirt was open to expose the tender flesh. Nelson caressed my shoulder, reaching to release it from my gown.

Gently, I pulled away from our embrace. "Let me 'elp you," I murmured, then stood up to untie my dress and stays. Slippers, hose, and linen followed.

Awestruck at the picture before him, Nelson whispered, "You are the most beautiful woman I have ever seen." He rose and came over to me, wrapping his arm about my waist.

"I do love my macaroni and champagne," I jested self-consciously. "You don't find me too fat?"

Kissing me passionately first, he replied, "I find you perfect."

I led him back to the settee, where I divested him of his shoes and hose. Kneeling before him, I began to unbutton his breeches. His hips were so slender, almost like a youth's. Removing his pants, I allowed my fingers to play upon his thighs and calves, and having disposed of the garment, I laid my head between his legs. I could feel him stiffen when his linen grazed my cheek.

"I am almost afraid to let you remove my shirt."

I smiled. "The only man in Europe not afraid of Bonaparte fears what I might think when I see two naked shoulders but only one bare arm?" He swallowed and looked away. "Then let's put an answer to't." Nelson raised his left arm and I lifted his shirt over his head. His nearly hairless chest was well made, though not muscular.

"Well?"

Tenderly, I kissed his "fin," then caressed it that I might learn every inch of the poor disfigured anatomy. "It is a sight I 'ave been waiting years to get my fill of."

"Come here," he murmured. Obligingly, I returned to the settee and nestled into the crook of his left arm. "Kiss me."

I loosened his queue with one hand while the other began to meander below his waist. "I am neither disgusted, nor am I dismayed, Nelson. I find you *magnificent*." Kneeling once again, I removed his linen. He grew hard at my slightest touch, and I brought my fingers and lips to him, enjoying the giving of the pleasure as much as I could tell he enjoyed the receiving of it.

At length he placed his hand upon my wrist, then tipped my chin to raise my head. "I need to feel your skin against mine. If I don't, I think I shall go mad."

The sheets were cool against my back. I was so hungry for Nelson that I had become a furnace. And finally, after so many months of torment, here we were. In the late-morning light, there was no disguising Time's hand upon our bodies and the price that each had paid for the pleasure of seeing so many days. Flaws and all, we came to each other, two worldly people of middle age, who saw nothing in one another but perfection.

Nelson wanted to touch, to kiss, to explore every part of me, from my eyelids to the backs of my knees. He wrapped a lock of my cascading hair around his hand and lingered at my breasts and belly, and then at the smooth, sugared flesh between my thighs. And I had lain with more than my share of men in the past to know that this experience, beyond my having waited so long for it, was something extraordinary. Physically, we were an unlikely pair: slender, almost-frail Nelson, and Emma, beginning to become Junoesque. And yet our mutually passionate natures, so blazing, so intense, such a perfect meeting of the minds and souls and hearts as we shared, could not help but translate into a combustible coupling in the boudoir. When his lips touched my sex for the first time, I thought my body would melt into his mouth and drown him. And when he eased himself on top of me and slipped inside, with the first thrust, I never wanted to be anywhere else in my life ever again; and then I feared to drown him with my tears, for never had I been so happy.

"Will they let you come back from Leg'orn?" I whispered fearfully as we lay together facing each other, unable to leave off caressing.

"God, I hope so. And I wouldn't leave you ever, but that I must. I own that I have been often made to feel the hero I always wanted to be, but never until now have I felt the most exquisite sensations that arise from loving fully and completely and being so fully loved in return. Heavens, Emma—*my Emma*—you would walk barefoot across the Sahara to bring me a cup of water if you knew I was thirsty."

I chuckled. "I would, too. Quite literally. No figger of speech."

Nelson stroked my hair and kissed a fistful of it. "I know you would."

"And I am 'your Emma,' too. I 'ave been for some time already; just we didn't say it. And I will be until my last breath." .

He smiled wryly. "Death or Glory."

"But I'd prefer to think on the second part of the credo, if that suits you."

"While we're under the same roof, I never want to spend another night without you in my . . ."

"*Arm*. It's all right. A one-armed Nelson as my lover is better than all the two-armed men in the rest of the world. We must try to be discreet, then. It's not only the servants as concern me. I never wish to injure Sir Willum. 'E's a man of the world. 'E may suspect that there 'as already been a tendresse between us for some time now, or 'e may simply acknowledge its possibility. In any event, 'e is not the kind of man to openly broach the subject with either of us, and if 'e does let on that 'e knows, or at least suspects something, 'e will do so with the utmost discretion and diplomacy. Leastways, 'e loves you near as much as 'e loves me. 'E won't call you out. But 'e don't deserve even the slightest hint of 'umiliation. I owe Sir Willum everything and 'e has never been anything but dear to me."

"And never have I been able to call a man a dearer friend. Not for the world would I injure him. And yet, we are *betraying* him, even if we can manage to keep our love a secret."

I sighed and let my fingers play upon his chest. "My conscience torments me. But we cannot undo what 'as passed between us, nor do either of us wish it 'ad never 'appened. I can just hear Mam saying, 'Be careful, gal. Wunst you get what you've been wishing for, it's easy to get cocky about it, y'nau?' She's a canny woman. She'll read it in our faces long before Sir Willum sees it." I rested on my elbows. "Don't go to Leg'orn. Send Keith a letter and tell 'im . . . tell 'im whatever it pleases you to write, but I fear this is all a ruse to get you to quit Palermo, and *me*. And once they've got you in Leg'orn, they'll send you packing for Portsmouth."

Nelson's brow was rutted with furrows. "I fear being sent home just as much. For there is someone there I do not wish to see and I would prefer never to have the conversation with her which I must, perforce, engage in."

"Fanny."

"Fanny."

"It will take you a few weeks to put everything in order before your departure. My dearest, dearest, dearest love, can we not at least pretend the days we have left to us are one grand 'oliday?"

Cupping my breast, he brought it to his lips. "It's like pudding," he teased, fondling the pale, firm flesh.

"Is that supposed to be a compliment?"

"*Um-hm*. I love pudding." He navigated his way along my collarbone and throat until he reached my mouth, tasting my lips as if for the first time. "Sweet, adorable Emma, your holiday suggestion is the finest idea I have ever heard in my life."

Thirty-three

Recalled!

*I*n early January, as Nelson prepared to report to Leghorn, Sir William was discovering England's displeasure with *him* through a significantly less direct route.

One morning he opened his mail packet and read in an issue of London's *Morning Chronicle* that his request for retirement had been granted by King George.

"But I haven't made any rumblings about retiring for years!" My husband was stunned, his face as pale as if he had been knifed in the chest. "And to heap further insult upon injury, my replacement is to be Arthur Paget, a pup so young I daresay he's scarcely out of skirts. Paget has but a single year in Bavaria by way of diplomatic credentials, and I'll lay a wager with anyone who cares to take it that he speaks neither French nor Italian. And to read about it in the papers! Presented with a fait accompli—in *print*, no less! Back in London they must be sniggering behind their snuffboxes and hands of whist."

" 'E will prove a disaster, then! The fatal Paget!" Poor Sir William looked monstrous glum. "My dear Sir Willum." I embraced him and held him in my arms for several moments. "They are punishing you for being a partisan in Neapolitan politics. When the queen 'ears about this, she'll bost a stay, I warrant you."

"Unless she can somehow turn back the hands of Time and

undo my own sovereign's order, I fear there is little to be done but prepare to go home," lamented Sir William, "for I do not wish to remain in either Naples or Palermo as a private citizen."

As my husband weighed his options with regard to his diplomatic career, my lover, who had sailed on January 16 for Leghorn, was tormented by our separation. I was no less sensible to the anxieties placed upon our mutually aching hearts. Our love had so lately reached a new and higher plateau, only to be painfully interrupted by Nelson's departure. The parting had been agonizing for both of us, and fraught with tears. "Duty, love," Nelson had reminded me, though his voice was cracking with emotion and he was hardly willing to wrest himself from our embrace.

"It's deliberate," I insisted. "I am sure that if Keith wished it, he could put his queries to you in writing and allow you to respond to them without leaving Palermo. The Admiralty are flexing their muscles, to show that they will always have more power over Nelson than Emma ever could."

But of course, he did have to leave my arms. And I lived for every word I would receive from him:

Wednesday, 29th Janry, 1800
Separated from all I hold dear in this world what is the use of living if indeed such an existence can be called so, nothing could alleviate such a seperation but the call of our Country, but loitering time away with <u>nonsense</u> is too much. No seperation, no time my only beloved Emma can alter my love and affection for you, it is founded on the truest principles of honor, and it only remains for us to regret which I do with the bitterest anguish that there are any obstacles to our being united in the closest ties of this worlds rigid rules, as we are in those of real love. Continue only to love your faithful Nelson as he loves his Emma. You are my guide, I submit to you, let me find all my fond heart hopes and wishes with the risk of my life. I have

been faithful to my word never to partake of amusemt: or to sleep on shore.

Thursday, Janry 30th: we have been six days from Leghorn and no prospect of our making a passage to Palermo, to me it is worse than death. I can neither eat or sleep for thinking of you my dearest love. I never even touch pudding you know the reason. No I would starve sooner. My only hope is to find that you have equally kept your promises to me, for I never made you a promise that I did not as strictly keep as if made in the presence of heaven, but I rest perfectly confident in the reality of your love and that you would die sooner than be false in the smallest thing to your own faithful Nelson who lives only for his Emma.

Friday: Last night I did nothing but dream of you altho' I woke 20 times in the night. In one of my dreams I thought I was at a large table you was not present, sitting between a Princess who I detest and another, they both tried to seduce me and the first wanted to take those liberties with me which no woman in this world but yourself ever did, the consequence was I knocked her down and in the moment of bustle you came in and taking me in your embrace wispered I love nothing but you my Nelson. I kissed you fervently and we enjoy'd the height of love. Ah Emma I pour out my soul to you. If you love any thing but me you love those who do not like your N.

Nelson returned to my eager arms a few days later, only to learn that, pursuant to Keith's orders, he was to sail for Malta on February 12.

On the eve of his departure we lay together for the entire night. Moonlight streamed through Nelson's bedroom window onto his back while I gazed into his eyes, enjoying the length of him deep inside me, memorizing the planes of his narrow face with my fingers and lips, from the bump on the bridge of his nose—imperceptible unless you touched it—to the gentle bow of his upper lip and the soft swell of his fuller lower one. We made love well into the wee hours of the morning, giving and taking pleasure in every kiss and caress. When a lark heralded the dawn Nelson and I were still nestled together, and I could feel him grow hard against the hollow of my back as his hand cupped my breast. "Nelson," I breathed, "are you awake?"

"I've been awake all night. Are you all right?"

We spoke in hushed whispers. "I suppose so. You?"

"I am now. I won't be in a few hours when I have to leave you."

"Nelson . . . ? Let's 'ave a child. I want to 'ave your baby."

His cry of joy startled the bird on the sill, which flew away in haste. "You do? Really? Emma, my beloved, darling Emma, I never dreamed you might. I cannot imagine a greater blessing than to be the father of my Emma's child." He rolled on top of me, balancing himself against the mattress with his hand. "I leave at eight," Nelson added as I helped to ease him inside me. Our bodies melted together, and a mischievous smile played across his lips. "We have no time to waste."

Mr. Tyson, Nelson's secretary, corresponded with me regarding naval affairs and the state of Nelson's health, for I was anxiously inquiring after it in my every dispatch. In March, I received an alarming letter from him. Nelson had "dropped with a pain in his heart and was always with a fever." Oh, that I could commandeer a boat and sail out to find him! I could not rest until I knew he was out of danger. After consulting with Mam as to the surest remedy for such an attack of the heart, I wrote to Tyson by the next dispatch. "Hot stupes," I told him. "Soak rags in boiling water and turpentine and apply them to his chest. My mother also advises you to rub his chest with packs of baked salt, and dose him with opium. And for God's sake, write by the next post to tell me how he is!"

While my heart was utterly filled with Nelson, Nelson, Nelson, my hands were filled with Sir William. Though Paget was now in Palermo, my husband—maintaining his promise not to remain in the Two Sicilies as a private individual—refused to relinquish his diplomatic credentials until such time as we were ready to depart for England. Nelson had promised to bring us home, and at present he was somewhere in the Adriatic.

A livid little Paget blamed me for the queen's reluctance to entertain his requests for a meeting with herself and King Ferdinand. I was fiercely loyal to Sir William, believing he'd been horridly wronged by his king and country—embodied by the inexperienced pup who stood before me, puffing up his importance.

"You are not the ambassador yet. What call 'as 'Er Majesty to greet a tourist?"

The fatal Paget grew florid. "You are poisoning the Neapolitans' minds against me! How will I ever be able to get anything accomplished at my post?"

I smiled as wide as a Nile crocodile. "I 'ave no idea, my dear sir. I will not be around to see it."

On April 17, 1800, Sir William formally returned his credentials to Their Sicilian Majesties. I felt as though I were attending a funeral. He had received those credentials on August 31, 1764, and had arrived in Naples on November 17 of that year, taking up his post before the Honorable Arthur Paget was even born.

As a parting honor to Nelson, the king established the Order of St. Ferdinand and Merit, proclaiming him the first knight of the order. Nelson was now beribboned all over, with three stars on his jacket and three medals about his neck, as well as the Turks' diamond *chelenkh*, which he wore on his hat.

A few days later, with heavy hearts, we loaded all of our possessions, our wardrobes, and our hopes onto the *Foudroyant*. The anchor was raised and Sir William and I bade a tearful farewell to a life, and a place, the likes of which we would never know again.

Joining us were Mam, of course, and Miss Knight, who had resided with us at the Palazzo Palagonia, though, being a scribbler, she most often kept to herself. Her mother's long illness had finally carried her off the year before. Maria Carolina, several of her children, and an entire retinue of nursemaids and ladies-in-waiting accompanied us as well. The queen had finally concluded that she would never regain the Neapolitan throne, and wished to return to Austria with her children, there to remain in the bosom of her large family. She and Ferdinand, who had recently begun to assert himself as a sovereign, no longer saw eye to eye on the political future of the Two Sicilies. They quarreled constantly, and I believe the queen was ready to acknowledge that their marriage was as doomed as their thrones. She requested Nelson to take her party as far as Leghorn, from whence they would travel overland to Vienna.

We celebrated my thirty-fifth birthday on board Nelson's flagship. Knowing how low my spirits had sunk, Nelson insisted that his officers and crew throw me the grandest gala possible. Miss Knight rewrote the lyric to an old chestnut and presented me with it, having spent the entire afternoon teaching Nelson's crew to sing it. One of the men grabbed his accordion and played a hornpipe, and I linked elbows with Nelson's left arm and Sir William's right one and together we danced until our legs gave out and our sides were bosting from merriment.

I wanted to make love with Nelson on my birthday, but the utmost prudence was necessary. Because of the watches, there were always men awake and alert for the slightest departure from the normal course of duty. Sir William and I shared a cabin and he was not a sound sleeper. The planks creaked. Were Nelson and I fooling ourselves into believing that no one knew we were shipboard lovers? Or perhaps, because we also believed we were the souls of discretion, everyone turned a blind eye.

He always left his sleeping cabin unlocked for me. And how he managed to redeploy the marine assigned to stand guard outside his quarters was beyond my ken. That night, barefoot, I padded through his great cabin in my nightshirt and tiptoed into the room, parting the silken hangings about his bed. A single candle guttered on the small table. Nelson was already awake, as breathless with anticipation as I. He held out his hand to me and I climbed in beside him, trying not to laugh in amazement at the way we both managed to squeeze into the narrow suspended berth. But all romantics know that passion and true love are never daunted by something as pedestrian as logistics. "Happy birthday," he whispered as our bodies met. "Happy birthday to the wife of my heart."

Upon our departure from Palermo, Nelson proposed a cruise to Syracuse before we made for England. Two days after my birthday, we anchored there, spending another two days visiting the city and its environs. Sir William was quite excited to tour the many ancient ruins. Nelson was eager to visit Bronte, for he had never seen his own dukedom.

We were all extremely surprised by the inhospitality of the estate's terrain. Much of it was more rocky than verdant; we had expected the volcanic soil to be more conducive to farming. Nor was the dukedom terribly majestic. In fact, it reminded me more of Hawarden, with its ramshackle stone farmhouse and long, low outbuildings standing gloomily amid the vineyards. On closer inspection, the farmhouse was abandoned and the furniture inside it broken and moldy. I was unhappy for Nelson's sake that his royal demesne was neither grand nor noble. He deserved far better. This Bronte was more of an insult than an accolade.

"Well, at least the chestnut groves are lovely," Nelson sighed. But he was dismayed at the state of the tenants' welfare. They lived in near-abject poverty, prompting him to declare that any income from the estate be put right back into it, in the form of agricultural improvements and social amenities. "I daresay His Sicilian Majesty did not give me much of a gift after all," he muttered, "but at least I can try to provide my tenants with a proper living." Setting about this aim with alacrity, he engaged as a steward Sir William's old friend John Graefer, who had been one of the landscape designers of the English Gardens at Caserta.

On May 4, the *Foudroyant* anchored in St. Paul's Bay, in Malta. Czar Paul of Russia was now the Grand Master of the Order of Malta, because he had offered the order's knights sanctuary in his own country after the French had confiscated their property. In order for one to be made a Knight of Malta, one had to prove noble lineage going back for five successive generations, on *both sides* of one's family. However, the czar bestowed the Maltese Cross upon Sir Alexander Ball, the island's governor, on Nelson, and upon me, as a gesture of thanks for an act of mercy and political expedience. Earlier in the year, as an "ambassador without portfolio," I had been instrumental in getting shiploads of corn delivered to the starving Maltese.

What an astounding honor! What would my dear gammer, now with the angels in heaven, think of her wild little Emy now? The grubby child who had stood by the Chester Road with a lump of coal in her besmirched hands now cradled a Maltese Cross, the first Englishwoman ever to be made a Dame of the Order of the Cross of Malta! It thrilled me to write to the College of Arms in London, for they had to record all enrollments in the order. My honor entitled me to commission the design of an escutcheon. I was to have my very own coat of arms! I could have danced on air.

On the return journey from Malta to Palermo, though the seas were relatively calm, I felt dreadfully unwell. Nelson, despairing for my health, commanded every officer and member of his crew to tiptoe about the decks and rigging. "Not a sound should disturb Lady Hamilton," he warned them, "or I may be compelled to consider the lash." To complain of seasickness now, when I had proved myself such an excellent and indefatigable sailor during the tempest that had blown us from Naples to Palermo, was to betray my condition. But what could I do? Before the officers and crew of the *Foudroyant*, I put it down to influenza—and anxiety that we should be returning to an uncertain future in England after so many years abroad. The latter was, in fact, true.

Nelson was anxious as well about returning to England. The man who had first found Naples to be a country of fiddlers, poets, scoundrels, and whores now could scarcely bring himself to quit the land of apples and music and golden sunshine, particularly for one of fog and gray . . . and Fanny.

We had news from London that did nothing to allay our collective trepidation. The outspoken Whig leader Charles James Fox had denounced Nelson in the House of Commons for alleged atrocities and executions carried out in the Bay of Naples during the summer of 1799. Although the hero of the Nile was still the hero of John Bull, he was losing ground among the members of the upper classes, who had also caught wind of the gossip about Nelson's insubordination in the face of Lord Keith, and his conduct in Palermo, particularly as it involved Lady Hamilton.

On the eighth of June, following a week of preparations, Nelson gave the order to weigh anchor, and we set sail for England. I suddenly remembered the inscription on the wall of Sir William's study in the Palazzo Sessa. He had pointed it out to me the day I arrived in Naples, fourteen years earlier. *La mia patria è dove mi trovo bene*; "My homeland is where I feel at home." My eyes welled with tears and I swallowed hard to fight the catch in my throat, having acknowledged in that moment that I wasn't headed for my homeland; I was leaving it.

Thirty-four

The Toasts of the Continent

In Leghorn, I prepared myself to say farewell to the queen. As a grown woman I had never been closer or more important to any other woman, save Mam, and I knew I should miss her dreadfully. After all, we saw each other several times a day for years and had guarded one another's deepest confidences. I felt especially vulnerable and emotional, for by then I was certain I was carrying Nelson's child. Our fondest wish had come true. I was deliriously happy about it, though I regretted being able to share this ecstasy with him alone. Mam, of course, had figured it out even before I did.

"I've been through this with you before, y'nau," she'd reminded me. "Don't worry, gal. I won't breathe a word of it to either of 'em: Sir Willum or the little admiral."

My fragile sensibilities, which swelled and dipped like the sea, had been in large measure responsible for my decision to lop off all my hair, for so many years my crowning glory. It was too difficult to keep clean on shipboard, its density and length suddenly made me feel too hot all the time, and I suppose with so many endings occurring all at once, chopping off my auburn tresses became just another one of them. I feared that Nelson would despise my looks now that I was shorn of several feet of hair, especially since he had so admired it. Perhaps it had all been a dreadful mistake to cut it—

what had I been thinking? I felt heavy and hideous. But the dear man soothed my trepidation, assuring me that he found me just as beautiful and as magnificent as ever.

We were all still aboard the *Foudroyant* on June 19, when Nelson and I received word of the Austrian defeat at the Battle of Marengo five days earlier. The queen feared to disembark, and rightly, Nelson refused to put her and her party ashore when Boney was on the march.

Lord Keith had something to say about the situation, however. He commanded Nelson to dispatch all of his ships to Genoa to reinforce the British fleet stationed there, and to relinquish command of the *Foudroyant*, which needed to be sent to Minorca to be refitted. My lover had no choice but to obey. He moved his flag to the *Alexander*, yet refused to send that ship to Genoa along with his others. Keith became apoplectic.

"He told me in no uncertain terms, 'Lady Hamilton has ruled the fleet long enough.' I wished to tell *him* to damn himself to hell," Nelson confided.

Learning that the *Foudroyant* was no longer to continue on to England, and fearful of the political climate in northern Italy and Austria, the queen asked that the eighty-gunner take her back to Sicily, where she would bide her time in relative safety. She and I employed all our feminine wiles to convince Keith to grant her request. He refused, stating that the Royal Navy was not to be abused by foreign monarchs, nor its vessels to be treated as private passenger ships. Keith suggested that Maria Carolina make haste for Vienna overland or else avail herself of a Neapolitan vessel. This time, *she* refused. Nelson sulked, Sir William fretted, my every changing emotion was worn on my sleeve, and Mam had her hands full with all of us.

Sir William's last collections of virtu were moved from the *Alexander* to the *Serapis*, which was bound for England. We all remained in Leghorn, though by now we had quit Nelson's ships.

But a few weeks later, we learnt that the republican army had marched into the nearby village of Lucca. Fearing they might become Boney's next target, an armed mob of Livornese imprisoned Maria Carolina in the Governor's Palace, vowing to keep her there until Nelson provided his personal guarantee to help them defend themselves against the French.

The queen was beside herself with anguish. "I don't know what to do, miledi. What do these people want from me? Have I not suffered enough? All I want to do is take my children home to Austria where it is safe. Tell me, what shall I do?"

"You don't fret, ma'am. I will speak to 'em and set 'em straight." I stepped out onto the balcony of the governor's residence and raised up my hands to quiet the people. "Lay down your arms," I demanded. "It is unwise for you to 'old 'Er Sicilian Majesty for ransom, as Nelson will not treat with criminals. Return your weapons to the arsenal immediately, and then 'e will consider your situation."

No one was more astonished than I that the Livornese listened to me! The thing was done, to our immense relief. The next morning at first light, the queen departed for Florence. Our little quintet—Nelson, Sir William, Mam, Miss Knight, and I—followed her route, departing in two carriages the day after, on July 17.

Our overland journey took us from town to tiny town. We endured flea-ridden mattresses in filthy posting inns, sweltering heat, and Boney within striking distance of us at every stop, until at last we gained Vienna on the eighteenth of August. But in short order we discovered that the mood among some of the people there was not entirely an elated one. Although the Viennese had, ever since the Nile victory, sported elegant black capes that they called "Nelsons," and silly bonnets that looked like crocodile snouts, vicious gossip such as Troubridge had alluded to had somehow traveled north. Not everyone was kind to us.

"Pray, sir, have you heard of the Battle of the Nile?" Nelson demanded to a particularly discourteous dinner companion one night. "That, sir, was the most extraordinary one that was ever fought, and it is *unique*, sir, for three reasons: first, for its having been fought at night; second, for its having been fought at anchor; and thirdly, for its having been gained by an admiral with one arm."

We gritted our teeth and jutted our chins and braved the occasional chilliness, for there were indeed many who were happy to meet us. Thirteen nights in succession we attended the theatre, because each one of the playhouses wanted to offer a performance in Nelson's honor and he did not wish to offend any of the proprietors. There were dances and galas galore, all for us, with never fewer than seventy guests in attendance. *They* could not get enough of Nelson, the only man in Europe to have inflicted serious damage on the Corsican menace. Trumpets blared and cannons roared throughout the city as glasses were raised in toasts to his health and success.

As had been the case in Bath when Sir William and I visited there just before our wedding, I became a fashion plate. Many Viennese women were keen to copy my ensembles: my Nelson caps (which did not resemble crocodiles) and my neoclassical gowns such as those I had donned for years when I performed my Attitudes. The truth was that these loose-fitting frocks were worn with only the lightest of stays beneath them—and because the gowns could be easily adjusted through the torso, they suited my burgeoning form.

My sweet tooth was well satisfied, for the Viennese puddings were exceptional, and they had a penchant for topping everything, including coffee, with a generous helping of vanilla-flavored whipped cream. As my changing figure began to reveal my secret, the only way to disguise it was with prodigious gourmandizing so that people would think my increasing embonpoint was due to a surfeit of fine food and copious drink.

At Eisenstadt, the country estate of the Prince and Princess of Esterhazy, we were introduced to Haydn, the court composer. It was a glittering soiree, where one was free to move about from room to room, like at the Neapolitan conversazioni, enjoying the music in one room and a hand of cards in another. We were treated to a performance of Haydn's "Nelson Mass," a most glowing tribute to the hero of the Nile. I wish'd at once to learn the soprano's part, for I found it most beguiling.

I was as impressed with Haydn's talent as he was with mine. The great maestro accompanied me on one or two lieder and a bit of *Nina*. Haydn, whom everyone affectionately called "Papa," then composed a number of songs for me, including "The Spirit's Song," which he bestowed upon me at Eisenstadt on September 9, 1800. What an honor! What a gift! I still cherish the autographed original of the sheet music, inscribed to me by Papa.

"My husband says you put him in mind of Dido and Calypso," Princess Esterhazy told me. "And I must compliment you on your German. It is quite good for an Englishwoman. In fact, had I not known, I would have taken you immediately for a Viennese!"

Vienna's old-world ambience had by and large remained untouched and untainted by Jacobinism. Elaborately dressed powdered wigs and voluminous brocaded dresses with wide-caged underpinnings *à l'ancien régime* were still the fashion. Men still carried diamond-hilted swords at their hips. Life for the upper classes was a bit like living inside a candy box. Everything was mirrored or gilded, or both. At night, the thousands of perfumed wax candles were reflected tenfold. Maria Carolina, being a Hapsburg herself, settled into the atmosphere with ease. Her imperial manner restored, all her fears for her own kingdom seemed to evanesce.

I had a harder time of it. My natural ebullience and vitality (even now when I was more than four months pregnant) had been well suited to the raucous and flamboyant Neapolitan court, but the Hapsburgs were different. Austria was extravagant, to be sure, but its rarefied atmosphere was one of fine and subtle decadence, far closer to what I had so briefly glimpsed in Paris than to the ambience of Naples and Palermo.

As our party was to continue on to Dresden, it was in Vienna that Maria Carolina and I ended up exchanging our final farewells. "I shall always cherish our friendship, miledi. The name of Lady Hamilton will be on my lips and in my grateful thoughts as a dear friend and a munificent woman. And most assuredly, my loyal countrymen and -women shall long remember your service to the crown, for you are too great a lady to be forgotten." As a token of her esteem, she offered me an annual pension of one thousand pounds, but on Sir William's advice not to take money from a foreign monarch, I refused to accept it. In its stead, she gave me a letter in her own hand, recommending me to the Queen of England, with the unspoken hope that it would help me gain acceptance at the Court of St. James.

I tried not to weep, but I could not help myself, remembering her many kindnesses, most especially her encouragement of Sir William's wish to marry me. "Your Majesty, you 'ave already given me the greatest gifts a woman can receive: respect and respectability, for without them I should never have *been* Lady 'Amilton."

Having just departed from a queen who esteemed me so greatly, I was ill prepared for our reception in Dresden in early October.

The only good to come of our time in that dreary city was that Johann Schmidt rendered Nelson and me in pastels. Schmidt's portrait of me immediately became one of Nelson's favorites. It is the only depiction of me with my hair chopped off—and rare enough for that alone—and it is the sole portrait done whilst I was pregnant. I have always thought of this image of me, clad all in white save for my Maltese Order, as being titled *Emma Carrying Nelson's Deepest and Most Wish'd-for Secret.*

We spent our time at Dresden in the company of Sir Hugh Elliot, His Britannic Majesty's envoy there. Sir Hugh and his thin-lipped biddy of a wife lacked all sense of mirth and merriment, and were quite put out of sorts by all our laughter, our fondness for parties and entertainment, and our appetite for music and champagne. At a dinner the Elliots hosted in our honor, they were shocked silly when Sir William, Nelson, and I behaved just as we had done in Palermo, with ribald jokes and boisterous laughter, as I sang and clapped, and Sir William, all of seventy years old, demonstrated his vigor—after numerous glasses of champagne— by hopping about the room on his back, alternately flailing his arms and kicking up his heels, with his Order of the Bath flying about his neck.

Lady Elliot and her houseguest Melesina St. George Trench gossiped about me behind their fans. I was fat; I was coarse; I was uncouth. Their sniggering wounded me to the quick. But I shut their gobs when I performed my Attitudes for 'em. In those days I would wear a high-necked, long-sleeved calico frock instead of a diaphanous gown; nevertheless, I portrayed the characters with a depth of interpretation that they, by the looks on their awestruck faces, had never imagined me capable of. Sir William, as always, was both moved and charmed beyond all measure. "Mrs. Siddons be damned!" he cried out. "My wife is the best actress in Europe!"

The next day, we wished to be presented to the Saxon elector, and decked ourselves in gallant trim against the occasion. We had already called for our carriage when Sir Hugh appeared to explain that there must have been some mistake, for there was to be no court during our stay in Dresden.

"*Indeed* there must be some mistake, for that is not what we have heard," replied Sir William smoothly.

Sir Hugh drew my husband aside. There was much muttering and glancing in my direction, with the words "electress" and "former" and "dissolute" popping out of the conversation.

"Lady Hamilton, I misspoke. What I should have said was that the Dresden court is known throughout Europe to be deadly dull, and the presentation to the elector and electress would have been nothing but a quick bow and curtsy. Nothing to see, nothing to do, no banquets . . ."

"What, no guttling?!" I exclaimed, for when my hackles was up, I tended to become as vulgar as they all thought I was anyway.

"The truth of the matter is," an uncomfortable Elliot told us, "that the electress will not welcome Lady Hamilton at court, on account of her former dissolute life."

I exploded. "Former! *Former!*"

Nelson got his back up as well. "Sir, if there's any difficulty of that sort, Lady Hamilton will knock the elector down, and damme, I'll knock him down, too!"

Thus ended (without my knocking anyone down) our Grand European Tour. Nelson and I had tried at every step to take our time in getting back to England, for neither of us was sure what would happen once we reached Albion's shores, other than knowing in our hearts that we never wanted to be parted from each other.

On October 31, 1800, we boarded the *King George* mail packet bound from Hamburg for England, but en route to the pier, Nelson insisted on stopping the carriage at a mantua-maker's. "I shan't be but a minute," he assured us. True to his word, he emerged from the shop barely sixty seconds later, bearing a small parcel wrapped in brown paper. "Some lace for Fanny," he said sheepishly. "She would think ill of me if I came back from three years in Europe empty-handed."

Circe

1800–1805

Thirty-five

A Hero's Welcome

"Land ho!"

November 5, 1800. A cry went up. The eastern coast of England had been sighted. I asked the man on the watch if I might borrow his spyglass to glimpse it for myself and he readily obliged me. It had taken us five months from the day we departed Palermo to reach this point. I was now a little more than six months with child and had prepared myself against the day of our arrival home with an ensemble stitched especially for the hero's welcome: a white muslin gown that bore on its hem the words *Bronte* and *Nelson* embroidered in pendants suspended from anchors, with a crown atop each anchor, all joined with a repeating garland border of oak leaves (the symbol for true friendship), worked in gold thread and sequins.

The sleepy port of Great Yarmouth bustled awake when we stepped off the ship the following morning. It looked as though the entire town had turned out to greet us in their Sunday best. Huzzahs echoed off every facade, and a clatter arose when our horses were unhitched from the carriage and replaced by a number of strapping residents, who drew the coach all the way to the center of town, depositing us with a thump at our destination, the Wrestler's Arms. We could scarce get inside the inn, for everyone had their hands and arms outstretched trying to touch Nelson as though he were a sacred relic. Their cheers and cries filled the streets. "Speech, Speech!" the voices cried as one. "Nelson! Nelson!"

When their hero bowed to *them*, they went wilder still. Medals were struck immediately to commemorate Nelson's return. At a local church, we attended a thanksgiving service and the organist struck up "See, the Conquering Hero Comes." In the evening, celebratory bonfires were lit in the streets and we were serenaded by citizens singing patriotic songs under our windows.

"Just imagine the reception we'll get in London!" I exclaimed.

"There is a large part of me that would gladly trade it all to remain here," Nelson replied. The agitated movement of his stump betrayed his inner turmoil. "For though I am elated to have won the people's hearts, there is one among them I wish to avoid. Emma—my beloved Emma," he murmured, bringing his lips to my swollen belly, "every ounce of glittering tin on my chest is nothing to our love. All the glory I have gained is best enjoyed when you are at my side."

Fully aware that rumors had reached her ears, I, too, was anxious about meeting Lady Nelson. And our triumphal procession into London was beset with bad omens. With Nelson in full regalia, we entered the city on November 9, in the midst of the most freakish storm in living memory, our horses dodging hailstones half the size of my fist. Tiles blew off the facades in Fleet Street, flowerpots tumbled to the street from Grosvenor Square windowsills, roofs were ripped off of churches with no thought spared for the worshipping congregations gathered beneath 'em, and the north windows of the foundling hospital were blown clear in. Parapets crumbled and people were knocked into one another like Punch and Judy puppets. Our team reared up in fear as our driver struggled to control the reins.

The storm lasted but twenty minutes, yet left marked devastation in its wake. Nelson and I were more shaken than the others, for once the carriage pulled up in King Street, we knew not what would happen once we set foot inside Nerot's Hotel.

They were waiting for us in the quietly furnished public parlor: a slim, plain woman—looking like a matron with a fear of colds, in a simple high-waisted, high-necked gown, with a white bonnet tied in a tight bow beneath her chin—and an older gentleman who somewhat resembled Nelson, dressed in the manner of a clergyman. The chill in the air was not warmed by our reception. The gentleman rose and extended his arms in greeting. "Horace!"

"Father." Nelson entered his embrace rather stiffly. "I trust you are well." The woman with the small, gray eyes remained seated, taking in the scene as though she was holding her breath.

"We expected you three days ago, Horace. In fact, we expected you to come straight to Suffolk—to Roundwood. Fanny and I had the house scrubbed top to bottom and planned a festive dinner against your arrival. But of course"—the man glanced at Sir William and me—"you evidently had other plans in mind."

"Father, allow me to name Sir William Hamilton; his wife, Lady Hamilton; her mother, Mrs. Cadogan; and Miss Cornelia Knight." Having gestured toward each of us, he added awkwardly, "My father, the Reverend Edmund Nelson . . . of Norfolk. And my wife, Lady Nelson."

"I am sorry we did not have better weather to welcome your arrival," she murmured. Where were her soft, if not ebullient, words of congratulations for her husband, the nation's greatest hero? Where were her expressions of admiration for his great deeds? Had my beloved been away at sea for upward of three years—nay, but three hours—I should not have greeted him by discussing the climate! I should have flung my arms about his dear neck and covered him with kisses!

"Why are you sorry, Fanny? 'Twasn't as though you could have done anything about the weather. Tell me, how is your cold?"

"I am in tolerable good health. Under the circumstances." Her remark, being cryptic, left me to wonder whether she referred to the sudden hailstorm or to my presence.

"Oh, I mustn't forget!" exclaimed Nelson, removing the parcel of lace from his coat pocket. "A gift for you from the Continent. Perhaps it can dress up a gown or a bonnet, or whatever it is you women do to decorate yourselves."

There was not an ounce of trim on Fanny's pearl gray gown. She opened the package as she simultaneously surveyed my hem, with Nelson's name and title embroidered upon it. Her voice was pinched. "Thank you, husband. I am sure that I shall put this to excellent use." To strangle me with it, perhaps.

"Come, Horace. Our rooms are ready upstairs. Have been for more than a day, I daresay."

"Our good father is right," said Fanny. "Time to bid a good day to the Hamiltons and their . . . retinue."

"We will dine with the Hamiltons this evening," Nelson replied, his tone brooking no dissent. With little choice but compliance, Fanny emitted a disobliging little snort. Nelson bowed to us. "Until five, then. We shall sup in our rooms."

Sir William's cousin William Beckford graciously allowed us the use of his town house in Grosvenor Square until we might find a residence of our own, but within a day of our arrival, Miss Knight received a letter and, after perusing its contents, packed her trunks and bolted. I had a powerful feeling that it warned her of associating too closely with the tainted reputations of the *tria juncta in uno*. I sent word of her sudden departure to Nelson at Nerot's.

> *Altho she is clever & learned, she is dirty, illbred, ungrateful, bad mannered, false, and deceitful. But my Heart takes a noble vengeance. I forgive her.*

Nelson was less charitable. *What a b— that Miss Knight is!* came the swift reply.

That day, Nelson paid his official call to the Admiralty, lecturing them on his strategy to defend the Channel coast, should Napoleon attempt to invade by that route. The following night, we received an enthusiastic reception at the lord mayor's banquet, where Nelson was presented with the sword of honor. Fanny was conspicuous by her absence, but Nelson, accepting the accolades and approbation of his peers, was in his element.

Sir William accompanied Nelson the next day to King George's levee.

"Well, 'ow did it go?" I inquired excitedly upon his return to Grosvenor Square, certain of another triumph.

"Rumped!" he exclaimed. "The greatest man England has ever produced and His Majesty rumps him!"

"I don't understand, Sir Willum? What 'appened at Windsor?"

"There Nelson stood, with all his medallions and orders about his neck, and the stars on his chest, the sultan's *chelenkh* in his hat, and the king approaches him. Naturally, Nelson and I expected some effusion, some 'Saved our necks from the frogeaters, eh, wot-wot?' His Majesty goes to greet him, Nelson bows, and all Farmer George can find to say is, 'Have you recovered your health, sir?' And Nelson replies that he is quite well, thank you very much, Your Majesty, and begins to mention the contributions to the Crown of the absent Lady Hamilton, whereupon the king turns his back on him to converse with some decorated redcoat about military strategy! Rumped him right in the middle of the room, for all to witness! The snub could not have been more pointed, my dear. And to heap insult upon injury, the king's third son, the Duke of Clarence, who Nelson served with years ago in the West Indies, comes up to him, huffing and puffing in that Hanoverian way, and says, 'Nelson, my man! Allow me to be the first to shake your

hand!' whereupon he goes straight for the hero's right arm, only to
be tripped up by an empty sleeve. I tell you, we were mortified and
could not leave soon enough. Nelson's in a black mood if ever I saw
it, and not least of which, my dear, is because he was unable to raise
the issue of your being presented at court."

I was angered, wishing I had been there just so I could whap
the king as I had threatened to sock the Saxon elector. "You poor,
poor Sir Willum. How dare the king treat 'is most noble subjects
so rudely?"

Sir William sighed. "*Because* he is the king, my love."

It was an inauspicious opening to a new chapter in all our lives.
As the days progressed, I was shocked to discover that the warm reception we had received from the masses was in direct contrast
with the greeting we received from many of the People Who Mattered. The ladies who had visited us in Naples would call upon me,
but none of the other English noblewomen would pay a call or
leave their cards with our servants. At the dinner parties and the
theatrical performances that we attended with the Nelsons, there
was as much sniggering behind fans and remarks upon my girth
(particularly vis-à-vis Sir William's increasing gauntness) as there
were huzzahs. Hypocrites they were, in the worst way, for the *haute
ton* thought nothing of hopping from bed to bed, forsaking their
marriage vows and taking lovers and mistresses with impunity. The
love that Nelson and I bore for each other was no different from
that of Lord Sandwich, who, while First Lord of the Admiralty, enjoyed a lengthy amorous liaison with the singer Martha Reay. But
I was not only lowborn, with an unfortunate past; Nelson was their
god, the greatest national hero since King Arthur. Our mutual admiration, so honest in its openness, was considered by them to be
the height of indiscretion. That these two-faced toadies should
consider us pariahs galled me to distraction, and often to tears, for
at times I found it very difficult to put a brave face on it.

Soon after our arrival in London, the four of us spent an

evening at the opera, joined by Captain Hardy, and the Reverend Edmund Nelson. In the front row of the box sat Nelson, with Fanny to his left and me on his right. Fanny had not wished to attend at all, and had argued bitterly with Nelson about it, but Nelson insisted that she could not be rude to his two dearest, closest friends in all the world, and to insult us was to insult him, adding, "It will not be tolerated, madam."

Perhaps in an effort to assert her much-celebrated dignity and her position as Lady Nelson, Fanny looked more elegant than I had ever seen her, gowned in white, with a violet-colored headdress. Before the curtain was rung open, the orchestra struck up "Rule Britannia," the song I had claimed for my own ever since Nelson's brilliant victory at the Nile. I rose to my feet and sang out as if I were Britannia herself. To my immense delight, the ovation for Nelson lasted longer and was louder than anyone could remember and it was many, many minutes before the opera could begin.

But if Fanny had not already guessed my secret, I surmised that she had an inkling of it when I fainted during the fourth act. Afterward I put it down to the excitement and the stifling heat inside the theatre, but there was no disguising her husband's immediate reaction to my swoon, for he was panicked and concerned and tender all at once.

As we quit the opera house, Nelson and Fanny began to quarrel. "How could you have ignored dear Lady Hamilton's distress, Fanny? Where is your womanly feeling, your compassion?" Nelson asked his wife angrily. "Dear Lady Hamilton has been nothing but good to me. I'faith, she is to be credited with saving me from the fever when I came back to Naples after the Nile victory. Had it not been for her tender ministrations, I daresay I might not be here to discuss it."

"I am tired of hearing about that woman!" cried Fanny. "I will not stand for such ill use. Chuse, Horace. Chuse between your *dear*

Lady Hamilton and myself, for I will have all your heart or none of it!"

"You already have my answer, madam," Nelson replied stiffly.

I felt poorly that he should be so cross with Fanny, for too well I knew what it was to suddenly lose the man you thought was the center of your world. Uppark Harry had ignored me entirely, and Greville's perfunctory replies to my desperate entreaties were near as curt as Nelson's. To her credit, Fanny was in fact more dignified than I had ever been about the whole business when I was in her shoes. So, for a brief time, I tried to befriend her—if not to make her a bosom companion, at least to turn incivility into acquaintance. I could never part with Nelson's heart now, but I cannot say I accorded her too much blame. Fanny was a genuinely scorned woman and behaved as such at every possible opportunity, her famous self-control slipping away by the day.

We frequently dined *en famille* with the Nelsons in their modest apartments in Dover Street as well as out in company, much to Fanny's continual mortification. One such dinner is indelibly printed upon my memory. The four of us had been asked to sup at Admiralty House with Lord and Lady Spencer. I had been terribly unwell all day, yet never would I have missed that most prestigious invitation.

A bowl of walnuts was served with the puddings and Nelson was having difficulty cracking open the nuts with his left hand. "Here, allow me, Horace," Fanny said attentively, taking the morsel from his hand. With maternal solicitude, she began opening the walnuts for her husband, placing them before him on his plate.

"Damme, woman!" Nelson exploded tetchily, "I am no suckling infant that needs to be coddled!" He tossed the plate like a discus, smashing it to bits against the damasked wall and sending walnuts flying about the eating room.

Fanny burst into tears. "Whatever have I done to upset or disappoint you, Horace?" she asked him. "Have I ever given you cause to be dissatisfied with me as a wife?"

Lady Spencer quickly dismissed the servants from the room.

"Love, madam, is, I believe, an integral ingredient for the recipe that is a happy marriage."

"You did love me once. Or made me believe so. I still have the letters you wrote to me after you left Nevis."

"At the time, I had naturally never entertained the possibility that our bed could grow so cold, given the warm climate in which you had lived for so many years. Madam, you made me feel like an outcast onshore."

Sir William and the Spencers were shocked that they should quarrel so frankly before us, referring in particular to Fanny's long-standing distaste for sexual congress. But Nelson had a temper, and his soul had been tormented with guilt since our arrival in England. He had been horribly out of love with his wife for some time and wished to extract himself from their marriage as quickly as possible, even if the parliamentary procedure involved in the getting of a divorce rendered that event a near impossibility.

A few moments later, I found it necessary to excuse myself from the eating room, availing myself of a basin I found in a commode just off the boudoir. I could not disguise my retching, and soon found myself in the company of Sir William and the Nelsons, the Spencers having wisely elected to maintain a discreet distance.

"My dear Lady Hamilton, pray, what can I do to alleviate your discomfort?" Nelson, ever solicitous toward me, glared at his wife. "Fanny, ask Lady Spencer to see that a cup of chamomile tea is prepared for her ladyship."

Fanny could scarce swallow her humiliation, but a woman dares not disobey her husband, no matter what demands he made of her.

After successfully digesting the tea, I felt well enough to go home, and Sir William and I made for Grosvenor Square, where we retired to our separate bedrooms, as had been our arrangement for the past couple of years. Sir William's increasing age—for he was seventy now—and his numerous infirmities had contributed to a loss of interest in the acts that had so delighted him in the past. I could not even recall the last time we had played at "all fours." Since Nelson and I first became lovers in Palermo—after many, many months of celibacy within my marriage—Sir William had never uttered so much as a single word about it. It was as if the time had come for him to pass me on to the man he most esteemed— the man in the better position to satisfy me—just as his nephew had done so many years ago. Would this always be my destiny? With a touch of sadness I remembered the beautiful blue Barberini Vase he'd sold to the Duchess of Portland, now in display at the British Museum for the entire public to admire: loved by many, and owned by none.

In the middle of the night, our entire household was awakened by an insistent thumping at the door. I followed Sir William as he pattered downstairs to answer it, admitting a terribly fagged Nelson, who was clutching his head in pain. He fairly collapsed into the nearest chair. "I cannot live with the woman anymore. That much is plain. I would not impose upon your hospitality, Sir William, but I have been walking the streets of London all night in search of a solution to my dilemma."

"My dear, is it all right with you if we take Lord Nelson in? What say you?"

I pondered the idea, for my desires and the exigencies of propriety were most distinctly at odds. "I daresay we could fix up Miss Knight's old room for tonight, for we cannot possibly let 'im continue to roam the streets like a wayfaring stranger, but you must 'ave considered this as well as I 'ave. . . . To take 'im in permanently . . . 'ere in London . . . *bienséance* and all . . . would it not present an odd appearance to the world?"

Sir William glanced at his dear friend, slumped miserably in the chair. "At the moment, Emma, it would appear that he cares not a fig for the world."

Thirty-six

Horatia

In the light of day, Nelson recognized the impracticality of the arrangement, returning to Dover Street the following morning, but he viewed his capitulation as temporary. His plan was to secure his own lodgings as soon as possible, and in any event, he expected that a new commission would soon be forthcoming. I despaired of his being at sea when I gave birth, but Lady Hamilton's lying-in was most assuredly not among the Admiralty's chief concerns.

In early January, Sir William and I found a charming house of our own opposite Green Park, at 23 Piccadilly. I sold my jewelry to buy our new furnishings. We reckoned the jewels' value at over sixty thousand pounds, but to our immense disappointment they fetched a paltry twenty-five hundred. We were told, somewhat apologetically, that the market was already flooded with the jewels of French émigrés seeking to forge a new life on English shores.

Nelson, having been promoted to vice admiral of the blue, was given a reprieve from his misery at Dover Street, dispatched to Torbay as second-in-command of the Channel Fleet, under Lord St. Vincent. I received a mournful letter from him with bad news from the ship's surgeon regarding his eyesight. Could I possibly whip up a batch of green eyeshades? But of course! Though I was nearing my confinement, I leapt to the task with alacrity, for I could not bear to think that Nelson was in pain or suffering for a single moment.

On January 16, Nelson was appointed second-in-command of His Majesty's North Sea fleet. He had hoped for supreme command, and was mightily displeased that Sir Hyde Parker, a dreadful footdragger, was preferred above him. Damn excuses and damn seniority! I was certain they were punishing Nelson for loving me.

Nelson hated to be so far away as I neared my time, for he was horribly anxious for my health. My relatively advanced age, as well as our necessity for the utmost secrecy, greatly increased the dangers of childbirth, and neither Nelson nor I was insensible to it. I was called upon to behave as normally as ever, or else hazard censure—or, worse, exposure. Well into my ninth month, I maintained as active a social calendar as ever, for it would never have occurred to anyone that a woman about to give birth was making the rounds of dinner and theatre and card parties. It simply was not done.

Aware of the inadequate security of the postal system, and that his letters might be lost, stolen, intercepted and read by just about anyone, Nelson devised a persona, an alter ego whom he identified in his missives as a poor "Mr. Thompson." This fictional sailor had left a pregnant sweetheart back in England, and had asked his compassionate commander (Nelson) to urge the gracious Lady Hamilton to intercede for him by ascertaining news of his sweetheart's well-being and reporting upon it in her letters to Nelson. Nelson destroyed all of my correspondence to him that it might not fall into the wrong hands, but I saved every one of his passionate letters.

I took to bed with a "very bad cold" on the twenty-sixth of January. We could afford no telltale signs of my lying-in: no straw upon the front steps, no muffled door knocker. Sir William, who was not insensible of the truth, though we never discussed it, found it convenient not to disturb me during my "illness," taking the opportunity to spend as much time as possible at the Dilettanti Society or at his club. Even the servants were not privy to my secret. Only Mam was present when on the chilly gray morning of January 29, after a remarkably brief period of labor, I brought into this world a healthy baby girl. There was never a question about her name. Of course, she would be Horatia.

The little beauty seemed to know her place from the moment she took her first breath, for she was not a fussy babe. Obediently she went to my breast and obligingly refrained from bawling. Nelson was in ecstasies, delighted that I had given him a daughter, and relieved beyond measure that Horatia and I were both hale and in good spirits. His letter to me of February 1, written as if his alter ego sat beside him as he penned it, was filled with elation:

> *I believe Mrs. Thompson's friend will go mad with joy. He swears he will drink your health this day in a bumper. I cannot write. I am so agitated by the young man at my elbow. I believe he is foolish; he does nothing but rave about you and her.*

Though my body was fagged beyond comprehension, I forced myself to resume my social evenings almost immediately, the better to give the lie to my condition, as well-bred women recuperated from childbirth for weeks, if not months, and I knew all eyes had been upon me ever since we returned to England.

A few days after Horatia's birth, Mam quietly handed me a slip of paper with an address on it. On February 7, I swathed myself to the eyes in furs, wrapped Horatia as warmly as I could, hired a hack, and brought her to 9 Little Titchfield Street, a mile from 23 Piccadilly, delivering Horatia into the hands of Mrs. Gibson, a widow with a young daughter of her own. "I am Lady 'Amilton," I told her, "and this little girl was born last October twenty-ninth to a poor young woman under my protection who finds, to her most profound dismay, that she cannot care for the infant 'erself."

Mrs. Gibson gave me the fish eye. Clearly she didn't believe that the little bundle in my arms was already three months old. But Nelson's guineas spoke louder than my lies. Mrs. Gibson was to secure a wet nurse and look after Horatia with all the kindness of a foster mother, providing me with frequent reports of her health and progress. I was all sensibility, for my body still bore the signs of my recent ordeal. It took every ounce of nerve to refrain from weeping as I bade farewell to tiny Horatia, for Mrs. Gibson was never for a moment to suspect that I was the girl's mother.

I stained my furs with tears throughout the bumpy ride back to Piccadilly. I had brought two daughters into this gray world, only to bow to *bienséance* and part with both of them.

⟨∼⟩

I have been the world around, and in every corner of it, and never yet saw your equal, never one which could be put in comparison with you. You cannot think how my feelings are alive towards you, probably more than ever, and they never can be diminished. I want not to conquer any heart, if that which I have conquered is happy in its lot: I am confident, for the conqueror is become the conquered. My hearty endeavours shall not be wanting to improve and to give us new ties of regard and affection. For ever, ever yours, only yours.

Such were the words of a proud and loving papa who wrote to thank me for the lock of Horatia's hair I had sent him, even more in love with the baby's dear mama than ever he was. Nelson then altered his will, leaving property to any child of his, whether born in or out of wedlock, thus insuring little Horatia a legacy.

Settling financial matters still left him with sleepless nights, for he missed me something dreadful and longed to see our daughter. *I am really miserable; I look at all your pictures, at your dear hair, I am ready to cry, my heart is so full.*

Sir William had begun to campaign for his retirement pension, expecting the customary sum of two thousand pounds per annum, though he had also run up thousands of pounds in debts from his many years of good service in Naples. He'd sold his own diamonds to help make ends meet, but still required a reimbursement of eight thousand pounds from Whitehall or he would remain in distress to the end of his life. "My mother look'd after us both; the same nurse suckled us," he reminded our sovereign. "Having passed my whole life in the service of my king and country, I do not ask what is more than common justice." The prime minister ignored his pleas, and His Majesty, though not unsympathetic, informed Sir William that whenever he might receive his pension, and whatever amount it should be, the sum would not revert to Lady Hamilton upon his death. Sir William bore this news far better than I, for he would not be around to witness the outcome. "They continue to insult us!" I fumed.

My husband then conceived the notion that it might do well for him to count the Prince of Wales as a friend and ally, for though the heir and his father were ever at odds, if not at each other's throats, "Prinny" would one day, of course, be king.

But the news that we might entertain England's most notorious rake under our roof sent Nelson into a panic. He scribbled letter after letter to me, full of his fears that I might succumb to the prince's seductions, and accusing Sir William—referring to him as my "uncle"—of trying to sell me to the prince in exchange for his pension. My poor lover was beside himself, at one moment praising me for my fidelity and, in the next, fearing that I might play him false, particularly when it came to His Royal Highness, whose reputation as an "unprincipled lyar" he traduced in nearly every sentence. England's bravest hero displayed the full measure of his vulnerability, mindful that his letters might be intercepted and yet heedless of all but his own torment. Nelson wrote daily, and sometimes oftener, his words and anxieties tumbling pell-mell, one upon the other, like the rocks disgorged in a violent volcanic eruption. He confessed to being sleepless over the whole shoddy business, blinded by anger and tears, his fears for my virtue driving him to such distraction that he could not eat for days.

Nelson's passionately despairing correspondence reminded me all too well of the raft of fearful and frantic letters I had dispatched to Greville twenty years earlier, when I'd been pregnant with little Emma, and revived my memories of the fifteen panicked missives that I'd sent Greville back in 1786 when I first arrived in Naples. How could I fault my beloved for his epistolary onslaught when our tenderest sensibilities and heightened passions, even our mutual tendency toward the dramatic, were so simpatico?

That night, Nelson wrote another letter from the *St. George*, with a postscript to "Mrs. Thompson."

> *Your friend is at my elbow, and enjoins me to assure you that his love for you and your child is, if possible, greater than ever, and that he calls God to witness that he will marry you as soon as possible, and that it will be his delight to call you his own. He desires you will adhere to Lady H's good advice and, like her, keep those impertinent men at a proper distance. He behaves, I can assure you, incomparably well and loves you as much as man ever loved woman, and do you, my dear, believe me your dear friend.*

As "Thompson," he was all love and passion, but as Nelson, he remained all despair.

The coda on the Prince of Wales dinner was an anticlimax, though anything would have seemed so after Nelson's frantic barrages. I pleaded a headache on the Sunday fixed for the soiree and took to my bed with it, and there spelt an end to the matter. Talk about a tempest in a teapot!

On February 23, Nelson wrote to "Mrs. Thompson" in a holiday mood, full of flirtatious double entendres, so eager to make love with me he hinted that his most noble parts were full enough to make him twice as potent.

> *To the Care of Lady Hamilton.*
>
> *My dear Mrs. T, poor Thompson seems to have forgot all his ill health, and all his mortifications and sorrows, in the thought that he will soon bury them all in your dear, dear bosom; he seems almost beside himself. I daresay twins will again be the fruit of your & his meeting. The thought is too much to bear. Have the dear thatched cottage ready to receive him & I will answer that he would not give it up for a queen and a palace. Kiss dear H. for me, etc.*

That very day, he was granted three days' leave, and made posthaste for London. The Dover Street flat was shut, Tom Tit—my nickname for Fanny—being in Brighton, so Nelson took rooms at Lothian's Hotel. Together, we visited Horatia at Mrs. Gibson's, and what a joy it was to see Nelson cooing over his little "pattern of perfection," as he called his tiny daughter. But how painful it was for the two of us not to be able to let on that we were her parents.

"I do believe Horatia's eyes and brow resemble your own," Nelson said affectionately once we had safely rounded the corner of Little Titchfield Street.

"Do you really, now?" I chuckled. "I think she's the spitting image of 'er father! Not a trace of Emma in 'er little face. I'd scarce believe I was 'er mam 'ad I not seen the little mite wriggle out from between my legs. Why, 'er every feature, even the shape of 'er face, is pure Nelson!"

Nelson grew doleful. "I received a letter from Fanny when she learnt I'd gotten leave."

"And what did Tom Tit have to say for 'erself?" I asked anxiously.

"Tom Tit? I've been meaning to ask you, why in heaven's name do you call her that?"

"Tom Tit?" I bosted out laughing so hard I almost snapped my stays. "It's Cockney rhyming slang, something I 'eard plenty of when I first came to London as a girl. *Tom Tit* is cant for *shit*!"

Nelson erupted in laughter as well. "And here I thought it was because Fanny is pigeon-breasted! I told her not to bother. In response to her letter about coming to London to meet up with me."

Our talk turned serious. Nelson's doctor was concerned about his health. It wasn't just the failing sight in his left eye, but his constitution that was suffering as well. "He tells me my digestion ain't good," Nelson muttered. "Eat but the simplest of foods, avoid wine and porter—I might as well be tossed back into the nursery! And then he cautions me—in order to preserve my sight, he says— that I write as little as possible, a thing that positively cannot be done, and to sit in a darkened room for as much of the day as I can, wearing my green eyeshade! Now, I ask you, how am I to command a fleet from my cabin?"

"You *can* watch your diet, y'nau? Of course I couldn't do without wine or porter, but you've always been more disciplined about a thing than I."

"I've suffered the heart spasms again, too, from time to time," he admitted sheepishly. "I hadn't wanted to tell you, for I knew you'd worry yourself sicker than I."

" 'Ave you been applying the 'ot stupes against the palpitations?"

Nelson nodded. "And my lungs have been doing poorly as well. It's all the fears I have for you, my love, every moment of the day— and now for Horatia as well. Perhaps my time has come."

I grew terribly anxious. "What do you mean? You're not talking . . . ?"

"No, God forbid. I wish to be with you forever, not to leave you. Perhaps it's time to go to Bronte, to move there. The rumping I received from His Majesty still smarts. This England is a shocking place. Better to be shot by a bandit in Italy than to have your reputation stabbed in England."

"Do you think you are more ill-treated than I? Queen Maria Carolina's letter recommending me to Queen Charlotte went unanswered. I am still persona non grata at court, unacceptable because of my background—as if I am the only woman in England 'oo 'as been someone's mistress!—while the journalists and caricaturists take *me* to task for my absence! 'Ow dare they? Everything I 'ave done for country and Crown—all of it counts for naught with these too-nice Hanovers," I fumed, emphasizing my *H*'s, "whose *own* brood of sons could give Hogarth's rake a run for 'is money!"

"And every time I raise your name, no less to praise it, they all look askance or give me the fish eye as if to wink at the reason behind it. Hypocrites, all of 'em! I shall not bear to have your name and munificence abused and traduced. To my mind, Sir William has become one of the worst offenders, for he would see you lose your reputation if it gained him his pension."

"Yes." I smiled. "I 'ave already gotten quite an earful, or I suppose I should say, eyeful, of your opinion on that subject!"

Nelson's leave went by in a twinkling, without a truly private moment to ourselves. To be able to look yet barely to touch, let alone make love, was a torment. How we yearned for our bodies to melt together while the rest of the intrusive world disappeared for a few hours. We dreamed of a future together as a family, and it was hard to imagine that there had ever been a moment in time when Emma knew not Nelson, when she had been so foolish as to spend her heart's credit on another. So much precious time had been lost, and there was so much catching up to do.

By Saturday, February 28, he was back in the admiral's cabin aboard the *St. George*, preparing to sail to Copenhagen. His mission was to push the Danes out of the "League of Armed Neutrality," which was hostile to Britain.

That very afternoon, missing me dreadfully, he wrote:

> *Would to God I had dined alone with you. <u>What a dessert we</u>*
> *<u>would have had</u>. The time will come, and believe me, that I am,*
> *for ever, for ever, your own. . . .*

And filled to bosting with love, later in the day he added:

> *Now, my own dear wife, for such you are in my eyes and in the*
> *face of heaven, I can give full scope to my feelings, for I daresay*
> *Oliver will faithfully deliver this letter. You know, my dearest*
> *Emma, that there is nothing in this world that I would not do for*
> *us to live together, and to have our dear little child with us. I*
> *never had a dear pledge of love till you gave me one, and you,*
> *thank God, never gave one to anyone else. I think before March*
> *is out you will either see us back, or so victorious we shall insure*
> *a glorious issue to our toils. Think what my Emma will feel at see-*
> *ing return safe, perhaps with a little more fame, her own dear lov-*
> *ing Nelson. You, my beloved Emma, and my Country, are the two*
> *dearest objects of my fond heart—a heart susceptible and true. . . .*
> *My longing for you, both person and conversation, you may read-*
> *ily imagine. What must be my sensations at the idea of sleeping*
> *with you! It setts me on fire, even the thoughts, much more would*
> *the reality. I am sure my love & desires are all to you, and if any*
> *woman naked were to come to me, even as I am this moment*
> *from thinking of you, I hope it might rot off if I would touch her*
> *even with my hands. No, my heart, person, and mind is in per-*
> *fect union of love towards my own dear, beloved Emma—the <u>real</u>*
> *<u>bosom</u> friend of her, all hers, all Emma's, etc.*

After such a wildly romantic, passionate, even erotic letter, how
could I possibly ever tell Nelson that I'd had a child *before*? It would
forever remain the only secret between us.

Thirty-seven

Copenhagen

I worship, nay, adore you, and if you was single & I found you
under a hedge, I would instantly marry you, Nelson wrote on
March 6, followed later by:

> *I shall soon return and then we shall take our fill of love. No,*
> *we can never be satiated. . . . The sight of my heaven-given wife*
> *will make me a happy father and you a mother.*

Now that we were in England, it seemed harder than ever to be
the consort of a hero—to have to share him with king and
country—yet he should not have been Nelson if those were not
as dear a priority to him as myself and Horatia. He panicked
when he learnt that her wet nurse had taken ill, and consequently had made our daughter sick as well. The woman must
be replaced!

Pray write and promise me you shan't catch cold, I scrawled. *I do hope*
it will not take long for you to talk some sense into the Danes, that you
may return to me with all dispatch. How can the man who bestowed
our Maltese Crosses be so foolish as to truck with the French when he
has had the pleasure of meeting the great Nelson?

Under pressure from Russia, Denmark was denying England access to the Baltic and it was imperative for Britain that these waters remain open to His Majesty's Navy, as well as to our merchantmen. The Russians had been seizing every British vessel in the area—ostensibly under orders from Czar Paul. The Frenchies had been known to smuggle arms and other war materials aboard neutral nations' merchant vessels sailing in the Baltic, and England had asserted its right to inspect these so-called neutral ships for such contraband. The Danes, along with the other League nations—Sweden, Russia, and Prussia—refused to comply, and King George wanted an explanation for it.

My "simple sailor" wrote a poem for me a few days before the Baltic fleet was set to weigh anchor.

LORD NELSON TO HIS GUARDIAN ANGEL

From my best cable tho' I'm forced to part,
I leave my anchor in my angel's heart.
Love, like a pilot, shall the pledge defend,
And for a prong his happiest quiver lend.

In all my life, no one had ever written a poem for me! I was touched beyond all measure. I had been immortalized in oils by Europe's finest portraitists, and Papa Haydn had composed lieder in my honor, but this tender and heartfelt quatrain from my own dear matchless Nelson, my soul's heart, was far grander to me than all the professional artists' tributes. I replied in verse as well:

ANSWER OF LORD NELSON'S GUARDIAN ANGEL

Go where you list, each thought of Emma's soul
Shall follow you from Indus to the Pole:
East, West, North, South, our minds shall never part;
Your Angel's loadstone shall be Nelson's heart.

> *Farewell! and o'er the wide, wide sea*
> *Bright glory's course pursue,*
> *And adverse winds to love and me*
> *Prove fair to fame and you.*
> *And when the dreaded hour of battle's nigh,*
> *Your Angel's heart, which trembles at a sigh,*
> *By your superior danger bolder grown,*
> *Shall dauntless place itself before your own.*
> *Happy, thrice happy, should her fond heart prove—*
> *A shield to Valour, Constancy, and Love.*

As if Nelson didn't have enough to occupy his mind as he prepared for action, an unnecessary distraction arrived from an unexpected county. Francis Oliver, who had been one of Sir William's private secretaries in Naples, now performed those duties for Nelson. Oliver, looking to change professions, had asked Nelson for a recommendation to a writership in the East India Company, which Nelson was prepared to provide until he discovered that there was a consideration for such things, the customary sum being one thousand pounds. Recognizing that this exorbitant figure amounted to no less than a bribe to some nabob at the East India Company, Nelson refused to submit the recommendation. Enraged and embittered, Oliver threatened to ruin him; yet to my astonishment, he remained in Nelson's employ.

The fleet hoisted sail on March 12. My heart was breaking, for every time Nelson was charged with engaging the enemy, I despaired that he would never return to me. It was too much to bear. I poured out my heart in another poem, sending it to Nelson that morning.

> *Silent grief and sad forebodings*
> *(Lest I ne'er should see him more),*
> *Fill my heart, when gallant Nelson*
> *Hoists Blue Peter at the fore.*

On his Pendant anxious gazing,
Fill with tears (mine eyes run o'er)
At each change of wind I tremble
While Blue Peter's at the fore.

All the live-long day I wander,
Sighing on the sea-beat shore;
But my sighs are all unheeded,
When Blue Peter's at the fore.

For when duty calls my hero
To far seas, where cannons roar,
Nelson (love and Emma leaving),
Hoists Blue Peter at the fore.

Oft he kiss'd my lips at parting,
And at every kiss he swore,
Nought could force him from my bosom,
Save Blue Peter at the fore.

Oh, that I might with my Nelson,
Sail the wide world o'er and o'er,
Never should I then with sorrow,
See Blue Peter at the fore.

But (ah me!) his ship's unmooring;
Nelson's last boat rows from shore,
Every sail is set and swelling,
And Blue Peter's seen no more.

At Copenhagen, Nelson proved himself a hero once again. Though the battle on April 2 lasted several bloody hours, and our losses of both men and ships were enormous, they would have been far greater and significantly more devastating if Nelson had obeyed Sir Hyde Parker's orders to discontinue the engagement. My lover knew that if they had attempted retreat on Hyde Parker's signals, the wind and the water would not have been in their favor and the men would likely have ended up caught upon the shoals, sitting ducks for the Danes. Nelson saw better than his commander-in-chief that victory was nearly theirs, and he could not allow his men to become cannon fodder whilst he had it in his power to win the day, despite his superior's signals.

One of Nelson's officers asked him, had he not seen the C-in-C's signal? "You know, Foley," Nelson replied, "I have only one eye; I have a right to be blind sometimes." He raised his spyglass to his right eye and turned toward the flagship, HMS *London*. "I really do not see the signal!" he added. "*Leave off action?! Damme if I do!*" Then several other captains followed Nelson's lead, enabling the British to gain the upper hand.

Nelson then managed to convince the proud Danes to agree to an armistice.

> *I received as a warrior all the praises which could gratify the ambitions of the bravest man, and the thanks of the nation, from the King downwards for my humanity in saving the town from destruction. Nelson is a warrior, but will not be a butcher. I am sure, could you have seen the adoration and respect you would have cried for joy; there are no honours can be conferred equal to this.*

But here in London, there were no illuminations of public buildings after news of the victory reached our ears. The City formally voted its thanks to His Majesty's Army and Navy in Egypt, but there was no mention of the Danish defeat, and in fact the daily newspapers accorded greater prominence than usual to the lists of those killed and wounded at Copenhagen. The Admiralty awarded only the paltriest of prize money for the Danish ships and no medals were struck to commemorate the victory.

Good news and bad news tumbled upon one another like so many rocks in a landslide. The government agreed to grant Sir William's pension, but the sum would be only twelve hundred pounds, rather than the two thousand per annum that was the customary sum for retiring ministers. However, our heavy disappointment was somewhat relieved when the wonderful news arrived that the best of William's vases had turned up in London! By some twist of fate those crates had never been placed aboard the *Colossus*. They had been found aboard the *Serapis* when she docked in London in October 1800, and had been left forgotten in a quayside warehouse. Sir William was overjoyed to see his old friends, as he called them, but their reunion was rather brief; he could not afford to keep them when he was so deeply in debt. Dismayed, he put them on the block.

Nelson was still in the Baltic when the Christie's sale of Sir William's paintings took place. My lover had commissioned his prize agent, Alexander Davison, to bid in his behalf on the portrait of me as St. Cecilia. As Nelson was not a wealthy man, he had authorized Davison to go no higher than three hundred pounds for it, but he could not bear to see me "sold," especially by my own husband. And "if it had been three hundred drops of blood, I would cheerfully have parted with it," Nelson assured me.

Taking a mighty loss on their value, but with little choice in the matter, Sir William netted only some sixty-five hundred pounds from the Christie's auction, buying back some of his own lots when they failed to meet the reserve. He managed to secure another four thousand pounds from a private sale of the antique vases from the *Serapis*. Yet we were still quite constrained financially. In Naples and Palermo we had been accustomed to a lavish lifestyle, one we could not easily relinquish. Expectations ran high for those in our position, and appearances had to be maintained. By the end of

April, Sir William had managed to raise enough to settle his six-thousand-pound debt with his bankers, Ross & Ogilvie, but not enough to satisfy his Italian creditors as well, if we were to live better than paupers.

Meanwhile, Mam took off for a visit to Hawarden, with the intention of stopping in Manchester to look in on Emma Carew. "Send me every particular about 'ow I am to proceed about the little girl," she instructed me.

"She's not little anymore, Mam, y'nau? She's now a young lady of nineteen—older'n I was when I brought 'er into this world. See that she is well and 'ealthy. Give 'er these ribands and this reticule that she might dress 'erself up a bit—though don't tell 'er they're from me. I don't know whether she 'as cause to own any indulgences and fripperies, and a young girl deserves 'em to pretty 'erself."

"And if she asks me about 'er own mam? Emy, gal, the subject's bound to come up. She knows I'm *your* mam, y'nau?"

I sought my handkerchief to blot away the falling tears. "It's too late. She's been settled for so long now, 'as a life she's accustomed to. . . . I'd want 'er to be proud of 'er mam, 'oo she is and all, but I can never think on 'little Emma' and not think on 'ow she came to be, in the first place. That girl's mam was a wild and giddy girl 'erself, not the woman who is now Lady 'Amilton."

Mam and I held each other tightly. "Emy, *I've* never been ashamed of you, no matter what kind of scrapes you got yourself into. You've got the biggest 'eart in all of England. And what I'm reckoning is that little Emma would excuse all, if you could only give the girl the chance, by forgiving yourself. What's done is done, gal, and it all 'appened a long time ago. Now, husht thee naise, and dry your tears."

Thirty-eight

The Countryside Beckons

I did try to see my other daughter as much as propriety would permit under the circumstances. When Sir William was out at a meeting, or hobnobbing at one of his societies, I would have Mrs. Gibson bring Horatia to me at 23 Piccadilly. We had carefully scheduled these arrangements to avoid unpleasant embarrassments, but one day Sir William, having developed a raging headache while at the Dilettanti Society, came home sooner than expected. He climbed the stairs to greet me in my rooms, only to find me holding Horatia and endeavoring to make her laugh by pulling a series of silly faces, while a stranger, seated in the corner, looked on.

Sir William remained in the doorway, observing for some moments the odd little domestic scene unfolding before his eyes. "I appear to have arrived at an inconvenient time for you, my dear," he said stiffly. He blinked away the moisture in his eyes and, without another word, quit the room. I felt dreadful over it, but to say something to him would have made the situation even more awkward and agonizing for the both of us. To discuss it was to acknowledge the unpleasant reality of the thing, and after that, there could be no hiding our heads in the polite safety of the sand.

Mrs. Gibson rose immediately. "I expect it's time for us to be going, your ladyship." I handed off Horatia to her. "You'll be in touch with me, of course, when you want me to bring her again." She dropped a slight curtsy and I gave her a guinea for her extra pains.

Nelson's service in the Baltic did not go entirely unrecognized. In May, he was made a viscount, and took the title "Viscount Nelson of the Nile and of Burnham Thorpe," the seat of his birth, although if *he* had been commander-in-chief of the Baltic fleet, and not Sir Hyde Parker, I am certain his victory at Copenhagen would have gained him an earldom. However, the new title brought with it no financial recompense. My hero's pension woes were in the same sort of boat as Sir William's. So he remained at sea, now the commander-in-chief of a special squadron charged with defending the Channel coast, though miserable to be once again separated from all he held dear.

He charged me with finding a place outside London where he might settle. Since he had left Fanny, making over half his income to her, he was dependent on letting hotel rooms whenever he found himself onshore. The house was to be paid for with his money, with the title in his name, but it was intended for the rustication of the entire *tria juncta in uno*. I accepted my commission with zeal, looking hither and yon for the perfect property, and I found it but an hour's drive from Westminster Bridge. Merton Place was just six miles outside of London, nestled amid the rustic and unspoilt Surrey countryside. It had but an acre and a half on its own. Mr. Cockerell, the surveyor, thought I was mad to say I would take it, for he took one look at the dirty little canal that meandered past it—a tributary of the River Wandle that I thought perfect for Sir William to fish from—and declared it most likely unsanitary. "I daresay your husband would be taking his life into his hands to eat a creature from that muck," he insisted.

Nor did the surveyor think the house itself a good prospect. The redbrick, rather antique-looking Merton Place, currently occupied and meanly furnished, was on the whole rather dark, and had but one large room on the ground floor, the rest being too tiny to be considered parlors, dining rooms, or sitting rooms. Upstairs, only one room was "fit for a gentleman," according to Cockerell, "and even that wants a dressing room. In short, it is altogether the worst place under all its circumstances that I ever saw pretending to suit a gentleman's family." He went on to elaborate the unsuitability of the property—lacking stables and gardens, and surrounded on all sides by public roads, so as to offer not the least bit of privacy. The soil was poor, the house itself in need of major renovations and repairs just to make it habitable.

What a narrow mind has this Mr. Cockerell! I thought. Such possibilities existed for this dear, sweet little place. "I will have it!" I declared ecstatically.

The property, with its very modest parcel of land, cost ninety-four hundred pounds. It would not have been a hardship for Nelson to afford had he won his case against Lord St. Vincent, but the lawsuit had come to trial while Nelson was still in the Baltic. The dispute was over the thirteen thousand pounds in prizes taken from the 1797 Battle of Cape St. Vincent. Nelson's barristers were appealing the verdict, yet only time would tell whether he would be awarded the damages he sought.

Yet once the decision to purchase Merton had been taken, it took longer than either Nelson or I had expected to make the thing a reality. His shares in the three percents yielded but two-thirds of the purchase price, and he had to appeal to Alexander Davison to loan him the remaining three thousand pounds. Then there was the matter of convincing William Haslewood, Nelson's solicitor, to permit his client to put all his eggs in the basket Nelson had begun to call Merton Farm.

But Nelson trusted me above anyone else, and if I thought a little spit and polish would turn Merton Place into a paradise on earth, he was all for it and would hear no words of discouragement

from any quarter. As he was still at sea, the task fell to me to prepare the property against his arrival. One tetchy matter was that of
the removal of the present occupant. The widow Greaves dug in
her heels and refused to quit Merton until Nelson's arrival in October. Truth told, I believe she wanted to meet the hero. I dipped
into my own purse to compensate Mrs. Greaves, and off she finally
went. Then came the business of turning Merton into a place fit
for a proper country squire. The property swarmed with builders
and painters, and Mam acted as the foreman of all of them, over-
seeing the renovations with her sleeves pushed up past the elbows,
her mobcap covered in brick dust.

The Wandle tributary, which I had rechristened the Nile, was
cleaned out, and where it widened into a lake, we stocked it with
fish for Sir William. Hedgerows now bordered the property where
it met the public roads. Mam and I planted a kitchen garden, set
up pigsties and hen coops, and added a flock of sheep—which
would have more room to graze if Nelson could persuade the adjacent landowner, Mr. Axe, to sell his acreage.

We had plate glass installed on nearly every window, and several of the walls were hung with mirrors to bring in more light and
create the illusion of space and depth. The rest of the walls were
covered with Nelsoniana and other mementos of our relationship.
"It's looking a bit like a shrine, y'nau?" Mam remarked.

"I know! Isn't it wonderful!"

"I dunno what Sir Willum will 'ave to say about all this."

"Sir Willum isn't paying a farthing for it. Nelson won't even
'ave any of Sir William's furnishings here, not so much as a chair or
a dish or a vase or a single volume of literature. It's all to be 'is, and
Sir Willum and I are to be naught but 'is frequent houseguests."

Mam chuckled. "Frequent as in 'living 'ere all the time'?"

"Well . . . when Sir Willum and I don't need to be entertaining
in town."

"Hmmm. Well, don't let your 'eart run away with your 'ead,

straight into your 'usband's bad graces, is all I can say. You know I can be as plucky as a summer day is long, but you never know what can 'appen in this world, and Sir Willum is just about the most patient man I've ever known—not to mention 'e's never been anything but good to the both of us. 'E's a gentleman from 'is 'ead to 'is boots, acting for all the world like nothing bothers 'im, and if 'e don't seem troubled by certain things, why, then there must be nothing in the world to be troubled by. Sir Willum's always been good at chusing to overlook a thing if it prevents an inconvenience. But I see the way 'e looks at you. 'E's still a man, and 'e's still got a man's 'eart, now matter how detached 'e likes to act or 'ow much 'e's privately made 'is peace with the present situation. 'E's like that volcano of 'is: all bubbling up inside and like to bost open at any time, y'nau? There's not a soul in this life I love more than you, Emy, gal, and I want to see you protected."

On October 24, 1801, Nelson drove down from London in a post chaise, entering Merton Place for the first time, under a triumphal arch. Sir William, Mam, and I had already ensconced ourselves in the modest manor. What a day it was! Dressed in their Sunday best, every resident in the quiet country village had turned out to greet him, lining the lanes and cheering his carriage as it rumbled toward his new home. He alighted from the post chaise, struck to tears by the sight before him, for here was the farm of his dreams.

I could scarce wait to take him upon the grand tour of his property. "The Nile!" he exclaimed, on seeing the meandering stream. "Is that little boat mine, too?"

I nodded. "Well, the admiral needs to embark upon the waters on occasion, don't 'e? With someone to row 'im about. Don't you think I'd make a fine bo'sun's mate?"

Nelson inclined his head, his words intended for my ears alone. "I think you'd make a fine *Nelson's* mate."

The "Nile" and the quaint Italianate bridge, the rose garden, and the little kitchen garden had left him in raptures, the livestock delighted him, and the house itself, complete with its alla Nelson decor and cozy furnishings, prompted exclamations of utter ecstasy. "Is this really all mine?" he asked repeatedly, dabbing at the wayward tear or two. "Oh, my dear, clever, magnificent Emma, do you know I have never truly felt I had a home to call my own? To my mind I always seemed to be imposing upon the kindness of my family at Burnham Thorpe, or even upon Fanny, when I'd come back to roost after so many months or years at sea. But this! My only love, you have indeed created the paradise of my fantasies. I am already in love with everything I see, and couldn't possibly wish for anything different!"

That first night, the entire village was illuminated, as though Nelson's arrival among them was an event worthy of as big a celebration as a victory at sea. From the start, Nelson took an interest in the welfare of the villagers as he had done, if but briefly, at Bronte. He quickly befriended the Reverend Mr. Lancaster of the local parish, and began regularly attending church. I accompanied him, but Sir William, ever the humanist, preferred to remain at Merton, ensconcing himself in the library, or fishing the "Nile."

For Sir William, Merton soon became an English version of the idyll he had left behind at Posillipo. Less than two months shy of his seventy-first birthday, he had finally acknowledged that a return to Naples was now naught but a pipe dream. He wrote to Samuel Ragland, his agent there, instructing him to close up Villa Emma in Posillipo, and to dismiss the servants from the Palazzo Sessa. But Sir William still owed back rent, as well as back payment to the servants and a number of Neapolitan tradesmen. The sale of our remaining furnishings there yielded but a fraction of what was owed. My poor husband was forced to sell 1,000 pounds of government stock in an attempt to cover the shortfall, but he suffered a huge

loss on that as well, for the sale of the consols yielded him only 673
pounds.

I was torn in two between my devotion to Nelson and my
growing concern for Sir William's increasing introspection. I endeavored to raise his spirits at Merton, but as the weeks wore on,
he became more withdrawn, preferring solitude to the bustle and
gaiety of our evening entertainments. What we had all envisioned
as a quiet retreat soon became as popular as our homes in Naples
and Palermo. With Nelson in residence, Merton bosted at the
seams with company night and day, and my poor philosopher husband wanted little to do with any of them, feeling like a spare appendage and craving nothing but peace and quiet, with ample time
for fishing and reflection.

The house was filled with the sounds of laughter and merriment, of tinkling crystal and clinking silver, of outlandish sea tales
and ribald country humor (saving the two Reverend Nelsons' respect) because Nelson and I could not, even in his own home, be
seen to be keeping private company. With my husband and mother
as my constant companions, I was considered as much a guest as
Nelson's sisters (the vivacious Katty Matcham with her brood of
six, and Susannah Bolton with her family of eight); my lover's
brother the Reverend William Nelson; his twittering wife, Sarah;
and their two children, Charlotte and Horace; or any of my Welsh
Connor cousins. I chaperoned the young people to parties and
balls, tutored them in French and Italian, listened to their sagas of
romantic woe, and dried the tears of the brokenhearted.

It has always been my nature to require a grand project in
which to immerse myself. Now that Naples was behind us, I spent
my energies on all improvements at Merton, that Nelson's every vision for his farm should be fulfilled. I wrote to a friend, *We are very
busy planting, and I am as much amused with pigs and hens as I was
as the Court of Naples' Ambassadress.*

We welcomed nabobs from the Admiralty, visiting foreign dignitaries, journalists, my singer friends from Naples, and even Maria Carolina's son, Prince Leopold.

We loved them all, for a house had become the home the itinerant Nelson had so long craved . . . but at bottom it was all an elaborate ruse of sorts: the only way Nelson and I could see each other every day, without censure. And never to pass another minute apart—*that*, above all else, was what we lived for.

Thirty-nine

Addio, il mio Marito

At the end of March 1802, Lord Cornwallis returned to England, having reached a peace treaty with the French. Though it was called "the peace everybody is glad of and nobody is proud of," no one in all of Britain could have been happier about it than I. It meant that my beloved Nelson would remain home!

But just as he believed himself the happiest man in England, in April my lover received some sorrowful news. After a brief illness his father had passed away. Fanny had flown to the Reverend Nelson's side when she learnt he had taken ill and she was with him in Bath when the sad event of his passing occurred. Yet neither she nor Nelson attended Edmund Nelson's funeral, held at his rectory in Burnham Thorpe, each not wishing to encounter the other. I feared that Nelson's spirits would not rally and suggested that we postpone our progress through the countryside, but he was quite adamant that our plans should not go amiss. A couple of months after his father's death, we commenced our victory tour, beginning in Oxford, where Nelson was given the freedom of the city, and in full convocation he and Sir William were made honorary doctors of civil law. But things swiftly slid downhill from there. At Blenheim Palace, the Duke of Marlborough refused to admit our little party for fear that the scandal swirling about the *tria juncta in uno* might taint his family. But His Grace had the temerity to send out some light refreshments, that we might pic-nic—like a group of nonentities—on his manicured lawns. At Merthyr Tydfil in Wales, Nelson was accorded a hero's welcome and we were noisily feted, but a cannon went off by mistake, killing a fourteen-year-old boy.

"May I suggest that we now return home?" Sir William asked quietly. Unlike Nelson—and me—he did not have it in his character to derive oxygen from accolades. More than anything, he wished to leave off the hustle and bustle of whirlwind tours. The expenses of the recent excursion had mounted precipitously, and Sir William feared spending the twilight of his days in poverty.

Greville poured pestilence in Sir William's ear, for at bottom he did not wish to see his inheritance squandered on concerts and guttling. The man who had once praised my thrift now decried my extravagance. Out of politesse I oft invited Greville down to Merton, for Sir William missed his company, but Greville always declined.

As the months had worn on, Sir William increasingly resented all the hullabaloo that surrounded our lives. He grew concerned about our expenditures, and yearned for peace and quiet: no raised voices, no large dinner parties. Marital tensions rose to the surface. If we were in London, Sir William wished to fish quietly at Merton. If we were all in the country, he missed his societies and the intellectual stimulus of the city. If we went sea bathing, or on some other excursion, he desired to be anywhere else but where we'd stopped. He took to leaving letters for me to read, rather than speaking with me directly. Still the diplomat, he avoided face-to-face confrontations that might prove unpleasant for all parties.

My dear Emma . . . there is no being on earth that has a bet-
ter understanding or better heart than yourself, if you would but
give them fair *play, but . . . you must excuse me if my having*
lived so long has given me Experience enough that the greatest

fortunes will not stand the total want of attention to what are
called trifling Expences. . . . Believe me, happiness is in a much
narrower compass than most people think. But my Dear Emma
let us cut this matter short. Do not then strain the bow too tight,
least the string should break.

Ponder well my Dear Emma these lines, let your good sense
come forward—as to me it is perfectly indifferent what may hap-
pen! I shall be Patience in Purity. Ever yr. W. Hamilton.

What a pedant he'd become! It saddened me greatly that our marriage, which had begun as a model of domestic felicity, had dwin-
dled over the past few years into pettiness. Truth told, our most
primary colors now surfaced—Emma, the wild and carefree prof-
ligate, and William, the coolly detached cynic—each of us selfish
in our own way, and we irked *each other* in no small measure.

The Merton expenses continued to mount and the number of
guests never seemed to diminish, for Nelson, having never had the
opportunity till now to gather his entire family about him and
come to know them well, desired they should visit us as often as
possible. After all, Merton was *his* home. He more than had a right
to host whomever he pleased and for however long he chose to do
so. And so the unspoken, though copiously documented, marital
strife continued. And I was torn in my allegiances to each of the
two men, like Helen caught between her passion for Paris and her
duty to Menelaus.

Sir William, who had believed that over the months he had
made his opinions perfectly plain, once again laid out his positions
and his terms for amity, writing to me one day in November 1802
sounding, not like a husband, but as if I were his opposite number
at a diplomatic conference.

I have passed the last 40 years of my life in the hurry and bus-
tle that must necessarily be attendant on a publick character. I

am arrived at the age when some repose is really necessary, and I promised myself a quiet home, and although I was sensible, and said so when I married, that I should be superannuated when my wife would be in her full beauty and vigour of youth. That time is arrived and we must make the best of it for the comfort of both parties. Unfortunately our tastes as to the manner of living are very different. I have no complaint to make, but I feel that the whole attention of my wife is given to Lord Nelson and his interest at Merton. I well know the purity of Lord Nelson's friendship for Emma and me, and I know how very uncomfortable it would make his Lordship, our best friend, if a separation should take place, and am therefore determined to do all in my power to prevent such an extremity. I mean to have a light Chariot or post Chaise by the month that I may make use of it in London and run backwards and forwards to Merton, &c. This is my plan, and we might go on very well, but I am fully determined not to have more of the very silly altercations that happen but too often between us and embitter the present moment exceedingly. If realy we cannot live comfortable together, a <u>wise</u> and <u>well concerted</u> separation is preferable; but I think, considering the possibility of my not troubling any party long in this world, the best for us all would be to bear those ills we have rather than flie to those we know not of. I have fairly stated what I have on my mind. I know and admire your talents and many excellent qualities, but I am not blind to your defects, and confess having many myself; therefore let us bear and forbear for God's sake.

Sir William's prophecy had come true at last. I was indeed in the prime of life, while my husband, ailing and crotchety, was but a shadow of the vital, virile man I first met back in 1783, made love to in 1786, and married in 1791. He got his chariot, though he had not ceased reminding me of the consequences of my extravagance. Not long after, when I was at my toilette one morning, he delivered a letter from my bankers at Coutts. "This must be an error," I said, puzzling over it. "They seem to believe that there is but twelve shillings and elevenpence in my account."

"I am afraid the balance is correct, my dear," Sir William replied. "And here is a second letter, which they copied to me as well, with regard to your overdraft of seven hundred pounds."

I was aghast. "Wherever will I get such a sum?"

Sir William kissed the top of my head. "Your husband is not the ogre you have of late believed him to be. I directed that the sum be paid out of my own funds."

I rose and threw my arms about his neck. His body was thin as a rail now, truly the figure of an old man. "My dear, dear Sir Willum! Thank you! Whatever 'ave I done to deserve you?" I wept.

His lips formed a faint smile. "I have asked myself the very same question on occasion, my dear."

Just a few weeks later, in February 1803, Sir William fell seriously ill. We had hosted a rather grand concert evening, after which my husband collapsed and needed to be carried into his bedroom by a pair of sturdy manservants. Mam and I nursed him round the clock and in several days' time he rallied. We thought it best that he recuperate in the country air, so we brought him out to Merton, but late one day in March, Sir William collapsed again. This time we conveyed him posthaste to 23 Piccadilly, where his trusted physician, Dr. Mosely, attended him. For six days and nights I would not stir from his bedside. Nelson, too, kept vigil every day. On March 30, I wrote to Nelson's elder sister Susannah, admitting exhaustion. But my husband needed me now; there would be time for sleep in the future.

On the morning of April 6, at the age of seventy-two, Sir William died in my arms, with Nelson at his side. I threw myself across his lifeless body and drenched it with miserable tears. *Un-happy day for the forlorn Emma ten minutes past ten Dear Blessed Sir*

William left me, I wrote in my diary. A noble heart had indeed crack'd, and taken with it half of Emma's life. He had been my savior and my Pygmalion, my teacher and my beloved. More than all, he was my *husband*—the only word in all the wide world that bestows upon a woman society's greatest gift: respectability. Sir William had risked his own character to make me honest and virtuous, and in his waning years I had not repaid him well. What a man, what a husband! Would God ever see fit to forgive me?!

Forty

Widowed

I *n every respect an extraordinary person; a lover and con-*
noisseur of the arts; he had in the highest degree the gift of
being agreeable to everyone; with his candor and honesty he
drew people to him in such a winning fashion that each
among all his numerous acquaintances believed him his best
friend. He was a man of the world who knew how to acquire
and enjoy the amenities of life. Not a moment passed him by
unused. . . .

Such were the words of Sir William's dear friend the painter Wilhelm Tischbein, but they make a fine eulogy. The newspapers
published Sir William's actual obituary on April 7. It was compli-
mentary to the point of effusiveness, and through my tears I was
touched with pride at how the journalists, who so often derided us,
had seen fit to honor our marriage.

About twelve years ago, he married Lady Hamilton, and never
was a union productive of more perfect felicity. The anxious so-
licitude, the unwearied attentions, the domestic duties, joined to
the uncommon talents and accomplishments of Lady Hamilton,
were the sources of the purest happiness to them both, as well as
of delight to the circle in which they lived.

The hatchment was affixed to the door of 23 Piccadilly, announcing a death within. I spent 185 pounds on black mourning attire for myself and our servants, and another 170 on a suite of jet mourning jewelry. As was the custom, we remained in seclusion.

My monetary woes commenced almost immediately. Greville, who was Sir William's executor as well as his heir, confided to me that he held out little hope of my ever seeing a penny of Sir William's pension. I did have a few supporters at Whitehall—Nelson's friend in the Treasury, George Rose, and the prime minister, Henry Addington—to whom I wrote regarding my claim, but they apologized for the need to concentrate their attentions on more pressing matters, such as the shaky state of the Treaty of Amiens and the likelihood of resuming the war. Queen Maria Carolina sent a belated, and very formal, letter of condolence on Sir William's death, but—after everything I had done for her—added nothing supporting my claims to Sir William's pension. I was already in low spirits, this epistolary equivalent of a Sicilian rumping stunned me to the quick. In a fury, I flung the jewelry she had given me against the wall. I had been there for Her Majesty, holding her hand through every hour of her darkest distress, but when my own despondency was at high tide, she royally ignored my despair. "By gad, if she can forget Emma, I can forget her!" Nelson thundered, with all the vehemence of Bronte.

On the afternoon of Sir William's death, Nelson dispatched a letter to Alexander Davison, doubting that I would be "left properly." He thought Sir William's nephew, not merely greedy, but also jealous that I had *more* than merely made something of myself—I had *triumphed*—since his caddish jilting of me so many years earlier. Nelson also wanted to ensure that William's deed of gift to me of the furniture at 23 Piccadilly was read aloud before a full conclave, for he was certain that Greville would try to take the furnishings, which I'd purchased myself through the sale of my jewels, along with the title to the property.

I had known the contents and terms of Sir William's will as
early as 1801. I was aware that he was leaving me three hundred
pounds in a lump sum upon his death, plus additional payments
of eight hundred pounds annually, to be paid in quarterly installments from Sir William's Welsh estates—"clear of all deductions."
Perhaps it was a passive, ever-diplomatic form of revenge from the
grave for my sin of loving Nelson, for Sir William must have realized that he was leaving me in relative penury.

Sir William did provide for a payment of 250 pounds against
my present debts, which at the time of his death had shot back up
to 700. To Mam, he left a hundred pounds at his death and another hundred per year. In his will, Sir William described Nelson
as his dearest friend, "the most virtuous, loyal, and truly brave man
I have ever met with," bequeathing him a snuffbox with a miniature version of Vigée Le Brun's portrait of me as a reposing bacchante set into the lid. It all appeared so petty and penurious to me
now, for Nelson had arranged to give his estranged wife eighteen
hundred pounds a year (at which sum Tom Tit—installed at 54
Wellbeck Street and calling herself Duchess of Bronte—griped vo-
ciferously), and he was no richer a man than Sir William.

The *Morning Herald*, always keen to take a swipe at the *tria
juncta in uno*, reported;

> Lord Nelson has received his celebrated picture of <u>Emma</u> by
> Madame Le Brun, conformably to the Will of Sir William
> Hamilton: another beautiful piece is also said to have devolved
> on his Lordship, in consequence of the demise of that friendly
> Connoisseur!

On April 12, Sir William was buried in Pembrokeshire, according
to his wishes to be laid beside his first wife. Neither Nelson nor I
traveled to the funeral. Though I had known about the arrangements for years, Sir William's returning to Wales to be reunited

with Catherine felt like a final nail in the coffin of *our* marriage. It was almost as if his spirit had visited me in my sleep and held up his hand to say, "You cannot follow me here, my dear." And I suppose he was right. The dead belong with the dead, and the time for the living to bid them good-bye is while they yet breathe.

Nelson was quite correct not to have trusted Greville to see me properly placed in my widowhood, for Charles *did*, in fact, deduct income tax from my annuity, prompting Nelson's vitriol.

> *Mr. Greville is a shabby fellow. . . . It may be law, but it is not just, nor in equity would, I believe, be considered as the will and intention of Sir William. Never mind! Thank God you do not want any of his kindness; nor will he give you justice.*

And then Greville dealt me another blow. *How soon can you quit 23 Piccadilly?* read his terse note. I bit my tongue and set my jaw and packed my belongings. Within a few weeks of Sir William's death, I found quiet and modest lodgings at 11 Clarges Street, just around the corner. Though we now lacked the verdant view, Mam and I still had the pleasures of the Green Park at our disposal, our little household could attend the nearby Church of St. James, and the temptations of the Bond Street emporiums were no farther from our doorstep than they had been at 23 Piccadilly. I browsed for books at Hookham's, patronized Mr. Atkinson for my perfumes, cosmetics, and creams, and placed my trust in the sage apothecary at Paytherus and Company.

By this time, Charlotte Nelson, the reverend's daughter, had already been living with us for several months. She was fifteen when she came down from Norfolk because I thought she should be introduced to a more sophisticated life than she had been accustomed to. After all, she was the niece of the nation's greatest hero, and many young men would be eager to make her acquaintance. It was my office to keep the cads at bay. Though our backgrounds could not have been more different, there was a protective and maternal streak in me that did not want her to end up as her "Aunt Emma" had done at the same age. And, looking back on those years, I suppose I missed having a daughter then. I had brought two into this world, yet could publicly acknowledge neither of them. Having a young girl to fashion into a proper young lady delighted me no end. Though I could scarce afford to look after Mam and me on our meager income, it gave me great pleasure to outfit Charlotte for dances and dinners and squire her about to museums, the opera, and the theatre.

The Treaty of Amiens, which the French had been treating as a grand joke since November of 1802, had completely crumbled, and Boney was now as big a threat as ever. On May 6, my lover received his orders to prepare to return to duty. Nelson was anxious that Horatia be christened, and wanted to be assured that his daughter would receive the sacrament before he departed. Unfortunately, it was too risky for either of us to stand up for her in the church, even in our guise as godparents. By now, Horatia was two and a half years old, and despite her puppy fat, the facial resemblance to her father was palpable.

Mrs. Gibson brought Horatia to St. Marylebone Church, the very place where Sir William and I had exchanged our wedding vows. I recalled then that the sanctuary was too small for a permanent baptismal font. At Nelson's instructions, I impressed upon Mrs. Gibson the vital importance that no parents' names be inscribed on the baptismal certificate, and in fact, the baptism itself was to be struck from the church record. A double fee was provided for the rendering of this favor, but Mrs. Gibson entirely misunderstood us and thought the double fee was for the purchase of a copy of the baptismal certificate. Thus, the St. Marylebone records list one Horatia Nelson Thompson, born October 29, 1800, baptized May 13, 1803. No parents' names are enumerated on the certificate, though it does list Lady Emma Hamilton and Lord Horatio Nelson as godparents.

Three days later, Nelson reported to Portsmouth, where he was made commander-in-chief of the Mediterranean fleet. On the eighteenth of May, England declared war on France.

In the past year, John Bull had all but forgotten his animosity toward Lord Horatio Nelson Bronte, Viscount of the Nile and Burnham Thorpe. Such a cheering throng gathered to see him off at Portsmouth that in order to preserve his person from being torn to pieces, he was drawn out to the longboat in a bathing machine. *I had their huzzahs; now I have their hearts*, he wrote to me.

Naturally, I never wanted to let him go, and if there was ever a man torn between desire and duty, it was Nelson. He was my sun and my moon. And to him I was more than his beloved. I was Britannia. He set off aboard the *Victory* on May 20, writing to me that very day:

> *You will believe that although I am glad to leave that horrid place Portsmouth, yet the being afloat makes me now feel that we do not tread the same element. . . . Be assured that I am thinking of you every moment. My heart is full to bursting. Believe me, my dear Emma, although the call of honour separates us, yet my heart is so entirely yours and with you that I cannot be faint hearted, carrying none with me.*

Every time I received a letter from him, I would place a rose in my hair, for it was truly a gala day. It always made me feel like we were a bit closer when I wrote to him of every little thing: of my trips to Norfolk to visit his family, of chaperoning his niece Charlotte, of the progress of our dear Horatia. Though I cried myself to sleep every night, I tried to keep my missives full of light and love. And Nelson seemed so happy to receive every scribbled word, assuring me of his complete and unswerving devotion and his desire to marry me. Nothing in the world could have made me happier, for I suspected that I was once again with child, the delightful outcome of our parting evening. More than anything I wanted to retire to Merton with him and our cozy little family. How I longed to sign my letters *Emma Nelson*! I used to practice on sheets of foolscap and then burn my romantic efforts so the servants should never see them.

Of paramount concern to Nelson was the placement of netting, about three feet high, around the "Nile" at Merton, to prevent Horatia from falling into the water. More than once he reminded me whom to speak with about it, for they had told him where such a commodity might be purchased, adding, *I shall be very anxious until I know this is done.* In one letter, he told me of his plans to settle four thousand pounds on Horatia—through a trustee—*For I will not put it in my own power to have her left destitute; for she would want friends if we left her in this world. She shall be independent of any smile or frown!*

Though he was kept prodigiously busy by the exigencies of his commission, Nelson always had time to write to me. I had told him that we were once again going to be parents, and on August 23, 1803, he composed a passionate and somewhat agonized reply:

> *My Dearest Beloved, To say that I think of you by day, night, and all day, and all night, but too faintly expresses my feelings of love and affection towards you. The call of our country is a duty which you would deservedly in the cool moments of reflection, reprobate, was I to abandon: and I should feel so disgraced by seeing you ashamed of me! No longer saying, "This is the man who has saved his country! This is he who is the first to go forth to fight our battles, and the last to return!"*
>
> *"Ah," they will think. "What a man! What sacrifices has he not made to secure our homes and property; even the society and happy union with the finest and most accomplished woman in*

the world." I shall, my best beloved, return—if it pleases God—
a victor; and it shall be my study to transmit an unsullied name.
There is no desire of wealth, no ambition that could keep me
from all my soul holds dear. No; it is to save my country, my wife
in the eye of God. . . . Only think of our happy meeting. Ever,
for ever, I am your's, only your's, even beyond this world. . . . For
ever, for ever, your own Nelson.

Forty-one

This Time We're Not So Lucky

My body was not taking as comfortably to this pregnancy as it had done when I was carrying Horatia, and I was having a far rougher go of it than I did when I was a mere girl myself, with little Emma in my belly. This time, I was gaining a tremendous amount of weight, my stomach was always agitated, and my legs felt like they was cast in lead. Halfway through my time it was becoming an effort just to bend down to scoop up my lapdog. The caricaturists were having a grand old time at my expense.

Missing him something dreadful, I wrote to Nelson suggesting that I might (with young Charlotte accompanying me as a sort of ward) journey down to the Mediterranean and join him on the ship. He scotched the idea immediately. My health, his health, and the general impracticability and unsuitability of the whole arrangement, all were reasons he enumerated for my staying put, not the least of which was our unpopularity: *As for _living_ in Italy, it is entirely out of the question. Nobody cares for us here.*

Worrying for Nelson's ailments put my mind off my own. My poor love complained of toothache and headache, eyeache, writing, *My sight is getting very bad, but I* must not *be sick till after the French fleet is taken*, and heartache—both literal and figurative. The lingering odor from the fresh coat of paint that his flagship *Victory* had received before her departure was making him ill as well . . . and he mentioned to me that he had more than once been seasick.

"What's all the Peruvian bark for if you won't avail yourself of it?" I lightly scolded, endeavoring to conceal the depths of my anxieties.

Toward the end of 1803, I took to my bed with a cold and a cough. It was more than a month before my time, but in truth, I felt too unwell to maintain my energetic entertaining. I lacked enthusiasm for just about everything and wanted to see no one but Mam.

On January 20, 1804, my babe arrived prematurely. The pain was excruciating; I bit down on cotton towels that my shrieks should not shake the house to its rafters and affright the servants.

"It's another girl," Mam whispered. I was almost too spent to take her in my arms. She was too small; I could see that. "Please heaven, let her live," I mumbled before I fell into a deep sleep with the tiny mite on my chest.

Where I had been up and about within a day of Horatia's birth, I could barely stir after bringing Nelson's second daughter into the world. *If it's a girl, she must be Emma*, he had written ecstatically when he first learnt of my pregnancy, *for what else could she be, after our first pledge of love was called Horatia?* I had still never told him about the first "little Emma," nor could I ever do so now. The newborn Emma was to be left with Mrs. Gibson, but this time, the foster mother had to be let in on the secret. There was no credulity in my appearing on the woman's doorstep for the second time in three years with another foundling in my arms. I was to inform her that Lord Nelson would certainly settle a small pension on her, providing she never broke her silence. Even Horatia should be kept from the knowledge that the new arrival was her sister.

I had remained mostly bedridden since baby Emma's birth, attended by Dr. John Heaviside, who dwelt just around the corner from me in George Street, Hanover Square, as something had happened to me during the birthing. Dr. Heaviside had prescribed the insertion of a pessary to support my womb, for he had diagnosed my condition as a dropped uterus. This, he said, was causing my unbearable back pain and the pressure I was feeling every time I went to the commode. Though I could complain of illness, I could not tell my dear Nelson just what a mess I was in, for I was convinced he would have said "Damn the French!" and heeled the *Victory* for home. As much as I wanted to hold him in my arms forever, never did I try to keep him from his duty to king and country.

One morning in mid-March, we received a note from Mrs. Gibson regarding my girls. They was suffering from the smallpox. I insisted on rousing myself from my sickbed to see them, for they was Nelson's children and I could not live with my shame were I to put my health above theirs. I hired a hack and set off for Little Titchfield Street. There I found Mrs. Gibson, dabbing at her eyes, and Horatia, feverish and covered in spots. I knew that Nelson, once he learnt of it, would accuse me of disobeying his instructions that the child be vaccinated. I had asked Mrs. Gibson to see that it be done, but perhaps it was not done proper.

"Where is baby Emma?" I whispered.

Mrs. Gibson looked stricken. "Not fifteen minutes ago, the Lord took her for His own." She bosted into tears. "I am so sorry, your ladyship. There was nothing to be done for her. The doctor came, but he didn't think she'd pull through, such a weak little thing."

I could not rail at her. I had to believe that she'd indeed done her best and fulfilled her obligations to look after the girls as best she knew. Baby Emma, still wrapped in her blanket, was placed inside an apple crate, the box was closed, and I returned with it to Clarges Street, my mind in such a haze that I scarce remembered the drive home.

Mam sussed up the situation immediately. "My poor gal," she

wept. "Poor Emy. The both of you." I immediately took to my bed. "What do you want to do with 'er?" Mam asked gently.

"Bury 'er, of course."

"I may be old, but I'm not daft, child. Do you want the world to know 'ow you came by that apple crate?"

I shook my head. "But I cannot allow a child of Nelson's to be placed in unconsecrated ground." I thought it over. "I'd always wanted to bring little Emma—Emma Carew now—to live with us in Edgware Road, y'nau? So if we take baby Emma to St. Mary's Church at the edge of Paddington Green, at least one of 'em will get to live there. Sort of."

"St. Mary's is Papist, y'nau? Since when 'ave you developed a fancy for popery?"

"So many years in Naples, I suppose," I sighed.

"And *we* ain't taking baby Emma to St. Mary's. You're too ill to be running about. I'll take 'er there. I don't get out much, so it's not likely I'll be recognized, specially when I'm wearing heavy mourning. And I pay the priest double to lay 'er in an unmarked grave and strike everything from the parish register. There won't be no slipups if your own mam attends to it."

Then I set pen to paper and imparted the news I despaired to write, telling Nelson that Horatia and I had been at death's door; and with the heaviest of hearts, I added that baby Emma had passed through it. Truly, I wrote, when I learnt of the unhappy event, it was the saddest day I had known since Sir William's death.

Horatia did survive the smallpox, but after such a scare, Nelson became adamant that she be removed from Mrs. Gibson's as soon as possible, and come to live with us at Merton.

And Nelson, as brokenhearted as I at the death of our baby girl, and acknowledging the emotional cost of all our subterfuge, as well as the fact that his letters could be read by others before they ever reached me, assured me of my place in his affections:

> *. . . I do not say all I wish; and which, my Dearest <u>beloved</u>*
> *Emma (read that whoever opens this letter and for what I care*
> *publish it to the world), your fertile imagination can readily*
> *fancy I would say, but this I can say with great truth: that I am*
> *<u>for ever yours</u>.*

To cheer me, he sent me charming birthday presents from
Sardinia—a Spanish comb and an unusual pair of gloves with a
muff made from the golden beards of mussel shells. He also enclosed a banknote, and sent gifts for Horatia as well: a pretty gold
watch set with seed pearls around the case to wear on Sundays and
special occasions, and a pendant. Horatia had once asked him for
a dog, but Nelson had written to me saying he could not possibly
have promised her such a thing, as they had no dogs on board his
ships. However, he settled the matter as he might have done a dispute between two of his men: he sent his little daughter a delicate
openwork medallion of a greyhound on a golden chain.

Once again, I tried to rouse my spirits by surrounding myself
with life. Nelson's sister-in-law Sarah Nelson and I had become
close over the past couple of years. I called her "my jewel," and she
had become something of a confidante, though there were certain
secrets she was never to know, for she did love to talk—incessantly,
in fact, and at stunning velocity. Sarah suspected the truth about
Horatia's parentage long before anyone else did, for being an ob-
servant sort (or at least the sort who gives a thought to anyone beyond himself—unlike her husband, the reverend), she had noticed
the child's resemblance to Nelson when we was all at Merton over
Christmas in 1803. After Sir William's death, she offered to entertain us at their rectory in Canterbury whenever I chose. I did enjoy
their company, though her husband was rather a prig, and he constantly leered at me. The hypocritical William Nelson was appalled
when I proposed a champagne-drinking contest one night. But my
heart was broke when invitations would arrive for some rout or ball

addressed to Dr. Nelson and his family with "but not Lady Hamilton" written across them.

"You know *we* want you, dear," Sarah insisted. But I had my pride, and I packed my things and returned to London, where I was more than appreciated. I wrote to Nelson, much amused, that I had received offers of marriage from the second son of a viscount, and from an earl. "But my being, body and soul, heart and mind, so completely belongs to you, that I cannot even spare a look for another."

As far as expenditures at Merton went, there were so many projects I planned for our dear farm, and I was eager that everything should be in place for Nelson's next homecoming. However, my beloved cautioned against my opening my own purse against the improvements, nor to spend my money "to please a pack of fools," for he was certain that my bountiful nature was abused by all and sundry and I was too naive to know when I was being taken advantage of. Yet what else could I do?

Following several months of negotiations, our neighbor Mr. Axe was convinced to sell Nelson his lands. After the small matter of the exchange of eight thousand pounds, Paradise Merton became an estate comprising 115 acres. Nelson had borrowed the entire sum, getting half from Alexander Davison and the other half from his brother-in-law, the handsome adventurer and entrepreneur George Matcham, out of Katty's marriage portion.

Once again the tradesmen descended upon Merton Place. Modern water closets were to be installed, and the wooden doors that opened onto the garden and our raised "quarterdeck" would be replaced with glass ones, in order to bring in as much light as possible. There was to be plenty of nursery space added as well. I wished Merton to be more than a paradise for lovers; it should be a true family home, where Nelson would never have a care in the world.

We would improve the kitchen with the addition of a Rumford

stove, which had fitted ovens for cooking and baking, a water boiler with its own tap, and plenty of shelves, enabling more than one thing to cook at a time. The hearth was to be much increased in size so that the hotplates could be heated by a flue running from the chimney, conveying hot gases to the fire. Mam, for one, was overjoyed. Our perpetual entertaining would be so much easier from now on!

A modern washhouse was to be built behind the servants' quarters. I had an icehouse erected in the garden, and ordered the construction of a brewery on the property that we might make our own beer, though we would still bring in stout, as well as all our wines, from London. We could soon rely on our own vegetables as well. In short, dear Merton was becoming a county squire's idyll.

Having not heard from Nelson in some weeks, I despaired. Where was he that he could not dispatch a letter? Was all well? In October, I sent a note to Davison, sharing with him the depth and breadth of my love for Nelson, for I could not keep my emotions locked away any longer, and I knew that Davison was not only aware of our situation but sympathetic to it. I was miserable. How ridiculous it all was that Nelson should still be wedded to a woman he did not love, whilst he and I should suffer so. I would have settled for dying in two hours if I could have been Nelson's wife for one. How I wished with every fiber of my being that our love could be completely out in the open. Priggish Admiralty! Damn the hypocrisy of society! Had not Nelson done enough for his country that they should let him love in peace?!

> *. . . I am anxious and agitated to see Him. I never shall be*
> *well till I do see him, the disappointment would kill me. I love*
> *him, I adore him, my mind and soul is now transported with the*
> *thoughts of that Blessed Extatic moment when I shall see Him,*
> *embrace Him. Ours is not a common, dull love. It may be a sin*

to love, I say it might have been a sin when I was another's but I had then more merit in trying to suppress it. I am now <u>Free</u> and I must sin on and love Him more than ever, it is a crime worth going to Hell for. May God only spare Him and send Him safe back. I shall be at Merton till I see him as He <u>particularly</u> wishes our first meeting should be there. . . .

Forty-two

Paradise Regained

Nelson was unwell again. He was suffering from a rheumatic fever and he wrote that he could feel the blood rushing up the left side of his head like water through a pipe. He'd been coughing so violently that he'd hacked up a ball of phlegm that he vowed had been the size of his fist. Night sweats and intense pains in his side rendered him sleepless. The shipboard physician had told him that the wound he had sustained during the Battle of Cape St. Vincent was a hernia. *If God in His mercy sees fit to send me home, I hope He won't mind if His poor Nelson chuses a less active means of service in future. What would you say, my dearest Emma, if I was to tell you that I've been thinking it would not be such a bad thing if I was to go into the Admiralty?*

I was overjoyed. If the Admiralty would have him, Nelson would remain by my side forever and we could indeed live our dream at Merton Place. But my pragmatic side told me that Nelson and the Admiralty would take to each other as well as oil does to water: they would never meld without a great deal of stirring.

At least I had a bit of good news to share with him. Lord Melville had spoken to Prime Minister Pitt about my pension, suggesting the figure of five hundred pounds a year. It was less than half Sir William's pension, but I was up to my arse in bills and anything at all would have been a boon. The upkeep of homes in town and country, entertainment at both, travel expenses, Horatia's care, my wardrobe and jewelry, presents to Nelson's family and my own—all greatly exceeded Sir William's annuity of eight hundred pounds and Nelson's gift to me of twelve hundred pounds a year.

Nelson, who in April was promoted to vice admiral of the white, already had his hands full, though even during the ugly business of war, he was able to spare a loving thought for me, pining for him at home. On March 16, he wrote from the *Victory*: *Your resemblance is never absent from my mind, and my own dearest Emma I hope very soon that I shall embrace the substantial heart of you instead of the ideal, that will I am sure give us both real pleasure and exquisite happiness.* But duty interrupted this most felicitous reverie. On March 29, in heavy fog, the French fleet slipped through the British blockade at Toulon and headed for the West Indies. As he set his fleet on a course for Gibraltar to chase down the French, Nelson wrote to me of his concerns for Horatia. First, he would make good on his intention to settle an annuity on Mrs. Gibson provided she had nothing more to do with Horatia, either directly or indirectly, nor was she to speak to anyone about her ever having cared for the child. Further, he was instructing Haslewood to hold four thousand pounds in trust for Horatia, in an account that would be beyond my reach. Had he hit me with a full broadside, I should not have been so wounded. I was cut to the quick. Not to trust me! It was as if to accuse me outright of squandering our daughter's inheritance!

Beside myself, I sat down to reply in anger to his letter, but found my ire melting by the moment. I responded with a poem instead.

> *I think I have not lost my heart,*
> *Since I with truth can swear,*
> *At every moment of my life,*
> *I feel my Nelson there.*

If from thine Emma's breast her heart
Were stolen or thrown away,
Where, where should she my Nelson's love
Record each happy day?

If from thine Emma's breast her heart
Were stolen or thrown away,
Where, where should she engrave, my Love,
Each tender word you say?

Where, where should Emma treasure up
Her Nelson's smiles and sighs,
Where mark with joy each secret look
Of love from Nelson's eyes?

Then do not rob me of my heart,
Unless you first forsake it;
And then so wretched it would be,
Despair alone would take it.

There was no more talk of the arrangements for Horatia's annuity. In a calmer mood I realized that perhaps Nelson did have sound reason for his actions, for he never did a thing in his life—even his "spontaneous" maneuvers during a battle—that he had not fully thought through.

Frustrated by the incompetence of a fellow admiral who had let the Frenchies slip right past his fleet near Gibraltar—necessitating Nelson's mad chase across the Atlantic to the West Indies—he expressed the most vehement wish to be sent home. He immediately added—with further fury—that Whitehall would not *let* him return. Then, his anger vented, and his undying love vowed to me and to Horatia, he fell frighteningly silent.

Meanwhile, I tried to quiet my nerves. As ever when I was

under extreme anxiety, my rashes returned; in late July I took a brief sea-bathing excursion, for that was the only cure that availed. I had just come home from a week or so away and was going through the correspondence that had mounted during my departure when I came across a letter from Emma Carew, saying she had reason to believe that she was a relation of mine; as she was coming down to London in August and understood that I was often to be found at Merton entertaining both friends and family, might she call upon me?

My pen was poised to compose a reply, but I hesitated. What should I say? Would it be better to see her after all these years, or tell a white lie and apologize that I would be unable to receive her, as I planned to be visiting in Norfolk or Canterbury then? A splash of ink spread across the page.

"Excuse me, ma'am." A soft, though unfamiliar, voice startled me. Another splotch dropped from my quill.

I turned to discover a pleasant-looking young woman, tall, with ash-blond hair and unremarkable features. "Can I 'elp you?"

"I hope so," she replied with a shy smile. Her speech was good, with just the slightest hint of Mancunian. "My name is Emma Carew."

My hands quivered, my jaw trembled, and it took all my nerve to steady myself from the shock.

"Did you not get my letter, then? I had written to you more than a week ago, but when I had no answer, I took the liberty of coming down here on the chance you might be receiving."

"I—I just opened your letter," I stammered, "and was about to send you a reply. I'm just lately back from sea bathing at Ramsgate, you see, and"—I indicated a stack of papers—"I've only just begun to peruse the correspondence that awaited my return."

An odd look crossed "little Emma's" face. "Sea bathing. I see."

Oh, dear God! Without thinking, I had touched upon a memory that 'twas best left buried. I changed the subject. "Well . . . of course you are welcome to stay 'ere, especially as you have come all this way from . . . ?"

"From Manchester. I am a governess up there. Does Mrs. Cadogan reside here as well? It was she who told me—"

"Told you what?"

"That we were related, of course."

I let this sink in. "Perhaps a cousin to the Connor side of the family?" I suggested, my countenance open and placid. "Or maybe the Lyons? Or is it the Kidds? My gammer was a Kidd." Mam could never have mentioned to Emma that the girl was my daughter . . . could she? "Mrs. Cadogan is out back, I believe. Allow me to fetch her. I am sure she will be delighted to learn of your arrival."

My outward show was all politesse; inwardly, I was in utter turmoil. I found Mam on her hands and knees in the kitchen garden digging up turnips. "Mam, Emma Carew has just arrived. Tell me, and tell me true: did you plan this?"

Mam rose unsteadily. Why she insisted on rooting about the garden at her age and with her bad hip taxed all common sense. "No, Emy, gal, I didn't. Though it might be time to think about telling the child the truth now that she's all grown."

"She says 'twas you as told her we was kin. What exactly was it you told 'er about the nature of our relations?"

"I said she was a distant cousin—of mine—which makes 'er once more removed from you. 'Twould make 'er kin to the Kidds when all is said and done, as far as the fiction is concerned. We *are* taking 'er in, I 'ope."

"Well, of course we are! Only I 'ope I never 'ave to answer too many questions. My 'eart won't be able to stand up to it, y'nau?"

I had lived the lie for so many years, I was surprised to find that it was not as difficult to maintain as I had expected, or rather dreaded, it would be. Little Emma was everything her own mam was not: grave where I was enthusiastic, well-bred—which I had never been—and properly educated, where I'd got what learning I had, piecemeal, as an adult. I admit it was quite pleasant having the dear girl under my roof, though maintaining the fiction prevented me from gushing with pride at the sweet creature she had become. Overwhelmed with regrets, I did not deserve to admit to her that she was my daughter.

On August 18, we was all thrown into a state at the news that Nelson was home! He had written from Spithead to say he expected to be released from quarantine the following day and would fly back to Merton! It had been two years and three months since we had parted. How my heart rejoiced! I ached to show him every devotion that my soul and body could devise.

Immediately, I dashed off letters to the William Nelsons, the Boltons, and the Matchams, and drove posthaste back to town to claim Horatia from Mrs. Gibson. I owed her thirty pounds for back care, and I gave her an additional twenty on Nelson's behalf, representing the annuity he had promised her for releasing his "adopted" daughter into my care, that I might be her guardian from now on. Mrs. Gibson agreed to the terms, acknowledging in writing that she would have nothing more to do with Horatia.

What scurrying I did to be sure that everything was in order against Nelson's arrival. My heart had begun pounding wildly in my chest from the moment I read his letter. To embrace him again! To feel his skin against mine, to bury my face in his scent! His room was to be a shrine to our love. A fine new Kidderminster carpet covered his bedroom floor. Laid upon his mattress were the enormous goose-down feather bed and bolsters he had requested me to purchase on his behalf from the London upholsterer Mr. Peddison—who also happened to be an undertaker, and who, at present, was in possession of the coffin Captain Hallowell had made from *L'Orient's* mainmast.

Nelson arrived at Merton on August 20. His entire family was there to welcome him home. Such laughter and tears spilled forth that day; as for myself, I could scarce leave off kissing him. I had to escort him on a private tour of all the improvements I had made to Merton in his absence, in order that we might steal a few moments together.

"I'm sure you've already noticed that the naked statues that was in the gardens last time are gone. Because they so offended you, I gave 'em all away, every last one of them! And there," I said, pointing to the charming new summerhouse, "is your 'poop deck.' But, come, you must first see what we've done with the Nile!" I exclaimed, leading him down to the tributary. It had been filled in on two sides, allowing for better access to all the new meandering gravel walks about the property. The grounds had been landscaped with gentle grassy slopes and planted with plenty of shade trees. It was a lovers' paradise. "Wait till you see all this in the fall," I said, gesturing toward our arboretum. "Imagine it in russet and gold and every color in between."

He'd slipped my arm through his, then held my hand as we sat on the bankside. I drank in every inch of him, noticing that his dear hair had grown quite gray over the past three years. "You are the most beautiful, wonderful, magnificent woman in the world," he whispered. "My dearest, beloved Emma. Was there ever man on earth as fortunate as I, to be loved by Emma Hamilton?"

Our lips met. Neither of us cared who might have been watching. For a long time we just tasted each other, simultaneously reconnecting and exploring. " 'Love' is too small a word. I don't believe there exists one weighty enough to bear my feelings. Right now I should be 'appy to say that I should never want you to quit my sight. You 'ave been gone from my arms for so long that if you was to step into the kitchen garden, it would be a world away."

He rested his head on my shoulder, and together we gazed at the water and just allowed ourselves to *be* for a while, listening to the whispers of the elements. "Look!" Nelson chuckled, pointing to the pond. "Look at those pikes!"

The fish were opening and shutting their enormous mouths as if to gobble up anything that came within reach. " 'Ow do you reckon we've got the Nile to stay so clean? I think of 'em as aquatic goats!"

"Life is not worth preserving without happiness. I love everything today!" Nelson sighed, "Even your silly lapdog, but if he comes near my ankles again, I may not be responsible for my actions. The Forest of Arden could not have been a more perfect idyll than this. I do believe I could safely say that there is not a dearer place on earth, nor a dearer soul to me, than Merton Farm and Lady Hamilton. And I wish never to quit 'em both."

I brought my lips to his. "Then don't, my love. Then don't."

We spent much of every day within the scope of each other's gaze. At night we held each other and made love, finding delight in every kiss and caress. The mornings came too soon. The house was filled to bosting with Nelson's family, and we had all his friends to dinner: Captains Hardy, Ball, and Fremantle, and so many others! Such conviviality! Four-and-a-half-year-old Horatia adored the funny one-armed man who bought her an enormous rocking horse, and a little silver cup from Salters' with her name engraved upon it, and the words *To my much loved Horatia* with the date, *21 August 1805*, and below it an engraved facsimile of his signature of *Nelson & Bronte*. Nelson sat her upon his knee and finally told her that he was her real papa, though I was still to be called Lady Hamilton and was her guardian, just *as if* I was her mother. I had introduced Emma Carew to my lover as a "distant cousin," and as there was so little resemblance between us, he never thought to question it—though it should be said that Nelson never thought to question *any* thing I told him.

On September 1, a Sunday, we drove into London, for Nelson wished to discuss Britain's and the enemy's naval strategy with the prime minister and the First Lord of the Admiralty. Pitt, always a sympathetic ear where Nelson was concerned, listened attentively and promised to give the matter serious attention. On the following day, Nelson sat down with a number of other prominent men to share his convictions (both intuited and reasoned) regarding the combined fleet's future movements.

After his meeting, Nelson and I took a stroll together, finding ourselves utterly mobbed as we walked in Piccadilly. His name was cheered with each step we took. Nelson grew a bit red-faced from all the attention.

"Why, you *like* to be applauded; you can't deny it!" I quizzed. "Look 'ow they all love you! And what else do you notice about 'em?"

"Many of 'em could do with a good wash?"

"Now I know you're teasing me, for there's several that look quite well turned out to me. Think on't! Not a one of 'em 'as 'ad an unkind word for Lady Hamilton walking by your side. They've read the newspapers; they've seen the caricatures; it's not as if they 'aven't heard the rumors that you and I might as well be one. But they don't seem to give a gray rat's arse about it. Which makes them plenty better bred than those 'Anovers up at Windsor."

"You're still smarting about not being permitted to be presented at court."

"You bet I am!"

"If it's any consolation to you, my love, I am, too."

The household was awakened the following morning at five thirty by Captain Henry Blackwood, a pleasant-looking man of thirty-five, bearing news that the French fleet had been sighted off Cádiz. Just three hours earlier, in the dead of night, Blackwood had delivered this intelligence to the Admiralty, which had immediately dispatched him to Merton. Not only had Nelson been right about the enemy; he had been anticipating such news.

After Blackwood's departure, I found a pensive Nelson pacing his "quarterdeck" in the crisp dawn air. I laid my hand upon his arm. "What's troubling you, my love?"

"I wouldn't give sixpence to call the king my uncle," he cryptically replied. "You heard enough of what Blackwood said to have sussed out the situation."

I tried to swallow the lump that had risen in my throat. "If the nation needs you, you must go."

"I am torn—beyond torn! I feel my body stretched upon the rack. For here we have the most perfect domestic felicity that ever man could imagine. And how could I ever be compelled to quit your side again, but for my duty to my country? Whatever may be my fate, I have no doubt in my own mind but that my conduct will be such as will not bring a blush on the face of my friends. The lives of all are in the hands of Him who knows best whether to preserve it or no, and to His will do I resign myself. My character and good name is in my own keeping. Life with disgrace is dreadful. A glorious death is to be envied, and if anything happens to me, recollect, my dear Emma, that death is a debt we must all pay, and whether now or in a few years hence can be but of little consequence."

"It's a very pretty speech," I sniffled. "You can employ it to rouse your men, like Henry V. But it is of *great* consequence to *me* when you pay that inevitable debt." I placed my hands on his shoulders and faced him squarely. "Nelson, if you're planning on dying this time, then I'm not letting you go!"

He pressed on in the same morbid vein, as though he were insensible of my tender feelings. Was he trying to prepare me, no matter how resistant I wished to remain? "There is a song you always sang on the *Foudroyant*. You used to accompany yourself on the Irish harp." He began to sing it softly.

> *Fly not yet! 'Tis now the hour*
> *When Beauty reigns with her magic power*
> *Then stay! Oh Stay! Hours like this so seldom reign*
> *This hour we never can regain*
> *Oh, wherefore go we hence?*

"My voice is dreadful, I fear. I sound like a tree frog. Emma, my love . . . I wish the sheet music to be placed in my coffin and for you to sing that for me at my funeral."

I nearly became sick. "No!"

He was all confusion. "No? You most angelic perfect creature, who refuses me nothing in life, will not sing my favorite melody at my memorial service?"

"Do you really think I should be able to speak, let alone sing, at such a miserable occasion? I 'ope to 'eaven that such event never arises during my lifetime, for I should wish to be struck dead immediately if you go before me." I blinked back tears. "Now, husht thee naise. There'll be no more talk of death. I forbid it."

Nelson's departure was both unavoidable and imminent. One morning I wept into my breakfast, while Susannah Bolton tried to comfort me. "You poor, sweet pet. I wish I could offer words of comfort, but you know as well as I that we can say 'Do not worry; all will be well,' but in truth we know nothing of the kind."

I pushed my coffee away. "It seems as though I 'ave 'ad a fortnight's dream and am awoke to all the misery of this cruel separation. But what can I do? 'Is powerful arm is of so much consequence to 'is country." I rose from the table, my appetite entirely vanished. "But I cannot say more. My 'eart is broken."

So much had to be prepared against Nelson's leaving. He went up to London to see Peddison, paid him the thirty-two pounds he owed for the feather bed and bolsters, and asked that his name be engraved on the *Orient* coffin lid, grimly adding that he thought it highly probable he would require it on his return from Cádiz. He picked up a new pair of spectacles from Mr. Dolland, and called upon Barrett, Corney & Corney, lace makers and embroiderers to Their Majesties, commissioning from them five sets of silver embroidered stars of the Orders of St. Ferdinand, the Crescent, St. Joachim, and the Bath. Mam and I spent the evening stitching a full set of stars onto each of Nelson's five coats.

There were rounds of parties and invitations, for everyone was anxious to have the opportunity to say good-bye. Even Greville thought to host a dinner in Nelson's honor, but as Nelson's time had grown so limited, he was genuinely sorry to have to decline. An entire wagon bound for the *Victory* was packed with food and drink: bottles of wine and double brown stout, twenty hams, kegs of tripe and pickles, sauces, mustard, pepper, and other condiments. When it set out for Portsmouth, I could not hide my tears, for his own departure was that much closer.

"I can't bear it," I told Nelson. "Every hour I find myself thinking that there will be one less of them until you are torn from my sight."

"Let's go to the church," he told me. "You are already my wife in the eyes of God, and before I leave, I don't think it would go amiss to remind Him of it."

The Dowager Lady Spencer was down at Merton when we chose to visit the church. She attended the service alongside us, and was our witness when, after receiving the host, Nelson took my hand and, facing the priest, said loud enough for the dowager countess to hear without her ear trumpet, "Emma, I have taken the Sacrament with you this day, to prove to the world that our friendship is most pure and innocent, and of this I call God to witness."

I believe God *then* witnessed, tho' the Dowager Lady Spencer did not, our surreptitious exchanging of *fede* rings: identical gold bands resembling a pair of clasped hands.

Nelson's departure was set for the night of Friday, September 13. The *Victory* had been all fitted up and was waiting for him at Portsmouth. That afternoon, we dined *en famille* with the entire Nelson-Bolton-Matcham broods, as well as with Lord Minto and the editor of the *Morning Chronicle*, my old friend James Perry. The family was courteous in retiring early, but Perry and Minto kept Nelson talking past sunset. I could not wait for them to quit the house!

Finally, they made for home, and Nelson and I made love for the last time before our parting. I was more sensible than ever to the pressure of his lips on mine, to the taste of him, to the sensation of my bare skin against his, to the way my eager body received the gift of his own. I must have kissed and caressed and honored every pore of his dear anatomy.

The tears coursed down my cheeks, bedewing his chest with salt water. My face was an honest picture of the sufferings of my heart. "God knows when we next shall see one another."

He reached up to stroke my cheek, catching the falling drops with his knuckles. "Brave Emma," he murmured.

"But I'm not. I'm not the slightest bit brave, and you know it."

"Nonsense," he said, forcing a chuckle. "I daresay you're the bravest woman in England. If there were more Emmas, there would be more Nelsons."

With great reluctance I helped him dress. We tiptoed into Horatia's room, where she slept the sleep of the innocent, her chubby arm embracing a fluffy toy bunny. Ever so gently, Nelson kissed her, then knelt and prayed beside her bed.

We exchanged the most tearful of farewells, and Nelson dashed off to his waiting chaise. But scarce had he got through the front door when he turned and ran back to me, drawing me so close to his bosom that I could feel the impression of his embroidered orders against my bodice. We held each other wordlessly, for we were too emotional to utter any. Then Nelson forced himself to break away from me, and once more made for his carriage. Again, he returned to my arms, and after resolving to leave in earnest, he got no farther than three feet from the house before he came back to me for a fourth time.

"There is no one on earth I love so well as you," he murmured. His own face was stained with tears. He knelt at my feet, raised his hand to God, and asked Him to bless me. "Amen" was the last word he spoke. Then he turned and strode resolutely toward the open door. This time he made it to the chaise without even looking back; I heard the *thumpf* of the closing carriage door, the turning of the latch, and the crack of the whip. The gravel crunched as the horses clip-clopped down the drive. It was ten thirty in the evening on Friday, September 13, 1805.

I never went to sleep that night. My mind was haunted by an anecdote Nelson had once told me. Many years previous, Nelson, superstitious as all sailors tended to be, permitted a Gypsy woman to tell his fortune. The scryer foretold, year by year, Nelson's losses as well as his triumphs, but when she reached 1805, she exclaimed that the crystal ball had suddenly gone dark. "I can see no farther," she had said.

Forty-three

Nelson Lost

At sea, Nelson would be in command of twenty-seven ships of the line as well as a handful of frigates, sloops, and other smaller vessels. He had 2,148 guns at his disposal, and all told, 17,000 souls sailed for Cádiz. Thomas Masterman Hardy was to be his flag captain aboard the *Victory*, with 820 men under his aegis, in addition to dozens of officers and midshipmen, and 31 boys. The entire fleet had painted their ships alla Nelson: with yellow horizontal stripes on the lines of the gunports, and the ports themselves painted black, the hulls resembled floating checkerboards.

The night before he sailed from Portsmouth, Nelson hosted a dinner on board the *Victory* for his friend George Rose from the Treasury, and Canning, the Treasurer of the Navy, during which he made Rose swear to interest Pitt in my claims to a pension. Even with the combined fleet of the enemy on his horizon, my beloved was ever my champion.

On the day after Nelson's departure I wrote to his secretary, John Scott, confiding my despair: *All these three short weeks of happiness seems like a dream—in short I am all most disturbed. . . . Poor little Horatia cryed out at breakfast for good papa, but I cannot describe to you—you can imagine all our wretchedness.* I could not bear to be too long alone in his absence, so I traveled to Canterbury to visit the William Nelsons for a few weeks, leaving Horatia under the tutelage of Cecilia Connor, who was proving to be a capable governess. Despite the odd display of temperament now and again, Horatia was quite the apt little pupil, already reading, with still three months to go before she saw her actual fifth birthday. The child possessed Nelson's sense of duty, which was already serving her well. I confess that her temper, and the rashes on her knees and elbows, were among the few things she had inherited from me.

Emma Carew returned to Manchester a week before Nelson departed. Mam had suggested to me that since "little Emma" was making her way in the world as a governess herself, it might do the girl a good turn if we was to employ her instead of taking on Cecilia.

"After all, we've been telling 'er she's our cousin, and if we're asking Cecilia, 'oo's got no experience in teaching, we might as well give little Emma the income instead, y'nau?" But I could not bring myself to hire one of my girls to educate the other, and neither one to know they were my daughters. My heart could not have withstood such a situation, nor could I handle being ever on my toes that the least thing might slip from my lips.

I urged the husband of my heart to write to me of every little thing; he should not spare a single detail. On October 22, I received a letter from him dated October 1, in which he told me he prayed that the ministry would send him more ships of the line but that he hoped to prevail nonetheless. He apologized for the brevity of his letters since his departure. *But had I a ream of paper at my disposal, all I might write could be comprised in one short sentence: I love you dearly, tenderly, affectionately.* He did find the time to write a poem for me, which he enclosed with the October 1 letter.

HENRY (OFF CÁDIZ) TO EMMA

The storm is o'er,
The troubled main
Now heaves no more,

But all is silent—hushed—and calm again,
Save in this bosom—where a ceaseless storm
Is raised—by love and Emma's beauteous form.

No calm, at sea,
This heart shall know,
While far from thee,
Midst lengthening hours of absence, and of woe,
I gaze—in sorrow, o'er the boundless deep,
With eyes—which were they not ashamed would weep.

But hark, I hear
The signal gun.
Farewell, my dear.
The Victory leads on. The fight's begun.
Thy Picture, round this cannon's neck shall prove,
A pledge—to valour, sent by thee and love.

Should conquest smile,
On Britain's fleet,
(As at the Nile,)
With joyful hearts, upon the beach we'll meet.
No more I'll tempt the dangers of the sea,
But live, in Merton's groves, with love and thee.

Horatio Nelson

Our letters always had a way of calming each other. Just knowing how much we were beloved in each other's eyes was a balm to the troubled soul. I had suffered many anxieties whilst Nelson was away this time, but his poem arrived as a reassuring caress. I folded the sheet of paper and wore it every day tucked beneath my stays, next to my bosom. I knew that beneath his shirt and stock, about his neck he wore a chain, and from that chain hung a miniature copy of me as Vigée Le Brun's *Reclining Bacchante*. It was the image he always wore by his heart, while the Schmidt pastel of me graced his great cabin and Romney's *Emma as St. Cecilia* blessed him nightly from one of the walls in his sleeping cabin.

On November 6, I was lying in bed at Merton when I thought I heard the Tower guns, for it was quite possible that such a loud report could travel the six miles from London. Susannah Bolton knocked upon my bedroom door, having heard the noise as well, and surmised that it heralded a happy victory. If that was true, soon, then! Soon, Nelson would be coming home!

Four minutes later, a carriage clattered up to the front door. The horses whinnied and snorted. As I was dressing, I sent to inquire who was arrived. They brought me word, Mr. Whitby, from the Admiralty. "Show him in directly," I said. I threw on a dressing gown—I was far too impatient to be laced into my stays—and dashed downstairs.

Captain Whitby, an older gentleman, was standing in the front room in full dress uniform, his hat in his hand and his countenance grave. "We have gained a great victory," he said, his voice faint and feeble.

All I wanted was news from my beloved Nelson. I had not heard from him in weeks. "Never mind your victory! My letters—give me my letters!"

Captain Whitby was unable to speak—tears in his eyes and a deathly paleness over his face made me comprehend him. I believe I gave a scream and fell back, and for ten hours after, I could neither speak nor shed a tear.

"Her heart has been shocked by grief, Mrs. Cadogan. It's a catalepsy induced by the dreadful news of Lord Nelson's passing. I've seen one or two cases of a similar nature in my time. I regret that there's nothing I can do for her, nor nothing any of you can do, but remain by her side and offer her every possible tenderness."

"Thank you, Dr. Heaviside."

"I don't want your guineas, Mrs. Cadogan. I couldn't live with myself if I was to charge you a fee for coming down here. I daresay the whole country is in mourning. In London there is not a dry eye in the streets. When the news came, there were people who stood stock-still wherever they were when they heard it, bawling as if they'd just lost their mothers. They'd never heard of 'Traffle-gar' before today, but the word was on everybody's lips. Lord Nelson was greatly loved, ma'am. And he will be sorely missed by his countrymen."

"There's no one going to miss him like my Emy." Mam was sobbing so hard her shoulders heaved up and down as if she were a marionette.

"I do suggest that you bring Lady Hamilton back to London as soon as possible that I may be just a few steps away, should you need my services again."

I could hear them, but I felt as if my body were inside a glass dome trapped underwater. Everyone around me was weeping, but there was no salt water for *my* eyes. Not then. Not yet.

I do not remember being dressed. I do not remember being bundled into the coach. I do not remember the journey up to town. I do not remember how I came to be in my bed at Clarges Street, but when my senses began to return, I found myself propped up against the bolsters, with a ring of concerned faces about me: those of Mam, and Nelson's family, my dear friend Lady Betty Foster. Cecilia Connor was to mind Horatia back at Merton. In such a state as I was in, I could not properly attend to her, nor did I feel it meet to disturb with my grief the routine of a child who was not yet five years old. The time would come soon enough—and I despaired of it—when I should have to tell our daughter that she would see her dear papa no more.

"What shall I do? 'Ow can I exist?" They told me that these were the first words I spoke when I came out of the catalepsy. Completely stunned, I repeated those two questions over and over again, searching the faces around me. One . . . two . . . three . . . four . . . fifteen countenances I counted, and not one of them had an answer for me. They stared back at me like figures in a wax-works. " *'Ow can I exist?* *What shall I do?*" I shouted.

Captain Blackwood, who had commanded the frigate *Euryalus* during the action at Trafalgar on October 21—that fateful day when my heart was torn from me—was, along with Captain Hardy, the first among Nelson's men to pay me a call. Blackwood had been aboard the *Victory* pacing her quarterdeck with Nelson right before the battle commenced.

I could not stir a leg to come downstairs and I asked that the captains be shown up. Blackwood came up alone, and I dismissed those who had kept so constant a vigil over me. "Tell me, tell me everything that 'appened, and do not spare a single detail," I insisted.

"I fear for your ladyship's delicate condition, should I—"

"I must know everything. 'Ow he spent his last hours. What my beloved Nelson said in 'is last breaths."

"Your name was on his lips, milady." The usually stalwart Blackwood reached for his handkerchief. "You were on his mind and in his heart at the very last. But Hardy can tell you exactly what it was he said. He was with Nelson when he . . . when he departed this earth."

"Hardy . . . was there? You know that 'e and I did not always . . ."

"He wants to speak to you directly," Blackwood confided. "Hardy may have spoken his mind on former occasions more freely than you could have wished, but depend upon it that the last words of our lamented friend will influence his conduct. He desires me, in the most unequivocal manner, to assure you of his good intentions towards you. This, I hope, will ease your mind."

Hardy was then sent up, by my request. He came bearing a large satchel and a packet of correspondence, including my own letters, written during October, that had never reached Nelson, and the last of Nelson's letters to me.

"His very last was begun two days before the action," Hardy said gently. I sifted through them and found my lover's final words to me.

> *Victory Octr 19th: 1805 Noon*
>
> *My Dearest, beloved Emma the dear friend of my bosom the Signal has been made that the Enemy's Combined Fleet are coming out of Port. We have very little Wind so that I have no hopes of seeing them before tomorrow. May the God of Battles crown my endeavors with success at all events. I will take care that my name shall ever be most dear to you and Horatia, both of whom I love as much as my own life and as my last writing before the battle will be to you, so I hope in God that I shall live to finish my letter after the Battle. May Heaven bless you prays your Nelson & Bronte. Octr. 20th in the morning we were close to the mouth of the Streights, but the Wind had not come far enough to the Westward to allow the combined fleets to weather the shoals off Trafallgar, but they were counted as forty Ships of War, which I suppose to be 34 of the Line and six frigates, a Group of them was seen off the Lighthouse of Cadiz this Morng, but it blows so very fresh & thick weather that I rather believe they will go into the Harbour before night. May God Almighty give us success over these fellows and enable us to get a peace.*

I bosted into hysterical sobs as I read it, the which neither officer begrudged me in the slightest, for their own eyes was misty as well, and it was many minutes before I could regain any semblance of composure.

I kissed the letter and pressed it to my bosom. Then I touched my lips to each of Nelson's other letters to me. "Tell me, now," I urged them. "That I might learn for myself 'ow my brave, beloved Nelson won the day . . ." My voice dropped to the merest whisper. "And 'ow he lost his life." Hardy and Blackwood exchanged glances. "The Admiralty would keep me in the dark, I am certain. But you, if you loved Nelson, as I know you did—and do—you will tell me 'ow it 'appened."

"The fleet was sighted on the morning of October twenty-first, with the nearest enemy ships just under two miles away. Nelson and I were on the *Victory*'s quarterdeck when the shout went up. He turned to me and said, 'Blackwood, I'll now amuse the fleet with a signal. Do you think there is one yet wanting?'

"I could not suppress a chuckle, ma'am, for I replied, 'I think the whole of the fleet seems to understand very clearly what they are about.' For Nelson always sat down with his captains before a battle; every man was apprised of his duties and responsibilities, so that when the action commenced, each knew just what was expected of him, and that Nelson entrusted him to carry it out. He called it the Nelson Touch . . . but I expect you know that."

I nodded. "But *was* there a signal hoisted then?" I wanted to know.

"Nelson walked over to Pasco, the signal officer, and ordered him to raise a signal to the *Africa*, which was sailing towards us over on the larboard beam, near the head of the enemy's line. ENGAGE THE ENEMY MORE CLOSELY, it was to say, and then he commanded Pasco to run up another for the entire fleet to PREPARE TO ANCHOR DURING THE ENSUING NIGHT. He thought for a bit—no more than a few seconds it was, I daresay—before telling Pasco, 'I wish to say to the fleet, ENGLAND CONFIDES THAT EVERY MAN WILL DO HIS DUTY,' adding, 'You must be quick, for I have one more to make, which is for CLOSE ACTION.' Now, Pasco puzzles it over for a moment or so, and finally tells Nelson, 'If your lordship will permit me to substitute *expects* for *confides*, the signal will soon be completed, because the word *expects* is in the vocabulary'—Popham's telegraphic vocabulary, that is—'and *confides* must be spelt.' 'That will do, Pasco,' Nelson replied. 'Make it directly.' Thus, ENGLAND EXPECTS THAT EVERY MAN WILL DO HIS DUTY was the phrase carried in each brave heart as we prepared to engage the combined fleet.

"The crew was clearing his furniture and personal effects out of Nelson's cabin to make room for the guns, and he was very anxious that the seaman transporting your picture—the only one I've ever seen where you have short hair, ma'am—should honor it properly. 'Take care of my guardian angel,' he told the youth, who then was careful to handle the frame as though you yourself were inside it and he feared to drop you. Not a few minutes earlier, Nelson had gazed upon that picture and told me, 'This is what inspires me; she loves glory and will either triumph in my fame or weep over my grave.' "

A sob caught in my throat. " 'E really said that?"

"Had you a Bible, milady, I would swear upon it." Blackwood mopped his brow. "Forgive me, Lady Hamilton. I fully appreciate how difficult the hearing of this news must be for you." He looked shattered.

"I am not insensible to the pains it must cause *you* to relive it for me. But pray continue. It's all I 'ave. Even the saddest news of Nelson keeps 'is name upon our lips."

"The combined fleet had formed themselves into a surprisingly haphazard pattern, when suddenly, at half past eleven, they hoisted their colors and began firing," Hardy said. "The action progressed well, though we were receiving heavy fire at close range." The large man's voice began to quaver a bit. "A lot of carnage on deck, milady. Perhaps I should omit—"

"Omit nothing, Captain 'Ardy. I am already dead. Nothing you say can kill me."

Hardy blinked a few times to scare back the threatening tears. His pale blue eyes were rimmed with red. "At fifteen past one in the afternoon, Nelson and I were walking the quarterdeck. He was wearing his admiral's frock coat, with all the stars and orders stitched upon it—"

"I stitched 'em on myself."

Hardy looked at me, and for the first time in our long acquaintance I thought he finally saw the woman before him as Nelson's true wife. "I urged him to go below and change his coat, for he was a walking target with all that glitter upon him—"

" 'E couldn't 'ave done," I interrupted softly. " 'E 'ad five coats, all identical. At 'is request Mam and I made 'em so. Where was 'e when it 'appened, and 'oo did it that I might pray 'is soul is forever consigned to hell?"

Hardy inhaled the courage to continue. "We were so close to the *Redoutable* then that her rigging was tangled amid the *Victory*'s. Nelson was in the act of turning near the hatchway when a sharpshooter positioned in the mizzen of the *Redoutable*, fired upon him. The ball traveled about fifteen yards, striking Nelson's left epaulet." He paused, and looked away from me.

"But 'ow could anyone make out Nelson—or any man—in all the smoke from the bombardments of cannon and musket?"

"That's why the sharpshooters are in the rigging," replied Blackwood. "They're above much of the direct fray. In the odd moments when the smoke clears enough for them to get a decent view of the enemy, they take aim. And Nelson's golden epaulet, catching the light . . ."

"The musket ball went clean through the shoulder to penetrate his chest," Hardy said. "He fell to the deck on the exact spot where his secretary, Mr. Scott, had been torn in two by a cannonball. A pool of Scott's blood was still warm upon it. 'They have done for me, Hardy,' he whispered to me. 'I hope not,' I replied. 'Yes, my backbone is shot through.' Two marines lifted him up and brought him down the companionway, where he noticed that the tiller ropes had been shot through, and—a commander to the last—

ordered them replaced immediately. Then, afeared that his men should lose heart if they saw him in such bodily distress, he asked that a handkerchief be opened to the fullest and spread across his face and decorated coat that he should not be recognized." Hardy reached into his pocket, withdrew a white linen square, and handed it to me. There was no need to explain its provenance.

"He insisted on waiting his turn for the surgeon, but Dr. Beatty attended to him right away. It was a butcher's shambles down there, and I cannot conscience further disturbing your sensibilities, ma'am, to tell you what bloody horrors I saw before me. When I left Nelson there on the orlop deck to return topside, he was calling for relief and water and air, saying 'fan, fan, drink, drink, rub, rub' over and over. They brought him water, lemonade, and watered-down wine to soothe his suffering. Dr. Scott, his chaplain, remained by Nelson's side, rubbing his chest. Nelson had continued to call for me, and until I returned to the orlop and stood before him, he refused to believe that I was not killed myself.

"He was so relieved to see me and took great comfort when I told him that fourteen or fifteen of the enemy's ships had struck their colors and were now ours. We were winning the day. 'Come nearer to me, Hardy,' Nelson whispered, his voice so faint I had to kneel beside him to hear his words. He was propped up against a bolster. 'Pray let my dear Lady Hamilton have my hair, and all other things belonging to me.' He asked that when he departed this world I should remove your portrait from about his neck and return it to the original. 'God be praised, I have done my duty,' he murmured, squeezing my hand. 'By your leave, sir, I should return to the deck,' I said, though I hated to quit his side. The pain was so severe that Nelson said he wished he were already dead that he might not be sensible of it. 'Yet one would like to live a little longer, too. What would become of Lady Hamilton, if she knew my situation?' "

I had opened Nelson's handkerchief across my palm and was caressing the fabric as if my own flesh beneath it were his dear, dear face. "What indeed?" A tear splashed into my hand.

"I returned to the orlop a second time," Hardy said, "to report to him of our great victory. Not fifteen minutes after Nelson was hit, the *Redoutable* herself struck her colors. 'Anchor, Hardy, anchor,' he said as emphatically as he could manage. 'Shall I have Collingwood assume command, sir?' I asked him." Hardy's voice became more choked with emotion. " 'Not while I live, I hope,' he replied. His spirits seemed to rally. 'If I live, I'll anchor.' Then his thoughts turned inward. 'Don't throw me overboard,' he begged me, and added, 'Take care of my dear Lady Hamilton, Hardy; take care of poor Lady Hamilton.' " The brave Hardy, now racked with sobs, took my hands in his. "And then he said, 'Kiss me Hardy,' and I knelt beside him and touched my lips to his cheek. 'Now I am satisfied,' he said. It seemed to be a sort of benediction he'd requested. 'Thank God I have done my duty,' he whispered. I kissed him again, on the forehead. 'Who is that?' he asked, as if a fever had suddenly taken hold of his senses. 'It is Hardy,' I replied. 'God bless you, Hardy!' he exclaimed, mustering another burst of strength."

I clutched Hardy's hands, for he was one of the last to touch Nelson's skin. He had no more words for me.

"As Dr. Scott is God's witness, he was with Nelson in his final moments," said Blackwood. "Nelson said to him, 'Doctor, I have not been a *great* sinner,' to which the chaplain made no reply."

I brought Nelson's handkerchief to my swollen eyelids. "If God is Love, 'ow can it be a great sin, if any sin at all, to love with all one's 'eart?"

"He then told Scott, 'Remember that I leave Lady Hamilton and my daughter, Horatia, as a legacy to my country; and never forget Horatia,' and he continued to call for relief and exclaim, 'Thank God I have done my duty.' Dr. Scott rubbed Nelson's stomach until Dr. Beatty touched his shoulder. 'You cannot help him anymore,' Beatty said, for Nelson had by then breathed his last." Hardy fell silent for a moment. His lips were quivering. "He expired at sixteen thirty, after the British victory had already been secured. Lady Hamilton, he died as he lived: a hero."

Hardy opened his satchel and handed me a parcel wrapped in brown paper. I opened it to discover Nelson's effects: the silver drinking cup I had given him on his fortieth birthday and which he had used every day since; the miniature portrait of me that Nelson had worn every day about his neck; his queue, gray from worry, for he was only forty-seven when he died; and the blue naval coat he was wearing when he was shot. The musket ball had ripped a hole in the fabric. It was rimmed with dried blood. I held it against my chest, wishing his dead body were alive inside it and had returned to my arms.

"There is as well a pair of shoe buckles which I took off his feet. To you I know they will be doubly dear as he so often knelt at yours. And there is a box downstairs with your larger portraits in it, milady. We wanted you to have everything that was Nelson's before the Admiralty got their hands on them, for there is no more proper legatee than yourself. Chevalier, his valet, took the liberty of honoring one of Nelson's final requests as well. Nelson asked him to remove the gold ring from his finger and see that it was returned to your ladyship." From his pocket, Hardy produced a scrap of black velvet and, within it, the golden band that I had given Nelson at the little parish church in Merton a few days before our parting. I kissed it and slipped it on my little finger, for it was too small to wear just above its twin, my own ring.

I could not take my hands from his damaged coat, caressing every inch of fabric, as though my touch could restore its owner to life. "Where is his dear body?"

"He wished to be buried in England and it has been the duty of his men who loved him so to honor his every dying wish, and damn the Admiralty if they see things different!" said Blackwood.

"His body was removed of all clothing, save his chemise, and he was placed within a leaguer cask, filled with spirits—brandy, if you must know—as well as such other preservatives as camphor and myrrh, that he might be transported home with minimal deterioration to his—forgive me, Lady Hamilton, this is hard for me to speak of. We who loved Nelson as though he was a brother, are as grieved as—I dare not say as grieved as you, for I own that no one can know the depths of your pain at this time—but, brave and sturdy men though we are, we are not insensible to the irretrievable loss of the greatest man England has ever produced."

"The Victorys wished to be the ones to escort his body home. We would not permit any other vessel to bear him," Hardy told me. "But as the ship would never make it as far as Spithead without prodigious mending, she was taken first to Gibraltar, where the necessary repairs could be made."

"I will want to see 'im when the *Victory* arrives," I told the captains. "I must see 'is poor dear body and kiss 'is lips for the last time."

The men exchanged a glance. "Rest assured, Lady Hamilton, we will apprise you of Nelson's final return," Blackwood told me.

Hardy made a polite bow. "It shall be my constant study to meet your wishes, as it was our ever dear lord's last request to be kind to you, which, I trust, I shall never forget."

They rose to leave and kissed my hand in parting.

O miserable, wretched Emma! O glorious and happy Nelson! I scrawled upon his last letter to me. I feared my tears would wash away all traces of his final words.

On December 6, I read in the *Morning Chronicle* that the *Victory* had reached Spithead. I sent a note to Hardy once again requesting permission to say farewell to Nelson's body.

By return post he dispatched a letter dissuading me, in the politest terms, from engaging in any spectacles of public mourning, though he admitted that were I to insist upon viewing Nelson's body, he would not oppose it.

I had been much misapprehended, for I had thought that Nelson's men—especially Hardy, who had thought enough of honoring Nelson's wishes to bring me his effects—should not think to discourage me.

Had it begun already? Was England already beginning to forget Lady Hamilton's importance to Lord Nelson, hero of the Nile and Trafalgar? Were they already preparing to enshrine him as a model of manufactured chastity, as insensible to passion and emotion—to love—as a marble statue?

Britain had most certainly not forgotten Nelson's family. William, who to everyone's shock had blarted out to Sarah in company (which included the bishop of Chichester), "Never mind the Battle of Trafalgar, for it has made me an earl and thee a countess!" was granted a sizable pension along with the title. Grasping, greedy William Nelson, the parvenu who had never done a thing to earn it, was handed a greater title than the king had ever seen fit to bestow upon the hero himself! The Boltons and Matchams, too, had received tidy sums from the government. Even Tom Tit was voted a pension of two thousand pounds for life. For what? For making her husband miserable in what should have been his most joyous years? I was enraged.

On the ninth of December, Rose informed me that Dr. Scott had spoken with him regarding Nelson's dying words. The chaplain confirmed that he had never quit the hero's side during his entire time in the orlop, and that Nelson had told him "Remember me to Lady Hamilton; remember me to Horatia. Doctor—remember me to Mr. Rose. Tell him I have made a will and left Lady Hamilton and Horatia to my country." He told me that the document had been witnessed by both Hardy and Blackwood just

before the action at Trafalgar began. Why had the captains neg-
lected to speak of it to me?

I went down to Whitehall to see it. The will turned out to be a
codicil in fact, and Nelson had carefully written a prayer above it.

> *May the Great God whom I worship Grant to my Country and
> for the benefit of Europe in general a great and Glorious Victory,
> and may no misconduct in any one tarnish it, and May hu-
> manity after Victory be the predominant feature in the British
> fleet. For myself individually I commit my life to Him who made
> me, and may his blessing light upon my endeavours for serving
> my Country faithfully, to Him I resign myself and the Just cause
> which is entrusted to me to Defend—Amen, Amen, Amen.*

> *Whereas the Eminent Services of Emma Hamilton Widow of the
> Right Honourable Sir William Hamilton have been of the very
> greatest Service to our King & Country to my knowledge with-
> out her receiving any reward from either our King or Country,
> first that she obtained the King of Spain's letter in 1796 to His
> Brother the King of Naples acquainting him of his intention to
> Declare War against England from which letter the Ministry sent
> out order to Sir John Jervis to Strike a Stroke against either the
> arsenals of Spain or her fleets. The British fleet under my Com-
> mand could never have returned the second time to Egypt had it
> not been for Lady Hamilton's influence with the Queen of Naples
> to encourage the fleet being supplied with everything should they
> put into any port in Sicily. We put into Syracuse, and received
> every supply, went to Egypt, & destroyed the French fleet. I leave
> Emma Hamilton therefore a Legacy to my King and Country
> that they will give her an ample provision to maintain her Rank
> in Life. I also leave to the beneficence of my Country my adopted
> daughter, Horatia Nelson Thompson, and I desire She Will Use
> in future the name of Nelson only. These are the only favours I*

*ask of my King and Country at this moment when I am going to
fight their Battle. . . .*

Nelson & Bronte

On December 22, I rode out to Margate, where the *Victory* had
moored temporarily. The surgeon Beatty's postmortem of the body
had revealed the most remarkable things. For all Nelson's ailments
and complaints of ill health, his vital parts and organs were found
to be so healthy—even his heart, which Nelson continually believed had suffered numerous attacks—that they more closely resembled those of a youth than of a man of forty-seven who had
weathered the world. Had the sniper's bullet never been fired, Nelson might have lived to see a hundred, and we could have dwelt
many years retired together at Paradise Merton.

There was numerous friends of Nelson's, his officers, and minor
government officials crowded into the admiral's cabin, where his
dear body was on view. It had been so well preserved by the spirits
that he appeared a bit bloated but scarcely decayed. I had humbled
myself before 'em by promising that if they let me kiss his lips
once, I would neither cry nor speak. True to my pledge, I touched
my mouth to Nelson's for the last time.

Nelson had given his life for England; he had been silenced forever. Now England, in its envy of the greatest love story in her glorious history, wished to silence Lady Hamilton as well.

Ariadne

1806–1814

Forty-four

The Painful Losses Tumble Down

J had lost more than Nelson. I had lost myself. My heart and my head were gone. No longer the heroine of a hero, I felt rudderless.

At the end of the year, while my love's poor body was still en route to Greenwich, the Reverend William Nelson, made an earl upon his brother's demise, was already making rumblings about being presented to His Majesty, more interested in attending a levee than attending to funeral arrangements. His family—the first to cut Fanny in 1801 when it became quite clear that the entrée to Nelson's good graces was purchased only through kindness and respect to me—now dropped my acquaintance almost entirely and once more took up courting Lady Nelson's goodwill.

Nelson's body lay in state in the Painted Hall in Greenwich, and tens of thousands of mourners queued up as far as Deptford to bid farewell. The funeral was a two-day spectacle. On January 8, a vast flotilla joined the funeral barge that bore Nelson's body up the Thames from Greenwich to Whitehall. The entire river was a sea of black—the majestic gondolas, the extravagant canopies, the thousands of people clad in mourning—with the only sign of color being the Union Jack, which flew from many of the vessels. Nelson's *L'Orient* coffin, which also contained the sheet music to my beloved's favorite ballad, had been placed inside a splendid ebony catafalque—originally intended for Cardinal Wolsey—that was placed on public display in Pall Mall.

This casket, draped with a black cloth of sumptuous Genoa velvet, was studded with no fewer than ten thousand double-gilt nails. The eight handles and the corner plates were gilded as well, the latter engraved with the crests and orders with which Nelson in his lifetime had been honored: Britannia and Neptune; the British Lion crushing the Gallic Cock under its mighty paw; and the Order of the Bath, with its most resonant motto, *Tria juncta in uno*.

The following day, the saddest Thursday in living memory, Nelson was honored on land as he had been on the chilly Thames. Heading the procession of mourners to St. Paul's Cathedral was the hearse, shaped like a ship of the line with the winged victory at her prow, and drawn by six coal blacks with violet plumes upon their heads. Following on foot came the Prince of Wales, leading the solemn cortege of dignitaries, nobles, and military men, marching, on horseback, or conveyed in carriages. The Chief Mourner was the eighty-three-year-old Sir Peter Parker, who'd mentored the young Nelson aboard his ship, the *Bristol*, and had promoted the promising young seaman from lieutenant to master and commander to post captain. No women took part in the procession. Everyone who attended Nelson's funeral service at St. Paul's received a printed admission ticket signed by the bishop of Lincoln, who was also the dean of the cathedral.

After the entire cortege had passed, an empty, unmarked black coach forlornly brought up the rear. Though Lady Nelson did not attend the funeral, she had sent her carriage as an emblem of respect, its vacant compartment representing the void left by Nelson's permanent absence. The bells of St. Paul's, which had been rung at funerals only if the deceased was of royal birth, now sounded for Nelson.

After the funeral service, Nelson's dear body was entombed at

St. Paul's and his name passed into immortality even as it remained fresh on everyone's lips and enshrined in every heart and mind.

I, too, did not attend the funeral, nor had I been among the thousands of common citizens who came to say farewell when Nelson's beloved body lay in state, first at Greenwich and then in Pall Mall. Even now, I am unsure what would have pained me more: to know that I was unwished for there, or to acknowledge that the memorial service was to be the final good-bye. Rather, I memorized every detail of the ceremonies as described in the morning papers.

Many of my old friends endeavored to improve my spirits by inviting me to concerts and the theatre, but everywhere I went there were elegies and homages to Nelson, which made my wounds bleed afresh. Mam determined that it was best for me to remain quiet at Merton, for then my broken heart might be more gently treated. She was right, as always, and in the country, at what had been our idyll, I drew comfort from Nelson's image on every wall; I slept with his bloodstained coat in my arms, and of course the most palpable reminder of our love was Nelson's "dear pledge" of it, little Horatia. I tried not to overindulge her for Nelson's sake, for I didn't wish her to become spoilt, and the horse, once out of the barn, cannot be called back. His only issue should always remain a credit to his name. Horatia was progressing remarkably well in her schooling for one so young. Many was the time when out of habit I reached for paper and quill to write to Nelson of her improvement, only to collapse in sobs over my blotter, bitterly acknowledging the impossibility.

On December 5, 1805, the earl had come into possession of Nelson's pocket-book, the little volume of memorandums that contained, among other items, the codicil he had written shortly before his most tragic demise. The pocket-book was then to have been delivered to Pitt, but the prime minister's sudden death on January 23, 1806, was a shock to the nation. His untimely passing struck a mighty blow to my campaign for a pension, for he had been sympathetic to my claims and might have been my Galahad in Parliament. At first, William Nelson had pretended to a cordiality with me, expressing his hope in writing that my claims to a pension might be granted. But no sooner did William Wyndham, Baron Grenville become prime minister, toward the end of February, than the earl began to demand the personal effects that Nelson had bestowed upon me—by will and codicil—as well as those that had been brought to me by Captain Hardy. We tussled mightily over them—it was monstrous unpleasant—with an unfortunate outcome that fully satisfied no one. The earl allowed me to retain Nelson's bloodstained coat, but I was to forfeit to him the diamond aigrette, the Turk sultan's *chelenkh* that the Kelim Effendi had conferred upon Nelson on the fateful night in Naples when we all took flight for Palermo.

Rather than presenting my case to Parliament, Grenville held on to Nelson's pocket-book well into the spring, and then returned it to the earl, saying that nothing could be done for me. The earl conveyed this news not without some glee. "The PM informs me that had your claims been presented to the government at the same time as Nelson's family had presented theirs, your pension might have been granted. Alas, it appears there is nothing to be done; for it is ever a surety that the early bird catches the worm."

What colossal poppycock! They were all playing me false, for Grenville *had* been given the pocket-book containing Nelson's codicil soon enough after his death, no thanks to the earl; but the new prime minister had sat upon this evidence—deliberately, I am sure—for nearly half a year, and then had the temerity to claim I was too tardy!

We was clashing too, over Bronte, for Nelson had also legally bequeathed to me the income from the dukedom. The earl claimed that Bronte had been in arrears for years before Nelson's death, and therefore, any income currently being derived from it must be used to satisfy the estate's many creditors. Consequently, I was not seeing a penny of Bronte's yield. George Rose had counseled me to rely upon Nelson's will. His codicil was, in fact, finally approved on July 4, 1806, so Lord Grenville would no longer be able to forestall me with lies and subterfuge. Like the Americans, on that day I toasted my independence—from debt—for I believed that my financial worries would soon be a thing of the past.

In June 1808, after I'd struggled for two and a half years to hold on to my precious home, Merton was put on the auction block. Almost a year later, in April 1809, the estate was sold for thirteen thousand pounds, and for the first time in months, if not years, I felt able to breathe fully. As the year wore on, however, Mam grew unwell, and I became increasingly plagued by my own health issues. I developed jaundice, which Dr. Heaviside attributed to a liver condition, although I had been suffering from touches of jaundice now and again ever since I'd pushed poor baby Emma into the world in 1804. Nelson's sister, Susannah Bolton, sent me the kindest note wishing me a swift recovery. *You are too great a lady*, she wrote, *to quit this world so soon.*

I was still ill abed when I received a letter from Francis Oliver, who had been Sir William's, and then Nelson's, secretary for a time. Oliver had couriered our love letters, and his correspondence to me was full of dark threats to publish everything he knew about my relationship with Nelson. He had also tried to court me after Nelson's death though I'd rebuffed him soundly. Now his attempt at blackmail sent me into a fury.

"You'll make yourself sicker if you worry it to pieces, y'nau?" As ever, Mam offered sage advice. "Tell the bastard you'll send copies of Nelson's letter about that 'ole East India business to the papers, and you'll tell them as well about 'ow 'e came a-wooing after Nelson died saying as 'e'd 'ad designs on you all these years. That should scare the stuffing out of 'im. And if it don't, it buys us a little time to come up with something else to affright 'im with."

She was right. I penned a very strong reply to Oliver and we never heard another word from him.

Greville had invited me to call upon him toward the close of the previous year, but I had been feeling too ill to see him. I missed the chance to say good-bye, for he died on April 23, 1809, at the age of sixty—a bachelor to his last breath. I was overcome with regret when I heard the news, for I should have ignored my ailments and accepted the opportunity to compose the coda to our lengthy and complicated connexion.

"Will you miss 'im?" Mam wanted to know.

I dabbed at a tear. "I suppose this spells my answer," I replied, referring to the moistness in my eyes. "With Greville, died a carefree, giddy girl 'oo changed her name to Emma to please 'im, and who scarce 'ad a worry in the wide world, as long as she believed 'erself beloved. I daresay I will miss *'er.*"

As 1810 dawned, Mam fell ill with pneumonia. Her poor body had endured two episodes of apoplexia over the years, and her joints had given her no end of troubles for decades. On January 14, she closed her eyes for the last time. I had lost the dearest friend in all the world, and the only person in my life who had known every single one of my secrets. Through it all, she had always placed my happiness above her own.

I laid her to rest in a private manner within a vault beneath St. Mary's Church in Paddington Green, built two years after Mam and I had departed Edgware Road. I could not afford an engraved entablature, but as the years passed I would visit the crypt from time to time, laying yellow flowers on the stone that marked her grave.

Forty-five

Within the Rules

Emma Carew had sent me a heartrending note of condolence after she learnt of Mam's death, expressing the hope that I would see her.

> *"Sunday Morning"*
>
> *It might have been happy for me to have forgotten the past, and to have began a new life with new ideas; but my memory traces back circumstances which have taught me too much, yet not quite all I could have wished to have known—with you that resides, and ample reasons, no doubt, you have for not imparting them to me. That I should persevere in it is what I owe to myself and to you, for it shall never be said that I avail myself of your partiality or my own inclination, unless I learn my claim on you is greater than you have hitherto acknowledged. But the time may come when the same reasons may cease to operate, and then, with a heart filled with tenderness and affection, will I shew you both my duty and my attachment. In the meantime, should you really wish to see me, I may be believed in saying that such a meeting would be one of the happiest moments of my life, but for the reflection that it may also be the last, as I leave England in a few days, and may, perhaps, never return to it again. I remain, etc.*

Little Emma had guessed the truth, of course. Of that, there was now no doubt. And after all that had passed, with a heart so buffeted, she was still willing, nay, anxious, to be a loving and dutiful daughter to me. My firstborn was a veritable Cordelia, and like Lear, I did not deserve her unswerving devotion. I did not return her letter, nor agree to see her again, for it would have broke my heart even more to tell her all (since her letter left me little room for continued denials) than it did to take the decision to remain forever silent. My intention was never to be cruel; quite the opposite, in fact. Full of shame as deep as the Thames, I felt that I'd had naught to give the darling girl when, no better than I should be, I'd first brought her into this world, and now, when she wish'd to form a deeper attachment, my fortunes and estate were once more at an ebb. I wanted the very best for her. But with my constrained finances, and continual picking up and moving from pillar to post, I truly did believe that when all was said and done the dear young woman would be better off without me. More importantly, I thought she would attain a better position in society if her prospects, and her potential for happiness and security, remained entirely untainted by my own tarnished reputation.

As the months wore on and Nelson's death receded into memory, my numerous creditors began to lie in wait for me. Writs were served and for days remained tacked like a hatchment upon the door before I mustered the strength to remove them. Over Christmas, Horatia came down with the whooping cough and I was too afraid to summon a doctor for fear of divulging my presence to my dunners. What a ghastly predicament we were in! The Sword of Damocles, in the guise of myriad debts, hung perilously above my head. In my despair I ceased all correspondence, for I had no words of cheer to impart and was certain my friends wished to read no more of Emma's unhappy straits.

Yet the creditors located me all the same, for at the beginning of 1813, the sword finally fell. At a friend's country home I was arrested for debt, bodily taken—along with Horatia—to live in a spunging house Within the Rules of the King's Bench, a proscribed area two and a half miles in circumference of the prison itself.

Five roads converged upon an obelisk on the Surrey side of the Thames across Blackfriars Bridge, the same bridge Jane Powell and I had sneaked across in the dead of evening on our way from the Budds' house to our nocturnal balladeering escapades at Cocksheath Camp. I was set up at No. 12 Temple Place, one of the terrace houses in the Magdalen Circus area, which when all was said and done—apart from the disgrace of being thrown into debtors' prison—was better than some of the lodgings Horatia and I had been compelled to let since the death of her father. Saddest of ironies was that one reached my new address by passing the recently christened Nelson Square.

The King's Bench prison itself was three blocks away from Temple Place. Also within a stone's throw were the Magdalen Hospital for penitent prostitutes and the Westminster Lying-in Hospital, which was open to all women, regardless of their ability to produce a marriage certificate. The nearby orphan asylum took in the children of Irish parents or of those whose parish was not easily determined. Also close at hand lay the Philanthropic Institution, whose mandate was to prevent vice by educating the children of convicts so they might not be tempted to follow in their parents' criminal footsteps. In short, the entire neighborhood was a little ghetto for society's outcasts and undesirables.

The air seemed even browner and heavier there, the miasma thick with sorrows. In the Magdalen quarter one could not escape the stench of refuse. Even the nearby brewery of Barclay & Perkins gave off an unpleasant odor that threatened to put me off porter forever.

Not only was I charged a daily rent of four shillings, sixpence, payable to the marshal of the King's Bench, but for each additional mouth to feed within my establishment—which included two serving women and Miss Wheatley, Horatia's singing mistress—I would have to forfeit a fee to the keeper of the spunging house. If I wished a fire, I had to purchase coal, another expense, for I began my sentence in January. Naturally, all food, beer, and spirits had to be bought as well, and a washerwoman had to be hired. It was a near-impossible challenge to pay off one's debts while still being compelled to make so many expenditures necessary for subsistence. The only consolation about being placed Within the Rules for one debt was that the debtor could not be arrested for any others.

A number of my possessions and effects were auctioned off that I might begin to diminish my encumbrances. But what truly ruptured my heart was the painful relinquishing of my two most treasured assets: Nelson's bloodstained coat and the inscribed silver christening cup that he had given to Horatia. The latter I brought to a Bond Street silversmith for sale. During every painful minute of the transaction, I felt like I was betraying Horatia, but she was still whooping; what else could I do but sell it to purchase a doctor's care? Nelson would never have preferred a corpse to a cup.

Inspecting the treasure for flaws, the merchant turned the cup over and over in his hands. "It's a beautiful piece, I'll warrant you that," he said. "A shame you have to part with it, for I'm sure that its provenance is quite precious to you. Tell me," he added with a wink, lowering his voice and leaning over his glass and mahogany countertop, "who was the girl's mother, then?"

I had inclined my head to hear his whisper, but his words caused me to rock back upon my heels. My carriage stiffened. "Horatia Nelson's mother is too great a lady to be mentioned," I told him firmly. When I pocketed the money from the sale of Horatia's cup and left the silversmith's, I felt as though I had sold my soul.

Nelson's younger sister, Katty Matcham, wrote to say that she was worried at not receiving a line from me in some time, and to express her concern for Horatia's whooping cough. It embarrassed me greatly to have to reply to her letter from Within the Rules, but I explained our situation in detail. She responded with great delicacy, first informing me that she was sending down some food, then inviting me to send Horatia to live with them, at least until I could regain my financial footing, for they loved her as dearly as if she were one of their own daughters and would surely care for her with all the love it was possible to bestow. It was a magnanimous gesture and one that I am certain, knowing the Matchams, came straight from their hearts, but I could not give away Nelson's daughter as if she were a coat or a cup. I had promised Nelson that I would be the one to raise and educate Horatia; never had there been a discussion of sending her away to live with his family, even to the dearest of his relations. She was all I had left in the world of him—and of course she was my flesh and blood, too.

To my astonishment, I discovered that I had friends in high places Within the Rules. Alderman Joshua Jonathan Smith had been lord mayor a few years earlier, and in fact we had celebrated Horatia's sixth birthday in his presence. Much enchanted with her, Smith had allowed her to climb upon the table and deliver a speech. Now Smith was president of the Borough Council of Suffolk, and the Rules were within his district's purview.

Soon after my possessions had been sold off, Alderman Smith brought me a parcel wrapped in brown paper tied with a length of twine. "I hope you won't think ill of me for having taken the liberty of purchasing you a gift, Lady Hamilton."

"A gift? For me?" My smile was as puzzled as it was grateful. "What does Mrs. Smith 'ave to say about it?"

It was the alderman's turn to smile. "I think Mrs. Smith would understand."

I opened the package to find Nelson's bloodstained coat. "Oh—dear God! Oh, my—his—" I bosted into tears on the spot, raining kisses on the treasure I had thought lost to me forever. "Oh, sir, there is assuredly a place reserved for you at God's right 'and, for you are the kindest man on earth!" In thanking him, I learnt that Smith's esteem for Nelson was unbounded and unalloyed—as well as long-standing. The alderman was a senior partner in a firm of sugar refiners and had known Nelson back when he was just a young captain on commission in the West Indies. Sometimes the great wide world is smaller than one could ever imagine!

Entertaining my old Neapolitan friends was the only thing that brought me any comfort, but this, too, made it near impossible for me to continue to economize. My bankruptcy was the laceratingly painful price of some little cheer. As I insisted on comporting my-self as though I were still the mistress of the Palazzo Sessa, *Sua Eccellenza l'Ambasciatrice*, few, including those of Nelson's extended family, believed I was in such dire straits. But it was the only way to preserve my dignity. Could I allow the princes of the blood, my frequent guests the Dukes of Clarence and Sussex, to learn that the woman they fancied to be all music and sunshine, all shimmer and starlight, had been reduced to penury? No! It would never do! If nothing else, my pride prevented me from showing them the dark side of the coin; perhaps it was an old habit from my days at Mrs. Kelly's in Arlington Street: never let them see you suffer.

In February, I began to compose a series of open letters to the prince regent and the king. These "memorials," lengthy recitations of my numerous services to king and country during my years in Naples—which had *still* gone unacknowledged and uncompen-sated after all these years—were published in the *Morning Herald*.

On March 6, as I had amassed enough capital to settle my debts, Alderman Smith secured my release from the Rules, and I became free to quit the squalor of Temple Place. My little distaff ménage was once more ensconced at Bond Street, my lodgings at No. 150 having remained empty since our departure at the end of 1812. On that same day, I received two letters in response to my memorials. The first was from George Rose, and the second letter was from Lord Sidmouth, the home secretary. The messages were essentially the same: the prime minister, Lord Liverpool, had made it clear to them that my pension would not materialize, as the money was needed for matters of national importance—though he regretted all the embarrassment Lady Hamilton had been put to of late. My arse, he did! A paltry thousand pounds or so a year would scarce bankrupt the government. Boney would not be prevented from invading Albion because Parliament had deigned to finally furnish Emma's remuneration!

Infuriated, I sent another letter to the Prince Regent. As time progressed, my debts were remounting. *I am harassed by extreme embarrassments; tradesmen are clamorous and cruel,* I told him, spelling out all my expenses in Naples and Palermo, including the thousands of pounds taken from my privy purse to supply corn to the starving Maltese so that they might remain allies of the British Crown. I begged the prince to grant me the funds necessary to properly raise and educate the only issue of Nelson's blood.

A reader of this memoir should not form the misapprehension of my character that I was grasping or greedy. 'Twas nominated in Nelson's will and codicils—instruments that had been properly witnessed—that Horatia and I be provided for; and to ignore his dying wishes was to flout the law. The legacy was legitimate. Not only that, I had *earned* a pension for all my years of service to the Crown; verily, it was my *due.*

In my despair I sought solace in the temporary comforts of the bottle, though Dr. Heaviside had cautioned me against the consumption of too much wine and champagne. I had never been one for spirits, despite the caricaturists' enjoyment of depicting me with a gin bottle in my hand.

Horatia and I began to quarrel with increasing frequency. Now twelve years old, she resented my—as she put it—dragging her hither and yon, dwelling in occasional squalor and perpetual embarrassment, whilst she might be living happily and comfortably at Ashfold Lodge with the well-to-do Matchams. "You give and give to people like the earl's family," she said, "and all they do is take advantage of your bounty; yet you are fundamentally incapable of accepting real love and generosity when it's offered to you by the likes of the Matchams and Miss Carew, who, for all your faults, think the world of you!" She accused me of being both blind and selfish. If I loved her as much as I professed to, I should not be ruining her young life, she insisted. What claims had I upon her anyway? I was merely her guardian whilst Katty Matcham was her aunt! And not only was I naught but her guardian; I was an embarrassment to her, a fat and slovenly tippler who dwelt in the past, caring more about my private memories of Lord Nelson, whatever they might be, than about his own daughter who lived and breathed before her eyes!

On Easter Sunday 1813, at the end of my tether with her continual moping and whining, and wounded to the quick by her churlish insults, I took a leaf from Sir William's book, expressing my anger and disappointment in her conduct by writing her the sternest possible letter.

> *18 April, 1813*
>
> *Listen to a kind, good mother, who has ever been to you affectionate, truly kind, and who has neither spared pains nor expense to make you the most amiable and most accomplish'd of your sex. I have weathered many a storm for your sake, but these frequent blows have kill'd me. Listen, then, from a mother who speaks from the dead! Reform your conduct, or you will be detested by all the world, & when you shall no longer have my fostering arm to sheild you, whoe betide you! You will sink to nothing. I grieve & lament to see the increasing strength of your turbulent passions; I weep & pray you may not be totally lost. I shall go join your father & my blessed mother & may you on your death-bed have as little to reproach yourself as your once affectionate mother has, for I can glorify, & say I was a good child.*

Can Horatia Nelson say so? I am unhappy to say you CANNOT.
No answer to this?
    P.S. Look on me now as gone from this world.

She had no need to know that at her age I was in truth just as petulant and twice as wild. At first, upon reading this letter, Horatia
was not contrite, as I hoped she would be. "You're so awfully dramatic," she said, almost sneering, then added, "and you're *not* my
mother. Not my *real* mother, anyway, and it's cruel and evil of you
to say so."

Her remark stung like a slap, but I still could not permit myself
to tell her the truth. For one thing, if she so detested me now, I was
certain she would not abruptly become proud of me were she to
become suddenly enlightened. "I am the only mother you will ever
'ave, Horatia," I replied stiffly. "Your father charged me with raising you, and by 'eaven I will keep my promise to 'im, if it takes my
last shilling to do so."

In May, my collection of silver and plate was sold off, including a silver dinner service engraved with Nelson's arms. I retained
only a few trinkets and some gold cups, yet I always carried a Nelson ha'penny in my purse. The coins, bearing the likeness of my
beloved, had been issued in 1812 and I vowed never to spend
mine. Nelson remained my guardian angel, keeping me secure in
the knowledge that there would always be money in my pocket;
thus I managed to hold my head high through every reversal of fortune.

But in June, three different litigants sued me for debts, listing
their claims in the judgment book of the King's Bench. As I lacked
the means to honor them, by the end of the month I once more
found myself in debtors' prison, back Within the Rules and calling
No. 12 Temple Place my home.

Forty-six

Denouement

At noon on July 8, 1813, by virtue of an execution from the sheriff of Middlesex, nearly all of my furniture and possessions from 150 Bond Street was auctioned off on the premises. The catalogue was eighteen pages long.

In accordance with the guidelines of the King's Bench, as a prisoner of the Rules I was permitted to retain enough items to make our little household at Temple Place tolerably comfortable, but anything and everything that might have brought a reasonable price was sold out from under me.

Like all proper ladies of the gentry, I began to pay regular "good works" calls at the Magdalen Hospital for penitent prostitutes. My visits to the Magdalen rekindled in me an interest in Catholicism that had been piqued by living so many years in Naples among devout, though profoundly superstitious, Papists. At Temple Place I began to entertain the visits of a priest named Father Peter, who offered me Communion there and educated me in the precepts of his religion. The more I learnt, the more it brought me comfort during a dark and difficult time.

Everyone's spirits were lifted that July when news reached England of Wellington's stunning rout of the French at Vitoria in northern Spain. Even Within the Rules, Londoners scrambled to obtain copies of the *Courier* and the *Gazette*, for they both carried full accounts of the battle. There were public celebrations every night, though prisoners of the Rules were prohibited from enjoying them. I could hear the hoopla from my open windows, and even from the confines of the Magdalen quarter we could see the nightly illuminations in the nearest public square. Government buildings and private balconies were bedecked with lamps, whilst the facades of theatres and shops were festooned with garlands and buntings. The words *Wellington* and *Victory* were spelled out in lights in several prominent locations throughout the city, including Carlton House, the Regent's residence, scene of a gala celebration that lasted for days. Even the Spanish consul's house in the Strand bore the letters VICTORY, JUNE 21, 1813.

How bittersweet that word—*victory*—tasted on my lips. Eight years too late for Nelson to enjoy in my embrace. Had he lived to see it, how happy he would have been, how proud for king and country, and how relieved to be able to tender his retirement on a glorious high note heard throughout the world, and return to Merton to live out the rest of his days in quiet comfort, with Horatia and me by his side. From Temple Place as I toasted our victory at Vitoria, I clutched his bloodstained coat to my heart as if Nelson himself were in my arms.

Outwardly, as ever, I endeavored to present a picture to the world of the Emma my old friends knew: the blithe spirit who always grabbed life with both hands and wrung every precious and wonderful moment from it. I refused to allow our reduced circumstances to deter us from living every day to the fullest. Gala days were still to be honored, and so we celebrated the anniversary of the Glorious First of August at Temple Place, serving up as fine a dinner as we could muster for Alderman Smith and his family. How I missed my gallant and tender Nelson!

That Christmas, with the grand news that peace negotiations were under way, I hosted a dinner party at Temple Place. The guest of honor was His Royal Highness the Duke of Sussex, who had been just plain old Augustus Frederick when he had visited Sir William and me in Naples so very long ago. What a caution it was when, upon realizing that there wasn't a carving knife to be had—I daresay they all must have been auctioned off—another of my guests, Sir William Dillon, a commander who had been a dear friend of Nelson's, ripped apart the Christmas goose with his bare hands, as we all bosted out laughing. "For those of you who never served in His Majesty's Navy," the commander joked, "this is what it was like to mess with a bunch of midshipmen! One of the first rules of the navy is 'Make do with what you've got.'"

"Oh, it can't be!" I laughed.

"Well, close enough, at any rate! Now, who's for a leg?" asked the commander, brandishing the goose limb, dripping with its own juices, as though it were a truncheon.

What a mirthful celebration we had that night! But only a week later, I fell quite ill again, spending the New Year holiday abed with what I believed to be another attack of jaundice, though Dr. Tegart, the Rules' physician, diagnosed me with dropsy, as well as edema, or "water on the chest," both symptoms of liver disease. I spent the first three months of 1814 in my bed, shivering like the devil throughout the month of February, when it grew so cold in London that the Thames froze over and a Frost Fair was held upon the ice. Horatia was miffed that I would not permit her to go skating upon it. The newspapers reported it as the coldest winter in twenty years. Travel ceased, and mail deliveries were halted unless the post was delivered by special messenger. Horses slipped and slid on London's frozen ruts and cobbles, and every exposed surface, including the shop windows, was frosted over with a layer of ice. It was as if the entire city lay under glass.

It was during my extended convalescence that I read the *Morning Herald*'s April 10 article regarding the two-volume publication by Harrison and Lovewell of *The Letters of Lord Nelson to Lady*

Hamilton, with a Supplement of Interesting Letters by Distinguished Characters. I am certain now more than ever that it was Francis Oliver who brought the copies of my letters to these scoundrels, for not only did he know the details of my relationship with Nelson, but Nelson's refusal to entertain the whole East India Company business, and my having spurned his amorous attentions gave him a double motive for attempting to ruin us in the eyes of all the world.

I wish to extend my grateful thanks to Alderman Smith for covering the spunging house's bill for "breakages" amounting to thirteen pounds, four shillings, eleven pence, incurred on April 10, as well as on the day I learnt that James Perry had refused to print my refutation of the volumes in the *Morning Chronicle.*

Many people believed those letters to be forgeries, for they were either incapable of accepting their national hero as a passionate lover or else unwilling to conceive that such a great and noble man as Nelson would disparage—and so emphatically traduce—the character of the Prince of Wales. These letters would most certainly render me persona non grata in the eyes of the Regent, from whom I have been seeking my pension, so it naturally availed me greatly to disavow them, claiming that all of us—Nelson and Sir William and I—were too much attached to the prince to ever speak ill of him. It is true, however, that until I read the *Morning Herald* on April 10, I had not the merest inkling that these letters were being published. It was assuredly done without my permission, and I don't stand to gain a penny from it.

I dare not know what to make of the irony that now, during some of the darkest moments of my life, England finally basks in the radiant glow of victory after so many years of war. Napoleon has been exiled to the island of Elba, and Britons may now cross the Channel in safety. Now that there is peace between England and France, the possibility of decamping to the Continent presents itself to me. I have been vilified since the public release of my letters, and once these memoirs are published I have little doubt but that I will be rendered completely friendless in my own country. At least my daughter—for once she reads this she will learn her mother's identity—and I might live quietly, unknown and unmolested, across the Channel on foreign shores.

On April 29, three days after I began to write this memoir, I applied to Earl Nelson for half my Bronte pension:

> *My Lord,*
>
> *It cannot be more disagreeable to you to receive a letter from me than it is for me to write to you but I shall be glad to know from your Lordship weather the first half year of the Bronte pension which Nelson left in his will I was to receive & which I never have received is to be settled. . . . Every sixpence is of the utmost consequence to me, on account of Horatia, the beloved Child of dear Nelson. I do not in the midst of poverty neglect her Education which is such as will suit the rank in life which she will yet hold in society & which her great father wish'd her to move in. I ask not alms, I ask not anything but right, and to know weather I am to receive my due or not.*

On May 6, I did receive 225 pounds from Earl Nelson, representing half the Bronte pension, less 25 pounds deducted for property taxes. Now that I am near to becoming a Catholic, I *do* believe in miracles.

When I began this memoir, on my forty-ninth birthday, all London was aglow with the celebration of Boney's enforced abdication. As I reach the final pages, it is the twentieth of May and the streets are once again filled with the strains of "Rule Britannia" and joyful revelry, the night sky resplendent with fireworks and illuminations in celebration of the tyrant's exile.

Now that the Bronte payment is enough to settle my present

debts, Alderman Smith has sent a petition for my release from the Rules to Lord Ellenborough, the chief justice of the King's Bench. Yet the funds are insufficient to secure my future and Horatia's, and in exchange for our freedom I leave my story as a legacy to the world. If I am ever to quit the Rules and raise Horatia with all the perquisites required to be a proper young lady, I must have a means of income.

The shape of my extraordinary life has imitated that of a farrier's horseshoe, which I suppose is sadly fitting, given my father's profession. It is indeed an odd sort of inheritance. I have seen enough of grandeur not to regret it, but comfort, and what would make Horatia and myself live like gentlewomen, would be all I wish, and to live to see her well settled in the world. You will not see me an ambassadress, nor in splendor, but you will ever find me firm and my mind uncorrupted.

Not too many years ago, Lady Melbourne remarked to me, "Anyone who braves the world sooner or later feels the consequences of it." Her ladyship is a veritable Sibyl, for I have learnt the hard way that in English society, you can do anything you wish to, so long as you remain discreet about it. An indiscretion, once revealed, spells ruin. So for all these years, I have kept my secrets from Emma Carew, kept them from Horatia, too, that the innocent should not suffer disgrace for their mother's past conduct. Perhaps the most dramatic—and the most heartbreaking—Attitude I ever assayed was *Emma Pretending* Not *to Be the Mother of Her Two Daughters.* I kept little Emma's existence a secret from Nelson, and endeavored to keep Horatia's existence a secret from Sir William, for I owed each of those great men so large a debt for my happiness that I could not have stood to see them suffer even the slightest degree of humiliation.

Alexander Pope once asked, "Is it, in Heaven, a crime to love too well?" Apparently it is so in England, as it is a crime to be too beautiful. Of these two transgressions I stand convicted and for years have served my sentence for it. With the publication of the whole story it is my intention to transcend my detractors. By hazarding all, I will rise far above them, living with my daughter in comfort and contentment. The only thing the English abjure more than a fallen woman is one who has risen. Emma Hamilton, however, shall be in France!

Afterword

On July 2, 1814, with only 50 pounds in her purse, Emma slipped away with Horatia and boarded a small boat, the *Little Tom*, which lay moored near the Tower of London. Embarking from London was a far less risky prospect than fleeing to Dover and chancing discovery and subsequent remanding to debtors' prison. Although Earl Nelson had finally paid her 225 pounds—half her Bronte pension (less taxes), which effected her release from debtors' prison—she still, in fact, had numerous creditors. If she could reach the Continent, she would be safe from their claims as long as she remained there. Emma and Horatia sailed for Calais, where Emma immediately took rooms at Dessin's Hotel, the city's poshest hostelry. For some months Emma entertained and received guests at Dessin's as though she were still an amabassadress. She continued to have Horatia schooled in music and languages by the finest instructors, though she spent several months suffering from a recurrence of her jaundice, most likely due to an enlarged liver from her excessive drinking. However, the money soon ran out and Emma and her young charge démenaged to a farmhouse outside of town, where they lived cheaply, but happily, and Emma herself took up Horatia's instruction in German and Spanish. Petitions to Colonel Robert Fulke Greville for her installments of William Hamilton's pension proved fruitless. Greville tartly informed her that creditors were claiming she had already pledged these sums to them. Finally, donations of forty pounds enabled Emma to settle herself and Horatia in a suite of dingy, if not outright squalid, rooms near the glamorous Dessin's. Emma's health continued to decline and she remained in her bed for days at a time, with Horatia keeping vigil. On January 15, 1815, Emma, Lady Hamilton, died. She was buried in Calais, after a proper funeral mass, having never received the government pension that Nelson had requested for her with his dying breaths. Neither did Horatia, who eventually wed a curate and became a proper Victorian. Throughout her life, Horatia never knew—or would deign to believe—that Emma Hamilton was her mother.

Author's Note

Too Great a Lady is a work of historical fiction, told from Emma Hamilton's perspective. To that end, certain events are recorded in the novel as they might have been seen through her eyes, and are based on what she would have known of those events at the time of their occurrence—depending on her own social and political inclinations, and on the sources from which she derived her knowledge and information. As a person, Emma was certainly jingoistic, and a fervent royalist; and in many ways, she was self-educated. Nelson, of course, could do no wrong in her eyes, so where modern historians might paint a more complex picture of his conduct, e.g., during the aftermath of the counterrevolution in Naples, or at Copenhagen, Emma herself would not have been privy to this research and information, nor would she have their detached and unbiased view. Also, she would have known what she read in the newspapers, and even in this day and age, journalistic reports of international conflicts often contain errors, or editorial agendas, and do not necessarily present the full picture!

Though my novel was extensively researched, I make no claim to being an historian. I am a fiction writer, and in *Too Great a Lady*, my aim was simply to play the role of Emma Hamilton and to tell her story from a deeply personal point of view.

—Amanda Elyot

Acknowledgments

Thanks to Claire Zion at NAL for sharing my vision and embracing Emma Hamilton's story with passion and dedication. Trends in publishing and a writer's initial story idea are not always in sync, however; I had so much exciting information to work with (and that I hated to eliminate) that the first draft of *Too Great a Lady*, at 715 pages, might easily (in my own view) have filled two books. So, thanks, too, to Irene Goodman for her tenacity and sound advice (even when the author didn't want to hear it!). One could never ask for a better agent. Thanks to den farrier (both a seafarer and a *Wunderkabinett* owner) for cheering the novel every comma of the way with loving encouragement and enthusiasm; to Justin Reay, Admiralty historian, for his myriad insights and for the rare opportunity to walk in Nelson's footsteps; and to Capt. Steven E. Maffeo for his extensive, informative, and insightful comments on the manuscript.

I am indebted to the numerous biographers of Emma Hamilton, Horatio Nelson, and Sir William Hamilton, whose various and several publications over the past century have illuminated so much about my principal characters' world. Primary source material, such as eyewitness accounts of the Battle of the Nile published just a few months after the famous victory, and the voluminous extant correspondence between the key parties, proved invaluable. And to the ladies (and gentleman) of the Beau Monde, I doff my bonnet in gratitude for their wealth of knowledge about the arcana and minutiae of the era.

ABOUT THE AUTHOR

Photo by Ron Rinaldi

Amanda Elyot is a pen name of Leslie Carroll, a multipublished author of contemporary women's fiction. An Ivy League graduate, and a professional actress, she currently resides in New York City. Visit www.tlt.com/authors/lesliecarroll.htm to meet the author online.

Too Great A Lady

Amanda Elyot

Dear Readers,

I hope that you find this guide helpful for your discussions about TOO GREAT A LADY, and that these questions will provide a springboard for stimulating conversation and passionate argument. To me, the most interesting questions are those you raise on your own, and you're welcome to share them with me. Enjoy!

—Amanda Elyot

QUESTIONS
FOR DISCUSSION

1. The passionate love affair between Emma and Nelson was real life that became romantic legend. Yet (and though divorces were extremely difficult to obtain during that era) both Emma and Nelson were committing adultery. How do you feel about that? Given the hypocritical moral standard of the day ("It's okay as long as you're discreet"), and the state of their respective marriages at the time Emma and Nelson began sleeping together, do you accept, or condone, their romance?

2. Given your discussion on the previous question, when soul mates find each other, should true love conquer all?

3. The three principal characters in the novel—Emma, Nelson, and William Hamilton—are drawn from actual people, and their fictional actions are derived from actual events. Each is undeniably flawed, as real human beings undoubtedly are. Do their flaws help you better understand their actions? Do these flaws (discuss them) make you sympathize with them—or not?

4. Emma and her mother have a rather atypical relationship, and yet an utterly symbiotic one. What do you make of it? Do you think Mam should have tried to be more present during

Emma's difficult teenage years, or do you think she did all she could under the circumstances (hers and Emma's)?

5. Bearing in mind the era in which this novel is set, do you agree that the life of courtesan or kept woman is preferable to an "honest" life as a servant, factory worker, or farm laborer? Do you think the former profession gives a woman more independence and autonomy than any or all of the latter trades mentioned? If you lived in the mid to late eighteenth century, which life would you choose, if faced with a dilemma similar to Emma's?

6. Do you think the British Crown and the Admiralty were right to come between Nelson and Emma and make life difficult for each of them, as a sort of "punishment" for their public displays of affection? Do you think Nelson's love for Emma had any impact on his nobility? Or on his ability to serve his king and country just as bravely and effectively as he did before he met Emma? Do you think the government should have stayed out of Nelson's personal life? Do you think they were right in ignoring his dying wishes and the terms of his codicil?

7. Do you believe that a leader's personal life—regardless of whether you agree with or condone his behavior—should have any bearing on whether he retains his position or remains a leader, as long as he continues to be effective? Can you think of more contemporary events than Nelson and Emma that follow a parallel?

8. Do you think societal hypocrisy and appetite for scandal is any different now than it was two hundred years ago?

9. Emma paid a terrible price for a past that she endeavored to overcome, proving herself a model of fidelity, particularly during the years from 1786 (when she traveled to Naples) to late 1799 (when she and Nelson commenced their affair). Yet royalty, and high society, scorned and shunned her, or refused to admit her into their homes (while still enjoying her Attitudes and her hospitality at Palazzo Sessa), citing not only Emma's former "dissolute" life but her low birth, which rendered her ineligible to mingle in their midst. How do you feel about the way Emma was treated?

10. If you lived in Emma's day, what strata of society might you have fit, or been born, into? How do you think others might have treated you?

11. Would you have shunned, or welcomed, Emma? Would she have been a friend?

12. Emma is a flawed heroine, as many of us might be, should our lives become the stuff of fiction. Which of Emma's many attributes do you find less than admirable? Which qualities do you admire?